Bella Rosa
Proposals

JACKIE BRAUN
BARBARA McMAHON
BARBARA HANNAY

MILLS &
BOON

Published in Great Britain 2013
by Mills & Boon, an imprint of Harlequin (UK) Limited,
Eton House, 18-24 Paradise Road, Richmond, Surrey TW9 1SR

BELLA ROSA PROPOSALS © by Harlequin Enterprises II B.V./S.à.r.l 2013

Special thanks and acknowledgements to Jackie Braun and Barbara McMahon for their contributions to BELLA ROSA PROPOSALS.

Star-Crossed Sweethearts, *Firefighter's Doorstep Baby* and *The Bridesmaid's Baby* were published in Great Britain by Harlequin (UK) Limited.

Star-Crossed Sweethearts © Harlequin Books S.A. 2010
Firefighter's Doorstep Baby © Harlequin Books S.A. 2010
The Bridesmaid's Baby © Barbara Hannay 2009

ISBN: 978 0 263 90556 4
ebook ISBN: 978 1 472 00129 0

05-0613

Harlequin (UK) policy is to use papers that are natural, renewable and recyclable products and made from wood grown in sustainable forests. The logging and manufacturing processes conform to the legal environmental regulations of the country of origin.

Printed and bound in Spain
by Blackprint CPI, Barcelona

STAR-CROSSED
SWEETHEARTS

BY
JACKIE BRAUN

Jackie Braun is a three-time RITA® Award finalist, a four-time National Readers' Choice Award finalist and a past winner of the Rising Star Award. She worked for nearly two decades as an award-winning journalist before leaving her full-time job to write fiction. She lives in mid-Michigan with her husband and their two sons. She loves to hear from readers and can be reached through her website at www.jackiebraun.com.

For Brady Williamson and his new sister, Alexandria

PROLOGUE

ANGELO CASALI stood at the home plate with his feet planted shoulder's width apart in the dust. The bat hovered in the air just beyond his right ear. It was the bottom of the ninth inning with two outs, and the Rogues were trailing by two. Anxious runners filled the bases waiting for New York's Angel to work a miracle. They and the fans knew the team's pennant hopes rested squarely on his shoulders.

The opposing team's pitcher glared at Angelo from beneath the bill of his cap. Kyle Morris had one of the best arms in the league. Only a handful of batters could touch his fastball. Angelo was one of them, which was why Morris had yet to bring the heat against him this game. In fact, the pitcher had walked Angelo his last two times at bat. Morris couldn't afford to do that now, and they both knew it.

The pitcher hiked up his leg and levered back his arm before bringing it around. The ball blasted free of his hand like a bullet clearing the barrel of a gun. Even so, Angelo was ready, his eyes tracking its trajectory. He timed his swing perfectly and put everything he had into it, shifting his weight to his right leg as he brought the bat around.

Crack!

The sound of red-stitched white leather meeting wood rent the air like gunfire. It was followed by a sickening *pop!* that only Angelo heard...and felt. Pain, wicked and white-hot, exploded from his shoulder. The crowd's deafening roar drowned out his cry.

It's worth it, he told himself. It's worth it.

Even as he dropped the bat and started toward first base, he knew there was no need to hurry. The ball was riding high in the clouds and showed no signs of dropping.

"And it's out of here!" the announcer shouted.

The fans were on their feet, clapping and high-fiving.

"Angel! Angel! Angel!"

Their jubilant chanting buoyed him. Along with the adrenaline streaking through his system, it allowed him to ignore the worst of the pain. He rounded the bases at a leisurely trot with his good arm raised in triumph. By the time he arrived at home plate, his teammates were out of the dugout, standing there en masse to greet him with whoops and careless back slaps that nearly sent Angelo to his knees. He kept his grin in place, enjoying the moment. How could he not? The Rogues had just sealed a berth in the playoffs. He was the city's hero.

Barely twenty-four hours, Angelo adjusted the ice pack on his shoulder and drank a beer in the solitude of his Upper East Side apartment. If he closed his eyes, he could still hear the crowd chanting his name as the video replayed on the big screen over the scoreboard. He'd watched it from the bench in the dugout, a spot he'd most likely keep warm for what little remained of the season. Most disturbing of all, though, was the thought that this time he might have to hang up his cleats for good.

He sipped the pricey imported brew he'd acquired a taste for his first year in the majors. What would he do then? The question nagged at him more than the pain from his shoulder.

His cell phone trilled as he debated having another drink in lieu of the medication the team doctor had prescribed. It was probably another journalist. Reporters were eager for an interview or even just a quote from the Angel. He snatched it off the coffee table, intending to turn it off. A glance at the readout stopped him. It was his brother, Alessandro.

He grinned as he flipped it open. "Alex. Hey."

"How are you?"

"Never better," Angelo lied.

"Except for your shoulder, you mean."

"Yeah." He shrugged the body part in question and immediately winced. "Except for that. What are you up to?"

"Drinking a beer. Been a long day."

"I'm doing the same. I know what you mean."

Angelo tossed the ice pack aside and started for the kitchen to retrieve another bottle. He wished his twin were there to share a cold one with him in person. It still amazed Angelo that Alex owned a ranch in San Antonio, Texas, and was as at home roping steer as Angelo was snapping up grounders in a major league ballpark. God knew their chaotic childhood hadn't lent itself to either profession. For that matter, it was amazing either of them had amounted to much of anything.

"So, is your shoulder as bad as the sportscasters are saying?" Alex wanted to know.

Angelo made a dismissive sound. "You know how those vultures are. They're milking the story to boost their sagging ratings."

His brother wasn't fooled. "You won't be back in uniform this season."

"No."

"And next year?"

"Sure. After surgery and some rehab I'll be as good as new." Angelo's shoulder throbbed, seemingly in contradiction. He silenced it with a gulp of beer and settled back into the leather recliner. "I'm too damned young to retire."

It was a lie and they both knew it. Thirty-eight wasn't old by most standards, but in baseball it was damned near ancient. Before the injury, Angelo had remained a powerhouse, but his legs weren't what they used to be. Things like that didn't escape the notice of the guys in the dugout, much less the guys in management. This injury didn't help. It was his second serious one in three years, and pulled tendons had taken him out for several games in June. No ball club wanted to pay top dollar for a player who'd ride the pine. Even his agent was getting antsy that when Angelo's multimillion-dollar contract expired in a couple months the team would cut him loose.

"Well, it sounds like you'll have some time on your hands."

"Yeah." He studied the label on his beer and scraped at the edge with his thumbnail. "Maybe I'll mosey on down to Texas and pay you a visit. I could get better acquainted with your bride-to-be and her little girl."

It still came as a surprise that the pretty single mom had knocked his brooding brother off his feet when she'd shown up at the ranch with her disabled daughter a few months earlier. Alex wasn't the sort to fall fast or hard. Yet he'd done both.

"I'd like that." Alex paused then. "But what I'd like even more is for you to use the time to go to Italy."

Angelo closed his eyes. "Not this again," he muttered after an oath.

For weeks his twin had been urging on him to reconnect with their estranged father and meet the rest of the Casali clan in Monta Correnti, the place of their birth.

"Go and make your peace. You won't regret it," Alex said.

"I have no peace to make. I'm fine with things just the way they are."

"Fine? You're ticked off, Angelo."

"That too," he agreed after a long pull on his beer. "Where were they when we were stealing to eat or getting dumped into yet another foster home? Where was Luca?" he demanded, referring to their father. "No one was inviting us to Italy to visit then."

The way he saw it, the old man had washed his hands of his sons when he had sent them to Boston to live with their American mother, who was more suited to partying than parenting. They'd been three years old then. By the time the twins were fourteen, Cindy had drunk herself to death and the boys had been made wards of the state. Not long after, they'd made their way to New York. His skin still crawled when he thought about how close they'd come to winding up statistics.

"They didn't know, Angelo. None of them, including Luca, knew that Mom was gone or that we were in and out of the foster system."

"They didn't know because they didn't care enough to find out," he shot back.

In Angelo's mind, it was all very cut and dried. In the past, when it could have made a real difference, his family had wanted nothing to do with him. Well, he wanted nothing to do with them now, regardless of how many olive branches they extended.

He'd already ignored the surprise e-mail from his half-sister, Isabella, which had kicked off this whole reunion quest. Talk about a curveball. He certainly hadn't expected to learn via the Internet that he had additional siblings in Monta Correnti, three of them born to Luca's second wife after Angelo and Alex's exile. He'd also passed on a wedding invitation from a cousin who'd grown up in Australia.

Family had been falling out of the rafters for the past several months, but it was all too little and coming far too late.

"Don't think Luca doesn't regret his choices," Alex said quietly. "He does. But he can't go back and change the past. He can only try to change the future. Go to Italy, Angelo. Spend a week in Monta Correnti. In fact, spend two. You could use a vacation. I've already booked you a flight and found you a place to stay. I'll e-mail you the information. You can pay me back later."

"I'll drop a check in the mail first thing in the morning, bro. But I'm not going."

Alex was quiet a moment before he pulled out his ace. "If you won't do it for yourself, then do it for me. I'm asking you to go."

"That's low." And it was. His level-headed and older-by-mere-minutes brother knew he was the only person who could get Angelo to do something he didn't want to do.

Far from sounding insulted, Alex's voice held a smile when he replied, "Sure it's low, but it's also effective. You'll thank me later."

"Thank you? Right. Don't hold your breath," Angelo snapped before hanging up.

CHAPTER ONE

ATLANTA JACKSON expelled a gusty sigh as she studied herself in the hotel suite's full-length mirror. Was the pale, hollowed-eyed woman staring back really her?

The hair was right, a long cascade of nearly white-blonde curls. But her skin was pasty and her body a tad too angular to carry off the bombshell label that was routinely applied to it. She was a good half-dozen pounds thinner than she'd been just a month earlier, and ten pounds thinner than she'd been the month before that. Forget the low-carb fad that was all the rage among Hollywood A-listers. She'd gone on the high-stress diet, guaranteed to melt off the pounds quicker than butter on Louisiana asphalt in August.

At least her dress, a simple navy sheath made of cotton, hid some of her new angles.

A smile bowed her lips. Zeke would hate this dress, which was precisely why she'd purchased it the day before at a pricy Fifth Avenue boutique, outside of which she had been mobbed by paparazzi and actually booed by a couple of passersby. Buying it and now wearing it out in public were acts of defiance.

Zeke Compton—her manager, mentor and, according to him, her messiah—hadn't allowed her to wear navy. It was too close to black, he claimed. Black being another forbidden color since it reminded him of mourning.

"What does America's favorite actress have to be sad about?" he'd asked the one time Atlanta's stylist had suggested a vintage Oscar de la Renta gown the color of onyx for a red-carpet event.

Wouldn't the public like to know? she'd thought at the time. Now she knew better. The public didn't want the truth, unvarnished or otherwise. They wanted romantic, rags-to-riches fairy tales and titillating scandals. They wouldn't accept that she was tired of being manipulated, tired of being dictated to and sick to death of living a lie.

Atlanta slipped on a pair of rounded-toe flats. Despite the fashionable little bow on them, the shoes were another no-no in Zeke's book.

"You're too short to wear anything less than a three-inch heel, love," he'd decreed one year into their professional relationship. By then, things between them also had turned personal, and she'd moved from her West Hollywood studio apartment into his Bellaire home, playing the dutiful Eliza Doolittle to his domineering Henry Higgins.

Atlanta was five-seven, hardly what one would consider petite, but she'd listened to him about clothing and shoes and pretty much everything else. She'd always listened to the men in her life, a habit that dated to her childhood.

Bad things happen to little girls who don't do what they're told.

The words echoed from her distant past. As she had done a million times before, Atlanta forced them and the black memories that accompanied them back. Then she glanced at her watch. It was time to go. Thank God, she thought, as she made her way out the suite's door. She was as eager to leave New York as she'd been to leave Los Angeles. Neither place was welcoming now that Zeke had poisoned the well of public opinion against her and made her a pariah among her peers.

In the elevator, she checked her purse one more time, making sure she had her itinerary, tickets and passport. Her luggage was waiting downstairs. The limousine she'd called for would be at the curb, only a gauntlet of paparazzi to run before she could relax in the relative privacy that its tinted windows would afford.

In a dozen hours she would be in Monta Correnti, Italy. Her stylist, one of the few people from her old life still willing to speak to her, assured Atlanta that the remote hillside village situated between Naples and Rome was the ideal place to drop off the radar, relax and rejuvenate.

God, she hoped Karen Somerville was right. Atlanta was wound so tightly these days she felt ready to explode. But first things first. Sucking in a deep breath, she donned a pair of dark designer sunglasses as the elevator's doors slid open.

"Show time," she murmured.

Eyes shaded with his trademark Oakleys, Angelo sauntered into the VIP lounge at JFK International as if he hadn't a care in the world. Image was everything, especially given all of the speculation swirling around his career.

The official line from the team was that Angelo was suffering pulled ligaments and severe tendonitis in his right shoulder, but that after rest and physical therapy he would return to the regular lineup in the spring. The truth wasn't quite as rosy as that. In addition to the start of osteoarthritis, he had a torn rotator cuff. Cortisone shots had kept the worst of the arthritis pain at bay in the past, but no shot would take care of the torn cuff.

As the team's physician bluntly put it, "You need surgery. An injury like this won't heal on its own. And, given your age, it might never heal well enough to take the abuse heaped on it by a major league ballplayer."

It all boiled down to a truth he wasn't ready to accept. Instead of scheduling surgery, he had embraced his brother's high-handed scheme for a family reunion. He was going to Italy, where he would spend the next couple of weeks. He had no intention of reconnecting with his father, but the gesture would appease Alex. As an added bonus, that little speck on the map was a good place to duck the press and figure out his future.

The bar area of the VIP lounge held only a smattering of patrons. None of them looked up when he entered. They were all important people in their own right—movers, shakers, captains of industry. They didn't get awestruck or if they did, they hid it well behind blasé attitudes. His ego certainly hoped that was the case with the gorgeous blonde sitting in front of the floor-to-ceiling window that overlooked the tarmac.

Despite the oversized sunglasses perched on her small nose, Atlanta Jackson was easy to recognize. The actress had starred in a dozen bona fide blockbusters. He took in the naturally pouty lips and the trademark blonde hair that tumbled just past her shoulders. Interest stirred. Again. He'd met her at a New York nightclub a few years earlier. They'd talked briefly. He'd flirted shamelessly, but to no avail. She'd turned him down flat when he'd asked her to dance. A couple of Angelo's teammates still liked to razz him about the fact that he, Angelo Casali, had struck out.

She shifted in her seat to cross her legs. The demure hemline of her simple navy dress pulled partway up her thighs. Interest turned to outright lust. Not many women were built as she was: long-limbed and slender, yet curvy in all of the places a man liked to rest his hands. A little less curvy than he recalled. He could guess why. Her image was taking a beating in the tabloids ever since she'd walked out on her much older manager slash boyfriend.

According to one story Angelo had read, the guy claimed Atlanta had betrayed him with a slew of lovers over the years, most recently bedding his twenty-year-old son.

Had she?

Maybe it was Angelo's ego talking, but the woman who'd turned him down flat in a nightclub a few years earlier hadn't seemed the sort to stray. With that in mind, he crossed to her table and waited until she looked up to speak.

"I'd offer to buy you a drink, but you'd probably turn me down. So, how about some meaningful conversation until one of our flights boards?"

He couldn't see her eyes behind the glasses, but her full lips twitched with amusement. "As lines go, that's very original, Mr. Casali."

"Thanks." He didn't wait to be offered a seat. He pulled out one of the chairs and straddled it backward. "So, you do remember me. I wasn't sure you would. It's been a few years."

His ego took another little hit when she replied, "Well, you've been in the news a lot these days."

"I could say the same about you."

Her mouth tightened fractionally. "Yes, I have."

"Is that why you're wearing sunglasses inside?"

"Maybe." She motioned to his Oakleys. "And you?"

"Definitely. This way no one can be sure I'm making eye contact with them. I find it discourages conversation."

A pair of finely arched brows rose over the top rim of her dark lenses.

"You find that ironic," he guessed.

"A little." She shrugged delicately.

"Here's the thing. Since you and I are the only two people in the lounge wearing shades I figure we probably should stick together. You know, play for the same team."

"Given all that is being said about me right now, are you sure you want me on your team, Mr. Casali?"

"The name is Angelo." He cocked his head to one side. "We'll consider this a tryout."

Atlanta laughed if for no other reason than the man's sheer nerve. A tryout? She hadn't had to read for a part in quite a while. The starring roles in her last three movies, each of which had grossed well over a hundred million dollars in the American market alone, had been written specifically with her in mind. Everyone in Hollywood knew that no one played the vulnerable vixen better than Atlanta Jackson. It was her niche. Her character type. She sobered at that.

"What if I don't want to be on your team?" she asked.

"You do."

She wanted to be turned off by his unflagging confidence or at the very least irritated by it. She found herself intrigued instead and maybe even a little envious. While she could portray confidence in front of the camera, she seldom felt it in real life. It was just one of the many things she was working to rectify.

"How can you be so sure?" she wanted to know.

"Everyone wants to be on the winning team."

"And that would be yours?"

"Of course. I've got the golden touch. The Rogues are in the playoffs because of me. We're heading to the World Series."

"That's only an assumption at this point."

"No. It's a fact, sweetheart. We'll be there."

Normally, she didn't care for empty endearments, but his casual use of sweetheart complemented his bravado so perfectly, she let it pass. Instead, she honed in on another matter.

"We? Are the news reports wrong, then?" Her gaze strayed to his shoulder. It didn't look injured. Indeed, nothing about the man's rock-hard physique appeared compromised...or compromising, for that matter.

"You know the media." He shrugged.

Atlanta might have believed that news of Angelo's professional demise was vastly overblown if he hadn't grimaced after making the casual movement.

"They're ruthless when they scent blood," he was saying.

Thinking of Zeke, she replied, "They're even more ruthless when they've got sources happy to help draw it."

Her image was being put through the shredder, and, while she wasn't all that sad to see some of the false layers she'd once agreed to peel away, she certainly didn't want them replaced with more lies and half-truths. Unfortunately, that was exactly what Zeke was feeding the hungry hordes these days, and they were eating it up, ravenous for more.

I made you. I'll ruin you.

Zeke's parting words. Foolishly, she hadn't believed he'd do it. She knew better now. He was doing a bang-up job of making good on his promise.

Angelo was apparently far less naïve than she. "The world is full of people eager to sell you out. You have to be careful who you trust."

"At this point, I trust no one." Surprised to have told him that, she asked, "Who do you trust?"

"My twin," he replied without hesitation. "Alex has always had my back."

"You have a twin?" Good heavens, there were two men on the planet as good-looking as this one? She'd worked with A-list actors, bona fide heartthrobs, who couldn't match Angelo's rugged male perfection. "Are you identical?"

"Not quite. I'm better looking."

"No doubt you're more modest, too," she replied dryly.

"Sure." Angelo wasn't put off. In fact, he pulled the sunglasses down the bridge of his nose and winked as he boasted, "I'm also better with women."

God help her. The man was every bit as sexy as she recalled from their brief meeting in a nightclub a few years back. He also was every bit as cocksure. She was used to being around oversized egos, her own included. Angelo, at least, tempered his with humor. He was harmless, she decided, especially here in a public place.

Which was what gave her the nerve to lean closer and say, "So, Don Juan, if I'm going to be on your team, perhaps you should explain the game we're playing."

"Distraction."

"Is that the name or the object?"

"Both."

"I'm intrigued. Tell me more."

He glanced at the chunky Rolex strapped to his wrist. "Here's the thing—I have an hour and forty minutes to kill before my flight departs. I could get my own table, order a drink and sip it alone while I wait. Or I could stay here with you and enjoy what is bound to be some fascinating conversation."

A lifetime ago, Atlanta had thought herself interesting, but it had been a very long time since a man had said so. "What makes you so sure the conversation would be fascinating?"

"You're a fascinating woman. What else would it be?"

Come-on or not, his reply caused her breath to catch. Clearly, being a pariah among the people she'd considered her friends had taken its toll on her self-esteem.

"I like your answer," she told him.

"Enough to let me buy you a drink?"

"Enough that the drink's on me."

Angelo waved over a server and they ordered their beverages—an imported beer for him and a glass of unsweetened iced tea for her. As the waitress left he was frowning.

"Is something wrong?" she asked.

"Not wrong. I guess I thought you'd order something… else."

"Such as champagne perhaps? And not just any champagne but Piper-Heidsieck by the magnum?"

"Or Dom. I read once that you bathed in it."

"I read that, too."

"It's not true?"

She shook her head. "Afraid not."

"I'm disappointed. I was going to ask you what it felt

like having all of those bubbles bursting against your bare skin."

His smile, set as it was on a mouth that would have been at home on Michelangelo's David, dazzled. Atlanta camouflaged her involuntary shiver by shifting in her seat. There was no camouflaging the gooseflesh that pricked her arms. She hoped he wouldn't notice it.

"My publicist made that one up. It enjoyed a lot of buzz for a while, and I even picked up an endorsement deal for another brand of champagne. The truth is, I prefer showers to baths of any sort and I don't drink."

"At all?" he asked.

"Rarely these days." She preferred to keep a clear head.

"Neither do I."

"You just ordered a beer," she reminded him.

The corners of Angelo's mouth turned down as if in consideration and he gazed out the window where a jumbo jet was lumbering toward a runway. "Special circumstances."

"You don't like flying," she guessed. It was a phobia Atlanta understood perfectly. She still experienced a burst of anxiety each time a plane she was on prepared for takeoff.

But Angelo was shaking his head. "Nah. Flying doesn't bother me. I do it all the time. But talking to a gorgeous woman? It leaves me tongue-tied." Again, the dazzling smile made an appearance.

"I don't know. You've managed fine so far without any fortification," she pointed out, well aware that she could do with a little of the false courage found in a cocktail right about now herself.

Apropos of nothing, he asked, "When's your flight?"

"Two forty-something."

"Around the same time as mine, which means I've still got an hour and a half left with the potential to humiliate myself. I don't want to take any chances."

"I'm sure if we keep the conversation light and neutral, you'll be just fine."

And she would be just fine, too. So, that was precisely what they did.

It was with regret that Angelo glanced at his watch a little over an hour later. He would have to leave soon. It wasn't only the thought of what lay ahead in Italy that disturbed him. He couldn't remember the last time he'd had an actual conversation with a woman that didn't include foreplay of some sort or other. Both he and Atlanta still had their clothes on, a good thing given their surroundings. But they had ditched their sunglasses.

"If you didn't have a plane to catch, too, I'd hop on a later flight just so I could spend more time with you," he told her.

"Sure you would." She humored him with a smile, apparently deciding she'd just been fed another line.

"I mean it." He reached across the table and caught her left hand in his. Her fingers were delicate and bare of any adornment. "To be honest, I didn't expect to enjoy myself as much as I have."

Her brows pulled together at the same time she pulled her hand free. "Gee, thanks."

"Sorry." He grimaced. "That was a pathetically backhanded compliment. I told you I get tongue-tied around beautiful women."

The truth was the only beautiful woman around whom he'd ever found himself at a loss for words with was Atlanta.

Chuckling, she shook her head. "You're forgiven. I think I know what you mean. I enjoyed being distracted."

That was all he'd had in mind when he'd sat down earlier, someone to take his mind off the problems at hand. Now...?

"Maybe when we both get back to the States we could get together. If you're going to be in New York, there's a new exhibit coming to the Met in October."

"The Met?" Her eyelids flickered. No doubt she'd figured he was going to suggest a sporting event of some sort.

"I'm a patron."

"Oh."

"I'm not exactly the quote unquote dumb jock whose only interests are those that happen on the diamond."

"I didn't think you were. Honestly, I don't know you well enough to draw that conclusion."

"That doesn't stop most people."

She sighed. "Look, Angelo, I really appreciate the offer, but I've got a lot on my plate right now. Dating isn't going to be a priority for a while."

He nodded slowly, bemused and a little disappointed. "You know, that makes twice now that you've thrown me out before I got on base. Forgive me for saying so, Atlanta, but you're hell on a man's ego."

"I think you'll survive." She smiled. It wasn't the high-wattage sort the cameras captured. This one was the genuine article.

"Glad I could make your day," he grumbled.

"You did, Angelo, but not in the way you mean."

Atlanta rarely did anything spontaneous. Spontaneity was too costly. She'd found that out as a child. Under Zeke's care and later his control, she'd learned to deftly plan out her every move. She didn't plan to kiss Angelo Casali. She just leaned across the table and did it, resting her lips against his for a brief, sweet moment during which neither of them closed their eyes.

Innocent. That was what the gesture was. It had been a long time since she'd felt that way around a man, which was what caused her to draw away.

She gathered up her handbag and reached for her small carryon as she stood. Even though her legs felt ridiculously shaky, her voice came out steady. "From one wounded ego to another, thank you."

Atlanta stopped in the restroom after saying goodbye to Angelo. Taking several slow, measured breaths, she regained the last of her composure. Then, with her makeup freshened and her emotions firmly in check, she dropped the dark glasses back onto the bridge of her nose and hustled to the gate. She arrived just in time for the final boarding call for Flight 174 to Rome's Leonardo da Vinci International Airport. A flight attendant helped stow her carryon in one of the overhead compartments. Atlanta let out a sigh and turned to find her seat.

"Cutting it a little close, aren't you, sweetheart?" a masculine voice drawled.

Her neck snapped around and her gaze locked with Angelo's. He was two rows behind her on the opposite side of the aisle. So much for restoring her composure.

"Wh-what are you doing here?" she asked inanely.

He tugged at the strap of his seat belt. "Preparing for takeoff."

"Are…are you following me?"

She immediately felt like an idiot for making the assumption and that was before Angelo replied, "And you claim to have a wounded ego. Seems perfectly healthy to me."

Her gaze darted around. Thankfully none of the other passengers in first class seemed to be paying much attention.

"So, you're going to Italy," she managed on a weak smile.

"Yeah. Is that seat next to you open?"

Angelo didn't wait for her to reply. He unbuckled and rose, grinning as he plopped down beside her. One thought came through loud and clear: The flight to Italy was going to be interesting indeed.

CHAPTER TWO

"SO, WHAT takes you to Italy?" Angelo asked once their flight was airborne. "A movie role?"

"A vacation, actually. I want some time alone without the media following my every move."

"So you picked a small town like Rome for that," he replied deadpan.

"Rome isn't my final destination." She lowered her voice. "I'm heading a little farther south to an isolated little village that I'd never heard of before. It's tucked up on a hillside, very remote and the people are very discreet when it comes to celebrities, or so I've been told."

No way, Angelo thought. What would be the odds? He had to know. "You're not talking about Monta Correnti, by any chance?"

"You know it?" Then her face paled. "You're...you're not going..."

"Yep." Angelo's laughter rang out loud enough to draw the attention of the passengers around them.

Distraction. In the airport's VIP lounge he'd told Atlanta it was the name of their game as well as its object. Apparently they were going into extra innings.

A couple hours into their flight, Angelo could no longer ignore the angry throbbing of his shoulder.

Atlanta was reading a magazine, or more likely pretending to since she hadn't turned the page in twenty minutes. He was no speed-reader, but even he could have finished the article on eyeliner dos and don'ts in that amount of time.

He twisted the cap off the mineral water he'd ordered when the flight attendant last came around, and as discreetly as possible popped a couple of the potent painkillers the team doctor had prescribed, washing them down with a gulp of the beverage.

"That bad, huh?" She closed the magazine and laid it on her lap.

"Just stiff," he lied. "I'll be all right." He had to be.

After the pills kicked in, he didn't wake until shortly before the aircraft was making its final descent into the larger of Rome's two airports. He was hungry, having slept through the dinner that was served during the flight, the medicine was wearing off and his overall mood wasn't much improved.

Through the thick glass of the plane's window, Angelo caught his first glimpse of Italy in thirty-five years. Even with the floral scent of Atlanta's perfume teasing his senses, he could no longer ignore his real reason for coming.

"Sleep well?" she asked.

"Like a baby."

"You moaned a few times. I thought maybe you were in pain."

"Erotic dreams," he corrected on a wink.

"My mistake." But she rolled her eyes.

"Sir, your seat needs to be in the upright position," a flight attendant stopped by to remind him.

He shifted and a moan escaped before he could muffle it.

"Apparently you have those dreams even when you're awake," Atlanta said dryly.

"Want me to share the particulars with you?"

"That's all right."

"Sure? I wouldn't mind."

"I'm sure you wouldn't, but I'll pass."

"How long are you going to be staying in Monta—?"

"Shh!" she admonished and glanced around as if she expected to find the other first-class passengers shamelessly eavesdropping. That was a virtual impossibility over the loud hum of the jet engines. Still, he obliged her by lowering his voice.

"So, how long?"

Her eyes narrowed. "Why?"

"Just curious how much time I'll have to wear you down. Eventually, even though you claim not to drink, I predict you and I will share a bottle of wine and some more fascinating conversation."

She chuckled. "What do you call this?"

"You're avoiding answering my question."

"Fine. I'll be there for three glorious weeks with an option to stay four." She sighed, as eager to arrive as he was to have the trip behind him.

"I'll be there two weeks tops. Might as well be a life sentence," he mumbled.

"Excuse me?"

"Nothing. You never said what made you decide to make Monta—" he caught himself before he finished the village's name "—MC your final destination. It's a speck on the map, you know."

If she heard the derision in his tone, she didn't comment on it. "That's why it's ideal."

"Ah, that's right. Hiding out."

A line formed between her brows. "That makes me sound like a coward."

"Sorry. I didn't—"

"No." She waved off the rest of his apology. "I guess I am hiding out. I just needed a place to go to recharge my batteries." Her expression turned rueful. "Someplace where I wouldn't have to deal with booing fans or the paparazzi at every turn. My stylist suggested the village. She visited it a few years ago. She was seeing a rather famous actor at the time and according to her they could go anywhere in town without worrying about drawing a crowd, much less paparazzi."

Frowning, Angelo said, "It's nothing like LA or New York, that's for sure."

"So, this isn't your first visit?"

He shook his head.

"What's it like?"

"It's been a while, years in fact."

Vague images of quaint, red-tile-roofed houses tucked into the side of a hill rose from his memory, accompanied by the scents of fresh basil, roasted red peppers and plum tomatoes. Angelo couldn't be sure if they were real or the result of wishful thinking. As it was, nothing of his childhood in Boston evoked anything worth recalling.

"I looked it up on Google," Atlanta was saying. "There's not a lot of information, but I did find some photographs. It's very picturesque and old-fashioned, like a snapshot out of the past."

His past.

Her gaze shifted to his shoulder. Her expression held understanding. "Are you interested in dropping out of sight for a while, too?"

"Not exactly." He took a deep breath before admitting, "My father lives there."

Atlanta blinked, not quite able to hide her surprise.

"Yes, I have one of those," he replied dryly.

"From the scowl on your face I gather the two of you aren't close."

"I haven't seen him in thirty-five years." And Angelo had no desire to see Luca now.

"Ouch. Sorry."

He laughed outright as a cover for the pain he couldn't admit to feeling. "It's no big deal. I didn't need him and I haven't missed him. Hell, I barely remember him."

"So, why are you going? If you don't mind me asking," she added.

He shrugged. The pain the gesture caused made him wince. "My brother booked my flight and my accommodations. Alex thinks that making peace with our father is important."

"But you don't share his opinion," she guessed.

Angelo caught himself before he could shrug again. "It's ancient history. What's to be gained?"

"I'm the wrong person to ask," Atlanta admitted. "I haven't seen my mother in years. My choice."

"You're smart. The only reason my brother is all for a reunion now is that he's met a woman and they're getting married. He's *in love*."

"From your tone I'd take it you're not a big fan of the emotion."

"I've got nothing against love. I'm happy for my brother."

How could Angelo not be? Allie, the woman Alex was marrying, was pretty, kind and intelligent. She had a daughter whom his brother obviously adored. Together they were a ready-made family. If that thought made him feel unbearably alone at times, it was his own problem. He'd get over it.

"Have you ever been in love yourself?" Atlanta asked.

"You're a regular Oprah. So many questions," he teased, stretching out his stiff legs. He hoped whatever accommodations Alex had arranged came with a jetted tub. He could do with a nice long soak.

"Sorry." She ruined the apology by adding, "Well?"

"No. I like women in general too much to commit to any one in particular." He sent Atlanta a wolfish smile that caused her to roll her sky-blue eyes.

"Gee, that's romantic," she said dryly.

"No, that's realistic. I could say something cliché like I haven't met the right woman, but I don't think the right woman exists."

"Your brother apparently disagrees."

Angelo held up a finger. "Let me clarify. I don't believe the right woman exists *for me*." It was a long-held belief, one that predated puberty. Commitment? His parents had gone that route and look how it had turned out. They hadn't been able to keep the promises they made to one another, let alone to the children they'd brought into the world. He grinned wickedly to banish the old bitterness, hiding behind the cockiness that was as much his trademark as Atlanta's bombshell looks were hers. "But if she did exist, she'd be blonde, about your height and have ridiculously long legs."

Atlanta crossed her arms and sent him a pointed look. "Do lines like that actually work for you?"

"Apparently not," he replied with feigned disappointment.

She shook her head. "You're incorrigible."

"I know. A judge told me that very thing before

sending me off to juvie when I was a kid." He said it lightly, though nothing about the incident could be considered fun or funny. Before she could comment he said, "I won't bother to ask if you've ever been in love. You lived with that Zeke guy for—what?—a decade?"

"Something like that," she murmured. Her gaze strayed to the window.

"But no ring?" he prodded.

"Not the kind you're talking about."

Curious, he asked, "What other kind is there?"

It sounded as if she said, "Through the nose," but he couldn't be sure.

"I find it hard to believe he didn't propose. If I were the sort of guy interested in lifelong commitments, I'd have been on bended knee after our first date."

Atlanta made a tsking noise. "Obviously you're not up on your tabloid reports. Zeke proposed dozens of times during the course of our relationship. Actually, begged is how I believe he put it. He wanted to marry me. He wanted to have a family with me. Heartless witch that I am, I repeatedly turned him down. I didn't want a husband and I didn't want babies. My figure is my fortune, you know. I'm nothing without a twenty-four-inch waist and flawless abs."

He'd seen pictures of the abs in question. Still, he said, "You sell yourself short."

She glanced over sharply, studied him for a moment. It might have been a trick of the light, but her eyes looked bright. "It doesn't really matter now."

The captain came on the public address system announcing the local time and temperature and the usual end-of-the-flight banter. Afterward, Angelo asked, "Should I apologize for prying?"

A ghost of a smile tugged at the corners of her mouth.

Even without her usual crimson gloss, her lips were full and inviting. "Are you sorry?"

Since she was striving to remain upbeat, he decided to oblige her. "No. I'm too curious to be sorry. You're quite an enigma."

"Me?" She laughed. "Everybody knows everything there is to know about me."

Did they? People thought they knew him, too. Since his injury, Angelo had begun to wonder if he knew himself.

Alex had assured Angelo that a driver would be waiting to take him to Monta Correnti. A rental car would be at his disposal in the village, but his brother figured Angelo would appreciate having someone else navigate the roads after a long flight. Alex had thought of everything, perhaps so that Angelo wouldn't have any excuses for backing out.

Atlanta had someone meeting her as well. Even so, they stayed together after deplaning.

"Want me to help you with your bags?" she asked.

"That's supposed to be my line."

She tilted her head to one side. "I'm not the one with a bum shoulder."

"It's fine," he protested through gritted teeth.

Her brows rose but she said nothing else as they waited to spot their bags on the conveyor belt. One by one, Atlanta's four pieces of matching designer luggage came around before Angelo's large suitcase. She snatched them off before he could offer.

"I thought you said you were going to be in Italy for less than a month?" he drawled as a bushy-haired porter hurried over with a cart. "From the amount of luggage, it looks like you're planning to move here."

"I like clothes and shoes."

"That's obvious. You could outfit the population of a small country."

She wrinkled her nose. "Sorry. I'm incredibly selfish when it comes to my shoes. I don't share."

"How many pairs did you bring?"

"Twelve, not counting the ones I'm wearing." She looked inordinately pleased when she announced, "Almost all of them have heels less than one inch."

"No stilettos?"

"Not a one."

"Damn." He spied his bag and moved closer to the conveyor to snatch it. She was at his side in an instant, helping him heft the bulky suitcase off.

"I've got it," he grumbled.

"Of course you do, big he-man that you are. You don't need anybody."

Angelo laughed, even if in truth he didn't want to need anybody. He'd learned a long time ago to rely on himself. The only people he trusted to help him out when needed were his twin and, of course, his teammates.

Assuming they were together, the bushy-haired porter added Angelo's bag to the cart stacked with Atlanta's.

"We're going to owe him a really big tip when it's all said and done," Angelo muttered as the man started off toward Customs.

"It's not like we can't afford it."

No indeed. She was one of the few women he'd ever met who actually made as much money as he did, perhaps more, since he didn't know what her cut had been on her past few movies.

Still, he had enough pride that he said, "I'll get this one since you picked up the tab in the lounge."

"Grazie mille," she said, batting her lashes at him for effect.

After they cleared Customs, she dropped the sunglasses back onto the bridge of her nose. Before landing, she'd pulled her hair back into a simple ponytail. Along with the navy dress and flat-heeled shoes, she hardly screamed high-maintenance Hollywood. But such raw beauty rarely went unnoticed. As low-key as she was trying to be, as soon as they passed into the main terminal she attracted a lot of attention and some of it was exactly the kind she wanted to avoid.

A couple of photographers began shouting her name. Even prefaced with the courtesy title of Signorina the intrusion was rude, especially since it was followed by a succession of near-blinding flashes. Atlanta held up her handbag as a shield. Just that quickly, the witty and surprisingly candid woman with whom he'd spent the past several hours was swallowed up by a monster of her own making.

Fame. Sometimes it grew fangs and bit you.

Angelo waited for the photographers to holler out his name, too. It was their lucky day. The parasites had a pair of American celebrities in their viewfinders. He patted his pockets in search of his Oakleys. He was as used to dealing with them as Atlanta was. On any given day, half a dozen of their ilk stood guard outside his Manhattan apartment building, their digital cameras trained on the exits in the hope of snapping a money shot or two for the tabloids.

"I'm going to duck into the ladies' room for a minute," Atlanta whispered. "You go on ahead to your car. Tell the porter to wait there with my bags."

"Divide and conquer?" he asked.

"Maybe we'll get lucky."

"See you in MC."

She didn't answer. They'd reached the ladies' room and she hustled inside.

Angelo turned. He'd found his sunglasses but needn't have bothered. With Atlanta gone, the paparazzi lowered their cameras. It came as a huge blow to realize that he hadn't been recognized. Baseball was a largely American game, he reminded himself. Neither it nor its players resonated much outside the United States, and apparently that was true in Italy.

He should have been relieved. It was a pain to be hounded by the paparazzi. Even so, he felt sucker-punched. Was this what his life would be like post-career? Would no one recognize him? Would no one care that for four consecutive seasons he'd led the league in runs batted in or that he was half a dozen homers from passing the current record? Would he return to the obscurity from which he'd come, a mere postscript in write-ups about the game that had literally saved his life?

The porter nudged him and said something in Italian. It was Angelo's native tongue, but he remembered none of it even if he found the accent and cadence oddly comforting.

"Sorry. I only speak English," he replied.

"Taxi?" the man said helpfully and pointed to an overhead sign designating the way to ground transportation.

"Ah, no. Someone is meeting me."

Several of those waiting to welcome passengers were holding signs with names written on them. One was printed with Angelo's. "My driver."

"Signorina?" The porter glanced back to the rest-room door.

She had her own transportation. She'd told Angelo to go. Yet Angelo told the porter, "We'll wait for her here."

He knew the moment she was out in the open. The paparazzi descended on her like a pack of wolves on prey. Long legs and irritation made her pace fast, but eventually, she had nowhere left to run.

"I told you to leave," she snapped, turning this way and that in an effort to avoid the cameras.

Angelo stood perfectly still. "I'm bad at following directions. It's a guy thing."

"This will make a fine headline."

"They don't know who I am."

"They will back home. You'll be labeled as my latest conquest."

"Yeah?"

"Don't look so smug," she cried. "That's not a good thing."

"From your point of view," he replied, hoping to see her smile.

Her expression remained grim.

"You need to get out of here," he told her.

"I would, but apparently my driver is late." Her laughter verged on hysteria.

"It's Italy," Angelo said. "I've been told they run on their own time here."

More camera flashes popped. Atlanta backed up, trying to put as much distance between herself and Angelo in the photographers' frames as possible.

"Come with me. We're heading to the same place."

He extended a hand. She declined both it and his offer with a shake of her head. "No, no. That's kind, but I have my own transportation. Or I will. Soon."

The photographers snapped off a couple more shots.

In addition to paparazzi they were drawing a crowd of onlookers, some of whom had pulled out their camera phones. Within a matter of hours this was going to be all over the Internet.

"Do you really want to wait around?" he asked.

"I…" She issued a heartfelt sigh. "God, no."

Along with the porter and driver, they made a mad dash for the exit. At the curb, Angelo peeled off some bills, trying to remember the exchange rate of dollars to euros. At the porter's broad grin, he figured the tip was as generous as intended.

He grinned, too, but for an entirely different reason.

CHAPTER THREE

ATLANTA assumed that the closer they drew to Monta Correnti and the villa she'd rented, the more relaxed she would feel. But just the opposite was occurring, probably because the small, isolated village was Angelo's final destination, too.

While it was entirely likely they would bump into each other a time or two during the next couple weeks, she didn't want it to become a habit. She was enjoying his company…a little too much. She found him funny and surprisingly interesting. He was far more than the inflated ego and one-dimensional jock she'd first assumed. She also found him intensely attractive. Their kiss kept coming to mind. It had her yearning for something she'd lost long ago. Something she could never get back.

It was just as well this wasn't a true vacation for either of them. He was in Italy to meet with his estranged father. She had come to escape the media's prying eyes. She had a career to save, a reputation to salvage. A life to start over without the guiding influence of a man. Any man. By the time the driver pulled the Mercedes sedan to a stop outside a sun-bleached two-story villa, she had rehearsed the lines in her head for her farewell speech.

"Great view," Angelo remarked before she could get the first words out.

The pre-World-War-II residence was bounded on one side by a cobblestone courtyard, part of which was shaded by a grapevine-draped pergola. Beyond it, the land sloped gently down before falling away completely to reveal a valley dotted with houses, farms and olive groves.

"Stunning," she agreed. "Well, thank you again. I hope you enjoy your stay here."

She reached for the door handle, intent on making her exit. Angelo ruined it by following her out.

"From what Alex has told me about the place I'm staying, it has an equally gorgeous view. It's farther up the hillside. If you want to stop by tomorrow evening, we can compare panoramas before going to dinner."

The invitation was delivered so smoothly that she nearly agreed. "I appreciate the offer, but I think I'll be eating in for most of my stay."

The driver had retrieved her bags from the trunk. Despite her objections, Angelo insisted on carrying one of them to the door. After the man returned to the car to wait, Angelo said, "I thought one of the reasons in coming to Monta Correnti was the discretion of the locals. Does that scene at the airport have you worried about being ambushed by paparazzi?"

"No. I just need time alone…to reflect and make plans. You understand, right?"

Angelo whistled through his teeth. "I can't believe I just struck out for the third time with you. You'd think I'd learn." The accompanying smile took the sting out of his words. Even so, Atlanta felt bad.

"I'm sorry. It's not you personally. In fact, I was just

thinking about how much I've enjoyed your company on the trip here. It's bad timing."

"For dinner?"

"You know what I mean."

"No." He set his hands on his hips. "Not really. I'm talking about a meal."

She changed tactics. "You're talking about avoidance, as in avoiding the real reason you came here. Your father."

"My choice. My business." His expression lost some of its easy charm, telling her she'd struck a nerve. So much for his earlier claim not to care about the estrangement. But the affable smile was back when he said, "What's the harm, Atlanta? We've already established that I'm not interested in a long-term relationship and you're not ready for one. What's wrong with a little… friendship?"

He stepped closer and ran his knuckles lightly down her cheek, making it clear he had more than friendship in mind. God help her, the simple touch stoked her pulse to life. Her feelings scared her almost as much as what he was suggesting. "We're two Americans in a foreign country. What happens here stays here."

He wound up his tempting offer with, "No one needs to ever find out."

Don't tell your mother. It's our little secret.

Bile rose in her throat, along with anger and a baffling amount of disappointment. But she kept her tone even when she said, "Let me put this another way: I'm not interested in continuing as your distraction, Angelo."

Indeed. She'd spent too many years being just that: A sick father figure's plaything. A powerful man's puppet.

Angelo frowned. "You just said you're not looking for strings."

"I'm not, but while I didn't mind being a distraction during the trip over, that scenario has played out." She took a step back. "To use your vernacular, the game is over."

He sucked in a breath and stepped back with his palms up in defeat. "Got it, sweetheart. Enjoy your stay."

She watched the Mercedes drive away. Should she have been so blunt? Could she have handled things differently, more diplomatically, perhaps? Though she was beset with doubts and some regret, one thing came through clearly. As angry and irritated as Angelo had been, he'd respected her decision.

As she stood on the steps replaying the encounter, the door behind her opened. A young woman stood just inside the entry. She wore a plain cotton dress and her dark hair was parted in the middle and pulled back.

"Miss Jackson, welcome," she said in heavily accented English. "I am Franca Bruno."

The name registered as Atlanta stepped inside. This was the owner of the house. "Thank you. I was just admiring the view. My travel agent said it was lovely and he wasn't mistaken."

The woman glanced at the bags before poking her head out the door. "Is my husband with you? He was supposed to pick you up from the airport."

"No. I caught another ride."

Franca's dark eyes narrowed and she rattled off something in Italian that didn't sound particularly nice. "He was late, wasn't he?"

"Maybe just a little," Atlanta hedged, not wanting to get in the middle of a domestic dispute. "Unfortunately, circumstances came up that forced me to leave in a rush. I was lucky to run into a friend who also was coming to Monta Correnti."

That snagged Franca's attention. "Another American?"

"Yes. Angelo Casali."

Franca nodded. "Luca's other son. I had heard that he might come. I am pleased for his father's sake that it is so. Signor Casali is a kind man…and far more reliable than my husband."

Franca helped Atlanta pull her bags inside. "Come, let me show you around."

In addition to the stunning view, the villa boasted three large bedrooms, three bathrooms, formal sitting and dining rooms, and what appeared to be a study. The furnishings were an eclectic mix of charming old-world pieces and modern conveniences such as the flat-screen television that hung over the fireplace in the study and the microwave oven that sat on the counter opposite a brick pizza oven.

Atlanta had everything she needed. Franca had stocked the refrigerator with food and had even gone to the trouble of preparing an antipasto salad in case Atlanta was too jet-lagged to go out later that evening.

"You will find bottled water and local vintage red wine in the pantry. I am happy to prepare any meals you request."

"Thank you. The antipasto will hold me over for tonight."

Together they walked back to the door and Atlanta followed the other woman outside.

"I hope you will enjoy your stay."

"I'll be hard-pressed not to." She spread out her hands to encompass the scenery. "It's truly lovely here."

"It is a special place," Franca agreed. "It belonged to my grandparents. My husband and I live just down the hill. I will be by each morning to freshen up the linens and take care of anything else you need."

After Franca was gone, Atlanta headed upstairs. The only thing she needed right now was a hot shower and a few hours of uninterrupted sleep. Unlike Angelo, she'd spent the entire flight wide awake and way too aware of not only the sexy man slumbering next to her, but her physical response to him.

The game is over.

Angelo mulled Atlanta's parting words on the way to his villa. He wanted to be able to shrug them off… shrug her off. There were plenty of other fish in the sea. He knew that firsthand. So, why did he feel so damned disappointed? Maybe because at times while they'd talked, it hadn't felt like a game.

It was the painkillers, he decided as the driver turned off the main road and passed through a gated drive. They made his brain fuzzy.

A turn-of-the-last-century villa came into sight. Its view of the surrounding countryside was worth every penny of the rent. His courtyard sported more than the cobblestones and grapevines that graced Atlanta's. His had a built-in pool and spa.

While the driver took his bags inside, Angelo walked over to inspect the amenities. The pool wasn't Olympic size, but he wasn't in any condition to swim laps anyway. The hot tub was more his speed, he thought on a grin. He could picture himself in it, the pulsating jets working the tension out of his muscles as he enjoyed a glass of red wine and watched the sun set. If he had to stay in Monta Correnti, at least he would be comfortable.

From what he'd seen so far, his brother had done well in choosing accommodations. He headed back to the house.

Alex hadn't said anything about meals being included, but when Angelo stepped inside he was greeted by the mouth-watering aroma of garlic, onions and assorted herbs. He inhaled deeply, letting the scents linger in his nose. Snippets of memories came to him before he could stop them, popping like corn kernels held over a flame. He recalled following his father to a nearby riverbed to pick the special basil that Luca said gave his tomato sauce its distinctive flavor. Alex was with them. Angelo swallowed now, remembering how happy the boys had been and how he'd basked in their father's attention. It was not long after that that Luca sent his sons away.

"No wonder I've never been a fan of spaghetti," he muttered with a shake of his head.

"Actually, I am making ravioli stuffed with portabella mushrooms and roasted garlic." A young woman stood on the opposite side of the room. Given her apron and her words, he assumed the door from which she'd entered must be the kitchen. She was dark-haired and lovely with surprisingly blue eyes. Eyes that were the exact shade of his, a trait he had inherited from his father.

"Isabella," he guessed, feeling mule-kicked.

So this was the sister he'd never met and had only learned about recently. Yet another reason to resent Luca. But it wasn't only resentment he felt. Emotions Angelo couldn't label, much less process, raced through his head. For so long he'd just had Alex. Now he was meeting a sister, and Luca had two other sons who shared the Casali name, as well.

Clearly, Isabella had more practice in handling the

surreal. While he stood gaping, she smiled warmly at the mention of her name.

"And you are Angelo." She crossed to him and rose up on tiptoe to kiss both of his cheeks. It was a standard Italian greeting, he reminded himself when a lump rose in his throat. "Welcome home."

"This…this is Luca's home?" He glanced around. Other than the aroma wafting from the kitchen, nothing about the place was remotely familiar.

"No. I meant welcome to Monta Correnti," Isabella clarified. "An American businessman owns this particular villa. He leases it out when he is not here, which is most of the time. Alessandro said he thought it would suit your needs."

Angelo nodded. Unsure what else to say, he told her, "Your English is very good."

"Better than your Italian?" Isabella's smile told him she already knew the answer to her question.

"It could use some work."

"So could your brother's when I met him. But he learned a lot during the time he was here." Her satisfied expression made Angelo think she was referring to more than the language. "Alessandro is a good man. I was grateful that he came, and I am even more grateful that he was able to convince you to come as well."

Angelo needed to set the record straight. "I'm not sure the outcome of my visit will be what you're hoping for, Isabella. Alex and I may look a lot alike, but that doesn't mean we think the same."

She took a moment to weigh his words before nodding. "You are here. That is enough for now. We will see about the rest later." She wiped her hands on her apron, a gesture that spoke of nerves more than necessity. "Come. You must be tired after your long journey. I can show you around."

"Actually, I'm not all that tired. I slept most of the way." He hated that he still felt a little groggy from the medication. Despite the returning pain, he was determined to forgo another dose. He had too much to process to be lost in the fog.

"Are you hungry, then?" Isabella asked.

He hadn't been since leaving the plane. Between the visit to come and Atlanta's intoxicating company, he'd been way too keyed up to think about food. Now, his empty stomach made its presence known with a loud growl, which she heard.

"I guess I am," he said sheepishly.

Isabella smiled, clearly pleased. "I was hoping that would be the case. I will set the table while you freshen up. You will find a bathroom down there." She pointed to a hallway that led from the room. "It's the first door on the right. You will find a larger one upstairs. Your rooms are on the second floor to the left of the landing."

Angelo opted for the former. A few minutes later, after splashing a little water on his face and adjusting his wrinkled clothes, he joined Isabella in the kitchen. Even though the villa had a formal dining room appointed with intricately carved mahogany furnishings, she'd set the wooden-plank table in what was a surprisingly plain kitchen. Plain and downright rustic, he thought, glancing around.

"I hope you don't mind," she said. "The other room is fancier, but so big and formal. We are family."

The word was as foreign to him as her accent. "I take it the American businessman who owns this place isn't much of a chef."

"No. On the rare occasions when he is here, he takes all of his meals in the village. But you are not to worry," she said, as if reading Angelo's mind. "You will find the master suite very comfortable. He has done what you would call extensive updating elsewhere in the house."

"And outside as well. It was kind of hard to miss the in-ground pool and hot tub."

"They look very inviting," Isabella agreed.

"So does this meal."

She motioned with her arms. "Then sit and enjoy."

While he lowered himself into one of the chairs, she filled his glass with red wine. He tried not to stare, but he couldn't help it. When she glanced up and caught him, they both flushed.

"I'm sorry. It's just…disturbing, you know?" When her brows pulled together in puzzlement, he added, "Seeing a resemblance in a stranger's face."

"The eyes."

"Yes, and our chins." At her startled expression, he laughed. "Don't worry. Yours is much smaller and far more refined."

"And this resemblance disturbs you?"

He decided to be frank. "For most of my life, it's been just Alex and me."

"But your mother—"

"Even then," he interrupted. Given Cindy's fair looks and her absorption with partying, it had been easy to discount her role in their lives. As for Luca, whenever Angelo had thought of their father, he hadn't considered the possibility of half-siblings. Or maybe he simply had been unable to process the idea that Luca could send away his twins and then someday have children he would keep. Confused and a great deal more curious than he wanted to be, he said, "You know, I'm a big eater, but there's enough here to feed a small army."

"I cook when I'm nervous," she admitted on a laugh.

"Why don't you join me and enjoy some of the fruits of your labor?"

A smile lit her face. "I would like that." As she took the seat opposite his it was obvious she knew the real reason he'd issued the invitation. "It will give us a chance to get better acquainted with one another."

He wasn't exaggerating about the amount of food. In addition to the pasta dish, which she'd served with the savory tomato sauce that had assaulted his senses upon arrival, the table included a loaf of thick-crusted bread, steamed green beans and a side of some sort of sausage that she told him was produced locally.

"This is excellent," he declared after his first bite of ravioli. It was no empty compliment. The flavors sang in his mouth. "You're an excellent cook."

"I cannot take all of the credit. The sauce is the real star."

"It's very good." In fact, he'd never tasted its equal, which made his aversion to bottled pasta sauce all the more understandable.

"It's very popular with our patrons."

"At Rosa." Despite his best effort, the name was hissed between clenched teeth. From Alex, Angelo had heard a lot about the quaint and rustic eatery their father owned and had named for their late grandmother. Far from taking pride in it, he saw the place as competition. After all, it was what Luca had squandered his time, love and attention on after shipping his sons off to America.

"I used to spend more time there than I did away,"

Isabella mused. Shook her head and laughed. "Scarlett, our cousin from Australia, manages it now. Her husband to be, Lorenzo, is the chef. But I am still there a lot."

"Why do you bother? Why do any of you bother to slave away for him?"

She sobered. "I have a full life, Angelo. As does Scarlett. I am married to a wonderful man and very happy. I work for our father because I enjoy what I do."

Angelo snorted. "You must to put up with him."

"That's unfair," Isabella objected. "You know nothing of Luca."

"Only because that's the way he wanted it," he shot back. "From what Alex has told me, the restaurant isn't doing as well as it could be these days. Money is tight."

Her face had paled. "That is true. He insists on using local produce and labor, and sometimes that has cost him more than if he'd outsourced."

The anger that had been simmering for the better part of three decades rolled to a boil. "So, call in the millionaire stepbrother to help save the day."

Isabella's cheeks flamed red now and she shot to her feet. She shouted something in Italian before she collected herself and, in a more moderated tone, replied in English, "I will apologize if that is the way it seems, but what you are saying is not true. Money is not why I sought out either you or Alex and asked you to come to Monta Correnti."

He wanted to believe her. Even so, he challenged, "Then why? Why now?"

"I only recently learned of your existence, Angelo."

He crossed his arms over his chest. "That makes

two of us. Again, Luca's choice. Or, should I say, his fault?"

He had her there and she knew it. But Isabella raised that small chin that was so similar to his.

"My motives for asking you to come here are very simple. I have two older brothers whom I wished to meet and a rift in our family that I wish to see mended. These are the reasons I sought Luca's permission to contact you and Alex in America." She unknotted her fingers from the cloth napkin she held and set it on the table. "If all I needed was money to save Rosa, Angelo, my husband would be happy to provide it. It is not beyond his means, and he has generously offered to do so on more than one occasion."

"But you've turned him down."

"Yes. *Family* is more important than the restaurant, but *family* is what it will take to save it."

She needn't have stressed the word. It would have struck him like a prizefighter's blow anyway. He'd never viewed family as the sort of savior she was implying it could be. Before he could respond, she was going on.

"We have a plan in mind. Our cousins and I. We want to combine our families' restaurants. They are joined by a courtyard. It is time they were joined in other ways."

"How does Luca feel about that?"

"He knows nothing of the plan. We want to surprise him. We want everyone who is descended from our grandmother, Rosa Firenzi, to come together. As I said, it will take all of us to make it happen."

He didn't question whether she was referring to funding now. He knew better.

Isabella rose to her feet. "I will leave you now to

finish your meal and to settle in. I have things I must see to."

"At the restaurant?" It was a low blow and he knew it. Shame stirred, making him wish it were possible to snatch back the words and start over.

Instead of answering his question, Isabella said, "If you want for anything, I wrote my number next to the telephone in the front parlor."

With that, his sister disappeared out the door. Angelo stood so abruptly that his chair tipped backward, clattering noisily on the tiled floor. He wanted to call her back so he could apologize. He felt horrible, putting her on the defensive, especially when she'd gone to such trouble to make his first day in Monta Correnti pleasant.

Besides, this wasn't her fault. None of it was. Luca was the one responsible for the rift in their family. Their father was the one who had screwed up all of their lives with his selfishness and single-minded pursuits.

Oh, Alex had tried to palm off some of the blame on Lisa Firenzi, Luca's older sister and the owner of the restaurant with which Isabella wanted to join Rosa. According to Angelo, if only their aunt had given Luca the loan he'd sought when the boys were toddlers, they could have remained in Italy rather than being sent to live with Cindy. Angelo wasn't buying it. Ultimately, the choice had been Luca's.

Angelo didn't go after his sister. Instead, he uncorked the bottle of wine and filled his glass to the rim. Then, without bothering to change into the swim trunks that were packed in the luggage the driver had toted upstairs, he went outside and lowered himself fully clothed into the hot tub.

It would be several hours yet before the sun set,

but, lost as he was in bitter memories of his fractured childhood, he really didn't give a damn about either his pricey clothes or the million-dollar view.

CHAPTER FOUR

ANGELO woke early the next morning with a pounding headache that was the result of jet lag, regrets and too much wine. He'd finished off the bottle the evening before. In fact, he'd sat in the hot tub drinking it. Now, not quite dawn, he was in his bed. His head was throbbing more than his shoulder, but not quite as much as his conscience.

He owed Isabella an apology.

Women. This made two who'd gotten under his skin in short order in ways that he hadn't thought possible.

Last night, after a second glass of wine and half an hour of bubbling hot water had mellowed his mood, he'd considered going to see Atlanta. He'd poured himself more *vino* and brooded instead. He'd never pursued a woman in the past. He'd never needed to. Yet he found himself practically chasing Atlanta and eager to see her even though she'd made it clear she wanted solitude. And that she didn't want him. He didn't care for the fact he was acting like some lovesick teen.

As for Isabella, his sister had welcomed him to Monta Correnti with a feast suitable for a returning prodigal son, which in a way he guessed he was. They were strangers, yet they also were siblings. Half, whole or otherwise, she hadn't felt the need to sever their kinship.

She'd made it clear all she wanted was a chance to get to know her long-lost brother. A chance to right a wrong and mend a rift. In return, all she asked of Angelo was for him to keep an open mind when it came to their father and the rest of the family.

He'd blown that deal before they'd finished eating the pasta she'd no doubt spent hours preparing. God, he was a heel. He had to make amends. He waited until it was a reasonable hour and called the number she'd left, only to find out she wasn't home.

The man who answered the phone told Angelo in heavily accented English that she was in the village running errands and he didn't expect her back for a couple hours.

"This is Angelo, no?" the man asked gruffly.

Guilty as charged, he thought. "Yes."

"I am Max, Isabella's husband."

Not sure what else to say, Angelo replied, "It's nice to meet you."

Max didn't bother with inane pleasantries. "Isabella was upset when she returned to our home last night."

"That would be my fault."

"*Sì*. She told me as much. You made her very angry." Max's voice softened when he added, "My Isabella is especially pretty when her temper flares."

Angelo had heard that tone before. His brother used it whenever the subject of his intended came up.

Max was saying, "As much as it was my pleasure to take her mind off family matters, it is my duty to look out for her well-being. I do not wish to see her distraught again."

Under other circumstances, the man's subtle threat might have irritated Angelo. In this case, he figured he deserved it. Besides, he'd already managed to get off on a bad foot with relatives. No sense making matters worse by getting into a verbal boxing match with Max.

So, he said, "Neither do I. In fact, that's why I'm calling. I'd hoped to apologize to her. I knew even before she left that I was way out of line."

"Good." Max sounded pleased. "If you happen to be in the village this afternoon, you can find her at Rosa."

And chance running into Luca? No, thanks, Angelo thought.

Max seemed to read his mind. "Your father will not be at the restaurant today. In fact, he is away from Monta Correnti on a buying trip to the coast for fresh seafood. He prefers to take care of important business in person."

Max's message was clear. Angelo should offer his apology to Isabella in person as well.

He was right, too, Angelo thought after ending the call. Hadn't Big Mike, the only foster father he'd ever considered worthy of the title, taught Angelo that very lesson right along with tips for how to steal a base when the pitcher wasn't looking?

Dressed and ready to eat whatever amount of crow was necessary, he started off for the village a little later. He figured he could poke around a bit before going to see Isabella.

In New York or while on the road with his team, Angelo left the driving to others. Here, he had a car at his disposal, a sporty little five-speed that his brother had thoughtfully rented on his behalf. He was itching to get behind the wheel, but he decided to walk. He could use the fresh air and exercise. Besides, he was too off-kilter to remember which side of the road he was supposed to be on.

The temperature was cool when he started out, the air still moist from dew. After a while, the sun poked through the filmy layer of clouds. Between its warmth and Angelo's physical exertion, by the time he reached the village he was regretting the jacket he'd pulled over his button-down shirt. He shrugged it off and slung it over his good shoulder as he made his way down cobbled streets that looked like something straight out of Brigadoon.

He navigated his way around what he figured was the main business district. With each turn, he discovered quaint shops and encountered the homey smells of fresh-baked bread and drying herbs. Based on his reaction the previous day to scent, he waited for some blast of recognition or sense of déjà vu to slow his steps. But while he definitely found Monta Correnti inviting and the smells mouthwatering, none of it was familiar.

Angelo told himself he was relieved. The last thing he wanted at the moment was to take a trip down memory lane. So what if the place of his birth didn't ring any mental bells? Why would it? He'd barely spent three years here. He and Alex had spent more than a decade with their apathetic mother in a Boston apartment building, and those memories were good and buried. That was how he preferred it. As far as he was concerned, his life had begun the day a scout from a small private college in upstate New York had come knocking at his foster family's door. It hadn't been the big leagues, but it had helped pave the way to them.

Lost in good memories, he took a moment to recognize the woman who emerged from the pastry shop at the corner. It was Atlanta.

She was wearing jeans, the faded boot-cut variety, and a ridiculously prim apple-green sweater set that did nothing to diminish her sex appeal. She might as well have been outfitted in skin-tight leather pants and a low-cut leopard-print blouse given the way his body reacted.

She's not interested, he reminded himself. She'd made that abundantly clear. He was just starting to turn in the opposite direction when she spied him and offered a tentative wave. He waved back and though he intended that to be the end of the encounter, his feet had other ideas. They started off in her direction.

"Good morning," he said when he reached her.

"*Buongiorno.*"

"Show off. You listened to Berlitz tapes before you came," he accused, finding it easier to distance himself from real emotions by hiding behind teasing humor.

For her part, Atlanta looked almost relieved.

"Actually, I had to learn a little Italian for a movie I did a few years back. I liked the language, so I brushed up on it before traveling." As she spoke, she tucked the little white pastry bag behind her back.

"What have you got in there?" he asked, craning to one side.

"N-nothing." She looked and sounded nervous. Not nervous, he amended. Guilty. But he'd be damned if he could figure out why.

"Did you knock over the pastry shop or something?"

Her mouth fell open and she sputtered a moment before finally managing a full sentence. "Why on earth would you say that?"

"Because you're acting suspicious." He retrieved the bag from her hands. "It's like you've got the Hope diamond stuffed in there or something."

She snatched it away before he could open it. "It's just a cannolo."

"A cannolo?" All that subterfuge for a damned pastry? He said as much.

She sighed. "Okay, two. I couldn't resist. They were fresh-made this morning."

"Mmm. Nothing like a freshly made cannolo." Angelo's mouth watered a little, but it wasn't the pastry alone that had whetted his appetite. "Were you planning to share with someone?"

"No. I bought them for me." She laughed and some of her nervousness leaked away. "I guess that's why I seemed so guilty. I can't believe I bought one cannolo, much less two and just for myself."

"What's so wrong with that?"

"I planned to eat them both. In one sitting." The last part was confessed in a near whisper with her gaze glued to the tips of her shoes.

"Is that a crime?"

"Yes." She shook her head then and her gaze reconnected with his. "No. Of course not. Unless you're Darnell."

"Darnell?"

"My sadistic personal trainer. Since I've been away from Los Angeles he's text-messaged me nearly every day to ask if I've been working out and sticking to my diet."

Though he knew he'd regret it, Angelo allowed his gaze to slip south. The woman had a killer body. It was perfectly proportioned, even if parts of it were a little less full these days. "I don't think you need to worry about a diet right now."

"I've lost a little weight," she admitted. "I call it the stress diet." She touched a finger to her chin, the pose intentionally thoughtful. "You know, maybe I should patent it and start hawking it to young starlets as a backup plan in case my career never recovers."

"That would be a waste of your talent. Besides, I like women with some curves."

"Some curves." She nodded. "But there's a fine line, which is why Zeke wouldn't let me..."

She flushed and didn't finish, but Angelo figured he could fill in the blanks easily enough. It sounded as if the guy had done a real number on her. Let it go, he told himself. Leave it alone. He had enough problems of his own to concentrate on without taking on Atlanta's, especially since she'd made it abundantly plain she was not interested in sharing a cannolo or anything else with him.

He hitched one thumb over his shoulder and took a step backward. "I should be going."

"Yes. I should, too."

"You wouldn't want those cannoli to get stale." He motioned toward the bag as he backed up another step.

"No." She forced out a laugh. "It was nice seeing you, Angelo."

He stopped. "Was it?"

His point-blank question caused her to blink. "I...I feel bad about yesterday. About...about how things ended between us."

"Well, as you said, it was time for them to end. The game was over and all," he drawled.

Atlanta winced. "That came out..."

"Wrong?" He shook his head. "I don't think so. Actually, I appreciate your honesty."

She blinked again, this time looking more piqued than perplexed. "I doubt that. You were clearly mad."

Royally ticked was more like it. But he smiled now. "Whatever. Water under the bridge."

"Then why bring it up?"

"I didn't."

"You did."

Damn. She had him there. He glanced past her up the block. A coffee shop caught his attention. He told himself it was only the promise of his first cup of java that caused him to say, "I want a cannolo."

"What?"

"A cannolo. I'll buy the espresso if you'll share your cannoli. It doesn't even have to be a whole one. I'll settle for a bite or two."

Her eyes narrowed. "You want a cannolo?"

"That's what I said." He held his breath, half expecting her to state the obvious and tell him to go buy his own.

Instead, to his surprise, she said slowly, "I guess that's a reasonable trade."

The coffee shop was small with limited seating inside and only half a dozen wrought-iron tables and chairs on its speck of a cobblestone patio. Most of the tables indoors were unoccupied, but it was too nice a day to sit inside. Outdoors, only two were empty. They took a seat at one of them and waited for the server to come for their order. Angelo went with espresso, the stronger the better in his opinion, especially given the rough start to his day. Atlanta opted for a cappuccino.

"In for a penny, in for a pound," she announced when their beverages arrived.

"What do you mean by that?" he asked.

She pointed to the rich froth that topped her cup. "This is steamed whole milk and the espresso isn't decaffeinated. Do you have any idea how long it's been since I allowed myself to have either?" She didn't wait for Angelo to answer. "And a cannolo!" She pulled one of the pastries in question from the paper bag. "I would be eating two if you hadn't talked me into being nice and sharing."

She tried to hand him one of the tempting pastries, but he refused to take it. "I've changed my mind. I want you to eat them both. And I want to watch."

"God, no! Please, Angelo. Save me from myself." Though the drama of her words was definitely for effect, he sensed a nugget of truth—and perhaps of fear—in them.

He leaned back in his chair. "What's to save, sweetheart? Everyone's entitled to a little indulgence from time to time."

Still eyeing the cannolo, she nodded. "I know."

"Do you?"

"Some habits are hard to break," she said softly.

"Zeke?"

She set the cannolo on a napkin and glanced away. "You think it's stupid that I let a man run my life to such a degree for so long."

"Is that what I think? Or is that what you think?" he asked, reneging on his earlier promise to himself to stay out of her business. He'd also vowed to steer clear of her. As the woman said, in for a penny, in for a pound.

"It's what I think."

"So, how'd it happen?"

Her brow furrowed. "It wasn't all at once. I thought I was free…"

"Free?"

She cleared her throat. "You know. Footloose and fancy free. God knows, I was all attitude when I first arrived in Hollywood. I didn't look in the rearview mirror when I left rural Louisiana. I was happy to kiss my hick roots and…and everything else goodbye."

The way she hesitated made him think there was more to it than that, but he commented on the obvious. "I thought you were born in Georgia?"

One side of her mouth rose. "That's what you're supposed to think. It was Zeke's idea after he came up with my name. Atlanta is one of his favorite cities, very cosmopolitan but with a bit of edge. He said it suited me."

"What is your given name?"

"Jane. Jane Marie Lutz."

It was a nice enough name, but it didn't fit her, Angelo decided as he took in the tumble of nearly white hair and the blue eyes that, even without the benefit of much makeup, were her face's star feature.

"Forgive me for saying so, but you don't look like a Jane."

Her laughter held little humor. "Zeke's words exactly. He wanted something exotic, something people would remember. A name that could be used all by itself and people would know who you meant."

"Like Cher or Madonna."

She nodded. "You got it. The idea of being that famous caught my attention, even if at first I wasn't too excited about being called Atlanta. Still, I was willing to do whatever Zeke suggested. He was a Hollywood big shot who had managed the careers of some of the hottest names in the business, and I was a nobody who wanted to be a star. I was grateful to him, pathetically so, for believing that I could be."

"I don't think he had to overtax his imagination. He

must have seen a spark of something that he knew would have broad appeal."

"He saw my body," she said dryly. "I was nineteen, wearing a G-string and pasties and performing onstage at a gentleman's club. Not my finest hour and definitely not the career I envisioned when I traded in my Podunk Ville address for a cockroach-invested walkup in Tinsel Town."

A G-string and pasties.

Angelo had too much testosterone not to hone in on those words and be turned on by the erotic image they evoked. Somehow, however, he managed to say in a remarkably normal tone, "It takes more than a hot body and pretty face to become a mainstay in Hollywood. Lots of actresses with only that to recommend them have come and gone, while you've remained a box-office draw. You're selling yourself short again."

He expected her to argue, but she didn't. Neither did she agree. Instead, she tore open a white packet of sugar and added it to her beverage. Another act of defiance, he was sure.

"So what does all of this have to do with a couple of cannoli and caffeine laced with whole milk and now some sugar?" he asked.

"Zeke was strict about what I could eat." She exhaled and shook her head. "And about what I could drink, wear…you name it."

"Controlling?"

"He claimed that he was only looking out for my best interests."

Of course he did.

"Controlling," Angelo said again, this time not as a question but as a statement.

"He was right about a lot of things, though. He got

me my first big break. I didn't want the part of Daisy Maddox." It was the role that had made her a bona fide star. "He insisted I take it and it wound up being my best-grossing movie."

"Are you defending him?" Angelo asked.

"No." She looked insulted. "I'm merely pointing out the hand he had in making my career."

"So, you're defending him."

"No!"

"He could have had the same impact on your career without treating you like a lump of clay to be molded to his exact specifications."

She shook her head. "You don't understand."

"Do you?"

"He managed what has been a very successful career for me."

"So, that meant he got to manage your life, too?"

"Of course not."

"As for your career, is it all you envisioned for yourself?"

He wasn't sure what made him ask the question, but he was glad he had when he saw her mouth drop open. "I...I have other ideas, other avenues I'd like to explore."

"Let me guess. He didn't want you to explore them."

Her gaze slid away. "Let's drop it."

"Sure."

Atlanta grew quiet. He considered apologizing, but he wasn't really sorry. She'd been under the guy's thumb for way too long. Angelo didn't want to see her slip beneath it again, even for a moment. No one deserved that kind of treatment.

She dipped the tip of her index finger into the custard

that oozed from the end of the cannolo and licked it off. All thoughts of Zeke vanished. In fact, thoughts of every variety except the lustful kind vanished. It was all he could do not to groan.

"That's a good start. But you can do better."

When she looked at him in question, he nodded to the cannolo.

She dipped her finger in a second time for another nibble. He snagged her wrist before she could and brought it to his mouth instead, taking his time licking off the last of the rich filling. The quick intake of her breath was all of the encouragement he needed.

"I know all about indulgence, Atlanta. You might say I'm an expert."

She pulled her fingers free and reached for her cappuccino. The hands holding the cup weren't completely steady. He knew the feeling.

"Seduced in Italy."

"Excuse me?" She gaped at him and his ego needed to believe she looked every bit as guilty as she had over the cannoli.

"The name of the movie you learned Italian for."

"Oh. Right." She smiled. "That was the one. It was shot on location in Venice. I loved it there."

"Was Zeke with you?"

"Only for the first couple days, then he had to fly back to LA for business."

"Perhaps that's why you enjoyed Venice so much. It's a city known for indulgence."

She shrugged, non-committal, and took another sip of her cappuccino. "I'm guessing you were on a date when you saw the movie."

"Why do you say that?"

"It's a chick flick. I can't see you going with a couple of guys from the team."

"You're right." His expression was unrepentant when he said, "I don't remember the woman I was with, but I remember the scene where you danced in the fountain in that really sheer top."

"What a surprise," Atlanta replied dryly.

Angelo was flirting with her again, although at times it seemed as if he was testing himself as much as her. Either way, flirting was harmless, she decided. Come to that, even though she'd had precious little practice at it away from the big screen, it was all but required when two healthy and unattached adults got together in an idyllic setting. In Angelo's case, it was second nature and indicative of nothing more than his interest in a romp in the sack. The man had a one-track mind.

He needn't bother. She was the polar opposite of her celluloid twin, the recent stirrings of her libido not-withstanding. With a crew looking on and a camera recording her every move and emotion, she'd enticed and seduced her leading man or fallen victim to his charms. In real life, however, she'd always been care-ful not to send out signals or offer come-hither glances and coy smiles. She considered that to be too close to her mother's method of operation when it came to men. Too close to what her stepfather had accused Atlanta of doing to assuage his conscience for the petting and pawing that had begun even before she'd hit puberty.

Even with Zeke, Atlanta had felt awkward and had approached sex with a straightforwardness that had siphoned off every last ounce of romance from the act. He hadn't seemed to mind, which she realized now was because for him romance had never entered into it.

"Is something wrong with your dessert?" Angelo's question roused her from her thoughts.

"No. It's fine. Delicious, in fact." She reached for her napkin and blotted the corners of her mouth.

"Then why are you frowning?"

"I wasn't aware that I was."

"You are."

"If I am, it's not the company." She said it automatically. She'd had a lot of practice placating men.

"Sure it is." Angelo's eyes narrowed. "I make you nervous."

"Please." She waved a hand. "What do I have to be nervous about?"

"You're attracted to me."

She huffed out an impatient breath to camouflage the truth. "Right. And that would make me nervous?"

"Yeah," he said slowly. "You're not as confident in real life as you are in your movies."

So, he'd figured that out, had he? Well, points to him.

"That's because I'm a person, not a character for whom every action and reaction has been scripted." She crossed her arms. "You, on the other hand, come across as grossly overconfident."

"It's not overconfidence if you can back it up with actions."

"I'm talking off the ball diamond."

"So am I."

"Is that so, *sweetheart*?" she drawled. "I hate to tell you this, but, all of your bravado aside, you're no more certain of yourself than I am. It's easy to flirt and throw out pickup lines, but you've admitted that you aren't capable of cultivating a real relationship."

"I didn't say I was incapable." The calf that had been

rubbing against hers under the table stilled. "I said it's not what I want."

"Uh-huh. The right woman doesn't exist for you. I remember the conversation. Have you ever *had* a relationship? And I'm talking about something that involves more than the exchange of apartment keys and regular sex."

A muscle twitched in his jaw. "As I said, that's not what I want."

"Why?" It was her turn to play therapist, and if it kept her out of the hot seat, all the better. "Is your life so perfect flying solo all the time?"

"That's right."

"No. That's what you want everybody to think. Most people buy it. I don't. What insecurities are you trying to mask? Hmm? What are your secrets?"

He shifted back in his chair, his gaze turning guarded. She'd struck a nerve.

"You know, I almost turned around and walked the other way when I saw you today," he admitted.

"Regretting that you didn't?"

He didn't answer.

"You don't like it when the shoe is on the other foot," she said.

"It's damned uncomfortable," he surprised her by admitting.

"Then maybe you'll resist the next time you're tempted to analyze me."

"Maybe. I probably should." He shrugged. "For that matter, I should probably leave you alone entirely. You've asked me to. I don't usually pursue a woman who tells me not to bother."

"Then why are you?"

She expected him to mention attraction again. What he said was, "I can't quite figure you out, Atlanta."

Her laughter was bitter. "No one else seems to have a problem."

"Yeah, I thought I had, too. But you're a bundle of contradictions. Strong one moment, vulnerable the next."

She shifted uncomfortably in her seat. "Maybe I'm both. Maybe I'm neither. I am an actress."

"Uh-uh. My turn to tell you I'm not buying it. This is you. Not an act. Contradictions," he said again. "Like the way you keep telling me no but—"

That was as far as he got. She shot to her feet, rapping her hip against the edge of the table and spilling both of their beverages.

"When I say no, I mean no."

"Atlanta."

"No means no!"

He reached out a hand in entreaty, but she shook her head, turned and fled.

CHAPTER FIVE

What was that all about?

Alone at the café, Angelo slumped back in his chair and replayed the encounter. Atlanta had surprised him twice. First, by turning the tables on him and questioning what his secrets and vulnerabilities might be. And then with her overreaction to his admittedly poor choice of words.

He was a firm believer that when a woman said no, she meant no, but that was in the bedroom. He hadn't been talking about sex, at least not directly; although where Atlanta was concerned, it was much on his mind.

"I should have walked the other way," he muttered.

He didn't have time to sort through her emotional baggage. As she'd already figured out, he had enough of his own.

Standing, he tossed some bills onto the table alongside her discarded cannoli and left to meander through the town. He had a little more time to kill before seeing Isabella.

Everyone he passed in Monta Correnti was friendly. From the shop owners to their customers to the people milling about on the streets, they smiled and called out polite greetings. But not one of them asked for Angelo's autograph. Not one of them asked him to stop and pose for a photograph. Almost absently, he rubbed his shoulder. Just as he had at the airport in Rome, he found anonymity disturbing. He also found his need for fame disturbing.

What insecurities are you hiding? Atlanta had asked.

"*Buongiorno.*"

He glanced up to find a young woman standing beside a pushcart of freshly cut flowers. The blooms were separated by kind and color and tucked into individual buckets of water. The overall effect was lovely, as was the cart's owner. He guessed her to be in her mid-twenties. She had a ripe figure, Sophia Loren eyes and mahogany-colored hair that tumbled halfway down her back.

"Hi, uh, *buongiorno.*"

She switched to English when she asked, "Do you see something you like, *signor*?"

The invitation in her smile was unmistakable, as was his appalling lack of interest. Here was the kind of mindless distraction he needed, yet the thought of spending time with her—clothed or otherwise—held virtually no appeal. Now, if she'd had blonde hair and blue eyes... He glanced past her to the cart.

"Um, how about some roses?"

"Roses." Her disappointment was clear.

"A dozen white." The perfect peace offering for his sister, he decided.

The woman gathered the blooms and added some greenery to the arrangement. Her movements were deft but her enthusiasm to make a sale had waned considerably. That much was all the more obvious when she thrust the bouquet into his hands and spat out a price.

He was reaching into his pocket for his wallet when a burly older man rushed over shouting something in Italian. The words were directed at the young woman, who cast Angelo a second appraising look before leaving.

"You are Luca's son, no?"

Despite the label's uncomfortable fit, Angelo answered, "Yes, um, *sì*."

"I am Andrea. I own the village floral shop. My daughter, Bianca, looks after the cart for me. I provide flowers for the tables at Rosa." He cast another dark look in her direction before continuing. "Luca, he is so good to me and my family. He is good to many of us in Monta Correnti. So, I give you these flowers for half the price."

Angelo fought the ridiculous urge to argue. Instead he offered a stilted, *"Grazie."*

After twenty minutes of brooding and walking, he arrived at his father's restaurant. The exterior of Rosa was just as his brother described it, a rustic stone façade with arched windows. Directly next to it was the more upscale eatery Sorella. Their aunt, Luca's older sister Lisa, owned it. The two restaurants shared a wall and a gated courtyard, but otherwise they had little in common.

According to Alex, Sorella's cuisine was contemporary and international, the sort of stuff that could be found at the trendy restaurants of New York. That sounded more like Angelo's kind of thing. A peek through the restaurant's wide windows revealed a stylish interior that leaned toward modern with its chrome and glass fixtures and sleek furnishings.

Definitely more my thing, he thought. The designer he'd hired a couple years back to make over his

Manhattan apartment had done the rooms in a similar style.

Both restaurants were open for business. Rosa's door was propped open. Music drifted from inside, something classical and soothing that probably was written around the same time the building was erected. Angelo stepped through the door and was immediately welcomed by the aroma of freshly baked bread and the same tomato sauce Isabella had made for him the evening before. His stomach growled.

A young woman stood at the hostess station. She smiled politely and offered a greeting.

"Ciao," he replied. "I'm Angelo Casali." His name, he figured, would say it all.

Based on the way her face lit up, it did. *"Sì, sì.* Yes. Welcome. Signor Casali is not here."

Which was exactly why Angelo was willing to set foot in the place today. He smiled.

"Actually, I was hoping to see Isabella. Her husband told me I might find her here."

"Isabella. *Sì.* She is taking a telephone call right now, but I will tell her you are here. Have a seat." The young woman pointed to a table near the front window that offered a view of the street. "Can I get you a cup of espresso to drink while you wait?"

The thought of more caffeine on an empty stomach held zero appeal. "Just water, please."

She returned a moment later with a bottle of sparkling water and a glass.

"Isabella said to tell you she will be with you soon. Also, your cousin Scarlett is in her office. Shall I get her for you?"

"No. That's all right. I don't want to disturb her."

He was bound to meet all of the Casali clan before

he returned to New York, but he wasn't in the mood to do it now. The young woman nodded and left him to greet a group of tourists that had just come through the door.

Though it was barely a quarter past noon, Rosa was already filling up with patrons. The place was popular, no doubt about it. He figured the rich aromas that had greeted him when he stepped through the door explained why. He'd come here on a mission. He didn't want to be hungry. Nor did he want to feel this odd sense of pride. But he did.

Someone arrived with a basket of warm bread. When he glanced up to offer his thanks, he saw that it was Isabella.

"Angelo. Hello. I hope you are well rested." The words were offered with a polite if restrained smile. His doing, he knew.

"Yes," he lied, even though nothing about the previous night had been restful.

"I wasn't expecting to see you here today. Luca is away."

"I know."

Her smile was sad. "Of course, you do."

Angelo decided to cut to the chase. "I came because I owe you an apology and I didn't want to let it wait."

Isabella's brows rose, but she said nothing. He took that as a positive sign and reached over to pull out the chair next to his. When she was seated he continued.

"I offended you yesterday, and for that I'm sorry. You were nothing but kind, fixing me a meal and making me feel welcome on my first day in Monta Correnti, and I was rude."

A smile, this one more genuine than polite, creased her cheeks. "Yes, you were."

Her teasing reply, as much as her impish expression, made it easy to accept they really were siblings. "Unforgivably so?" he asked.

"Never, especially if those flowers are for me."

He'd nearly forgotten about the roses. He picked up the bouquet now and handed it to her. "I thought it was a fitting gesture."

"And very sweet. I cannot remember our other brothers ever giving me such a peace offering. When we were little, Cristiano and Valentino used to tickle me till I forgave them." As she buried her face in the blooms Angelo almost could hear the echoes of childish laughter. It unsettled him because he regretted not having been a part of it. She smiled at him. "I think I like your act of contrition better."

"I'm just glad you're no longer upset with me."

"How could I be?" She set the roses aside and clasped his hands firmly in her much smaller ones. "We're family, Angelo."

He didn't argue, even though the concept still seemed so foreign. But he needed to make one thing clear. "I don't know that I can forgive him, Isabella. What Luca did, it's not the same as a surly mood. Sorry and flowers won't fix it."

She sobered slightly as she settled back in her chair. "I only ask that, when you are ready, you will listen to what he has to say."

Angelo nodded and sipped his water. Still, he had to know. "Why is it so important to you?"

She seemed perplexed by the question. "We are family, Angelo. *Familia*. What is more important than that?"

He envied Isabella's passion on the subject. This made twice in a matter of minutes that she'd referenced their shared bloodline. He wanted to be swayed by her argument, to get behind it with as much conviction. Even with half as much. But the truth was, "The only family I've had for a very long time is Alex."

Her gaze held compassion as well as empathy. "I understand from your brother that your mother died when you were teenagers."

"She drank herself to death," he said bluntly. "Cindy…" An embarrassing rush of emotions washed away the rest of his words. He shook his head and tried again. "She was never going to win any Mother of the Year awards, you know? But she was all we had."

"My mamma is gone as well. She died when I was young." Her gaze softened. "I still miss her."

Alex had mentioned that Luca's second wife, Violetta, had been killed in a tragic fall. Fate could be crueler than addiction, even though some might argue that it didn't matter since the end result was the same. But fate put things outside one's control. "That's rough. Sorry."

"I remember her a little, as does Valentino. He is the youngest. Cristiano, who is two years older than I am, has more memories." Her expression clouded.

"I get the feeling that even though you weren't the oldest, you took care of them." What little he knew of Isabella pointed to a take-charge person. After all, she'd been the one to initiate contact with Angelo and Alex. The peacemaker, the bridge-maker. He'd admire the characteristics more if they weren't running against his own goals.

"I did."

"And you helped out here." He made a circular motion with one hand.

"Yes. Our father was lost in his grief after Mamma died. He needed me."

Luca and his needs. It took all of Angelo's willpower not to sneer.

"Why aren't you bitter?" He hadn't intended to ask that question, so he shook his head. "Never mind. I came here to apologize to you, not to pick another fight."

"I will answer anyway. Bitterness serves no useful purpose, Angelo. I would have liked a different childhood, *sì*. One with fewer cares and responsibilities, but…" Isabella's shoulders rose.

"Well, you're obviously happy now."

"I am. Very." Blue eyes that were so like his own lit with an emotion that Angelo had yet to experience for himself.

"Alex said you're married, and to a real prince, no less."

Her smile grew wider. "Maximilliano Di Rossi."

"I spoke to him today. He wasn't very happy with me."

Her laughter was pleased and wholly female. "He can be very protective."

"So I gathered."

"You will meet him and some of the others at the—" Isabella broke off and blushed.

"At the what?"

"Party."

"Let me guess. I'm to be the guest of honor," he said dryly.

She wrinkled her nose. "Would you rather not have such a gathering? If that is your wish I can call the others and explain. They can meet with you individually during the course of your stay in Italy."

Now there was an even less appealing thought. Better

to get it over with in one fell swoop than prolong the agony over days. "No. A party is fine. When is it and where?"

"We thought we would give you a chance to settle in first, get to know some people. So it is planned for a week from Friday at eight o'clock. Our plan is to close Rosa early for the occasion. Valentino will be here. Cristiano, unfortunately, can't be. He's a firefighter and was injured during a blaze in Rome."

A strange feeling of concern stirred for this stranger who shared his bloodline. "Is he…okay?"

Isabella's smile was all-knowing. "He will be." Then, "You are sure a family party is all right with you?"

"Yes."

Her expression turned wily when she mentioned, "You could bring someone."

"Who would I bring?" he asked, though he had the feeling his sister had someone in mind.

She did. "How about Atlanta Jackson? I have heard from no fewer than three sources already this morning that you were spotted sharing cannoli with the pretty actress at the café up the street."

And Atlanta's abrupt departure? Had they mentioned that?

"Is everything all right, Angelo?"

"Fine. It's just that she came here hoping to get away. She doesn't want to draw any attention to herself."

"Nor will she," Isabella assured him. "The villagers are curious about her, but they will leave her be. No one will ask for autographs or pictures. The wealthy and famous come here because they know they can count on our discretion. In turn, they keep our economy going."

"Good. She's going through a rough patch professionally and personally. The last thing she needs right now is to find herself being tailed by the media, legitimate or otherwise."

"I have read some of the things her ex is saying."

"Lies." But Angelo didn't think Zeke's cruelty or control were the only demons she needed to exorcise.

Isabella tilted her head to one side. "You seem very... concerned about her. Have you and this Atlanta known one another for very long?"

"We don't really know one another at all," he said slowly.

His sister smiled before helpfully suggesting, "Perhaps you can remedy that while you are here."

Atlanta rubbed her throbbing forehead with one hand and pressed the telephone to her ear with the other as Sara Daniels, one of the few true friends she had in Los Angeles, confirmed her worst fears.

"I hate to tell you this, but you're still making headlines. When I stopped for coffee on my way into work this morning, I saw pictures of you and Angelo Casali together in Rome's airport on the front page of a couple of tabloids."

Even as she bit back a groan Atlanta forced herself to ask, "What are they saying about me now?"

"Hon, you don't want to know."

"No, I don't, but tell me anyway." Forewarned was forearmed.

Sara heaved a sigh. "Okay. The headline on the one in *The Scoop* is, um, 'Angel and the Tramp'. The article claims that the two of you have been involved on and off for years."

"Of course it does. And the other tabloid? What did it come up with for a headline?"

"Keep in mind the writer is probably a Rogues fan, okay?" Sara hedged.

"Okay." Atlanta's forehead throbbed more insistently.

"'New York's Angel falls under Hollywood seductress's spell.'"

This time Atlanta wasn't able to hold back her groan. Glutton for punishment that she was, she asked, "What does it say?"

"The usual tripe about how Angelo is another of your many conquests. It includes a quote from Zeke. He, um, says he feels sorry for Mr. Casali and is a little surprised you went after him considering that the ballplayer is past his prime and not likely to continue in the spotlight much longer, unless, given his recent injury, it's to do endorsements for over-the-counter pain medicine."

"God, he's a piece of work," she spat, insulted on Angelo's behalf. "If he wants to trash me, fine. But he has no right to drag anyone else into the mud."

"Speaking of Angelo, how exactly did the two of you hook up?"

"We haven't *hooked up*. We were on the same flight, headed to the same place and he was kind enough to share his car with me after I was spotted by those photographers."

"So, that was the end of it?"

"We bumped into each other again today." She swallowed, thinking of how she'd overreacted during their conversation. And she had overreacted. She could see that now.

"Do you plan to see each other again?"

After her earlier display? He probably thought her to be either the quintessential drama queen or a complete nut. Either way, it was for the best. He had her thinking things, remembering things, best left alone.

It's not your fault.

A therapist had assured her of that, although it hadn't been necessary. Atlanta had always known who to blame. Her stepfather. Duke had been an adult and a parental figure. She'd been but a frightened girl who'd had the misfortune to blossom early and live in a trailer with a man who believed he was entitled to do as he pleased and a mother who chose to look the other way because she was too afraid of being alone.

No means no.

Knowing that didn't automatically make everything all right, though.

Thankfully, acting out a love scene in front of a camera had never been much of a problem for her, perhaps because she knew exactly what to expect. She knew when it would start and when it would stop. She knew what her reactions were supposed to be. The one time a co-star had tried to ad lib a bit too much for her liking, she'd ended the scene and walked off the set. Being in control made it easier, it made it almost cathartic, and it helped to block out the bad memories. Still, she considered it a testament to her acting ability that she could make the world believe she was truly enjoying herself.

As an adult, it had taken a long time for Atlanta to actually have sex without getting physically sick afterward. After a decade with Zeke, she'd gotten to the point where she sometimes could enjoy herself, though she rarely wound up fully satisfied. She was fine with that. Or she had been…until recently. Angelo had her wondering what she might have been missing.

"Atlanta?" Sara's voice brought her back to the present.

"What?"

"I asked if you were going to see him again."

"No," she replied with conviction.

"Hmm. Too bad."

"Why do you say that?"

Sara's laughter came over the line. "Have you gone blind or taken vows with a religious order since you've been gone?"

"My vision is perfect and, no, I doubt I'll ever be a candidate for the abbey."

"Well, then, if you tell me that man isn't every bit as sexy in real life as he comes across on television, I'm going to be crushed."

Atlanta nearly shivered as she recalled the way Angelo had licked cannolo custard from her fingers. "It's no trick of the cameras. He's sexy, all right."

"I thought so."

To counteract her friend's smugness, Atlanta said, "And so is every male co-star I've worked with during my career. It doesn't mean I want to sleep with them."

"Who said anything about sleeping together?" Sara asked. "I merely asked if you were going to see him again."

"My answer hasn't changed. No."

"You could do a lot worse."

"Sara."

"Just saying. I mean, it's not like I could see the two of you together for the long haul. But for a vacation fling? A post-Zeke fling?" Her friend sighed dreamily. "He's perfect."

"I'm not here for a fling," Atlanta replied impatiently, but Sara was right about one thing: if she were the sort of woman who engaged in casual, no-strings encounters, Angelo would be perfect.

For the better part of the afternoon, Atlanta hung around the villa going through the stack of scripts she'd brought with her. None was written by an established name. That was half of their appeal. The parts hadn't been penned with her in mind. They didn't play to her known strengths, mainly her sex appeal. She would have to adapt herself to these parts, in some cases change physically to do the characters justice.

Cut and dye her trademark locks? Gain a dozen pounds? The very idea was scary but exciting, too. Zeke never would have allowed it, but how else would she ever prove herself as more than a sex symbol?

You sell yourself short.

Angelo had told her that twice now.

She set a script in her lap. Angelo. He was so different from Zeke. She didn't mean to compare the men, but it was impossible not to. Physically, they were night and day. Zeke was lean with an elegant build. He claimed to be six feet tall, but she suspected he was closer to five ten. He also claimed to be fifty-two, but she knew for a fact that he was fifty-seven. He looked good for his age, though, thanks to regular workouts, a little Botox to his brow line and regular appointments with his stylist to ensure that the hair on his head and in his goatee remained a youthful chocolate brown. He was fond of designer clothes, preferred silk to cotton and didn't own anything made from denim or, God forbid, a synthetic fiber. He regularly wore large diamond studs in both of his ears and carried a European handbag to accommodate his BlackBerry and assorted other electronic gadgets.

In other words, Zeke was the walking definition of the metrosexual man while Angelo was the walking definition of masculinity.

Atlanta couldn't see Angelo carrying a purse, regardless of the label one gave it, and she knew he didn't dye his hair because she'd spotted a few strands of gray around his temples. As for Botox, if he indulged in it, he wasn't getting his money's worth, but he was all the more ruggedly handsome for the lines that fanned out from his eyes, which most likely were the result of squinting into the sun to catch a fly ball.

For the past decade, Zeke had dominated Atlanta's life. Under his rigid tutelage, she'd been transformed from a mousy-haired, small-town girl with big dreams and some talent into a blonde, box-office bombshell. On screen, she melted hearts and left men salivating. More than once in real life, Zeke had accused her of being frigid. Given her past, she'd thought herself incapable of the kind of intense passion she portrayed on screen. But when Atlanta was around Angelo, she was never more aware of her sexuality or of her purely feminine response to him.

It scared her.

Angelo was ticked off. His lunch with Isabella had gone well, but when he returned to his villa he found a delivery from Luca. Tucked in the basket of fresh fruit was a note. It was written in Italian, so the only word he recognized was Papa.

He crumpled it up and shoved it into his pocket before grabbing the keys to the rental car.

Damn the man. Damn him.

He had no idea where he was going, only that he

needed to get out, get away. The problem with Monta Correnti, though, was it wasn't big enough to put much distance between Angelo and his troubles. After more than an hour of driving, mostly in circles, he wound up at the one place he knew he wasn't welcome. Oddly, that made it perfect.

Lost in thought, the unexpected knock at the villa door gave Atlanta a start. It was late in the afternoon and she wasn't expecting anyone. Probably Franca, she thought, smoothing the hair back from her face. The woman was super efficient and determined that Atlanta would enjoy her stay. But it wasn't her landlady who stood on the other side of the door. It was Angelo.

Atlanta's mouth fell open before she managed to sputter out a greeting. "I wasn't expecting...company."

Angelo's in particular, though she'd thought of him incessantly all afternoon. For a moment she wondered if she'd conjured him up. But no, he was flesh and blood and all brooding male.

"Sorry to drop by unannounced," he began. "I wasn't exactly planning to come here. I just was driving around and..." His words trailed away on a frown.

It was the frown that stopped her from inviting him inside. He looked none too happy to be there and, as such, she doubted he planned to stay. So she folded her hands and waited patiently for him to say whatever it was that had compelled him to her villa.

"Can you read Italian?"

The question came out of left field. "Can I read...?"

"Italian," he said impatiently.

"A little."

"Good. Decipher this for me, okay?" He pulled a

wadded-up piece of paper from his pocket and dropped it into her palm.

Atlanta smoothed out the worst of the wrinkles. Though her grasp of the language was rudimentary at best, she understood enough that she glanced up sharply.

"It's from your father."

"I know. Even I could figure that out." He closed his eyes for a moment. "Sorry."

"It's okay." She tapped the paper with one finger. "This is personal. Are you sure you want me to read it?"

His laughter was bitter, but not directed at her. "Personal," he drawled. "Isn't that rich. The first I've heard from him in practically forever and the guy writes it in a language I can't understand." Despite the firm set of his jaw, she saw bewilderment and pain in his expression. "Read it."

My Dearest Son,
Thank you for coming to Monta Correnti. I wanted to give you a little time to get settled before coming by, but I am eager to see you.

You have grown into a fine man from everything I have read and from what your brother told me. You cannot know how glad that makes my heart.

My hope is that, like Alessandro, you will come to forgive me and we can start fresh.

With love, Papa

"He sent me a damned fruit basket," Angelo muttered as he pocketed the note Atlanta returned to him. "Can you believe that?"

"What should he send?"

"Nothing. I don't want anything from him."

But it was so plain to her he did that her heart ached. She knew what it was like to want to be loved. Angelo was no big-egoed jock now. Perhaps that was what prompted her to ask, "Do you want to come in?"

He surprised her again by saying, "I do, but first I feel like I owe you an apology for today, even if I don't think I said anything out of line."

"You didn't. I overreacted."

He shoved a hand through his hair as he exhaled, giving her the impression he'd expected her to argue. "So...we're okay?"

Not exactly. There remained an unsettling amount of attraction that she didn't know what to do with. But Atlanta nodded and smiled. As an afterthought, she added, "Well, except for the cannoli. I didn't get to finish one, let alone two."

"I guess I do owe you an apology after all." He smiled as he stepped into the foyer, and she nearly regretted her impulse to invite him inside. "What can I do to make it up to you?"

"Buy me dinner." The words were out in a rush. Being out in public with him seemed the safer bet.

"I can do that."

"I can be ready in an hour if you want to come back."

"What's wrong with right now?"

"Right now? I'm not dressed for dinner." She was wearing the same jeans and sweater set she'd had on earlier. It was fine for kicking around the village or hanging out alone at the villa, but dinner? She always dressed for dinner. Zeke said...She notched up her chin. "I'm wearing what I have on."

"Fine by me. I wasn't expecting you to change."

Simple words, a simple statement. Yet her heart did a funny little flip. For good measure she added, "And I get to pick the place."

CHAPTER SIX

ANGELO felt nervous as he ushered Atlanta to the car. He didn't like it. When it came to women, he didn't get nervous. It was the same with baseball. He was a natural. So why did he feel so out of sorts right now?

It wasn't Atlanta's fame that had his palms sweating. He'd been with well-known women before, including a couple of supermodels and a wealthy socialite who was a fixture on Page Six of the *New York Post*.

Some guys, he supposed, would confuse the woman with the breathy characters she portrayed on the big screen. Before he'd had an actual conversation with her, Angelo might have, too. But it hadn't taken long to determine that, while Atlanta shared their vulnerability and some of their spunk, she wasn't some celluloid creation concocted to appeal to the masses. Especially the male masses. She was flesh and blood. Real. Her current set of troubles would not be neatly resolved during the span of a full-length feature film. And, if his guess was right, she had a past to contend with, too, some ugly secrets that refused to stay under the rug no matter how many times she swept them there.

The two of them had that in common.

He thought about the note from his father. Atlanta was privy to far more of his past than any other woman in his life had ever been. Maybe that was why he felt nervous. Hell, maybe that was part of her overall draw. It was rare to find someone with as much baggage as he had. It was rare to have someone call him on his. In fact, he couldn't think of a single woman who ever had. They'd accepted him as the fun-loving playboy he portrayed. Atlanta had spotted the troubled man behind the façade. It was that man she spoke to.

When they reached his car, he waited until they were both settled and the engine was humming before asking, "Where to?"

"I...I don't know."

"We'll drive around the village. When you see something you like, tell me to stop."

She turned to face him. "You don't mind?"

"What's to mind?"

"A lot of men—" Zeke was implied "—like to decide the destination or at the very least know what it will be before shifting the car into drive."

"Then a lot of men don't know what they're missing," he said casually before stepping on the accelerator.

They wound up on the far side of the village at a small eatery that was really more roadside diner than restaurant. It had a small dining room, but they sat outside, enjoying the view of the neighboring shops as evening settled in.

"You're sure this is okay?" she asked not for the first time even before their beverages arrived.

"Why wouldn't it be? I'm hungry. They serve food."

"It has nothing to do with what I mentioned earlier? You know, about Zeke."

"And his tendency to call all of the shots?"

She nodded.

"Maybe a little," he agreed.

Her lips pursed. "So, you're humoring me."

"I don't see it that way." Control was important to her right now. She needed to have it. She needed to exercise it. Besides, he was curious to find out what she would do with it. And if it helped him take his mind off his father, all the better. "As I said, I have no reason to object."

Mollified, she nodded. "Okay."

"For the record, when I find a reason to draw a line in the sand, I do and I'm not likely to cross it afterward."

"Stubborn?"

"So I've been told." Most recently by Alex.

"But you're not completely intractable."

"What makes you say that?"

"You're in Italy to meet your father," she reminded him.

"Only because my brother asked me to."

"Is that the only reason?"

He said nothing.

The waiter dropped off their drinks, sparkling water for both of them. When they were alone again, she said, "I briefly considered picking your family restaurant for dinner this evening."

He sipped his water. "Why didn't you?"

"Given your reaction to your father's note, I didn't want to push you into doing something you might not be ready for," she admitted.

Her concern touched him, though a part of him was eager to shake it off. "I wouldn't have cared. He's nothing to me."

"Angelo—"

"Less than nothing." The strident words scraped his throat, making him wonder who he was trying to convince.

"It's okay to be angry," she said quietly.

"Gee, thanks for your permission."

"You know what I mean."

"Yes. I do. Sorry." He exhaled sharply.

"So, when do you plan to see your father?"

He thought about the party Isabella had told him about. He tried *not* to think about the invitation his sister had told him he was welcome to extend to a guest. He mentioned neither to Atlanta. Rather, he said casually, "I'm in no rush. I've still got a couple of weeks to kill."

"What about the restaurant? Have you seen it?"

"I ate lunch there today after you and I…parted company," he finished diplomatically.

"By yourself?"

"With Isabella. I owed her an apology."

"Isabella, hmm? You work fast. I wouldn't have guessed you'd have had an opportunity to offend any of the local women already."

"Isabella is my sister."

He liked the way the announcement caused heat to suffuse her face.

"Sister," she repeated on a slow nod.

"Half, I guess is the more accurate description. Luca remarried after Alex and I were out of the picture. He had a second family." Bitterness welled. "He decided to keep this one around."

"And you didn't know about them," she guessed.

"Not until recently." He sipped more of his water. "Nor did they apparently know about Alex and me. It came as a bit of a surprise to us all, you might say."

"I'm sorry."

He shook his head and his tone was rueful when he said, "That was my line today. As you've noticed, I'm not handling this situation very well, which is why I owed Isabella an apology. All she did was to hold out an olive branch." He shifted in his seat. "My beef isn't with her. It's with Luca."

"Yet you're in no hurry to see him, confront him."

Her simple statement cut right to the heart of it. He didn't like what that said about him. Thankfully, she changed the subject a moment later.

"Oh, my God! I nearly forgot. Something's come up. Something…embarrassing."

That got his attention. "Embarrassing for me?"

"For both of us, I'm afraid. It seems that the paparazzi you saved me from at the airport the other day got their money shot. My arrival in Rome made headlines in a couple of the rags back home."

"Sorry, Atlanta. I'd hoped to shield you from that. I take it since I was in some of those shots I was mentioned."

"Yes and some, um, assumptions were made regarding our relationship."

"They assumed we're getting away together for some R&R—Romance and Recreation," he guessed.

"According to one of the stories, I've seduced you."

"Really." His eyebrows rose along with the corners of his mouth. "You seduced me, hmm? There's a thought that's going to keep me awake into the wee hours of the morning."

"This is serious, Angelo."

He sobered a bit. "From your perspective, I know that it is. For that reason alone, if I could get my hands on those photographers, they'd be sorry they ever bought their first camera."

Atlanta was no fan of violence, but his words warmed her. When was the last time, outside of a movie set, that a man had defended her honor, let alone offered to beat up someone for her? Back to the matter at hand, she chided herself when she realized she was staring at him, a sappy smile threatening to break out.

"Aren't you the least bit upset? You're being likened to a boy toy, and Zeke is claiming that you're merely another one of my many conquests."

"When you put it like that, okay, I'm a little upset. I'm no boy, Atlanta." No, indeed, he was all man. "As for the conquest remark, well, that rubs the wrong way, too." He scratched his chin thoughtfully. "But there's an upside to this for me."

"There is?"

He smiled again. "Unlike the other recent tabloids reports about me, at least this time no one is questioning my physical ability."

She laughed because she didn't have an off-the-cuff remark handy. Not to mention that the mental image of Angelo "performing" to his physical best left her a little tongue-tied.

The sandwiches they ordered came on thickly sliced ciabatta. The cold cuts and cheese were tasty, the bread good, but none of it could hold a candle to the stuff Angelo had sampled at Rosa earlier in the day, a fact that made him feel strangely proud and definitely uneasy.

The thing that helped banish both was watching Atlanta eat. She pulled off one of the two slices of provolone and half of the salami, setting them aside with the top slice of bread. No doubt she was tallying up carb and protein grams as she went. Afterward, she went after what remained of the sandwich with dainty nibbles that barely put a dent in the hefty ciabatta. It was the damned cannoli all over again. Angelo stifled the urge to comment. Instead he went after his own sandwich with a gusto that far inflated his actual enjoyment of it.

When he glanced up, Atlanta was watching him. He took another bite and added a few sound effects as he chewed. "Mmm-mmm."

Her gaze narrowed and she set her open-faced sandwich on her plate where she piled the rest of the ingredients back on, including the second slice of ciabatta. She lifted the finished product with a flourish, her expression as steely and no-nonsense as a gunslinger's. Then she brought the sandwich to her mouth. No dainty nip for her this time. She opened wide and came away with enough to keep her chewing for the next couple minutes. He watched her the entire time, that same odd mixture of pride and unease making his skin prickle.

She wasn't able to finish the sandwich. No surprise there since the portion had been generous. Still, she'd eaten more than half of it before calling it quits and even then had gone back to loot some of the good stuff from inside.

"I really enjoyed that," she admitted, settling back in her chair on a sigh that, to Angelo's way of thinking, seemed way too close to those issued during post-coital bliss.

"I enjoyed watching you."

"So how does it rate?"

Lost as he was in carnal thoughts, the question had his mouth dropping open. "Rate?" he repeated inanely.

"You know, compared to Rosa."

"Oh. Right. Food. And Rosa." The words marched out his mouth in staccato procession.

Atlanta laughed, enjoying him as much as she'd just

enjoyed her sandwich. "I'm not even going to ask what you thought I wanted you to rate."

"Wise move, though I'll be happy to tell you."

He was back to flirting. She decided to play along. "Fine. Tell."

His brows rose. Clearly, he hadn't expected her to call him on it. Would he back down?

The answer was clear as soon as he said, "We danced about it earlier today."

"Ah, attraction."

"Let's call it what it really is. Sex."

At the coffee shop she'd gotten all riled for reasons that had nothing to do with the man sitting before her. Did he think she would again? Was he testing her?

"So we were," she said nonchalantly.

He smiled, as if pleased by the way she was rallying. Then he asked point-blank, "How long has it been for you?"

"How long has…?" She sputtered out a mild oath before regaining her composure. She was offended, she reminded herself, even as heat curled through her. "Some questions are too rude to warrant an answer. Or are you one of those men who love to kiss and tell?"

Her reprimand left him undeterred. "I'm discreet. I see no reason to brag." Then he got back to her sex life. "I'm guessing it's been a while."

She was not going to have this conversation. But she heard herself ask, "What makes you so sure?"

"Even though you ended things with Zeke about six months ago, if things weren't going well, the two of you probably weren't sleeping together for a while before then. So, it's been months, perhaps more than a year."

"What about all of the lovers I've supposedly had?"

"I'm not buying it."

She swallowed, pathetically pleased and grateful. She was back to irritated when he said, "I'm not Zeke."

"I wasn't mistaking you for him."

His eyes narrowed. "But I'm betting you've done some comparing."

She flushed guiltily and was grateful they were seated outside under the uneven glow of hanging lanterns.

"For the record," he was saying, "I'm younger, fitter and a whole lot more accommodating."

"Thanks for the heads up."

He wasn't put off by her bored attitude. He leaned over the table, lowered his voice. "I like you. I'm attracted to you. I can't promise you that whatever happens between us will last beyond Italy. I never make any kind of promises. And you may be okay with that since you aren't looking for strings. But, given our individual circumstances, a few fireworks might be a welcome diversion for both of us."

Angelo was turning her inside out with his words, but she felt no shame, nor was she visited by any bitter memories. Even her current troubles blended into the background, until the only thing left was temptation and something akin to yearning. She recalled Sara's suggestion of a vacation fling. A post-Zeke fling.

"And you can guarantee those?" she asked as sparks showered her skin.

"With a little encouragement and participation, of course." He reached over to stroke the side of her face. "Lovemaking is all about give and take. It's not just about having control, but giving it to the other person. Both parties end up satisfied that way."

His words had heat suffusing her face as well as regions of a body that had been languishing in permafrost for far longer than he assumed. Give *and* take. In her experience only one of those two verbs had ever come into play, unless she was in front of a camera with a director calling the shots.

Her voice wasn't quite steady when she asked, "Are you finished with your analysis, Dr. Freud?"

"For now. The rest can wait for another time."

Because she found herself surprisingly eager for future tutelage, Atlanta decided to change the subject. "As fascinating as I find our conversation, I'm afraid jet lag is catching up with me."

"Does that mean you want me to take you home?"

She nodded. Then, tipping her head to one side, she asked, "Mad?"

"Disappointed, but it's just as well. I don't think either of us is ready for what our raging hormones have in store."

Not ready in the least, she knew. But that didn't stop her from dreaming about it when, later that evening, she fell asleep in her bed all alone.

From his prone position on the mattress, Angelo stared up at the bedroom ceiling. As his gaze idly traced the shadows thrown from the bedside lamp, he recounted the evening.

That wasn't something he did normally, even when the evening in question ended on a far more satisfactory note. Yet he didn't feel frustrated exactly, sexually or otherwise. Like a damned moth, he just felt drawn and more curious than ever about the woman most of the world thought they knew.

He flipped to his side, recalling the way Atlanta had looked when he'd left her on her doorstep. He'd waited, and, yes, he'd hoped that she would invite him inside. Whether for a nightcap or something more, he hadn't cared. He'd only known that he hadn't wanted the evening to end. But she hadn't invited him in. Instead, she'd smiled and bade him goodnight.

With a handshake!

Left with little choice, he'd taken her hand, pumped it delicately and released it so quickly it might as well have been a poisonous snake. Patience, he'd reminded himself. He was pretty certain she was a woman who'd had some bad breaks when it came to physical intimacy. Just when he'd convinced himself of that and had turned toward his car, she'd grabbed his arm and spun him back around.

The kiss that had followed hadn't been chaste. It had been downright greedy. He'd felt teeth nip at his lower lip and fingernails bite into the flesh of his arms. It hadn't ended slowly or on a sigh. No, she'd broken it off cleanly, her breathing labored afterward.

He'd considered a pithy comeback. Hell, he'd considered hauling her back into his arms and having a second go at it. Only her expression had stopped him. It had been neither smug nor frightened. Rather, she'd looked uncertain, confused.

For him, sex had never been complicated, partly because he was smart enough to know women often viewed the act differently. They tried to inject emotions into the mix, which could cause problems if a guy let things progress too far. Mindful of his parents and the disaster they had made of not only their marriage but of their children's lives, he'd been careful not to let that happen.

So, why was he feeling every bit as confused and uncertain as Atlanta had looked? He turned out the lamp and gave his pillow a couple of punches. It was going to be a long night.

* * *

Angelo had no firm plans for the following day, which was just as well. He woke in pain not long after the sun rose.

"Damned shoulder," he muttered, although it wasn't his only source of discomfort. "Damned woman."

He swung his legs over the side of the mattress and scraped the hand of his good arm over his jaw, eyeing the pills on the nightstand as he did so. In the end, he decided to do what he had for the past year of his career: play through the pain.

By mid-afternoon, with nothing more to occupy his time than Italian television programs and a couple of old *Sports Illustrated* magazines he'd brought with him, he was surly and sick of his own company, so he got in the car and headed out for a drive. He didn't plan his destination, at least not consciously, but he wound up at Atlanta's villa. This time, however, when he knocked at the door it was a dark-haired woman who answered. Given the wicker basket of linens on the floor at her feet, he figured she was there to do the cleaning.

"Hi... I mean, *ciao.* I was looking for Atlanta Jackson. I take it she's not here."

"No." But the woman's expression brightened. Her tone held a little awe when she said, "You are Angelo Casali."

Finally, someone recognized him. He grinned in return. "Yes, I am."

"It is such a pleasure to meet you."

"Thanks."

Her obvious excitement. The wide-eyed adoration. He lapped both up. He was just about to ask her if she wanted his autograph when she added, "I know your family well. I attended school with Isabella. I had a crush on Valentino."

Angelo's smile faltered. She knew his family, but apparently she'd never heard of his multimillion-dollar baseball career, which was fading as fast as the season. How ironic that the New York Angel's only claim to fame here was as Luca Casali's son.

The young woman was saying, "I met Alessandro while he was in Monta Correnti. He was at Rosa one evening when my husband and I dined there." She tipped her head to one side and studied Angelo. "You both have the look of your father. You have his eyes."

Angelo backed up a step. He cared for neither the comparison she was making nor the connection it defined. "I have to be going."

"Do you wish to leave a message for Miss Jackson?"

"No. I'll..." He shook his head and said a second time, "No."

The woman was still standing in the open doorway staring after him when he climbed into the car. He revved its engine to life, shifted into gear and hit the gas. The tires spat gravel and gave a little squeal as he sped away. He didn't care. He had to get out of there. Just as Atlanta had the day before at the coffee shop, Angelo found himself running from the past.

It was the present that caused him to slow down before he hit the first bend in the road, which was a good thing considering the sharp turns up ahead. Another fifty feet and the road became as curvy as the woman walking along the side of it.

Atlanta.

She was more strolling than walking, given the leisurely pace of her long-legged stride. She looked more relaxed than he'd ever seen her. Fresh air and the Italian countryside agreed with her. She held a bouquet of wildflowers in one hand. Her signature blonde hair was partly obscured beneath a cap that, upon closer inspection, he realized was emblazoned with the logo of a rival ball club. Even so, the sight of her made him smile. Some of his tension ebbed away, only to be replaced with a different sort of restlessness when she spotted him and waved. He pulled the car over and got out, leaning against the hood while he waited for her to reach him.

When she did he asked, "Getting in a little exercise?"

"That wasn't my primary objective, but yes."

He was glad to hear she didn't feel the need to walk off last night's carbohydrate indulgence. The woman who just the day before had been racked with guilt over a couple of cannoli was making progress.

"Are you heading back?" he asked.

She glanced at her wristwatch. "Not quite yet. My landlady, Franca, is there. She insists on changing the sheets every day, though I've told her I'm not that picky. I left because I didn't want to be underfoot."

"Interested in some company?"

She fussed with the ponytail that spilled out the back of the hat. "I wouldn't mind it."

Initially, Atlanta had gone for a walk to clear her head. The day was perfect for it, so sunny and warm. But how was a woman supposed to keep her head clear when the man responsible for clouding it up was now asking to join her?

She could tell him no. She'd turned Angelo down more than once, and for things more consequential than a stroll down a country road. Despite the bruises he claimed his ego had endured, it hadn't stopped him from coming back or from being a friend, even if it was clear he had more than friendship on his mind.

Still, the friendship was an unexpected gift. She'd never had a male friend before. For that matter, with the exception of Sara, Atlanta had precious few female ones. Hollywood wasn't the sort of town where one could cultivate deep bonds of any sort easily. Too many people had an agenda or an angle to work. Very little was ever as it seemed on the surface, a fact Atlanta knew all too well.

"I want to thank you," she said.

His brows shot up. "For what?"

"For being a friend."

He stuffed his hands in the front pockets of his jeans. "That's just what a guy wants to hear."

"Sorry, it's just that I don't have many friends and I really need one right now."

"I know." His tone was serious when he said, "Same goes for me."

"Oh." She smiled, pleased.

"Just to be clear, though. I still want to sleep with you."

She stopped walking and faced him. "Why do you do that?"

"Do what?"

"Hide behind macho come-on lines."

She expected him to deny it. Instead, he replied, "For the same reason that you fall back on your plastic Hollywood smile."

She sobered.

"Yeah." He nodded. "I can tell the difference between a real Atlanta Jackson smile and the ones you manufacture for the masses."

"Touché." She plucked at the petals of one of the flowers in her bouquet.

"How about we make a deal?"

"I'm listening."

"How about if we're real with one another?"

"Flaws and all?" she wanted to know.

"Why not? What's to lose? The way I see it, everyone thinks they've got us figured out based on all of the media hype. We both know they're wrong."

"So, you're not an arrogant athlete with more testosterone than intelligence?"

"No more than you are a self-absorbed starlet who uses and discards men by the dozen." At her startled expression, he said, "That was the quote I read on an Internet site the other day."

Her eyelids flickered. "God, we're a pair."

"Only if you believe the tabloids," he said. "So, deal?"

"Deal."

They started walking again. A few minutes later, Angelo bent to pick a flower similar to the ones in her bouquet. He handed it to her.

"Thanks."

"They're pretty."

"I thought so. I'm going to look them up online later, find out what they are."

"Is that how you're filling your time these days, trolling the Internet?"

"Yes, and, before you say anything, I'm loving it. I haven't had a real vacation, and by real I mean a do-nothing sort of vacation, in years. In fact, I don't think I've ever had one," she said wryly.

All of her downtime away from a movie set was spent promoting a project, a product or herself. That was

Zeke's idea. Two birds with one stone and all that. Even the supposedly romantic getaways the pair of them had taken over the years had included jaunts to public places where the paparazzi were sure to spot them. Indeed, Atlanta sometimes wondered if Zeke wasn't responsible for some of the anonymous tips to the tabloids that had divulged their locations and left her ducking for cover.

"Neither have I, and for good reason," Angelo was saying. "Two days with little to do and I'm going stir crazy."

"How can you be bored here?" She spread her arms wide.

"I'm not bored, I just feel...trapped."

She turned, not sure she'd heard him correctly. His frown told her that she had.

"I know about feeling trapped," she said quietly.

He was still frowning, but something in his expression had changed, softened in a way she couldn't quite define. "I think you do."

"Anything I can do to help?"

"A friend to a friend?"

"That's right."

Though the way he was looking at her suggested more than friendly feelings.

"Then, yes." His gaze grew intense as he studied her. Would he bare his soul and divulge some of his secrets? Would he kiss her? He did neither. Instead, he snatched the ball cap off her head. "You can set a match to this. God! The team manages to win one stinking World Series and suddenly everyone becomes a fan."

She knew it was his intent to lighten the situation, so she allowed her laughter to ring out in the late afternoon. Another time, perhaps she wouldn't let him off the hook so easily.

"Which team should I root for?"

"The best one out there."

"Yours?"

"The Rogues." Afterward, his expression darkened again, leaving her to wonder if it was mere clarification he sought with his answer or outright distance.

CHAPTER SEVEN

ATLANTA lost track of the time as they walked, but the lengthening shadows of the trees, as well as the indelicate protests of her empty stomach, told her it was getting close to dinner. Regardless, Franca would be done changing the linens by now.

They headed back to her villa, stopping when they reached his car. Though he probably found the gesture foolish, she handed him the flowers that she'd collected. They were drooping a little now.

"If you put them in water they should perk back up," she said, not at all confident that would be the case.

"Thanks."

He looked as ridiculous holding them as she would have looked outfitted in a catcher's pads squatting behind home plate. He'd probably toss them out the window before he hit the first curve. Men weren't sentimental.

Angelo surprised her by snapping the stem on one bloom. After tugging off her hat for the second time that day, he tucked the flower behind her ear.

"My Italian can use a lot of work, as you well know, but I'm aware of one word that applies in this case. *Bella.*"

Beautiful. She'd been called that before, in several different languages both on-screen and off. This time the compliment curled around her and she luxuriated in its embrace.

"Thank you."

The breeze kicked up. Without the ball cap he found so offensive, it sent ribbons of her hair across her face. The yellow blossom tumbled free from its perch at her ear. He caught it before it could hit the ground.

"It doesn't want to stay put," she murmured as her heart kicked out an extra beat. He was standing so close she could feel the heat emanating from his body.

"I guess I cut the stem a little too short."

"You could try another one."

"Yeah? You mean keep at it till I get it right?"

Atlanta swallowed, nodded.

"You know, you have a point," he said slowly, seriously. "Not everything works the way we want it to the first time." He leaned back against the car and rested his hands lightly on her waist. "Like last night."

"What about last night?"

"That kiss you gave me."

"You had a problem with it?" she asked, trying to sound insulted rather than insecure.

"I wouldn't call it a problem. It's just that if I'd been in control I would have done things a little differently."

Angelo's choice of words was deliberate, she knew. He was making a not so subtle reference to Zeke, as well as offering a not so subtle reminder that last night he'd let her call the shots, everything from where to eat to how to end the evening.

"You were a perfect gentleman, by the way, a fact I appreciated."

His gaze sharpened slightly. "Were you worried that I wouldn't be?"

"If I had been I wouldn't have agreed to have dinner with you," she replied seriously.

He nodded. "And what about tonight?"

Because she found the invitation to spend another evening with him way too tempting, she dodged it by asking, "When are you going to get around to visiting with the relatives you came to Italy to see?"

"When I can no longer avoid it," he said pointedly. "So, about tonight?"

"All right, under one condition."

His eyes narrowed. "What might that be?"

"You have to tell me something about yourself. Something no one else knows. I figure that's only fair since so much of my dirty laundry is out in the air."

He nodded slowly. "Okay, but I have a condition of my own. I get to pick the place tonight."

"Deal," Atlanta said, sure she'd gotten the better end of the bargain.

Back at the villa, she hurriedly changed her clothes. Angelo insisted she needn't bother, with the exception of the ball cap. But that meant she had to do something different with her hair and, while she was at it, it seemed a shame not to slip into one of the pretty skirts and new blouses she'd brought with her. So while he paced around the courtyard, she was in her room, primping for another evening out.

She wasn't sure what had happened to her resolve to steer clear of men in general and Angelo Casali in particular. Nor could she say why she'd told him things about her relationship with Zeke that she'd only admitted to a few people, and then with mixed reactions.

"Don't bite the hand that feeds you," her agent had warned when Atlanta had confided her unhappiness a year earlier. "You might be a box-office draw, but Zeke wields a scary amount of power in this town. So what if he likes to tell you how to wear your hair or which entree to order at Spago? Nine times out of ten, he's right. The guy has the Midas touch when it comes to building careers. A million other wannabes would be only too happy to heed his advice."

Angelo, however, had understood that it wasn't advice Zeke imparted, but rules. He'd created her, named her, handcrafted every aspect of her past and present. He'd controlled her, every bit as much as her stepfather had, caging her in and making her feel trapped, helpless.

But just as she'd broken free from her stepfather's grip, she'd wrested herself from Zeke's control. No man was going to bully her or boss her around. That included Angelo, even if she'd opted to let him pick the location for tonight's meal.

She felt confident and unconcerned when, once they were seated in his car, she asked, "So, where are we heading for dinner?"

He tapped his fingers on the steering wheel. "My villa."

"Your villa?" Her nerves kicked into high gear right along with the sports coupe.

"We can go somewhere else if you'd rather," he said.

His offer quelled her concern. Now Atlanta was intrigued, "Why your villa?"

"My sister made this incredible feast for me the other night. I have a lot of leftovers. More than I can eat in this lifetime. I thought we could dine *alfresco*. The view from my patio is five-star.

"Is that the only reason?" When he shook his head, she added, "I didn't think so."

She waited for him to make some flirty comment about wanting to be alone with her. He didn't. Rather, he sighed. "Monta Correnti is small. Everyone here knows my father or someone in my family."

"You should be used to being recognized," she reminded him. "It's not like you're anonymous when you go out in New York or anywhere in America, for that matter."

"That's just it. I'm not recognized here, Atlanta. No one here knows Angelo Casali." He was talking about the ballplayer. "Here I am only Luca's long-lost son."

"Angelo." Understanding the source of his pain, she reached out to him. Then she screamed, "Look out!"

Angelo had been watching her rather than the road, a dangerous proposition, especially on this winding stretch. As a result, he wasn't quite ready for the hairpin turn ahead. To avoid collision with a tree, he stepped on the brake and yanked the steering wheel to one side. The car skidded on gravel for what seemed like a lifetime before the tire found traction.

He grunted and bit back the worst of an oath as pain shot from his shoulder. As he cupped it with his hand he asked, "Are you okay?"

"Fine," Atlanta said. "But I don't think you are."

He tried to lie around a grimace. "I'm good."

She wasn't buying it. "Your shoulder is bothering you again."

"More like still," he admitted.

"Are you taking something for the pain?"

"When it becomes unbearable."

"From what I've observed that must be most of the time."

Angelo didn't deny it. Instead, he said, "The pills the

doctor prescribed make me tired and a little foggy. I've played through pain before."

"We're not talking about a baseball game, Angelo. This is your health, your quality of life. You can't keep on this way. Eventually, I'm guessing your shoulder is going to require surgery."

Surgery. The S word. After which would come the R word. Not rehabilitation, but retirement.

"Look, I'm fine," he said a second time. He didn't need to see her blink to know his tone carried an edge. "Sorry."

"No. I'm sorry. It's not my business."

It wasn't. Yet he heard himself say, "I'm scared, Atlanta."

Her gaze snapped to his. "Of having surgery?"

That was only a small part of his fear. He was far more unnerved that he might lose his overall identity. But he nodded. As he maneuvered the car back onto the road, he said, "Well, there it is. The secret no one else knows. I'm a big baby when it comes to the thought of going under the knife."

Her smile was the plastic Hollywood variety. She knew he was a liar.

The sun was just starting to set when they reached Angelo's villa. Atlanta was out of the car before he could come around to open her door.

"I didn't think it was possible to top the view from my place, but this does. And you have a pool. Very nice."

"I also have a hot tub."

"I'm going to have a talk with my travel agent when I get back."

"No need to be jealous. I'm willing to share. We can take a dip in it later if you'd like."

She pursed her lips in mock dismay. "Darn. I don't have a suit."

Blue eyes twinkled. "I don't mind."

She deflected his flirting by saying, "I bet the hot tub feels like heaven on your shoulder."

He scowled and started to walk away before turning back. Snagging her wrist, he hauled her close. "Let's get something straight. I may be on the injured list, but I'm not out of the game."

She wasn't put off in the least by his temper. "Are you talking figuratively or literally?"

"Both," he said, before bringing his mouth down on hers.

Atlanta expected his kiss to be hard, punishing even. Angelo was angry. He was scared, too. Not of having shoulder surgery, though that was his claim. It went beyond that, she was sure. Which was why she allowed the kiss, hoping, foolishly perhaps, that he would find some comfort in it.

It was clear he hadn't when he broke off abruptly and stepped away from her. Shoving a hand through his hair, he said, "If you want to leave now, I'll understand."

She frowned. "Why would I want to leave?"

"I shouldn't have done that. I…I know you have some issues regarding…control. And with, um, no meaning no."

Her throat ached as his words pierced the barrier protecting her heart. "I didn't say no."

"If you had, I wouldn't have kissed you," he said earnestly.

She nodded. "If I had, I wouldn't have let you."

"So, you want to stay?"

"I was promised a meal."

Angelo ushered her inside the villa. The main living

space was larger than the one in hers and, she decided from the well-appointed furnishings, professionally decorated.

"This is very nice." The quality of the pieces was obvious. The owner had expensive taste and the bank account to indulge it.

Angelo's tone was wry. "You might want to reserve your opinion until you've seen the kitchen."

She understood what he meant a moment later. Rustic was the word that came to mind. The stove was a big black behemoth.

"Oh, my God."

"Exactly, although Isabella managed to create a feast in here." His expression brightened. "Hey, didn't you play a chef in one of your movies?"

"Sous chef, but the operative word here is played. This is beyond my talents as either an actress or an amateur cook." She exhaled softly as she turned in a semi-circle. "I don't suppose there's a microwave stashed in one of the cupboards?"

"Nope. And, believe me, I've checked every last one of them. Apparently the guy who owns this place stopped short of renovating the kitchen. This is original to the house."

"So I can see. What's wrong with the owner? He's not a fan of eating?"

"He's not a fan of cooking. My sister said he doesn't spend much time in Monta Correnti and when he does, he takes his meals elsewhere." Angelo's brows drew together. "You know, I have a feeling that's what my brother had in mind for me when he booked my accommodations."

She chuckled. "Sounds like a bit of a set-up."

"I'll find a way to make him pay," he muttered as he crossed to the equally ancient-looking refrigerator.

While Angelo pulled out an assortment of covered bowls, Atlanta rooted through cabinets and drawers, and came up with plates and silverware. They decided to eat the pasta cold, pairing it with fat slices of thick-crusted Italian bread. She decided to indulge in what Zeke had considered an absolute no-no and combined olive oil and some dried herbs she found in the pantry in a shallow bowl to dip the bread in. Then she took the dishes, utensils, bread and herbed oil out to the patio table. Night had fallen. Hanging lanterns illuminated the pool and patio area, while down the hillside the lights from scattered homes mirrored the stars that winked in the sky. Angelo joined her a moment later with the pasta, a bottle of wine and two glasses whose thin stems were wedged between his fingers.

"No wine for me, thanks," she said.

Even so, he set one down in front of her plate. "Just in case you change your mind. Nothing brings out the rich flavors of a meal like a nice glass of wine."

"Okay, half a glass."

Before they finished their meal, Atlanta had consumed a second half. Angelo was right about the wine. It complemented the flavor of the tomato sauce perfectly. Indeed, she couldn't recall the last time she'd enjoyed a meal as much as this one.

"This is incredible," she said, forking up the last bite of pasta. "I've always been a fan of Italian cuisine, although I can't quite place all of the flavors in this sauce."

"It contains a special kind of basil. It's grown locally. Very exclusive." A deep groove formed between his brows. "When I arrived here the other day and smelled the sauce simmering in the kitchen, I remembered going out with Alex and my father to pick the herb. I would have been a preschooler."

"I've heard it said that smell is one of the most potent senses when it comes to memory recall."

"I believe it."

He didn't sound happy about it, so she didn't ask if the outing with his father and brother was a good memory. Even if it were, the intervening years surely would have soured it.

She'd finished off her wine. He pointed to the empty glass. "Would you like some more?"

"No, I've had enough."

"I believe the word they use here is *basta*," he told her.

"That's right." She nodded. "It's a handy word to know."

"Just be careful," he warned. "If you use it too often you're likely to miss out on a lot of…adventure."

Angelo expected Atlanta to say she wasn't up for any more adventure in her life. He wouldn't blame her for feeling that way, especially with a new scandal brewing over the photos that had been snapped of the two of them in Rome's airport. Instead, she studied him in the soft light that cascaded from the patio's scattered lanterns.

"I guess I'll have to use my best judgment, then."

"You do that."

Angelo finished his Chianti and leaned back in his chair on a contented sigh that morphed into a yelp of pain when he tried to stack his hands behind his head. He lowered his arms immediately and reached for his shoulder before he could think better of it.

Atlanta's eyes were wide with concern.

"Don't say it." His words held more of a plea than a warning.

"Fine. I won't ask about surgery or rehabilitation or quality of life," she promised. "But I am curious."

The pain was abating. He squinted at her. "About what?"

"What do you plan to do after baseball?"

After? The word hit him with the force of a fastball to the chest. There was no after. Just as he'd convinced himself over the years that there had been no before. Baseball was both his alpha and omega.

"I'm not going anywhere." Even before she raised her eyebrows, he knew he sounded belligerent. That didn't stop him from adding, "The Rogues still need me. I'll be suiting up next season, make no mistake."

"I'm not talking about next season. Or even the season after that. You can't play ball forever, Angelo."

It wasn't anything he hadn't heard from other people, including younger players speculating on what the future held for them post-career. Usually, Angelo deflected the conversation with a witty comeback. This time, seated next to Atlanta in the cool evening air, he not only accepted reality, he met it head-on.

Gazing up at the stars, he admitted, "I don't know what I'll do."

"You have lots of options."

He did. He could branch off into coaching. One of the farm teams had already approached him with an offer. He could buy one of the existing franchises when it came up for sale. Ownership certainly held appeal. Money wasn't an object. The endorsement well showed no signs of drying up, despite his latest injury. But…

"Baseball is everything."

"Not everything," Atlanta replied softly.

"To me it is. It saved me. Literally. Baseball and Alex, they were what kept me from becoming a statistic."

"What do you mean?" she asked.

This wasn't something he talked about freely, let alone with a beautiful woman who had her own set of problems. But the timing, the woman who was willing to listen, they both seemed right.

"I was bound for trouble and taking the express train to get there. I was too young and too stupid to care about consequences. And I was just plain ticked off," he could admit now.

"At your father," she guessed.

"Him, yeah. And my mom." Angelo snorted. "Hell, I was angry at everyone." The sky held a million stars. He concentrated on one of them and continued. "No one seemed to give a damn about my brother and me. Our mom came home drunk most nights. She worked in public relations as a consultant. She kept a roof over our heads and, when she remembered to go grocery shopping, food in the pantry. But, honestly, I don't know how she managed to keep a job."

"Not all alcoholics are falling-down drunks. Some are quite capable of leading dual lives, at least for a while."

"That was Cindy. She wasn't a mean person, just disinterested in motherhood and, I think, angry with Luca that their marriage hadn't worked out. From what little she said on the subject, they'd met while she was vacationing here, she got pregnant and they got married. They barely knew one another. Not exactly the recipe for long-term success."

"No."

"Anyway, I think she was desperate to stay young and free of responsibility."

"That's pretty hard to do when you have twins," Atlanta inserted.

"Yeah, well, it didn't stop her. She spent more time out partying at trendy nightclubs than she did at home with Alex and me."

Maybe, Angelo realized now, that was why he'd never cared for the fun-loving party girls who hung around outside the stadium after games hoping to hook up with the players. They were a little too reminiscent of Cindy and her irresponsible ways for his taste.

The star he was staring at winked as if urging him on.

"Some of our teachers tried to help, but they could only do so much without state intervention. Cindy was good at avoiding that. Whenever she was called in for a parent-teacher conference or visited by a social worker, she would ramp up the tears and promise to change her ways. They believed her. Hell, Alex and I believed her."

"Those kinds of promises are impossible not to believe coming from someone you need and love," Atlanta said in a voice that sounded both sad and knowing.

"Things would be good for a while, but then she'd start going out again."

The stars blurred out of focus. Angelo swallowed. His mother had abandoned her sons, too. Not physically, but emotionally.

"Didn't your father at least help out financially?"

He shook his head. "According to her, the reason Alex and I wound up in the States to begin with was that Luca was broke and couldn't provide for us. He was selling food from a roadside stand at that point." Angelo's tone turned frosty. "Eventually things turned around. He managed to open a restaurant, remarry and support a second family."

"He never contacted you and Alex?"

"Once. We were eighteen and already living in New York. He managed to track us down through some shirt-tail relative of our mother's. I was so ticked off at him that I hung up the telephone a few minutes into the conversation. Busted the receiver in two." He snorted out a laugh that held no humor.

"You had a right to be angry."

Hearing her say it opened the floodgate. During the past twenty years, he'd shared his private pain with no one except his twin. He found it surprisingly easy to tell Atlanta, "Luca forgot all about Alex and me. When you come right down to it, he abandoned us!"

His words echoed down the hillside.

"I'm sorry, Angelo." Atlanta reached across the table to lay one of her hands over his.

"It was a long time ago."

"Not so long that it doesn't still hurt."

And it did. The pain in his heart throbbed as intensely as the one in his shoulder. His throat constricted with emotions he rarely allowed to the surface. Not trusting himself to speak, he nodded.

CHAPTER EIGHT

"So, TELL me how baseball saved you," Atlanta said after a long moment. "Did you play for your high school's team?"

"No. I didn't have the grades to make the school's team. You had to pull at least a C average in all of your classes to suit up one week to the next. I was lucky to be passing. If not for a couple of teachers who believed in social promotion, I don't think Alex and I would have graduated the same year." He swallowed before saying, "I wasn't much of a studier and I have a hard time with letters. Some of them like to scramble up on me."

"You're dyslexic."

"They didn't use that term as much back then, but, yeah. I'm dyslexic."

"So, where does baseball enter this picture?" she asked.

"Not long after I hotwired a cherry-red Porsche."

"How old were you?"

"Fifteen."

"Fifteen? You can't drive at that age."

"Not legally, but I'd had a lot of practice." Some of his good humor returned and he sent a wink in her direction. "I'd had a lot of practice at other things by that age, too, sweetheart."

She shook her head on a weary laugh. "Just go on with the story, please."

"Okay. By then Cindy was dead, and Alex and I were in the foster-care system. We'd already run away from a home in Boston and had lived on the streets for a while, dodging social workers and police. You meet people there." He sobered as black-edged memories swirled in. "They make certain things sound...acceptable, even though you know they aren't."

"Things like stealing a car?"

"Yeah. They turn crime into a rite of passage for misguided kids looking for a place to belong. Alex wanted no part of it. To this day, he doesn't know how close I came to being completely sucked under," Angelo said quietly.

"How did you wind up in New York?"

"The people I was running with in Boston had friends in the Bronx. They said they could find work for me. Alex didn't like it. He went with me to New York, determined to keep me out of trouble. One night, I was supposed to deliver the stolen car to a chop shop. I got the street wrong." He shook his head. "Dyslexic, remember?"

"Then what?"

"When Alex came to see me in jail, social services swooped in. He was assigned a foster home in Brooklyn. The father was a no-nonsense former U.S. Marine. Big Mike, they called him. While I was awaiting my court date the guy pulled some strings and, after spending a few weeks in juvie, I got sent there."

This wasn't part of his official bio. Long ago, Angelo's agent had talked him out of sharing any of the truly unsavory particulars. Fans rooted for underdogs, but there was no sense in making them squeamish.

"Were you found guilty?" Atlanta asked.

He nodded. "Grand theft auto, a felony. Even though I was a juvenile I was looking at some serious time. I had already racked up a couple of other minor offenses back in Boston. This made me a repeat offender as far as the DA in New York was concerned. So he charged me as an adult. I was facing time in juvenile detention until my eighteenth birthday, after which time I would be moved to the state penitentiary to finish out the rest of my sentence. But Big Mike, he was the foster dad, he went out on a limb for me at my sentencing hearing. He told the judge not to write me off. He said I was smart and had potential to turn my life around, but tossing me in the pen with the adult population would all but ensure I became a career criminal. Mike felt what I really needed was a good attitude adjustment and to have my energy refocused."

"And the judge listened?" Atlanta asked, sounding as surprised as Angelo had been twenty-some years earlier.

"Mike's word carried a lot of weight with the court." He snorted out a laugh. "For good reason, as it turned out. The guy knew how to adjust attitudes and refocus energy. The first night I was in his home he sat me down at the kitchen table and point-blank told me that if I blew the second chance he'd just gotten me, he'd personally see to it that I wound up behind bars. That's not all he told me, but I'll spare your delicate sensibilities and won't repeat the rest of his lecture."

"You were scared straight."

"Damned right. The guy was huge and intimidating as hell. He meant business. He also cared. What really kept me on the straight and narrow, though, was base-ball. Mike coached a team in a recreational league. I'd always liked baseball. I'd always been good at it despite no formal training. But when I started playing on Mike's team…" He shook his head, words failing him.

Atlanta's expression softened with understanding. "So, baseball saved your life."

He nodded. "That's why it's all I can imagine doing, even though I know I can't do it forever. Given your circumstances, you probably feel the same about acting."

A shadow passed over her face. "I love it. And you're right. Acting saved me in a way, too." It was gone by the time she went on. "But if I never starred in another movie like the ones I've been making for the past decade, I'd be okay with that."

"Liar," he taunted, sure she couldn't mean it.

But her tone was emphatic. "I'm being honest, Angelo. I'm tired of the roles I've been playing. I've wanted to move in a different direction for a while now. During the past few years I've been approached by indie film makers with screenplays that have had me salivating despite the low pay and nearly nonexistent production budgets."

"What's stopped you from doing them?"

"Zeke." She shook her head then. "No. That's too neat of an explanation and not entirely accurate. The messier truth is I've been afraid. The moviegoing public loves Atlanta Jackson, the vulnerable vixen. But would they love me in a less-than-sexy role?"

Surprised, he asked, "Is that the kind of part you want to play?"

"If it had some real meat. I've also given some thought to directing. I've learned a lot from my time in front of the camera." She lifted her hands. "The bottom line is I want to be taken seriously, Angelo."

"I take you seriously."

His reply had her flustered again. She rallied quickly. "Thank you. Unfortunately, in my business, women, especially attractive women, only seem to earn accolades when their looks are diminished."

"You want more recognition in the industry?"

"Of course I do. But ultimately I want what that represents."

"Respect."

"Exactly. That's what I want from my peers in the industry."

"You don't think you have it now?" he asked in disbelief. "I'm betting most actors would give their eye-teeth to be you or to have the chance to work with you. You're one of the hottest properties on the planet, Atlanta. Plunk you in the lead role and, no matter what the movie is about, it's destined to become a blockbuster and rake in millions if not billions of dollars worldwide."

"That's not a commentary on my talent. It only means that fans like the way I look and they've gobbled up all of the poor-little-rich-girl stories Zeke planted in the media over the years. Don't get me wrong. I'm grateful for the opportunities I've had. At one point the money was enough to keep me happy and make me feel safe."

"Safe? That's an odd word choice."

"Um, you know, secure. Financially speaking." Despite the hasty clarification, he didn't think that was really what Atlanta meant. Since he'd just bared his soul, he couldn't help but feel a little disappointed that she was still holding back. She was saying, "I've got more money than I can spend in this lifetime, assuming Zeke's palimony suit doesn't leave me in the poorhouse."

"The guy is suing you for palimony?" he asked incredulously.

She rattled off a monthly sum that left Angelo

staggered. "He claims he neglected other business opportunities in order to put my career first."

"He's also claiming you did the horizontal mambo with his son and half the men in Hollywood. We both know the guy is delusional."

"Thank you."

"For what? For paying attention? I may not have known you long, Atlanta, but it's plain to me the kind of person you are…and the kind of person you aren't."

She swallowed and shrugged. "That's neither here nor there. Getting back to my point, despite being money-makers, only a couple of my movies received positive reviews. The majority were panned."

"To hell with the critics." Angelo fumed on her behalf. He'd endured similar armchair analyses from so-called experts over the years. "What do they know?"

She sighed. "They know good acting, and so do I. I'm capable of it, too. I just haven't found the right vehicle to stretch my talent. With Zeke, it became increasingly clear over the past few years that I never would. Every time I wanted to so much as read a script from a little-known screenwriter or got wind of a project that didn't require me to show my cleavage, he vetoed it."

"Is that why you finally left him?"

"I'd had enough," she said softly.

"Good for you."

"When I first met Zeke, I thought he was my savior, but it turned out I'd merely traded one male keeper for another."

"How so?"

She blinked as if just realizing what she'd said. He doubted she knew how haunted or sad she looked. It was her expression that kept him from pushing when she said, "We'll save that for another day. Do you realize it's nearly midnight?"

He stood and came around the table, where he offered her his hand. "Tomorrow then."

"Excuse me?" she asked as she rose to her feet.

"Tomorrow is another day. We can pick up where we left off. We could do dinner again."

"Angelo—"

"You don't have to tell me any deep, dark secrets. But if you do, you can trust me not to share anything I learn with another person." He lifted her hand to his mouth, kissed the back of it. "You'll find me a good listener, Atlanta. Every bit as good as you were tonight when I bared my soul."

"Then maybe you'll take a bit of advice. You're here to see your father, Angelo. You can't keep avoiding him by spending all of your time with me."

"You're the only reason this trip is tolerable." When Atlanta opened her mouth to protest, he added, "Don't worry about Luca. My father and I will have our talk. A family gathering is planned. I'll see him then and get to meet the rest of the clan." He couldn't quite keep the dread from his tone.

"I'm sure it won't be as bad as all that."

"Maybe not." He smiled. "You and I will skip out early. I see no point in staying for more than a few introductions and some small talk."

That had Atlanta blinking. "You're asking me to come with you?"

"I could use an ally."

"It's a family party, Angelo."

"They're strangers," he corrected. "The only thing we have in common is DNA."

He thought of Isabella and guilt nipped. The description didn't seem fair. His sister was kind, interesting and spirited. He liked her, admired her. The fragile bond he already felt went beyond the Casali blue eyes and a blunt chin. Under other circumstances…

But the circumstances couldn't be changed, which meant he was left to make the best of them.

"There's no need to give me your answer right now. You can think about it. As for tomorrow, I'll call early in the day, so you can figure out what our plans will be and what I should wear."

She tipped her head to one side. "You want me to tell you what to wear?"

"No. I just want to be with you. But if that's what it takes…"

He pulled her tight against him and kissed her with more passion than was wise. Was he testing her or testing himself? She sighed her consent as their lips parted. A moment later, however, her tone was no breathy whisper when she added, "We need to get one thing straight."

"And that is?" He ran his knuckles down the sides of her ribcage before resting his hands on her waist and was pleased when he felt her tremble.

Her voice remained steady and strong when she said, "We share the decision-making. Okay?"

As he lowered his mouth to hers for the second time, he whispered, "I've got no problem with that."

Atlanta was still in bed when Angelo called the following morning.

And the morning after that.

And the morning after that.

It became their habit to spend the better part of the day together and then share the evening meal. In addition to eating in, they'd dined at nearly every place in Monta Correnti. Except for Rosa and Sorella, of course.

Afterward, they talked, kissed and bade one another goodnight. It was unexpected and sweet. What was happening between them was neither friendship nor a fling. An exact definition failed her, but she knew one thing: it was becoming an exquisite kind of torture.

On this morning, Angelo's deep voice reached through the phone like a caress.

"Did you sleep well?"

She'd barely slept at all. Again. Between Angelo's increasingly bold kisses and her barely restrained responses to those kisses, she'd passed the better part of another night tossing and turning. While her legs had become tangled in the sheets, her mind had been free to roam. Time and again it strayed to sex…with Angelo. If the skill he'd shown with his mouth was any indication, the ultimate act would be good. Very good. At least from her perspective. But how would he rate the experience? Old insecurities bubbled back.

Zeke had been critical of her lovemaking.

"It's a good thing your male fans aren't privy to how inept you are in the sack, love. Ticket sales would tank."

The memory had her stammering as she tried to speak to Angelo now.

"I…I…"

"I know. Me, too."

His voice held humor, but it wasn't directed at her. She pulled the lapels of her silk pajamas together, gathered her wits and struggled to a sitting position.

"So, what do you want to do today?"

"Do you really have to ask? I think you know what

I'd like to do today. It's the same thing I wanted to do last night and the night before and the night before."

Atlanta levered the phone away from her mouth so he wouldn't hear her staggered breathing. Angelo broke the silence with a chuckle.

"Okay, I won't go there." Laughter rumbled again before he lowered his voice. In a silken whisper he added, "Yet. The day's young. There's plenty of time to revisit my original answer later on."

"Sightseeing!" she all but shouted.

"Sightseeing?"

In a less zealous tone, she told him, "The woman who owns the villa I'm renting said some medieval fortress ruins are located not that far away. We'd have to drive some and then walk a ways since they are on a remote hilltop, but I'm up for some exercise."

"So am I," he quipped. "Or at least I can be at a moment's notice."

Despite her popping hormones, she couldn't help but smile. "I'm talking about walking, Angelo."

"There are other, more stimulating ways to increase your heart rate, you know."

"Yes. A simple conversation with you is one of them." She waited for his comeback, something cocky and off-color, but the phone line remained silent. "Angelo?"

"You shouldn't tell a guy something like that," he said at last, sounding much too serious.

"Why?"

"It might give him ideas."

"From what I can tell, you have plenty of ideas already." Feeling emboldened, she took the initiative to flirt. "What are you wearing?"

"You want to know what I'm wearing?" It was apparent in his tone that her boldness took him aback.

She laughed. "I'm wearing a cotton sheet and a smile. So, what about you?"

"Apparently one article of clothing too many. But that's easy enough to remedy," he assured her. "Hang on a minute, okay?"

"Angelo?" She got no response. Had he put down the receiver? She heard a creaking noise. Were those... bedsprings? Surely not. Even so, her grip tightened on the lapels of her pajama top and she had to pull it out from her chest a few times to cool her suddenly heated skin.

Angelo came back on the line then. "Do you want to know what I'm wearing now, Atlanta?"

His words held a dare. She nearly backed down. *Basta.* She'd had enough of meekness.

"I think I can guess," she told him. "Hmm. Let's see. A smile?"

"That's a given. What else?"

The seductive voice that replied was one she barely recognized as her own. Even while filming a love scene on the set, she'd never sounded like this, nor had she ever felt this way around a man. Confident. Powerful. Sexy and in control.

You're worthless, Jane. Worthless. You can't do anything right. Just like your mother.

Body of a centerfold and no clue how to use it. Good thing your fans can't see into our bedroom.

She banished the ugly memories and embraced the moment instead. "You do know that that sheet is optional, right?"

"Same goes."

"I have a confession to make."

"You're not wearing a sheet."

"I'm not." She fingered the fabric-covered button

between her breasts. Before she could fathom what she was doing, she'd fished it one-handed through its hole. A second one followed before she asked, "Does this constitute phone sex?"

"No. It's more like phone foreplay. For the record, I prefer to do both in person. I can be at your villa in fifteen minutes if I don't bother with stop signs and get lucky on those hairpin turns."

"A tempting offer." She meant it. Should she say yes? She wanted to. But the power she'd felt just a moment earlier proved fleeting. Her hand stilled on the third button. "You can take your time getting here, though. The ruins aren't going anywhere."

"Sure?"

She chose to be obtuse. "They haven't in half a dozen centuries or so."

"Your next movie should be a comedy," he grumbled. She heard him exhale then and thought he might have cursed. "Let's say an hour. That will give me enough time to take a long shower of the cold variety."

They were playing with fire, Angelo decided as he hung up the phone and reached for the boxer shorts he'd just tugged off and tossed over the side of the bed. Even so, being burned was low on his list of concerns. Need held the top stop. He'd never met a woman who had tied him in such knots, and in so short a time. He was desperate to have her. More damning, he was desperate just to be with her.

It was crazy, outrageous. They'd known each other mere days, had only shared a handful of kisses and some sexy banter.

He dropped back on the mattress. No, he reminded himself. They'd shared much more than that. He'd shared his life story, laid out all of the ugly details for her inspection. She'd listened. More, she'd accepted and understood. She'd encouraged him to quit avoiding his father, to look beyond career.

What was her life story? He knew some of it from their conversations and he'd guessed a little more. To his surprise, he wanted to know it all, to return the favor of being a good sounding board. Professionally and personally, she was at the same crossroads as he. Despite his relationship with his twin, Angelo had always been a bit of a loner. He preferred it that way. *I'm scared.* At the time he'd made that confession, he'd been referring to his career. Now, it was the unprecedented press of emotions he felt where Atlanta was concerned that left him shaken.

He took his time getting to her villa, arriving an hour later than he'd planned. She was sitting at the wrought-iron table in the courtyard. She had what appeared to be a script folded open in front of her. The fingers of her right hand were curled around a tiny porcelain cup. She wore sunglasses, her lips were slicked with a sheer gloss and she'd pulled her hair back into a simple ponytail. She looked every bit as lovely as she did done up to the nines for the red carpet.

His heart knocked unsteadily, and the disturbing mix of emotions he'd spent the better part of an hour relegating to the background surged to the fore again. He took the seat opposite hers and pretended not to have a care in the world.

"Tell me that's espresso you're drinking and that there's more where it came from."

"Yes to both of your questions." She smiled. "I take it you want some."

"I do."

She set the script aside and started to rise, but Angelo stopped her by reaching for her demitasse cup and finishing off its contents.

"I couldn't resist." He set the cup back on its saucer and stretched out his legs, resting his size eleven sneakers on either side of her dainty navy-and-white skimmers. Keep it light, he ordered himself. Keep it casual. "I've got an espresso machine at home. It's this big, expensive thing that was imported from Italy. But the stuff I make doesn't come out tasting anything like yours. Maybe you should move in with me and every cup would be perfect."

Her expression dimmed. "I thought we agreed to be real with one another? That sure sounded like an old Angelo come-on line to me."

"It was. Habit." One that ensured a certain measure of emotional distance. He blew out a breath. "I'm sorry."

"Okay." She accepted his apology with a nod. "And for the record, I moved in with a man once before for all the wrong reasons. I don't plan to make that mistake again."

His gut clenched at the thought of her setting up housekeeping with someone else. Jealousy? He didn't want to think so. Curiosity was more like it. And so he asked, "Why did you move in with Zeke?"

"In part, because I thought he needed me. He did, too. Not as a life partner, not as a partner of any sort."

"But as someone to control," he finished for her.

"Yes." Her smile was sad. "That lump of clay you once referenced."

"You didn't appreciate my saying so, as I recall."

Was that really mere days ago?

"No. Despite everything, I guess I wasn't ready to

hear it, especially from someone else. The fact I allowed him to mold me is as much my fault as his."

"I disagree, but you know that. Did…did you love him?"

"Maybe. I wanted to." She swallowed and her gaze left Angelo's to focus instead on something behind him. "Even more, I wanted to *be* loved. That probably sounds so pathetic."

Not so pathetic, Angelo thought as realization dawned.

"I wanted to be loved, too," he began. "You and I just went about it differently."

Her gaze snapped back to his. "What do you mean?"

"When I'm standing at home plate, I never feel alone or…or rejected."

She covered one of his hands with her own. He could stop, he knew. She would understand how hard the words were for him to say. But he needed to say them. Aloud. Not for Atlanta, but for himself. It was time to finally accept that the great and glorious ride he'd been on for the past two decades was ending.

"When I've got that bat in my hand and the fans are chanting 'Angel, Angel, Angel,' it's not just a rush of adrenaline I feel. It's…it's validation," he admitted.

Though she said nothing, the pressure on his hand increased.

"I'm someone then, Atlanta. I don't want to lose that, but it's slipping away. It's not about being important or famous. It's…it's just about mattering."

When he glanced up she was nodding, blue eyes awash in unshed tears. "I know what it's like not to recognize your own worth and to see yourself as defined by things outside your control. But the fact is, Angelo, you do matter. You've always mattered, with or without a bat in your hand. And that will continue to be the case."

He squeezed her hand back. "I want to believe that."

"You will. It takes time. I'm still getting there."

The moment stretched as they sat holding hands. The emotional distance he'd always maintained narrowed precariously. He cleared his throat. "So, what about that espresso?"

"Sure." She rose and reached for her cup. "I'll just be a moment."

CHAPTER NINE

WHEN she was gone, Angelo scrubbed a hand over his face. Afterward, his gaze landed on the script she'd left on the table. The fact that it was upside down didn't help given his dyslexia. It took him a full five minutes to figure out the first few words.

"The Blue Flag."

He glanced up just as she placed the cups on the table. He hadn't heard her return, probably because he was concentrating so hard trying to make out the letters.

Easing back in his chair, he apologized. "Sorry. I'm being nosy."

"That's all right. It's nothing personal. Just a script I'm considering."

Glad to have something else to discuss, he asked, "Is it one of those indie projects you mentioned the other night?"

Atlanta nodded. "The title refers to a kind of wild iris that grows in swampy conditions."

"So, are you going to take it?" he asked.

"No. I want my return to the big screen to be memorable for the right reasons, and I think critics and moviegoers ultimately would have the same concerns with the story and its characters that I do."

She picked up the script and flipped absently through

the pages. "It's not a bad story. The leading role, which is what I would play, has some depth. The character is a young woman who's just discovered that she's pregnant and is struggling to come to terms with her younger sister's recent schizophrenia diagnosis. She's worried that her unborn child could be at risk for mental illness. She's also afraid to tell her husband about the baby since he basically thinks her sister, and all people similarly afflicted, should be locked away."

"How does it turn out?"

"Let's just say the ending is satisfying in a theatrical sense, but not terribly happy."

"It sounds dark." Far darker than anything Angelo could recall Atlanta ever doing. Of course, that was exactly why she was considering the script. She wanted to break free from the mold.

"It needs to be given the subject matter, but some of the scenes border on superficial and do very little to heighten the overall tension. To make matters worse, the husband's character is way underdeveloped. I can't figure out what motivates the guy, why he's such an insensitive jerk. For that matter, I can't understand why my character would stay with him."

"Maybe she's not as tough as you are. It takes guts to walk away."

Atlanta glanced up sharply, but when she spoke, it was to change the subject. "You know, we really should be going. It's sunny now, but the forecast is for rain later in the day. We should have no problem getting in our sightseeing before the weather turns if we leave now."

The ruins were indeed off the beaten path. During the last half-hour of the drive, they didn't pass so much as a roadside stand. Luckily, Atlanta had taken Franca's advice and packed a simple lunch for the two of them to share.

"Are you sure this is it?" Angelo asked after he pulled the car to the side of the road. A path opened up through the dense woods, but the only marker was a crude wooden arrow whose painted words were too weathered to read.

"According to Franca's directions. She said it wasn't a regular tourist destination."

"We don't have to go." His gaze flicked to her feet. Her shoes were practical for hoofing around the city, but not exactly designed for hiking.

Atlanta pushed open her car door. "No. We came all this way. Besides, it might be nice to see ruins on a grander scale than those in my life."

"Or mine," Angelo muttered as he joined her.

It was cooler there, perhaps because the trees blocked out most of the sun. Despite the occasional wayward branch, the path was wide enough for them to walk side-by-side. They started out at a brisk pace and maintained it even when the incline grew steeper and the ground more treacherous. Twenty minutes into the walk, Atlanta's heart was hammering, her leg muscles starting to burn and a blister had begun to form on her left heel.

"This is a regular workout," Angelo remarked, as if he could read her mind.

"Darnell would be pleased," she said, thinking of her trainer for the first time in days.

A moment later, she nearly tripped over an exposed tree root.

Angelo offered a hand to steady her. "Watch out," he warned with a laugh. "Given the shape of my shoulder,

I won't be able to carry you out of here if you sprain an ankle."

Though the words were spoken in jest, they represented a shift for him. He was no longer denying his injury and the effect it was having on him now or in the future, she thought, recalling his earlier candor about why he didn't want his career to end and his recognition that it was.

The trail ended a few minutes later at a clearing where the grass grew knee-high and was interspersed with prickly shrubs and the occasional tree. But it was the huge, grayish-white stones that commanded attention. They rose up from the vegetation like an army of ghosts, a haunting reminder of a time long past.

"It's not what I was expecting," Angelo said.

Once a fortress, it was now a pile of rubble. Atlanta had to use her imagination to picture it as it once had been, with high walls and towers and a thriving community living inside. "Nor I, but it is pretty amazing."

She rested her hands against one of the rough-hewn slabs. It was cool to the touch and partly covered in moss. Long ago, someone had labored to bring it and the others to this remote hilltop and create a wall that was intended to keep out invaders.

It had seen hard times, withstood the attacks of invaders for a couple centuries before falling into enemy hands. That was when the real damage to the structure had occurred, according to Franca. Yet part of it remained today, and it would be there long after Angelo and Atlanta were gone.

Some things defied the passage of time. The thought had her recalling what she'd told Angelo earlier about his worth regardless of his baseball career. She'd told him he would always matter. It had been on the tip of her tongue to add, *to me*.

It was a fact Atlanta could no longer deny.

They spent an hour strolling amid the ruins. The view alone was worth the hike. Even with a few clouds starting to darken the sky, or perhaps because of them, the vista was dramatic. Atlanta leaned her elbows on what remained of the fortress's exterior wall and gazed down at the valley below.

"Do you really see me as tough?" she asked, harking back to their earlier conversation on her patio. She turned to face Angelo. "And not, well, the man-eating shrew the tabloids are portraying?"

He settled one hip on the edge of a stone and studied her.

"You're a force to be reckoned with, Atlanta, and for all of the right reasons."

"When I was a little girl…I…I wasn't so tough. I vowed to myself I would never make that mistake again, yet I did with Zeke. The circumstances were different, but…" She shrugged.

"No one's tough when they're a kid, even if they want everybody to believe otherwise."

"Does that include you?"

He studied the calluses on his hands, no doubt the result of gripping a bat. "A week ago, I would have denied it, but yeah. That includes me."

"What's different now than a week ago?"

His expression turned oddly guarded and it sounded as if he said, "I'll let you know when I figure it out."

There wasn't much left to explore, but they stayed a little longer. The approaching storm made the view all the more compelling.

"I can't believe I forgot to bring my camera today," she said as, far in the distance, lightning streaked the sky.

"I've got my cell phone. It's got a camera." He unclipped it from his belt.

"Do you get a signal out here?"

"I haven't checked. To tell you the truth, I hope to God not. The only people likely to call right now are my agent, the team doctor or some reporter. I don't want to talk to any of them on this trip."

"Then why bring a cell?"

"Habit. A bad one." But then he was holding up the phone and instructing her to smile.

He glanced at the display afterward. "Gorgeous."

She dismissed his compliment with a shrug. "I'm photogenic is all."

"Actually, I don't think you look as good on film as you do in person."

She opened her mouth to dismiss his compliment once again. Instead, she heard herself ask, "Really?"

"Really." Angelo leaned one elbow against a boulder, the picture of masculine perfection. "They say the camera adds ten pounds. From where I'm standing, it's more like fifteen."

Atlanta was laughing too hard to be insulted. She attempted to slap him on the upper arm, but Angelo caught her hand before it made contact. He used it to pull her to him. Once she was in his arms, he slid his hands from her waist up to the sides of her breasts, eliciting a shiver.

"Maybe it is only ten." He leaned closer, kissed her neck. "You know I'm only kidding, right?"

"Yes, but only because the cannoli haven't caught up with me yet."

She turned her head to grant him greater access. He nipped her earlobe.

"God, I can't wait till they do. Don't get me wrong. You've got a killer body right now."

Eyes at half-mast, she muttered, "Zeke would say I'm too thin. Of course, if I gained back the weight I've lost, he'd get on me for letting myself go."

Angelo's breath was hot on her neck. "We've already established that Zeke is an idiot." His mouth detoured south to her collarbone. "You should eat two cannoli a day for the duration of your stay in Italy."

"Is that an order?"

"I know how you feel about those, so, no. Consider it more of a plea."

"A plea?"

"I'm not above begging when it comes to certain things."

At that moment, neither was she.

It was late afternoon when they returned to Monta Correnti. By that time the wind had picked up and the mass of billowing purple clouds was no longer far away, but directly overhead. Thankfully, Mother Nature waited to unleash her fury until they were almost to Atlanta's villa with the worst of the hairpin turns behind them.

Then the rain came down in a torrent. Even on high the car's wipers couldn't clear the windshield of water fast enough to provide decent visibility. Angelo navigated the last quarter-mile at a snail's pace. His knuckles glowed white on the steering wheel. When he finally pulled the car to a stop and shifted it into park, he let out a gusty sigh.

"That was an adventure, one I'd prefer not to repeat in this lifetime."

He had parked as close to the villa's main entrance as he could. Even so, with the way the rain was coming down, Atlanta knew she would be drenched to the skin before making it inside.

"Give it a minute," he said, stilling her hand when she went to unbuckle her seat belt. "It's bound to let up."

Slap! Slap! Slap! went the wipers in the quiet that followed, making a mockery of his prediction.

Atlanta glanced around the car. "I don't suppose you have an umbrella handy?"

He switched on the dome light, illuminating the rental's interior, and checked. "Apparently not. Sorry."

Slap! Slap! Slap! went the wipers.

Atlanta was a great believer in setting the scene. In her business it was vital, not only to involve those who plunked down cash to see the final product at their local theater, but to the actors as they worked to stay in character during filming. The storm, the close confines of the sports coupe and the intimate glow from the dome light—they turned the setting into something romantic rather than ridiculous.

Or maybe it was the man who was responsible for that. She'd fought this attraction since the beginning, terrified of it at first. But it was like fighting gravity—exhausting and, in the end, pointless. She glanced over to find him watching her. His hungry gaze caused a shiver and brought forth an appalling amount of need. Even as a flash of lightning rent the dark sky, followed by ominous thunder, his gaze didn't leave hers and his expression didn't change. All the while, the wipers continued to slap across the windshield with ineffective results.

"It's not letting up," she said quietly.

"No. I keep thinking it will, but…" He sounded bemused.

She moistened her lips. "You probably shouldn't drive back in this. The roads around here are difficult enough to navigate when they're dry."

"I could manage."

"I'd worry. Come in."

He sucked in a breath, exhaling as his thumbs tapped against the steering wheel. "Are you sure you want me to come in?"

They were talking about more than her providing him with shelter from the storm.

"Yes. No."

"Which is it?"

"I don't want you to leave."

He switched off the ignition and pocketed the keys. The car's interior went dark. The wipers went still. *Thump, thump, thump* went Atlanta's heart.

They stumbled through the villa's door together, breathless from their frantic dash. As she'd anticipated, they were both soaked. Angelo's shirt was plastered to his skin, outlining the hard contours of his athletic physique. Distracted, it took her a moment to realize that her own drenched clothing was providing a similar view. She tucked her arms over her chest. When she glanced up, he was watching her. He swiped his forearm over his face in a futile attempt to dry it. More rain dripped down from his hair.

"I'll…I'll go get us some towels," she said.

"In a minute. There's something I need to do first."

Angelo moved closer until barely a whisper of space separated their bodies. Slowly, he pushed the damp hair back from her face. His palms were warm against her cheeks. She savored his touch, reveled in the desire it had awakened from such a long slumber.

"You are the most beautiful woman I've ever seen." He whispered the words, almost as if he were speaking to himself rather than offering a compliment.

Atlanta swallowed.

You're a right pretty girl, Jane. The boys will be after you before long.

She refused to think about what Duke had said after that or what he'd done. She refused to think about Zeke and the face he'd turned into both of their fortunes.

Standing in the villa's dimly lit entryway with Angelo, she simply allowed herself to feel. For the first time in her life, what she felt was beautiful and feminine. It struck her as ironic, given her disheveled state. Her hair was plastered to her head. God only knew what had become of the mascara she'd brushed on her eyelashes that morning. Yet he found her beautiful and she felt the same.

Power surged through her, the origin of which she wasn't quite able to name. She reveled in it all the same. No longer was she Duke's terrified stepdaughter or Zeke's dutiful protégé. It was as if the rain had washed away the last clinging bits of dirt from her past.

She slipped out of her flats and kicked them aside. "I'm more than a pretty package, you know."

He nodded slowly, almost as if he liked hearing the clarification, almost as if he understood her reasons for offering it.

"I figured that out within five minutes of meeting you. And I'm talking about at that nightclub three years ago." He traced her lower lip with the pad of his thumb and the same lightning that intermittently streaked the sky outside shot through her.

"It took me a little longer." A lifetime, she thought ruefully.

"Better late than never."

His hands came up to frame her face and then his mouth found hers. Desperate to hold on as the kiss deepened, she fisted her hands in the wet fabric of his shirt and gave herself over to desire.

The worst of the storm had passed outside as well as in. Angelo and Atlanta lay exhausted on the metal-framed bed in her room. Like the thunder rumbling far off in the distance, her body still felt the aftershocks of their lovemaking. She'd played countless such scenes on screen and alone with Zeke. But she'd never experienced firsthand what she'd portrayed all these years.

Until now.

It wasn't just the sex, though it had been every bit as incredible as she'd hoped it would be. It was the man. His strength and his vulnerability. His generosity, not only as a lover, but as a friend. The emotions she was experiencing at the moment were every bit as new and unnerving as those earlier physical sensations. They'd been mounting since their first meeting, growing deeper, stronger and impossible to ignore.

I love you.

The words were on the tip of her tongue, begging to be said. She wasn't sure he would want to hear them, though, so she kept them to herself as she lay next to him in the dark.

She thought Angelo had dozed off until she heard him say, "You're quiet."

"Speechless is the better word."

He rose on his elbow and studied her in the dim light. "Was it…okay for you? You seemed…hesitant."

She stilled. "I did?"

"Just a little. And only at first."

The old Atlanta, weighted down with sexual hang-ups, would have excused herself and hidden away in the bathroom, mortified. The new Atlanta rolled on top of him, determined that whatever memories he took away from their time in Italy would be positive. Those were the only kind she wanted to have as well.

"Let's see what you think this time."

CHAPTER TEN

THE sun was up when Angelo woke. He stretched and reached for the woman who was responsible for the smile curving his lips. His hands found only cool sheets. He opened his eyes. The room was empty. A breeze wafted through the open windows bringing in the clean, earthy scents of the countryside. He preferred the lingering scent of the woman who was absent. He dressed and went downstairs to find her.

Atlanta was seated at the table outside, having espresso and reading another script. The cobblestones were strewn with leaves and debris, signs of the previous night's storm. She looked…peaceful. She smiled when she saw him, her expression at once that of the seductress and the ingénue.

"I was wondering when you were going to wake up. Sleep well last night?"

"I did." Partly because she'd been there beside him. He walked to where she sat and dropped a kiss on her mouth. "I liked being awake even better."

She flushed. "Me, too."

He took the chair opposite hers and nodded to the papers in her hand. "Another script?"

"Yes."

As he had before, he helped himself to her espresso. "Does it hold any more promise than the last one?"

"My character is a serial killer." She grinned wickedly. "She doesn't see herself that way, of course. She's a nurse and her victims are people who have little or no family. She thinks she's doing them a favor, relieving them of their loneliness."

There was an eagerness in her tone that he hadn't heard before. "You sound excited."

She smiled. "I guess I am a little. It's got some serious meat for me to chew. I'm only a few chapters into it, and I can already tell the characters are well developed."

"Sounds promising."

A shadow fell across her face. "The only problem is the guys who sent it to me have had a few big duds. As a result, they've had a problem attracting financing for their last few projects. If they land me, they can land a backer. I'm sure my bankability is a big part of my draw."

"What? You don't think you can handle the part?"

"I know I can." He found her confidence as sexy as her wind-tumbled hair. "Which is why I've spent the past half-hour seriously thinking about financing the picture myself."

"As in forming your own production company?"

"Exactly." Her brows rose and on a grin, she asked, "Well? Think I'm crazy?"

"I told you once you're a force to be reckoned with, Atlanta. All I can say is, watch out, Hollywood."

Her smile wobbled a little. "Thanks."

"For what?"

"For believing in me."

He nodded. "Same goes."

* * *

He left not long after that, eschewing her offer to make breakfast. Sharing a meal with her after a long night of lovemaking was just too domestic, especially since they'd spent the better part of the past twenty-four hours together. Still, it wasn't because he didn't like the idea that he declined. It was because he did…way too much.

On the way back to his villa, he stopped in town at the little coffee shop where he and Atlanta had shared cannoli their first full day in Monta Correnti. It seemed a lifetime ago. He'd changed so much since then. They both had changed, and so had their relationship. And not only because it had turned physical.

Last night, after they'd made love a second time, she'd asked him what would happen when they returned home.

"We resume our lives," he said evasively, rather than giving her the answer that had come so readily to mind. He wanted to keep seeing her, logistics and complications be damned. Things didn't have to end…in Italy.

He was returning to his car, lost in thought and balancing a cup of coffee and a pastry, when he heard his name called. He didn't recognize the raspy male voice, but he knew the speaker's identity in an instant. He stopped abruptly and he swore his heart did the same. As he turned, time reeled backward.

"Papa."

He whispered the name, but it scraped his throat as viciously as a blood-curdling scream would have. For one crazy moment Angelo was a confused and heartbroken little boy again, wondering what he and his brother had done to deserve being sent away.

I'll be good.

Bile rose in his throat. How many times had he made that promise in the days leading up to his ouster?

Now in his late sixties, Luca's light brown hair was streaked with gray at the temples and his expressive face was creased with lines. Those seemed to be his only bow to age. He remained a tall man, only about an inch shy of Angelo's six feet three, and, even though he wasn't as broad or as thickly built as his twin sons, he commanded attention. But that wasn't why he commanded Angelo's.

Papa.

He didn't say it aloud this time. He kept the name to himself. He wasn't quite as successful, however, at stopping the memories. They flashed in his head like an old film reel, a bit grainy from age, but clear enough to pry open what he'd thought were ironclad defenses. He recalled riding on his father's shoulders and climbing up on his knee. He remembered giggling riotously as Luca tossed him high in the air, and then begging for another turn after Alex had received the same treatment.

Ti amo, Papa.

Love in its purest form—that of a child for a parent—welled up. Anger, confusion, grief and fear helped banish it. They rose with the force of a tsunami to wash away the memories and the words he hadn't recalled in more than three decades.

So it was that as Luca drew even with him and broke into a smile, Angelo was clenching his teeth.

"Angelo! My son. I can barely believe my eyes." Luca smiled and extended, not his hand, but his arms, clearly expecting to wrap his long-lost son in a welcoming embrace.

Angelo took a step backward, not in retreat but to make a stand. He'd been sent away, exiled. He wasn't sure he could be as forgiving of that fact as his brother Alex was. Luca's expression faltered but he nodded as if he understood this reunion would not be so tidy after all.

"I've wanted to come by your villa after sending the welcome basket, but Isabella said I should wait, give you more time."

God bless Isabella. Even so, Angelo said quietly, "I've had thirty-five years of time."

Luca flushed. "I...I have no excuse to offer. Only an apology, which I hope that you will accept."

Angelo ignored the words. "Actually, I'm glad you didn't come by. I've been enjoying my stay."

Despite the implied insult, Luca nodded. "That is good. The company of a beautiful woman helps."

Of course he would know about Atlanta. "It does."

"Perhaps the two of you could come by the restaurant one evening and let me buy you dinner."

"I don't want anything from you."

"I only wish to buy you a meal," Luca pointed out, his reasonable tone in stark contrast to Angelo's petulant one.

He moderated his. "I'll bring her to Rosa for the meet and greet with the relatives that Isabella has planned. I assume you'll be picking up the tab for that."

Luca's expression was sad as he held out a hand in entreaty. "How I wish I could change the past."

Angelo's eyes stung. Because he wanted so badly just then to believe his father meant it, he shook his head. "But you can't, Luca. You can't."

Back at his villa, Angelo paced in agitation. Who did the man think he was acting so hurt, looking so sad and offering apologies that were three decades too late? Well, he wanted an apology even less than he wanted his old man to buy him and Atlanta dinner at Rosa.

"I don't want you in my life," he muttered. "I don't need you."

Stone by stone, Angelo rebuilt the wall around his heart where his father was concerned. If not for Atlanta, he would be packing his bags and making arrangements to return to New York. But they had plans for later. That was the only reason he was staying in Monta Correnti. Otherwise, his mission here was complete, as far as he was concerned.

He said as much to Atlanta when she arrived for dinner that evening. He'd had the meal catered, making the arrangements through Isabella with no mention of the meeting with their father, though he figured she'd probably heard about it. Just as she'd probably heard that he'd snubbed Luca's offer of dinner at Rosa. Angelo had paid in full for the meal, offering a generous tip to the young man who delivered it.

As they sat at the patio table Atlanta said, "I'm glad you're sticking around. Not just for me, for you."

He knew what she meant. On a sigh, he admitted, "I didn't think this was going to be so difficult."

"Confronting the past never is easy."

He angled his head to one side. Questions nagged. "You've never mentioned much about your family."

"That's because I don't like to talk about them," she said quietly.

"Neither do I, but I have."

She sipped her wine. "Let me put it another way. Luca is Father of the Year material compared to my stepdad."

Angelo snorted. "Right."

"Definitely. Duke was pure evil. I found it best to

make myself scarce whenever he was home, especially if my mother wasn't around."

Dread pooled in his stomach. *No. No.*

"I know what you're thinking," she said mildly.

"You do?"

"You're trying to match what I just said to the story the public has been fed."

God help him, he wished that were what he was thinking. Still, he said, "They don't add up."

"No." She sipped more wine. "My so-called humble beginnings were a little seedier than that."

"You said stepfather. What about your dad? Where does he figure in all of this?"

"He doesn't. The truth is I don't know my biological father's identity. Even my mother isn't sure. It could be one of a half-dozen different men. She wasn't terribly discriminating, especially if the guy had a few bucks in his pocket and could help her make the rent. Before she married Duke, a slew of 'uncles' lived with us.

"I don't tell many people this, of course. In fact, only one other person knows the truth."

"Zeke," he said.

"My attorney." That came as a surprise. "He sends my mother checks to keep quiet."

"What about your stepfather?"

"He died five years ago. Until then, I was sending Duke checks, too. He demanded more than my mother."

"Why?"

She said nothing, but her silence spoke volumes. It was a good thing the man was dead. Otherwise Angelo would have had to kill him.

"They blackmailed you."

"Yes." She pasted on a smile. "See what I mean. Your family is the portrait of normal by comparison."

"I wouldn't say normal, but…" He reached across the table for her hand. "I'm sorry, Atlanta. So damned sorry."

Angelo's touch, combined with the compassion in his eyes, was almost her undoing. She called on all of her acting skills to suppress her emotions.

"There's no need to be. I came to terms with the situation a long time ago. I'll never have a relationship with my mother other than as her meal ticket. She's made it clear that's all she sees me as. I never hear from her on my birthday or at the holidays. The only time she contacts me is through my attorney because she's running low of funds.

"As for Duke, I actually celebrated when I learned that he'd died of a heart attack. That's not something I'm proud of, but it's the truth." She fingered the stem of her wine glass. "I drank champagne. Half a bottle of it."

"Piper-Heidsieck?" Angelo asked.

She glanced up and smiled. "That would be the one. Not a magnum, though."

"I'd say you were entitled, even if it had been half a magnum."

"I thought so, too. Zeke was appalled when he arrived home and found me listening to old-school country music and well on my way to being snockered." She laughed dryly now at the memory of her ex pacing their bedroom and demanding answers while she'd giggled hysterically and done her best Tanya Tucker impersonation.

"Family is one big pain in the backside," he grumbled.

"I'd have to agree. Still, I wish it could be different."

At his surprised expression, she added, "I still fantasize about my mother coming to me, begging for my forgiveness and telling me that she's proud, that she cares."

"Make no mistake, Luca doesn't care. If he cared, he would have been there all of these years. Come to that, if he cared, he would have been the one to contact me and Alex, instead of leaving that chore to Isabella."

"Maybe he was afraid, Angelo."

"Of what?"

"Of your reaction. Maybe he was afraid you would reject him, again. You know how that feels."

"Don't."

But she pressed ahead. "He made a really bad choice and he knows it." Atlanta was thinking of her own poor decisions when she added, "Things like that haunt you."

He sighed. "I'm usually a pretty easygoing guy. I've been hit by pitches that were thrown with the intention of taking me out of a game. I shake it off. I've even been known to buy the pitcher a beer after the game just to show there are no hard feelings. But this..." He shook his head. "I can't get around the fact that Luca sent us away. I can't forget. I can't forgive."

"That line in the sand you once spoke of?"

He nodded. "Yeah."

Atlanta thought about Zeke and her stepfather. Both men had left her with scars, emotional, psychological and physical. Had she forgiven them? Would she ever be able to forget?

"Maybe it's enough just to move on," she said after a moment.

The meal was finished. The moon was rising. At least one of them had come to terms with the past.

"That hot tub looks inviting," she mentioned after a moment.

"Too bad you didn't bring your swimsuit."

Atlanta stood and reached for the hem of her shirt. "And here I was thinking, how fortunate."

Angelo's phone woke him the next morning. This made twice he'd slept with Atlanta. Twice he'd awoken alone. He didn't care for it, he thought as he untangled himself from the sheets to reach for the receiver. It was his brother.

"Hey, Angelo. How's everything going?"

"It's going," he answered slowly, trying to get his bearings. According to the bedside clock it was nearly nine.

"Have you spoken with Luca?"

"Yesterday, actually. I ran into him in town."

"You *ran* into him? That doesn't sound like you had much of a conversation."

"Close enough."

"Angelo—"

"Don't," he warned.

"Are you okay?"

"Why wouldn't I be?" he scoffed.

"It was a jolt for me, too, seeing Papa again."

"Don't call him that," Angelo ground out, stumbling back till he found the edge of the mattress.

"He's our father, Angelo. Like it or not, that much can't be changed. And Luca wants to be part of our lives now, whatever part we're willing to let him be."

"You know my answer."

"Then why are you there?"

"You strong-armed me into it."

Alex was quiet a moment before saying, "It was

strange for me, too, being in Italy. I didn't think I had
any real memories of the place or of Luca or that part
of our childhood, for that matter, until I was in Monta
Correnti. Then all of a sudden bits and pieces of the past
started coming back."

Angelo swallowed as some of the memories to which
his twin referred beckoned. "Do you remember going
out into the countryside to pick herbs?"

"Yeah." Alex chuckled. "Luca was very particular
about what he wanted. I remember that he turned it into
a game of sorts. Who could find the most perfect basil
leaves?"

"You always won."

"Only because you were too impatient to look."

"We took turns sitting on his shoulders," Angelo said.
"I felt like a giant up there."

"Yeah." They both fell silent. Then Alex changed
the subject. "According to the media, I see you're not
hurting for female companionship on this trip. How in
the hell did you manage to meet Atlanta Jackson?"

Angelo opted to keep it light. "You know how it is,
bro. No woman can resist my charm. You'd better marry
Allie quick before she comes to her senses and realizes
she's engaged to the wrong twin."

"Not a chance. She and I are perfect for one another."
He said it with such conviction that Angelo couldn't
bring himself to come back with an off-handed remark.
He walked to the window. Atlanta was outside. His heart
hitched seeing her, since he'd thought she'd gone.

"I'm happy for you, Alex. I'm happy for both of
you."

"Thanks. I've got to say, I'm a little worried about
you. There's a lot of unflattering coverage of Atlanta in

the press these days. Now they're saying some interesting things about you, too."

"You know the tabloids."

"Yeah, but it's not just the rags that are reporting these things. I saw a piece on the nightly news the other day that the two of you are holed up together at an undisclosed location in Italy. Baseball fans are wondering why you're not at the playoff games, even if you can't swing a bat. When the Rogues lost the other night, a couple of fans burned your effigy."

"What?"

"They were drunk and ticketed for disorderly conduct, but they aren't the only ones who feel like you've written off your team."

"That's not true," he yelled into the phone.

"It's not me you need to convince," Alex said quietly.

"It would kill me to suit up and sit on the bench, but I've followed the games on the Internet. I've been in contact with management and my agent. Hell, I even e-mailed that rookie outfielder with some advice and encouragement."

"The fans only see what they see. And right now what they're seeing is New York's Angel tramping about in Italy somewhere with Hollywood's Mata Hari."

Angelo let out a string of curses while his brother continued.

"One report claims you and Atlanta met a few years ago. Now the speculation is that you've been seeing one another behind her boyfriend's back and you're the main reason for their breakup."

"You know me better than that. I don't poach," he growled.

"Hey, don't shoot the messenger. I'm just saying there's a lot of speculation out there."

"Well, here's the truth. Atlanta and I did meet a few years back, but she blew me off completely." Muffled laughter rumbled through the line. Angelo ignored it. "Then we ran into each other at JFK on our way here. We barely know one another," he concluded. Even without glancing at the bed, he knew he was lying.

"A waitress from the airport's VIP lounge says she saw the two of you together. She said you looked very chummy and even shared a kiss."

"It was more like a friendly peck goodbye."

"Goodbye? You're still together," Alex pointed out.

"We wound up on the same plane, bound for the same place. Pure coincidence." Or was it fate?

"So, it's nothing?" Alex said.

Angelo watched Atlanta through the window and took his time responding. "I don't know what it is."

"That sounds serious coming from you."

"I…don't know."

"You can do better than a bimbo, Angelo."

If they'd been face to face rather than speaking on the phone, Angelo would have taken a swing at Alex. His anger came through loud and clear in his words.

"Watch what you say about her."

"It's like that, huh?"

"Like what?" he grumbled.

"Serious."

"It's not serious." Liar, his conscience argued.

"Are you sure?" Alex's voice lowered then. "I told myself that when I met Allie. Love is pretty scary and at times it's damned inconvenient, but it's worth it when the woman is right."

He sucked in a breath, feeling gut-punched. "I'm not in love."

Alex didn't argue with him. Instead, he said, "Be careful, Angelo. Be sure she's the right one."

The panic he'd felt at the mention of the L-word dissipated. "She's not who you think she is. Atlanta is very different from the women she plays onscreen, and she's definitely nothing like the woman the media are portraying her to be."

"Where there's smoke…" Alex said. Another time, Angelo would have realized he was being baited. Right now, he launched his attack.

"You're wrong. She's being set up by her ex. He's bitter and controlling. She's been his cash cow for the past decade and he's ticked that she's walked out on him."

"You sound awfully…involved in her business," Alex finished after a short pause.

Angelo huffed out a sigh. "I hate seeing anyone railroaded."

"What about the affairs?"

"Rumored affairs. And the rumors are bunk. Atlanta is no femme fatale."

"Then far be it from me to argue," Alex responded quietly. "Besides, your love life isn't the reason for my call."

"I'd rather talk about Atlanta than Luca."

Alex merely laughed. "I bet you would. Have you had a chance to meet anyone else from the family?"

"Isabella." Angelo's tone softened. "She was at the villa when I arrived. She welcomed me to Monta Correnti with a feast fit for a king."

"She's all heart, not to mention one hell of a cook," Alex agreed.

"I still can't believe we have a sister."

"And a couple of brothers, too." Alex chuckled. "Wait till you meet Valentino. He's the life of the party. He kind of reminds me of you. He's a thrill-seeking adrenaline junkie, not to mention a real player when it comes to the ladies. Not that he's doing that any more. Clara would have his hide."

Angelo mentally flicked back through conversations he'd had with his brother on this topic, conversations he'd dismissed at the time but now found himself wanting to recall. "Valentino's not really our brother, though, is he? I'm talking blood-wise. He's not a Casali."

"Don't let anyone there hear you saying that," Alex warned in a surprisingly stern voice. "Valentino may not be Luca's biological son, but that's a non-issue for all involved. He's family."

Family. Alex bandied the word about with such ease.

"So, Luca could father a kid he didn't, well, father, but conveniently forget all about us?"

"That chip you're carrying around has to be hell on your bum shoulder," Alex said dryly. "Speaking of which, what are you going to do about it?"

"The chip?"

"The shoulder."

Angelo knew. He'd always known. "Surgery."

"And then?"

"I'm thinking about coaching. Or I may try my hand at commentating."

"I'm surprised to hear you say that."

"Why? I love the game. I'll always be part of it."

"That's not what I find surprising." Alex was quiet a moment. "I'm glad you finally came to this realization."

He'd had some help, Angelo knew.

He decided to redirect the conversation. "Isabella mentioned that Cristiano is a firefighter and he'd been injured in a blaze in Rome."

"Yes. Although Isabella is playing that down somewhat—it was no ordinary blaze. Cristiano saved seven lives in the recent terror attacks in Rome. He's a hero. They're all very proud of him."

Respect welled a second time. Admiration followed. He found himself curious about this man, this brother, and wanting to meet him. In fact, he found himself wanting to meet Valentino. Family. When had the concept stopped feeling so foreign?

Alex's voice came through the line. "Hey, are you still there?"

"I'm here." Angelo rubbed his temple and admitted, "It's a lot to process, you know?"

"I know. I struggled with it at first, too. Allie helped me see what a gift I was being given."

"A gift." Angelo snorted.

"Give it time," Alex urged. Before hanging up, he added, "And give Luca a chance."

His brother's plea echoed in Angelo's head long after their conversation ended. Maybe their father was due a few more minutes of his time.

CHAPTER ELEVEN

HE JOINED Atlanta out by the pool. She was seated on the edge, her bare feet and legs dangling in the sun-dappled water. He settled beside her and gave her a kiss.

"I've got to tell you, I don't like waking up alone."

"Sorry. I'm an early riser. I didn't want to wake you. You looked so peaceful."

"Wake me," he said. The kiss that accompanied his request was longer than the first one. If not for the cool water lapping at his legs, he would have forgotten what he needed to say. He pulled back and cleared his throat. "There's been a change of plans for today."

"Has something come up?"

"I...I need to go see my father."

She blinked in surprise. "What made you change your mind?"

"Alex." He sighed heavily. "My brother just called. He thinks I should give our father a little more of my time."

Atlanta rested her head on his shoulder. "He's not the only one who feels that way."

"I know."

"I don't think you'll regret it, no matter what the outcome."

"The past needs to be confronted and all that."

"So, you have been listening." After giving him a kiss, Atlanta rose to her feet. "Call me later?"

"Count on it."

Despite his resolve, Angelo wound up taking his time going to see Luca, whom he knew from a call to Isabella would be at Rosa. It was late afternoon when he finally made it to the village. His footsteps faltered outside the restaurant and he jammed his hands into the pockets of his jeans. Five minutes passed and found him still standing in the same spot.

"He who hesitates…" a feminine voice remarked dryly.

He turned to find an older woman standing in the doorway of the restaurant next door. She was a stranger, but he felt certain of her identity. The infamous Aunt Lisa. The woman who'd apparently had the means to bail out her brother, but had chosen to let him send his sons away instead.

"I'm not lost," he countered.

"And yet you are still standing there." Her lips curved. She had classical features, the kind that defied the passage of time. She had to be around Luca's age, yet she remained a strikingly beautiful woman.

"I like taking my time."

"Then, by all means, carry on."

Neither of them moved. After a moment, he said, "I believe we're related."

"I believe you are right." Her gaze held a hint of amusement. "I am Lisa Firenzi."

He nodded as he mentally added another face to the list of names in his head. "You're Luca's older sister."

Her mouth tightened fractionally. Vanity, he decided. Few women appreciated having their age referenced in any way. Given this woman's sleek dark hair and fashionable appearance, it was clear she was determined to wage a take-no-prisoners battle against time.

"And you are Angelo, or, as they call you back in New York, the Angel."

"That's right," he said, and crossed to where she stood.

"I visited your city once and saw a photograph of you in the newspaper. You are quite famous, I gather."

"I'm good at what I do," he replied mildly.

Lisa wasn't fooled. "You are better than good, at least according to the newspaper clipping I read. I do not claim to know anything about this sport you play—"

"Baseball."

"*Sì.* But the article made it plain that you have many loyal fans."

How loyal? The very question that had niggled so persistently for weeks suddenly seemed unimportant. They'd remember him or they wouldn't.

Lisa was saying, "Why don't you come in to Sorella? Let me treat my famous nephew to an exceptionally fine meal."

He cast a glance back at his father's restaurant.

Lisa apparently read his mind. "Rosa isn't going anywhere and neither is Luca. Besides, I believe you might know one of my guests, a lovely young American woman who is sitting all alone." Lisa clicked her tongue. "Such a pity."

He peered past his aunt into Sorella. Atlanta was seated with her back to him at a table in the middle of the restaurant. His pulse picked up speed when he spied the familiar cascade of nearly white hair.

"I'll come in," he informed his aunt. "But I'll buy my own dinner."

"You are so like your father." The corners of her mouth turned down then and she shrugged. "As you wish."

"Fancy running into you."

Startled, Atlanta turned to find Angelo standing behind her. "What are you doing here?"

"Same thing you are. Planning to have an early supper." Angelo settled into the chair opposite hers, dwarfing its sleek chrome frame.

She lowered her voice, "So, how did it go, your meeting with Luca?"

"I haven't seen him yet."

"You've had all day," she said.

"I know."

He wasn't quite ready.

The same waiter who'd taken her order for chicken piccata came by again. Angelo requested linguine in white clam sauce and a bottle of wine. Courage, she decided.

The wine arrived at their table a moment later. Followed not long after by their entrées.

"I'm curious about something," she said. "When you spoke to your brother earlier, what did he have to say about me?"

Angelo halted mid-sip. Not a good sign, she thought.

"What makes you think we talked about you?"

She eyed him in challenge. "You didn't?"

"Maybe just a little. He read about us."

"God." Her fork clattered to her plate. "Tell me you set him straight."

"Of course I did. I made sure he knew that all that stuff is garbage." He reached across the table for her hand. "He's going to like you."

Angelo toyed with the last of his linguine as he mulled

what he'd just said. He'd never brought a woman around to meet his brother, yet he couldn't deny he wanted to introduce Atlanta to Alex and not only because he wanted his twin to see her for the woman she was, rather than the film sensation or the tabloid staple she'd become.

"You're frowning," Atlanta said softly.

"This thing with Luca," he evaded. "I don't like being at odds with my brother."

It was true, just not the whole truth. She picked up on that.

"But that's not the only reason you're out of sorts. In fact, Alex isn't the only reason you came to Italy."

"I'm looking for some answers," he admitted. Part of him wanted to make those meaningful connections he'd not only been denied, but had denied himself.

Family.

Despite his close ties to Alex, Angelo truly had never understood its importance or its staying power. He was starting to. It created connections, not only between people, but between the past and the present. Isabella and his cousins placed such stock in it they were rallying together to mend an old rift. Family also held out a promise for the future. Connections, he thought again, his mind turning to Alex and Allie and little Cherry.

"What's my legacy?" he asked softly, almost to himself.

Before coming to Italy he'd thought he knew. It was baseball—his stats at bat and in the field. It was a good bet he'd be inducted into the Baseball Hall of Fame. That kind of immortality was no longer enough.

"Your legacy is what you choose it to be." Her expression held understanding.

A feeling of rightness settled, only to be tempered by

fear. What if he loved Atlanta and she left him, too? She smiled a little uncertainly as he continued to stare.

"Are you okay?"

"Fine," he lied as emotions tumbled through him.

"You're not, but I understand."

"You do?" He swallowed, not caring in the least for this vulnerability.

"Go and see Luca. It's time, Angelo."

He should have been relieved she'd misinterpreted his thoughts. He wasn't. "We're not done with our meals."

"I'll have yours boxed and pick up the check. You can finish it at my villa later."

And finish this conversation, too, he decided. "Fine. But the meal's on me."

His act of chivalry wound up being a moot point. When he went to pay, he was told there was no charge. Damn his aunt. He glanced around to set her straight. He'd pay his own way. He wasn't sure why it was so important, just that it was.

It became doubly so when the hostess said, "It was Signor Casali. He stopped in a few minutes ago. He paid your bill."

Angelo had been irritated when he'd thought his aunt had paid for the meal. Now anger, whose origin dated back a few decades, surged to the fore. Next door, Rosa bustled with patrons. People laughed and talked over one another. Festive music played in the background. It struck him again how different the atmosphere here was compared to that next door. It was far less formal. More…homey. The thought added new heat to his anger.

He wound his way through the tables and headed to the kitchen. He stormed through the swinging doors like an outlaw looking for a gunfight. The white-coated chef whirled around and let out a stream of words in hard-edged Italian. The man clearly was not happy to have his territory invaded. Angelo was past the point of worrying about stepping on toes.

"I'm looking for Luca Casali," he announced.

The man's fierce expression subsided. "You…you are Angelo?"

"Yes."

A grin broke over the man's face. "I am Lorenzo. Lorenzo Nesta. I am head chef at Rosa. I also am engaged to your cousin Scarlett."

More ties, more connections.

"Can you tell me where to find Luca?"

"He is with Scarlett in the office." Lorenzo pointed toward a set of doors. His lips twitched a little when he added, "Maybe you could knock this time, *no*?"

Angelo had no intention of heeding Lorenzo's advice. Luca had barged back into his life without invitation. Why shouldn't he return the favor? So, when he reached the office, he turned the doorknob and sent the door flying open with enough force that it came back and banged him in his bad arm. That ticked him off even more.

"Angelo!" Luca blinked in surprise at his son's sudden appearance. The young woman sitting behind the desk appeared utterly startled.

"I came to return your money." He bit out the words.

Luca's face clouded with confusion. *"Scusi?"*

"There was no need for you to buy dinner for Atlanta and me."

"No need, *sì*. I wished to do it. I told you so the other day."

"Well, I *don't* wish you to do it. I want nothing from

you. Not a damn thing!" He pulled a wad of bills from his pocket and pressed them into his father's hand. The amount was more than enough to cover the check.

"Do you realize the insult of your actions?" This from Scarlett, who had risen to her feet and was coming around the desk. Her dark hair and chocolate eyes spoke of her Italian ancestry, but her English carried an Australian accent.

"Did he?" Angelo challenged.

"I can't believe your nerve—"

"It is all right, Scarlett." Luca held up a hand. "Angelo is entitled to his anger."

She huffed out a breath. "Is he also entitled to act boorish and ungrateful?"

"No." Angelo answered before his father could. His blinding anger had begun to dissipate. All too clearly he could see this exchange from his cousin's viewpoint. He *was* being boorish. He *did* seem ungrateful. "I apologize for barging in here. At the very least I should have knocked. The cook—"

"Chef," she inserted icily.

"Lorenzo, yes. We met in his kitchen. He's your fiancé, I believe." Scarlett's expression softened slightly. Angelo went on. "He advised me to knock first before coming in here, but I had already worked up a full head of steam."

"Over what? Your father wishing to welcome you home by paying for your meal at my mother's restaurant? Yes," she drawled. "I can see how that would offend you."

"He has more reason than that," Luca inserted quietly.

"No, Uncle, he doesn't understand—"

Luca took her hand, kissed it in a doting fashion.

"Can you leave Angelo and me alone for a moment, *per favore*?"

She looked torn, but finally nodded.

"I saw you and Atlanta through the window. I meant no offense in buying your meal," Luca began when they were alone. "It was intended as a gesture of goodwill."

Move on. Atlanta had told him that. Angelo swallowed. Some of his pride went down in the process.

"Thank you."

Luca's face brightened. "You're welcome. Did you enjoy your meal?"

"I did."

"Especially the company, I would imagine. She is a very beautiful woman."

"She's a hell of a lot more than beautiful."

"I felt that way about my Violetta," Luca mused before flushing.

"And my mother? How did you feel about her?"

Luca's expression turned thoughtful. "Your mother was lovely. She had an infectious laugh and a great love for adventure."

"She was the life of the party, all right," he replied dryly. "So, did you love her?"

"It happened so quickly."

"Did you love her?" Angelo bit out the words.

"I thought so at that time. She was an incredible woman. But life here was not what she expected. By the time she decided to go back to America, we both knew we weren't what the other needed."

"She left Alex and me here with you."

"She had a demanding career and lived in a big city. We both felt it would be for the best for you to stay here."

Twice abandoned, which made his tone all the more bitter when he said, "That was short-lived."

Luca closed his eyes on a sigh. "Of all the mistakes I've made in my life, sending your brother and you to live with Cindy is the one I regret most."

"Then why did you do it?"

"I was selling food from a roadside stall at the time," Luca began. "Money was tight. I...I had no means to keep you, no way to care for you."

He'd heard it all before from others. He still didn't understand. "So you sent us away. Even though you and Cindy had already decided we should stay here, you shipped us to Boston."

Luca nodded slowly. "I wanted you to have a stable home."

"Cindy was an alcoholic. I'm sure the stress of single parenthood didn't help. She drank her way to an early grave."

"I...I..."

Angelo didn't wait for him to finish. "A lot of nights, she didn't come home at all. Or she passed out on the floor before making it to her bed. Is *that* the stable home life you had in mind?"

Luca shook his head, looking like a doomed man. Even so, Angelo pulled forth another sharp-edged memory to hurl.

"Alex and I ate out of a Dumpster once. It was right after we ran away from the first foster home after Cindy died. We didn't like it there much."

"Alessandro mentioned that the father was not a kind man," Luca said quietly.

"Kind?" Angelo's laughter rang out bitter and harsh. "The guy would have beaten us senseless for the slightest transgression. That is, if he could have caught us. Luckily, Alex and I were fast on our feet."

Luca extended his hands palm up. "I am so sorry."

"Yeah. I'm sorry, too. Sorry that I let Alex and Atlanta talk me into coming here tonight and giving you a second chance to explain."

"Your brother found it in his heart to forgive me."

"Yeah, well, we may look alike, but Alex and I are very different people."

Luca wasn't put off. "So I can see. You play professional baseball for a living. Alessandro, he tells me you are very good at this game."

"It's more than a game. It's America's national pastime, as big as what soccer is here."

"And you are good at it." His father smiled.

Angelo let out a derisive snort. The lost young boy he'd been couldn't stop himself from bragging, "I'm better than good. I'm one of the best. I've got three World Series rings and I've been voted Most Valuable Player more than once. I'll be in the Hall of Fame someday. In the meantime, the Rogues pay me millions of dollars each season, and I make twice that amount a year endorsing everything from breakfast cereal to luxury automobiles."

"You have done well for yourself." Luca nodded. "I am pleased for you and very proud."

The words warmed him. He'd waited a lifetime to hear his father say them, which, in the end, was why he bristled. It was too late. Too damned late.

"Go to hell, Luca."

Atlanta was waiting for him just outside the courtyard the two restaurants shared. It bustled with people. Music played, laughter rang out over the din of conversation.

When he reached her, Angelo opened his mouth to speak. No words came. She stepped forward and wrapped her arms around him. It turned out no words were necessary. He buried his face in her hair and for the first time since he was a boy, he cried.

CHAPTER TWELVE

"URGENT!" read the subject line of the e-mail sent from her stylist. Atlanta opened it and immediately wished she hadn't.

"Make sure you're sitting down when you click on this link. I'm so sorry, sweetie."

Atlanta did as instructed. She sat first. Not that it mattered. Nothing could stop her from slumping to the floor once she'd read the story's headline.

"My daughter seduced my husband: Atlanta Jackson's mother's firsthand account of the star's dark side."

The accompanying photo was a grainy one of her and Duke. He had his hand on her backside and, though she recalled wanting to retch at the time, she'd smiled because her mother had told her to before taking the picture.

"Oh, God." It came out part moan and part plea. Not for the first time, her prayer went unheard.

Her first instinct was to stay curled up in a heap on the room's cotto floor. Her second one was the one she obeyed. Rising, she squared her shoulders. This time, she was going to fight.

Angelo arrived to find Atlanta's bags stacked in the entryway of her villa.

"What's going on?"

"Angelo. Thank God. I've been trying to reach you."

"My cell has been off. What's wrong?"

"I have to cut my vacation short."

"So I see." He motioned toward the bags and tried to give name to the flurry of foreign emotions hammering inside of him. The one beating most furiously was one he'd experienced before. He knew what it felt like to be left by someone he trusted.

By someone he loved.

"I've scheduled a press conference in Los Angeles for tomorrow afternoon." Her chin jutted up. "I'm not going to run away any more and let the lies go unchecked."

It made sense. He was proud of her for doing so, in fact. Though he still couldn't help feeling abandoned. So he asked, "Why now? What's being said now that you need to rush off?"

"Zeke somehow managed to contact my mother. Or maybe she sought him out." She rubbed her eyes. "I don't know. It really doesn't matter anyway. The bottom line is she's gone on the record claiming I seduced my stepfather."

"I can't believe she would accuse you of having sex with the guy."

Her throat worked convulsively. "But I did, Angelo."

"Atlanta."

He reached for her, but she shrank back. "Duke came to my bed every other night like clockwork from the day I turned eleven until I'd saved enough cash to leave for good."

It was exactly what Angelo had feared.

"Even before then, he'd started touching me inappropriately." Atlanta closed her eyes. "How could my mother not know what he was doing? She knew, damn her. Yet now she's pretending it was all my idea."

"I don't know what to say." Sorry seemed so trite in light of her revelation.

"You...you...don't need to say anything." She offered her fake Hollywood smile. He'd botched it, he knew. She needed reassurance. She needed his support. Before he could remedy his mistake, though, a car pulled up out front and a horn honked.

"Franca's husband is taking me to the airport. The sooner I confront this mess, the better. No more running. No more pretending. No more sweeping all of that ugliness under the rug. I don't give a damn about my career. If I never act again, it won't matter as long as I can look in the mirror and know I did all that I could to stand up for myself and set the record straight."

Despite her strong words, a tear leaked down her cheek.

"Atlanta." Just as she had for him the other day, he wiped it away. Before he could say anything else, she stepped away.

"I'm sorry about your family party. I wish I could be there for you tomorrow evening."

"Same goes."

"I'm going to echo what your brother said. Keep an open mind. Family, the real kind, is a rare gift. You'd be a fool to let it slip away. Your baseball career will leave you. Careers do. They're fickle, Angelo. Especially careers such as ours. Family—not my kind, but the real kind—it sticks around. So does love."

The driver honked a second time. "I've got to go."

"I'll help you carry these out." He pointed to the stack of bags.

"No. Your shoulder. Franca's husband will help me

get them." She opened the door and waved for the man to come inside. Here she was facing her problems head-on and Angelo was still trying to avoid reality.

Everything happened quickly after that. Atlanta's bags were stowed in the car's trunk. Afterward, she and Angelo stood together next to the idling vehicle.

"Have a safe trip."

"I will. Thanks."

"I'll call you."

"Please. I…I'd love to hear from you."

He brushed his lips against hers.

He stood in the driveway long after the car was gone. He didn't feel lonely, he felt empty. Atlanta wasn't merely a part of his life, he realized. She *was* his life.

"I can't make the party."

Isabella said something in Italian that sounded suspiciously like swearing, given her tone. "What do you mean?" she asked once she'd switched back to English.

"Something's come up. I'm booked on the evening flight to Los Angeles."

She cocked her head to one side and her expression turned less menacing. "Something? If you are going to Los Angeles, my guess is it's more like someone."

"Atlanta," he admitted. "She needs me."

His sister's eyes widened at that. "Is she all right?"

"No. Not yet. But she will be." His lips curved. "We're both going to be."

"I'll drive you to the airport."

Stunned, he asked, "Just like that? I'm ditching the family reunion party you planned for a woman you don't even know."

"You know her." Isabella smiled then. "And you love her."

"I...I don't..." Angelo started to deny it, but realized he would be lying. He loved Atlanta Jackson. What was more telling, though, was that he loved the woman who had once been Jane Marie Lutz. "I do."

Isabella's grin widened. "That makes her family."

Family. For so long, Angelo had found the word his foe. He embraced it now. He reveled in it.

"If I have anything to say about it, she will be," he promised.

Atlanta paced in the makeshift green room. The press was lining up in the hotel's largest conference room. Even so, some had been denied access in order to comply with the fire code. Her statement was going to be winging around the world via cyberspace and other electronic media before midnight. Everyone would know she'd been sexually abused by her stepfather and then had allowed herself to be manipulated by Zeke. The only person whose reaction she worried about was Angelo.

"We're ready for you, Miss Jackson."

She smiled at the young intern who'd come back to make the announcement.

As she had in New York, she murmured, "Show time," as she walked out the door.

Her purposeful stride and confident smile faltered when she spied Angelo standing at the bank of microphones.

"What are you doing here?" she snapped around her high-wattage smile.

"I'm being there. You know, like you've been there for me."

"Angelo, you don't need—"

He pressed a finger to her lips. "That's where you're wrong, sweetheart. I do. In fact, I can't imagine being anywhere else right now. You're too important to me."

The assembled media representatives had had enough of their whispered comments.

"Hey, Angelo. What's going on between you two?" one hollered boldly.

"This is Miss Jackson's press conference. I'm just here to lend support. Direct your questions to her, please."

They weren't put off, but they did ask the expected questions about her relationship with her stepfather. He stood beside her, proud of her courage as she offered up the ugly and unvarnished truth.

She glanced sideways at him as she finished.

"How do you feel about that, Mr. Casali?"

"I'm proud of her. She was a victim when she was a helpless kid. She's not a kid any more, nor is she a victim. As you can see, she's anything but helpless."

"Rumor has it the two of you are pretty tight these days," another reporter shouted. "What's the real story?"

"The real story? She didn't seduce me like some of the tabloid headlines claim." Some of the reporters chuckled. "But I have fallen in love with her."

Her mouth fell open and she gaped at him. "Angelo?"

"I didn't think I could fall in love. You proved me wrong, Atlanta. I love you." When she continued to stare at him, he added, "I hope to God you love me back or I'm making an incredible fool of myself."

At that she launched herself into his arms. "I love you, too."

One question made it over the din of voices. "What about your careers?"

With Atlanta in his arms, Angelo boldly asked, "What about them?"

"Some people are saying you're both washed up," the reporter went on.

"Not washed up. I'm retiring." The word was oddly much easier to say than he'd thought. "I've had an incredible career and I am very grateful to the Rogues organization, but I think it's time to move on."

"Unconfirmed reports say your shoulder—"

"I need surgery," he cut in. Atlanta had taught him how to face his worst fears. "I have a torn rotator cuff and some arthritis. I'll never be able to play at the level I used to. It's time to give some of the younger guys on the roster a chance to shine."

"What about Miss Jackson?" the same reporter asked. "Where does she fit in to your plans?"

She was watching him intently. Suddenly, he saw his future clearly.

"She doesn't fit in," Angelo said. "She's at the center of them. The heart. If she'll have me, I want to marry her. I want to make a family with her."

Family. There was that word again. This time, he understood it, embraced it.

"Miss Jackson?" The reporter was grinning now. "Can we get a comment from you regarding Mr. Casali's proposal?"

"There's only one thing to say to a proposal like that." But the reporters never heard her say the word yes. It was muffled against Angelo's lips during their kiss.

EPILOGUE

THE party with Angelo's family was rescheduled. Isabella had seen to all of the details. He expected it to be awkward. He expected to want to leave early. Neither was the case. With Atlanta by his side, he met just about every Casali and Firenzi and faced down the past that had been his nemesis for so long.

"I am glad you are here," Luca said toward the end of the evening. After his initial welcome, he'd kept to the sidelines. Now, with the party winding down, he returned to the fore.

"I'm glad I am, too."

"I know you haven't forgiven me, but—"

Angelo stopped him. "I've moved on. The past is...well, past. I'm concentrating on the future these days."

"Thank you."

"Thank Atlanta. She taught me that." But his expression softened. "You did what you thought was right at the time."

"Let's have a toast," Isabella called.

She began with Cristiano, who was being released from the hospital as well as being awarded a medal for his bravery in the line of duty.

All those assembled raised their glasses.

She smiled at Angelo when she said, "To family."

He smiled back before sipping his drink. With Atlanta at his side and the ghosts of the past laid to rest, he finally understood what the word meant.

"You are glad you came," she said a little later when she met up with him and Atlanta.

"Yes."

"And you will come back to celebrate with us again when the restaurants merge and reopen?"

His arm around Atlanta, he knew a moment of absolute peace when he said, "We'll be here."

* * * * *

FIREFIGHTER'S DOORSTEP BABY

BY
BARBARA McMAHON

Barbara McMahon was born and raised in the south USA, but settled in California after spending a year flying around the world for an international airline. After settling down to raise a family and work for a computer firm, she began writing when her children started school. Now, feeling fortunate in being able to realize a long-held dream of quitting her "day job" and writing full-time, she and her husband have moved to the Sierra Nevada mountains of California, where she finds her desire to write is stronger than ever. With the beauty of the mountains visible from her windows, and the pace of life slower than the hectic San Francisco Bay Area where they previously resided, she finds more time than ever to think up stories and characters and share them with others through writing. Barbara loves to hear from readers. You can reach her at PO Box 977, Pioneer, CA 95666-0977, USA. Readers can also contact Barbara at her website: www.barbaramcmahon.com.

**To First Responders everywhere
—thanks for all you do to serve and protect every day.
FDNY, we will never forget.**

CHAPTER ONE

MARIELLA HOLMES stood on the small stone patio and gazed at the lake. Some daredevil was racing the wind on a Jet Ski. A spume of water arced behind it. The soft rumble of its engine faded as it sped across the surface of the water. She glanced into the cottage. Dante was still sleeping. She looked back at the reckless idiot on the Jet Ski; if the noise had woken the baby she'd have been more than annoyed. It had taken her longer than usual to get him to sleep.

What was the maniac doing anyway? If he fell in the water he'd be frozen in no time. Late October was so not lake weather. Yet even as she watched, she felt a spark of envy. He looked carefree skimming along at warp speed. If he was on vacation, he was certainly making the most of his time.

She gazed around the tree-covered hills that rose behind the lake. This would be lovely in the summer. She could picture children swimming in the water, canoes or rowboats dotting the surface. Imagine even more daredevils testing their skills with the Jet Skis; chasing the excitement, exploring the limits of their skills. Her gaze drawn back to the man, she continued to watch as she hoped this one wouldn't crash. There was beauty in the arc of water spewing from behind him, in the soft wake that radiated from the path of the Jet Ski. Sunshine sparkled on the water, causing a misty rainbow when he turned.

She pulled her sweater closer and drank in the clean mountain air. Beautiful and peaceful. She had never visited this area before. She hadn't known what to expect. Forested hills, quiet lakes, small villages. It was enchanting. She wished she could explore everything, but they wouldn't be here that long. Whichever way things went, it would be a relatively short visit. She'd had a lull in work and so had acted on the spur of the moment when she'd decided to come see where Dante's father was from.

A loud smack of the Jet Ski on the water as it bounced over its own wake had her drawn again to the man. At this distance she could only see the dark hair and broad shoulders as he sat astride the machine. He seemed fearless as the engine roared louder and he went even faster. She could imagine herself flying along, the wind blowing all cares away.

Shivering, she stepped back inside the cottage. This would have been a perfect chance to call Ariana, tell her how much she was enjoying Lake Clarissa, and that she'd seen a man who fired her imagination. She still couldn't believe her best friend would never call her up again to talk a mile a minute about life. Would never get to hold her son or watch him learn to walk or start school. Mariella brushed the sudden tears from her cheeks. Ariana had been there for her when her own parents had died, but she was not here now. It was Mariella's turn to step up to the plate.

Time healed all hurts, Mariella knew that. She had gotten over the worst of her grief after her parents' untimely death when she'd been in New York during her first year at university. Her grief over Ariana's death would gradually ease too. She knew in her mind she'd remember her friend with love as the years went on. But sometimes she felt raw, burning pain. Ariana had only been twenty-two. Her life should have stretched out until they were both old ladies. Instead, it had ended far too soon.

Shaking her head to dislodge depressing thoughts, Mariella focused on the future. She had Dante. She had a job. She had a quest. One day at a time. It had worked so far. So what if she felt overwhelmed some days? Caring for an unexpected baby wasn't easy. At least they were both healthy, well fed and comfortable. And she was getting the hang of being a mother. She hoped Dante would never remember her inept first attempts.

Crossing the small living room, she checked on the infant sleeping in the baby carrier still locked in the stroller. Checking the time, she knew he'd awaken soon for a bottle. She had a few minutes to unpack the groceries she'd brought and prepare his next meal before the first stirring.

She'd booked the room for a week, thinking that would be enough time to wander around and get a feel for the place and see if anyone here recognized the picture she had of Ariana. If not, they'd move on to Monta Correnti. She had no firm clues, no certainty she was even in the right place. She only knew this was the place Ariana had spoken about. The only clue she had given about Dante's father.

Ariana had been so sick and afraid those last weeks. Mariella wished her friend had called upon her earlier, but she had waited until graduation and Mariella's return to Rome before sharing the prognosis for the disease that ravaged her body. And, despite all Mariella's pleading, she had not revealed Dante's father's name. Only the bare fact that he came from this area, and they'd spent a wonderful weekend at Lake Clarissa.

The only child of older parents, Mariella was now alone in the world—and the guardian of an infant to boot. She'd always wished for brothers and sisters, aunts, uncles and cousins galore. She wished that for Dante as well. Maybe she could find his father, tell him of his son and discover he came from a large loving family who would take the baby into their hearts.

She glanced over to him again, her heart twisting. She loved this child. But it was so hard to be suddenly a mom. If she found his father, would she be able to give the baby up? Would a big family be best for him? She was still uncertain. At least she didn't have to make any decisions today. First she had to see if she could even locate his father. She'd decide then what course of action to take.

Cristiano opened the throttle full blast as the Jet Ski skimmed across the waves. The air was chilled, causing his blood to pump harder to keep him warm. The thrill of speed, the challenge of control, the sun glittering on the water all made him feel more alive than he had in months. All other thoughts and worries and memories evaporated. If the Jet Ski could go even faster, he would have relished the exhilaration, however short-lived. He pushed the machine to the max.

The injured ankle had healed. He'd been unable to use the Jet Ski during the warm summer weeks, but now, in the waning days of fall, he had the lake to himself. Power roared beneath him as he bounced over the small waves. The shore blurred by as he pushed the throttle surging to that last bit of power. He felt invincible. He'd cheated death once this year. He would not be taken today.

Drawing near the shore, he slowly banked toward the right, not sharp enough to capsize, but enough to swerve away from the rocky land that was fast approaching. He could ease back on the throttle, but what challenge was in that?

The Jet Ski bumped over its own wake and he stood up

to cushion the smacks as it slammed down on the water. Now his ankle ached a bit, reminding him he was not yet totally fit. Another circle and he'd return to the dock. It was cold enough that his toes were going numb. But there were few enough sunny days at this time of year. He'd take all he could get to enjoy being on the lake.

A few moments later, he slowed the ski and made a figure eight, then angled near the shore to make a big sweep that would take him back to the dock. Lake Clarissa was empty, the beach deserted. He was the only person in sight. The summer tourists had long left and the few people who came in the winter had not yet shown up. He had the place to himself.

As he skied past the row of cottages the Bertatalis rented, he noticed the far one was occupied. Lake Clarissa didn't offer the nightlife that Monta Correnti did. Most people weren't foolish enough to venture into the cold lake at this time of year. They had more sense than he did. It was probably some older couple who wanted to watch birds or see the leaves change. It wasn't that far to Monta Correnti they couldn't still drive over for some nighttime entertainment.

He pulled the Jet Ski up to the dock and in only moments secured it in the small floating ramp in the berth he rented. He tied it down and headed back to land. His wet feet left footprints on the wooden dock as he walked to his motorcycle. Drying himself, he quickly donned the jeans and boots he'd left across the seat, and pulled on a heavy sweater. It felt good to get warm. Donning the helmet, he mounted the bike and kick-started it. The rumble was not unlike the Jet Ski. Did power equate noise? He laughed at that idea and pulled onto the street. The small amount of traffic still surprised him after his time in Rome. Vacations in Lake Clarissa had always been fleeting, too much work waiting at home when he'd been a child. Once grown, he'd preferred his exciting life travelling the world with his job, or the challenges of extreme sports, to spending much time in this little sleepy lakeside village.

Until the bombing had altered everything.

Shortly after one Cristiano got off his motorcycle on the side street by Pietro's Bistro. Lunch here would beat cooking for himself. His father would be horrified his own son didn't like cooking. It wasn't that he didn't like it precisely, it just didn't seem worth the effort for only one.

There was a wide patio for dining, empty this time of year. It wasn't that cool, yet the breezes blowing down from the higher elevation carried a chill. He entered the warm restaurant and paused a moment while his eyes got used to the dimmer light. Pietro's smelled like home. The restaurant he'd worked in most of his childhood, that his father still owned, was even of a similar rustic theme. Bella Rosa had more patrons and more bustle than Pietro's, but Pietro's was free of the ties to Cristiano's past he was trying to flee.

There were couples and groups eating at various tables— it was more crowded than he'd expected. Some people he recognized and nodded to when they looked up and waved. When Emeliano appeared from the kitchen, white apron tied neatly around his waist, heavy tray balanced on one hand, Cristiano watched. His arms almost ached at the remembered tiredness he'd felt after a long day at Rosa. He hadn't worked there in years, but some memories didn't fade. Even when he wished they would.

"Cristiano, sit anywhere. I'll be there soon," Emeliano called out as he deftly transferred the tray from his hand to the stand beside the table he was serving.

Cristiano walked toward his favorite table, near the big window overlooking the town square. It was occupied.

He walked past and sat at the next one, then looked at the woman who had taken the table he liked best.

She had blonde hair with copper highlights. She was cooing to a small baby and seemed oblivious to the rest of the restaurant. He didn't recognize her. Probably another tourist. Even keeping to himself, he still kept tapped into the local rumor mill— enough to know if someone local had a new baby visiting. Italian families loved new babies.

The woman looked up and caught his gaze. She smiled then looked away.

He stared at her feeling that smile like a punch to the gut. From that quick glimpse he noted her eyes were silver, her cheeks brushed with pink—from the sun or the warmth of the restaurant? Glancing around, he wondered idly where her husband was.

"Rigatoni?" Emeliano asked when he stopped by Cristiano's table, distracting Cristiano from his speculation about the woman.

"Sure." He ordered it almost every time he ate here.

"Not as good as what you get at Rosa," Emeliano said, jotting it on a pad.

"I'm not at Rosa," Cristiano said easily. He could have quickly covered the distance between Lake Clarissa and Monta Correnti for lunch, but he wasn't ready to see his family yet. Sometimes he wondered if he'd ever be ready to go back home.

"Saw you on the lake. You could get killed."

He and Emeliano had played together as kids, challenging each other to swim races, exploring the hills with his brother Valentino. Cristiano grinned up at him. "Could have but didn't." Didn't Emeliano know he felt invincible?

"You need to think of the future, Cristiano. You and Valentino, why not go into business with your father? If

Pietro didn't already have three boys, I'd see if he'd take me on as partner," Emeliano said.

"Go to Rome, find a place and work up," Cristiano suggested, conscious of the attention from the woman at the next table. He didn't care if she eavesdropped. He had no secrets.

Except one.

"And my mother, what of her? You have it great, Cristiano."

He smiled, all for show. If only Emeliano knew the truth—all the truth—he'd look away in disgust. "How is your mother?"

"Ailing. Arthritis is a terrible thing." Emeliano flexed his hands. "I hope I never get it."

"Me, too."

Cristiano met the woman's gaze again when Emeliano left and didn't look away. She flushed slightly and looked at the baby, smiling at his babbling and arm waving. Covering one small fist with her hand, she leaned over to kiss him. Just then she glanced up again.

"I saw you on the Jet Ski," she said.

He nodded.

"You fell in the water."

"But I didn't fall."

She shrugged, glancing at the infant. Then looked shyly at him again. "It looked like great fun."

"It is. How old is your baby?" He looked at the child, trying to gauge if it were smaller than the one from last May. He wasn't often around infants and couldn't guess his age.

She smiled again, her eyes going all silvery. Nice combination of coloring. He wondered again who she was and why she was at Lake Clarissa.

"He's almost five months."

A boy. His father had two boys and a girl. Wait, make that four boys and a girl. He still couldn't get used to the startling fact his sister shared a few months ago—about two older half-brothers who were Americans. Too surreal. Another reason to keep away from his family. He wasn't sure how he felt about his father keeping that secret all his life.

The infant had dark hair and dark eyes. His chubby cheeks held no clue as to what he'd look like as an adult, but his coloring didn't match hers at all.

"Does he look like his father?"

"I have no idea. But his mother had dark eyes and hair. Maybe when he's older, I'll see some resemblance to the man who fathered him. Right now to me he looks like his mom." She reached out and brushed the baby's head in a light caress.

"He's not yours?"

She shook her head.

"A nanny?" So maybe there was no man in the picture. Was she watching the baby for a family? She seemed devoted to the child.

She shook her head again. "I'm his guardian. His mother died." She blinked back tears and Cristiano again felt that discomforting shift in his mid section. He hoped she wasn't going to cry. He never knew how to handle a woman in tears. He wanted to slay dragons or race away. Unfortunately he all too often had to comfort women—and men sometimes—in tears at their loss. He always did his best. Always felt it fell short.

Emeliano arrived with a tray laden with rigatoni, big salad and hot garlic bread. He glanced at the woman, then Cristiano. "Want to sit together?"

"No," Cristiano said.

At the same time she replied, "That would be fine, if he doesn't mind."

"Oops," she said immediately. "I guess you do mind." She put on a bright smile. "I'll be going soon."

He felt like a jerk. He hadn't meant to embarrass her. "Come, sit with me. I could use the company while I eat." He tried to make up for the faux pas, but she just gave a polite smile and said, "No, thanks anyway, I have to be going. This guy likes to ride in the stroller to see the sights." She fumbled for her wallet and began pulling out the euros to pay her bill.

Emeliano served Cristiano, gave him a wry look and hurried away to look after another customer.

By the high color in her cheeks, he knew she was embarrassed. They'd been talking; it seemed churlish to refuse when his friend made the suggestion. Now he wished he had waited a second, thought before he spoke.

She rose and gathered her purse and a diaper bag and quickly carried the baby to the front of the restaurant without looking at him again. There he saw the stroller he'd missed when he first entered. In a heartbeat, they were gone.

His sister would have scolded him for his bad manners. His father would have looked at him with sadness. Of course his father seemed perpetually sad since their mother had died so long ago. He'd never found another woman to share his life with.

Cristiano began to eat. The food was good, not excellent, but good. What did it matter? Seeing the baby reminded him of his friend Stephano's young daughter. Too young to have lost her father. Cristiano still couldn't believe his best friend had perished in the instant the second bomb had exploded. Many days he could almost believe he was on leave and would go back to work to find Stephano and the others on his squad ready to fight whatever fires came their way.

But his friend was gone. Forever.

Cristiano ate slowly, regretting his hasty refusal of sitting with the woman with the baby. Learning more about her would have kept his mind off his friend and his other worries.

Mariella bundled Dante up and placed him in the stroller. She couldn't get out of the restaurant fast enough. She felt the wave of embarrassment wash over her as she remembered offering to have the man sit at her table. He had definitely been annoyed. He probably had women falling over themselves to gain his attention with those dark compelling eyes and the tanned skin. He looked as if he brought the outdoors inside with him. He towered over the waiter. When he'd sat at the table next to hers she'd been impressed with his trim physique, wide shoulders and masculine air. He had such vitality around him.

She'd also been too flustered to ask the waiter if he'd ever seen Ariana in the restaurant. She'd even brought the picture of her friend to show around.

A moment later the thought popped into her head that the man talking to the waiter could even have been Dante's father. He had the dark eyes and hair for it.

"So who's your daddy, sweetie? Did he live around here or only bring your mother for a visit?" she asked the baby as they moved along the worn sidewalk. Shops enticed, but it was difficult to maneuver the stroller through the narrow aisles of the small stores. She needed a better plan to try to find Dante's father than simply showing Ariana's photograph to every man she saw and asking if he'd known her. Why ever would anyone admit to it if there'd been a problem with their relationship?

Stopping near the church, she sat on one of the wooden benches facing the town square. It was peaceful here.

Dressed warmly, she was comfortable on this sunny afternoon despite the cooler temperatures. Checking on Dante, she was pleased he was warm and animated, looking around at the different buildings, up at the leaves on the tree partially shading the bench.

"Tree," she said. She knew Dante probably couldn't care less what that was called as long as she fed him on time and kept him dry and warm.

She still felt stressed dealing with the baby and hoped this trip would not only help her find out more about his father, but bring them closer together, too. She'd read every book she could get her hands on about newborns, had enlisted the help of a couple of friends who had children. But nothing had prepared her for the task of being an instant mom twenty-four-seven. At least most mothers had months to get used to the idea. Plans and dreams—usually with a partner—centered on the new life arriving. Psyching themselves up for the challenges.

Instead, Dante had been Mariella's instant baby. She had known about him for less than a month before she became his mother. No warning, no preparation, and definitely no partner to share the task.

Dante was dozing when Mariella thought about returning to the cottage she'd rented. He'd sleep better in the crib she'd had set up for him. And she could finish unpacking and settle in. They'd be here a week so she needed to get organized, then she could decide how to go on.

"I didn't mean to run you off." She looked to her left and saw the man from the restaurant. He paused beside her. The sun glinted on his dark hair. His dark eyes looked straight into hers and caused her heart to bump up in rhythm. For a moment she couldn't breathe. She felt a flare of attraction sweep through her. It made her almost giddy. Certainly not the way a mother should react. She hadn't expected to see him again—especially so soon after the restaurant.

"I was ready to leave," she said. She looked away. He was gorgeous—tall, tanned and fit. Was he on holiday? Why else would he be Jet Skiing and then taking a long lunch in the middle of the week? Or did he live around here and have the kind of job that allowed mid-week excursions to the lake? She wanted to know more about him.

He sat beside her on the bench, staring at the fountain at the center of the square. She flicked him a glance, but he seemed oblivious, still focused on the fountain. She noted no rings on his hands. She looked where he looked. The honey-colored stone blended well with the mountain setting. The cobbled street gave testimony to the age of the village. Surely he'd seen it all before. As if reading her thoughts, he turned and looked at her, offering his hand.

"My name is Cristiano Casali. Emeliano's suggestion caught me by surprise. You have a baby and I thought it best—never mind. I apologize for my rudeness."

She shook his hand and then pulled hers free. Tingling from the brief contact, she cleared her throat and tried to concentrate on what he said and not on the amazing feelings suddenly pulsing through her. He was just a man being courteous.

"Not to worry. I'm Mariella Holmes." She didn't dare look at him. Let her get her roiling emotions under some control first.

"So the mystery of the baby intrigues me. And if you knew about how things have been with me lately, that's surprising. How is he yours? You look too young to be a guardian of anyone." He glanced at the baby, then back at her.

"I'm twenty-two and old enough. I have friends who didn't go to university who married young and already have two children." She would never confide to a stranger how unprepared she felt being a new mother. If she'd just had more time to prepare, maybe she'd feel better suited to the role.

"Okay, you're old enough, but how?"

"His mother died. Before she did, I agreed to be his guardian. Ariana had no other family." She was proud she could say her friend's name without bursting into tears. Studying him as she spoke, she saw no start of recognition when she said her friend's name.

"The father didn't object?" he asked.

"I don't have a clue who the father is." She'd asked as many of Ariana's friends as she knew if they had known the man. No one had. It was a secret her friend had taken with her.

Cristiano frowned at her statement. Mariella elaborated in a rush, feeling the need to explain.

"Dante's mother was my best friend, Ariana. She met some guy and fell in love. Apparently when she told him she was pregnant, the man abandoned her. I didn't know any of this. I was in New York when I got her phone call shortly before Dante was born. She was sick and asked me to come back to Italy. I did, instantly. When she asked me to take Dante, how could I refuse? We were as close as sisters, yet she never told me his father's name though I asked many times." She looked at the child, feeling the weight of her commitment heavy on her shoulders.

"What happened to your friend?" Cristiano asked gently.

Mariella took a moment to gather her composure. It was still hard to talk about the death of her very dearest and longest friend. "She died of leukemia. She found out she had it while pregnant and refused any treatment until after the baby was born. He arrived healthy and strong, though a couple of weeks early. She died when he was two weeks old."

Mariella tried to blot out the picture of her friend those last weeks. Her thin cheeks, lackluster hair, sad, sad eyes. Ariana had known she wouldn't live to see her baby grow up. She'd implored Mariella over and over to promise to raise Dante for her. The day the guardianship paper had been signed, Ariana had smiled for the last time and soon thereafter slipped into a coma, which led to her death.

"You still seem awfully young to be tied down with a baby. Shouldn't you be out enjoying life at this stage?"

"Thanks for your concern, but I'm fine with being Dante's guardian." She didn't need some stranger questioning her ability to watch the baby. It was a huge responsibility, Mariella knew that already. And she often questioned her ability herself when lying awake at night, trying to anticipate all she needed to do to raise Dante. Mariella considered it an honor to be chosen to raise her friend's baby.

No one needed to know how overwhelmed she felt. And how while she loved Dante, it was not the deep maternal love she knew other mothers felt immediately for their child. Mariella loved this baby, but couldn't help feeling a bit cheated of her best friend. If Ariana had not been pregnant when she'd found out about the leukemia, she might be alive today. Mariella felt alone in a way she'd never experienced before; isolated even more by the demands of an infant.

Not that she'd tell anyone in a million years. What if it ever came back to Dante? She did love him. She did! But she had loved her friend for far longer.

"I need to go," she said, jumping up. She had to escape her thoughts. She could do this. She would do this. Or find his father and make sure Dante had a loving family to welcome him.

"Seems like I run you off at every turn," Cristiano said.

She started pushing the stroller. Cristiano rose and fell into step beside her. "Why are you here at this time of year? Most tourists come in the summer months, when they can use the lake," he said. Glancing at the baby, he added, "And they come when their kids are older and can play by the water. We'll be getting rain before long. It's already colder now than a couple of weeks ago. Not very conducive to sitting by the lake."

"I thought maybe I could find out about Dante's father. But now that I'm here, I'm not so sure." It had been a foolish thought. Clutching at straws, that was what. The man could have brought her friend here for a get-away weekend. She only knew Ariana had been happy at Lake Clarissa.

"What do you know about him?" Cristiano asked.

"Nothing. Ariana wouldn't talk about him at all."

They approached the small resort on the lake. Traffic was light on the street. The quiet of the afternoon was interrupted only by birdsong.

"You have the last cottage, right?"

"How did you know that?" Mariella asked, looking at him. He had obviously shortened his stride to stay even with her. She wondered if he'd come to the cottage and stay a while. She'd love to put the baby down and have some adult conversation—especially with a man so unlike others she knew.

"I saw it was occupied when I was skiing."

"Do you live here year round?" she asked.

"No." With that one word, he changed. She glanced at him, but his expression gave nothing away. He looked ahead as they walked, not elaborating on the single-word response. But she could feel the difference, the way he closed himself off. A bleakness in his eyes that hadn't been there before. What had she said?

"Visiting?" she probed. He'd asked enough questions, she could ask a few. Her curiosity grew. If Ariana had been around, she'd have called her up to tell her about the daredevil and how he was a poster child for sexy, virile Italian male. And speculate why he was at Lake Clarissa and discuss ways she might get to know him better.

"Staying a while," was all he said.

Her curiosity arose another notch. But she didn't know him well enough to pester with a lot of questions. Though a dozen burned on her tongue.

The path to the cottage was packed dirt lined with rocks. Bumpy and uneven. It was a bit of a struggle for Mariella to push the stroller, but Dante loved being bounced around. He gurgled and looked enchanted with the bouncy ride.

"Here, let me," Cristiano said at one point, reaching out to take the stroller. His hand brushed hers as he reached for the handle and she folded her arms across her chest, savoring the tingling. Walking beside him made her feel sheltered and feminine. This was how a family should be, father, mother and baby. She blinked. No going off in daydreams, she admonished.

"Thanks," she said when they reached the fifth cabin. The trees shaded in the afternoon. The small stone terrace had two chairs and a small table to use when sitting to watch the lake.

The wind had picked up a bit and it was definitely cooler than before.

"I can manage from here," she said with a smile. "I hope I see you in town again," she said, feeling daring. It would be too awful to have this be their sole encounter.

He stepped away from the stroller and looked at her.

Mariella had the feeling he wanted to say something. His eyes seemed full of turmoil. But he merely nodded and said, "Maybe you will. I come to town often. Goodbye."

She watched as he walked back along the path, his long legs covering the distance in a short time. One minute he was there, the next gone. And he took some of the brightness of the day with him.

She should have shown him the picture. Maybe he had seen Ariana. Where did he live? Why had her question caused the change? One minute he seemed open and friendly, the next closed and reserved. Not that it was any of her business. But she couldn't help the curiosity. Was he married? Separated or divorced?

She hoped she saw him again before she left.

Cristiano walked back to the square wondering if he was losing his mind. It had been months since anything had caught his attention as strongly as Mariella Holmes had. She was pretty—granted. But he'd seen other pretty women.

But not like her, something inside whispered. Her hair had that healthy glossy sheen that caught the light and reflected golden highlights. It looked thick and silky. He wished he could have touched it to verify the satiny feel. Her eyes were clear and honest. Her emotions shone through as they changed from steel grey to silvery.

He tried to ignore the image of her that kept flashing in his mind. Her gentle touch with the baby, her bright smile. The way she had of brushing back her hair when the breeze blew it in her face. Was he ready to risk a normal life now? Had things finally turned for the better? He had too much baggage to think of getting involved.

Yet she also came with baggage—a baby.

He'd never envisioned himself as a father. Or even a husband. He liked speed, challenges, adrenaline-producing activities that confirmed over and over he was alive and living life to the fullest. His job as a firefighter was exhilarating, but dangerous. Other men on his crew were married, but he'd never felt it fair to constantly risk his life if someone was depending on him.

He stopped along the sidewalk and gazed over the water. He knew he might never join his crew in battling a blaze again, or, then again, he might be fit to return to duty next week. No one knew what the future held. Maybe his held a silvery-eyed beauty. But he knew he had better be damned sure before going down that path.

Mariella Holmes had domesticity written all over her. She was not for a holiday romance. It'd be best for both their sakes to stay away from her.

Reaching the motorcycle, he sat on it a moment, watching neighbors and townspeople going about their business, shopping, greeting each other. Some waved to him and he acknowledged the greetings. Did they have secrets that would change lives? Did they have families who had kept secrets that were now coming out? Did they have sorrows and loss like those that had dimmed Mariella's smile?

Too philosophical for him. He put on the black helmet and started the bike. It was a short drive from the village of Lake Clarissa to the family cottage. He had liked being able to walk to the lake as a child. The happy times their family had once had seemed far away these days. Passing the driveway, he continued on, revving up his speed as if he could outrun the memories on the deserted mountain roads.

It was after dark when he pulled to a stop at the back of the family cottage. His excessive speed would give his father a heart attack. The harrowing hairpin turns provided a challenge he loved meeting. The fabulous scenery that raced by was a strong contrast to the smoke and dust and hell of his last weeks in Rome. He much preferred the vistas the hills offered to the memory of death and destruction and loss.

He entered the kitchen and ignored the dishes on the counter and in the sink. Going straight to the cabinet near the stove, he opened it and took down the bottle of brandy. It was far lighter than it had been last night. Not enough, now, to get rip-roaring drunk. He set it on the counter, reached for a glass, then stared at the bottle for a long moment. With a violent smash of his hand he knocked it on the stone floor where it broke into a thousand pieces, the smell of brandy filling the air.

He didn't need the stupor drink caused. Striding to his room, he stripped and went to take a shower, thinking of the bright smile on Mariella Holmes' face, and the love she showered on the baby. That was what he wanted. To feel connected. To feel passion and caring and hope for the future. To love. Dared he risk seeing her again?

CHAPTER TWO

MARIELLA rose at five to feed Dante. When he fell back asleep, she powered up her laptop and checked in on her clients, glad the rental cottage had Internet access. Working as a virtual assistant ensured she could work from home and at the hours that suited Dante's schedule. It was, however, a far cry from the work she'd thought she'd be doing after graduating from university.

She had often talked with friends in New York about setting up their own marketing firm. About setting New York on fire with their brilliant ideas and strong drive and determination. They'd fantasized about clients who would skyrocket them to the top of their field due to their impressive marketing.

Instead, she was quietly typing out another letter for a client miles away from the future she'd once envisioned. Yet she was grateful she'd found something that paid enough for their small flat and all their other needs. A baby was expensive. She could have been in worse shape.

By the time Dante woke from his nap in the late morning, Mariella had caught up on everything and had shut down her computer. Two of her major clients were away this week, which had freed enough time to allow her to start her search for Dante's father. It was a haphazard way to search for someone, but it was all she had to start with. Hiring someone would prove too expensive.

Bathing the baby when he awoke, then taking a quick shower after he'd been fed, she quickly prepared a light lunch. He was still awake and the day was lovely, so she took him in the stroller to the patio. Sitting on the wooden bench, she wished the cottage had come with a rocking chair. She had purchased one as soon as she'd known she would have Dante. It was soothing to rock the baby as he drank his bottle. Still, they'd only be here a week.

No daring Jet Ski riding today, she noticed. Or had Cristiano gone out earlier that morning and she'd missed him? She might have been busy with her work, but surely she would have heard the Jet Ski? She tried to ignore the pang of disappointment. She gazed at the deep blue of the water and the lighter blue of the sky. Contrasting with the dark green of the evergreen trees, it was an idyllic setting. She felt her heart lighten a bit. On impulse, she reached for the baby and held him sitting up in her arms as she absorbed the tranquility.

"Isn't this a pretty place?" she said, kissing the plump cheek. Dante gazed at her with wide brown eyes. Her heart expanded with love for her friend's child. He was such a precious little boy.

"Oh, Dante, what are we going to do?" she whispered. "I love you to bits, but I wish every time I see you that your mamma could see you. She loved you so much. One day I'll tell you just how much."

Then a noise caught her attention and she looked at the lake, almost grinning in surprised recognition. "It's him," she told the baby. "The man we met yesterday. Only you slept through most of it."

Cristiano sped across the water at a daring rate. She

watched, mesmerized. Did the man have no fear? She knew she'd be terrified to go at such speeds across the water.

He made it seem effortless. He and the machine seemed to be one as he banked and flew even faster toward the far shore. Soon she couldn't see him, only the arcing plume from the power ski. A moment later she saw the turn and then he was racing toward them. She stood, carried the baby to the edge of the patio and turned so Dante could also see the water. She had no idea if he was watching the Jet Ski, but she could scarcely take her eyes off the man riding. She remembered every inch of him—tall, tanned skin, dark hair shaggy and long. Remembering his dark eyes that had gazed into hers so intently had her heart racing.

She'd hoped to see him again. Wanted to learn more about him. Hear him tell about the village and the people who lived here. And tell her what he did in life, where he lived, what made him laugh. Was there a special woman in his life? She didn't think so, but would like to know for sure.

Was there any place in his life for her?

Foolish thoughts. She was only here for a short time.

As he approached the small dock in front of her cottage, he slowed, coming to a coasting stop as he cut the engine and glided to the wooden planks. Bumping slightly, he sat back and looked up at her.

She almost laughed in delight and, holding Dante firmly, she carefully followed the path to the dock, walking out the few steps to where he bobbed in the water.

"Hi," she said. "That looks amazing. How fast do you go?" She couldn't help her grin as she took in the broad shoulders, the muscular legs straddling the machine. For a moment she wished she'd checked her hair before coming out. But with the breeze, it would be windblown no matter what. Cristiano looked fantastic, tousled hair, ruddy cheeks, and those compelling brown eyes that about melted her heart.

"Not too fast. Want to go for a spin?" he asked with a cheeky grin, taking in the baby.

She laughed and shook her head, jiggling Dante a little. "Not with a baby, thank you very much. I'd never let him go on one of those."

"Maybe when he's older," Cristiano said, sitting casually on the floating machine, one foot on the dock anchoring him in place.

She eyed the machine with some wariness. "Too dangerous. Aren't you cold?" The breeze reminded her it was fall, no hot summer days to be refreshed by the water. With his dark eyes focused on her, she felt her temperature rise. The attraction that flared between them confused her. She'd never felt emotions like this with other men she'd known. Was Cristiano different in some way? Or was it just normal reaction after months of only dealing with Dante?

"My feet are freezing. I'm ready to head back. You going into the village today?"

Mariella hadn't been sure before, but this clinched it. "Yes. We'll be walking over in a little while. Are you planning to be there?" She gave him her best smile. Was she flirting with the man? Yes—and it felt great.

"I'll buy you an ice-cream cone." His eyes locked with hers, as if urging her to say yes.

She felt daring and excited at the same time. She nodded. "I'd like that." Trying to subdue the excitement from her voice, she said, "Don't fall in on your way back."

"No chance." He pushed off and in a moment the motor caught and he headed the short distance to the town's small marina.

She watched until she couldn't see him clearly.

"So, we've been invited to see him again," she said to Dante, hurrying back to the cottage to get the stroller. She could hardly wait.

Cristiano ran the Jet Ski up on the floating berth and turned off the motor. He'd left his clothes on the motorcycle again only this time didn't just pull them over his wet ones, but used the men's facilities at the public boathouse to change. He refused to examine closely why he'd stopped by the cottage to see her. He'd spotted her on the patio and impulse had driven him closer.

The only way to know if she was around, without being totally blatant about it, was to use the lake. When he'd seen her on the porch, the lure of the Jet Ski had vanished. He'd wanted to see her again.

Dressed, he bundled the wet clothes, strapping them on the back of the motorcycle. It would be a two-minute ride to the square. He had no idea if she'd already arrived. Maybe he should have gone home to get the car.

She was talking with the priest in front of the church when Cristiano entered the square. Stopping some distance away, he cut the engine and sat on the motorcycle as he watched, curious what she could be talking to Father Andreas about. The old man shook his head and then smiled down at the baby in the stroller.

In an instant the sunshine dimmed. Cristiano remembered the feel of the baby in the cradle of his arm, the small, terrified child clutched with the other. The baby cried and cried. The nightmare of smoke and darkness and wailing screams filled his senses. For a moment he was there, back in the tunnels of the metro, fighting for breath, for a foothold, for life itself with two children who were too young to die.

He could feel the heat of the fire behind him. Hear the shouts of other first responders, everyone trying to fight their way through hell. Screams of the dying, distorted shadows as the flames flared and waned. He could smell the smoke and dust as clearly as he had when his helmet shattered.

He couldn't breathe. He couldn't see. Which way was out? Which way lay sunshine and fresh air and life itself?

A shout sounded louder than the rest. Something bounced on his thigh and Cristiano blinked, looking down at the rubber ball that rolled away from where it had struck him. Two boys raced after it, their laughter and shouts echoing in the square.

He looked around. Mariella was pushing the stroller toward him. The priest was standing on the stairs leading into the old church smiling at the children who played around the fountain. The sun shone in a cloudless sky. A pastoral scene, one of peace and tranquility and the very fabric of life.

Taking a breath, he hoped he could keep his mind in the present. He'd thought he had these flashbacks under control. It had been days since—

"Hello,' she said as she approached, that wide smile holding his gaze.

No one seemed to notice anything out of the ordinary. Only Cristiano knew he'd had another flashback—thankfully brief this time. He never knew when they'd come, how debilitating they'd be. This one had passed quickly. Because of Mariella?

He didn't want her to know. They'd spend some time together today, enjoy each other's company and then he'd take off for the cottage, the bolt-hole he'd claimed when he had been released from the hospital. No one in his family had known he'd been injured far beyond the ankle that had broken.

"Are you all right?" Mariella asked when she reached the motorcycle, a questioning look in her eyes.

"Sure." He needed to change that subject quickly. "How do you know Father Andreas?"

"We just met. He was walking by and I showed him my friend's picture to see if he recognized her. He didn't."

She drew it from her pocket and held it out to Cristiano. He took it. The laughing expression on the unknown woman's face tugged at his heart. This was the young mother who had died. She didn't look as old as Mariella. Did Mariella feel the same tearing grief he felt whenever he thought about his friend Stephano? Did she regret time wasted when, if she had only known the future, she would have changed what she did in the weeks, days left before her friend's death?

Had he known Stephano would die in the bomb explosion last May, would he have done more in the days leading to that fateful time? Or would he have taken everything for granted as he had expecting them both to live forever?

It was a lesson well learned. No one could predict the future. Enjoy life while he could. As long as he could.

Handing it back, he said, "I don't recognize her. When was she here?"

"I don't know. Sometime within the last eighteen months is all I have. I thought at restaurants or shops someone would recognize her." She slipped the photograph back into her pocket and shrugged. "So far no one has."

"What are you going to do if you find him?"

"I'm still not sure. A baby should have his family around him. I'm hoping the father comes from a large family who would love Dante. I may never find him. But I want to tell Dante when he's older that I tried."

"Let your family be his."

She shrugged. "I have no family. Ariana was the closest thing to a sister I had. Both our parents are dead. Neither of us had any other living relatives. Maybe it's foolish to search for his father, but if it were me, I'd want to know. Easier maybe to find out about him now than when Dante is twenty-one."

Cristiano didn't know how he'd feel about finding out he had a child at some future date, after the child was grown. Had the man truly not wanted any connection, or had his initial reaction been panic that he now regretted?

In a way, his family's recent events paralleled Mariella's situation. He still didn't know how to deal with the newly acquired knowledge that his father had other sons, older than he was. They'd grown up a world apart. Would there be some connection should they ever meet? Would blood call to blood? Or would they forever be strangers?

Cristiano could never knowingly give up a child if he had one. How had his father done it?

He kicked down the stand and got off the motorcycle. "Have you questioned everyone in town?"

"So far only the priest and the proprietor at the resort."

"Come, I'll buy you an ice-cream cone and you can ask there. Seems to me your best bet would be restaurants and shops where visitors are likely to go."

"Maybe, but they could have simply come for a weekend at the height of the season when she'd have been just one of many," she said, pushing the stroller ahead as they walked around the square. The sun shone in a cloudless sky. The air was cool, but comfortable. And she was walking beside a handsome, attentive man. She didn't want to talk about Ariana and her lost love. She wanted to learn more about Cristiano.

The ice-cream shop was virtually empty.

"Not the time of year for ice cream. Want something else?" he asked.

"No. This will be good. I can give Dante a tiny taste. He's not eating real food yet."

They ordered, then went back into the square to sit on a bench in the sunshine.

"Did you once live here? The proprietress knew you," she asked.

"My grandparents were from Lake Clarissa. They had a small cottage nearby. We lived with them when we were children and papa was busy working. Summer days we would swim in the lake. Sometimes we'd camp out overnight in the forest."

He watched as Mariella licked her ice cream. The lonely existence he'd chosen these past few months melted away. He hadn't felt normal for a long time. What was it about this woman that changed that? He could forget the horror that haunted him when he was around her. Maybe he should take her home with him and keep her with him until the spell was broken.

Yet moments before he'd had another flashback. He looked away. He had no business coming to town. What if he had a major meltdown? He had to beat this thing before he could get his life back.

"Sounds like you had a lot of fun here," she said.

"Yes, we did, it was a happy time. My grandfather lived until I was almost an adult. He continued to live here even when we had all moved away from home, he was a part of the place. He gave our childhood an extra sense of fun and excitement, beyond playing in the forest or at the lake." Hard to think about the past when he listened to her voice, soft and lilting.

"Is that where you got your daredevil ways?" she asked with a teasing grin.

"Daredevil ways?" That grin felt like a kick to the mid section. For a moment he forgot where they were and wondered what she'd do if he leaned over and kissed her. Her eyes sparkled, there were freckles scattered across her nose, kisses from the sun. He looked away before he did something foolish, such as trail kisses over every one. They'd just met. It was too early to think about kisses.

Yet as the seconds ticked by, the thought would not fade. He'd like to take her hand and feel the soft warmth against his palm. Sit closer so he could feel every radiant bit of heat from her body. Lean in so she could only see him. Find out what fascinated him about her.

"Racing across the lake like you were trying to fly. I consider that amazingly like a daredevil," she explained, leaning closer.

Did she feel that same pull of attraction? He took a breath, taking in the scent of her, light and flowery. He held his breath for a moment to savor it. Then released it and shook his head. "I'm no daredevil. You should meet my brother Valentino. Now, he's the daredevil in the family. Today was just Jet Skiing."

She pointed to the motorcycle across the square. "That's a dangerous mode of transportation."

"Not if you know what you're doing. It's like flying along the road."

"So tell me about living here, especially during summer," she invited as they ate their cones.

Cristiano didn't want to talk about himself; he wanted to know more about Mariella. But if he offered something, he could have her reciprocate. He began recounting summer days playing at the edge of the lake, climbing around on the rocky shore and learning to swim. Then the nights he and Valentino had spent roaming the woods, feeling daring and grown up braving the darkness.

She laughed at his stories and from time to time admonished Dante to stop listening, she didn't want him to get ideas. The longer Cristiano talked, the lighter the world seemed to grow. He liked hearing her laugh. The more she did, the more outrageous he made the stories.

"Now, tell me about your summer holidays," he said when he'd wound down. They'd long since finished their ice cream. The baby had fallen asleep and Mariella seemed content to sit in the sunshine. It was as if she brought sunshine into his life where only darkness had once dwelt.

"We always went to places to learn more about history. My father was an accountant, but he loved history. So we visited Pompeii and Turin, Florence, of course, and Venice." She smiled in memory and Cristiano knew from her expression how much she'd enjoyed those vacations with her parents.

"Ariana went with us when we were teenagers. We flirted like crazy with the gondoliers in Venice. Of course they ignored us." She laughed, then her eyes unexpectedly filled with tears. "We should have had the chance to remember all those foolish activities when we were old with grandchildren running around. It's so unfair she died."

Cristiano wanted to comfort her, but only time would completely heal the pain.

"I had a friend who died last May. Life is unfair. I'm single with few responsibilities. He had a wife and two children. Why him? It should have been me."

She looked at him in shock. "Never say that. Who knows why some die young? But I have never thought it should have been me instead of Ariana. Life is too precious. We need to enjoy every moment. Maybe even more so because in a way we are now living also for our friends, experiencing life as they will no longer be able to."

The memories were threatening again. The fear he'd end up hiding beneath the bench they now sat on in the middle of the day, yelling for Stephano, was real. He had to get away before he cracked.

He stood. "I have to go.' The tightness in his chest grew. It was becoming more difficult to breathe. He held onto the present desperately.

"Thank you for the ice cream. And the conversation," she said.

He nodded and strode to the motorcycle. Staying any longer was flirting with danger. He knew his limits—and he'd passed them already. Time to get away.

He started the bike and looked over at Mariella. She was watching him, her head tilted slightly as if wondering what had gone wrong. If she only knew all that was wrong.

"Come tomorrow," he said.

She smiled and nodded.

Mariella watched Cristiano leave. He was the most perplexing man she'd ever met. She'd thought they'd been having a great conversation when he'd abruptly jumped up and left. She tried to remember what she could have said to cause such a reaction. They'd been exchanging memories and she had lamented the fact she and Ariana wouldn't grow old together.

So who was his friend who had died young? Such an odd thing for them to have in common, yet for a moment it brought her comfort. He was someone who could understand the sadness she felt for the loss of her friend.

The evening was quiet. Mariella played with Dante until the baby fell asleep. She liked this impromptu vacation. She was still working the odd hours to keep her clients happy. But she had more time to spend with the baby. And with several months' of experience behind her, she was growing more confident in her abilities than that first month as a stunned guardian with a tiny infant and no job.

She could not afford to stay in Lake Clarissa for long, however. She wanted to expand the search for Dante's father before she had to return to Rome. Stopping in a few shops, speaking with the priest didn't encompass all of the village. Tomorrow she'd make a concerted effort to visit more places. Then if she had no results, the next day she'd move on to Monta Correnti.

After the baby was asleep, she checked her laptop for any new assignments, then surfed the Net. She put in Cristiano's name on a whim and was startled when pages loaded. He was a firefighter. He'd been a first responder to the bombing in Rome last May. She read the compelling newspaper articles. The man was a hero. He'd gone down into the bombing scene time and again. He'd saved seven lives, become injured himself and still fought to bring a baby and small child through the smoke-filled metro tunnel to safety that last trip.

Wow. She read every article she could on the bombing. She'd been finishing up finals in New York when the terrorist attack had hit Rome. Once she'd been assured none of her friends had been injured, she'd relegated it and all other news to the back of her mind as she madly studied. Even if she'd seen Cristiano's name back then, she never would have remembered it.

She had suspected he had some physically demanding job. He was strong, muscular and fit. He moved with casual grace in that tall body. And being around him gave her a definite sense of security. She searched further hoping for a picture, but the only ones she saw were of firefighters and police in uniform, battling for people's lives.

It was late when she shut down the computer. Checking the doors and windows before retiring, she realized how much it had cooled down in the cottage. She switched on the wall heater and went to get ready for bed. Dante was fast asleep in one of the fleecy sleepers she used for him at night. She covered him with a light blanket and shivered; her fingers were freezing. Fall had truly arrived. At least the baby would be warm through the night, and once she was beneath the blankets she'd be toasty warm herself.

Cristiano sat upright with a bolt. He became instantly awake, breathing hard, the terror still clinging from the nightmare. He took deep gulps of breath, trying to still his racing heart. It was pitch dark—not unlike the tunnel after the bombing. Only the lights from their helmets had given any illumination in the dusty and smoky world.

He threw off the blanket and rose, walking to the window and opening it wide for the fresh air. The cold breeze swept over him, jarring him further. He breathed in the crisp air, relishing the icy clean feel. No smoke. No voices screaming in terror. Nothing here but the peaceful countryside in the middle of the night. The trees blotted out a lot of the stars. The moon rode low on the horizon, its light dancing on the shimmering surface of the lake, a sliver of which was visible from the window.

He gripped the sill and fought the remnants of the nightmare. It was hauntingly familiar. He'd had it often enough since that fateful day. Gradually the echoes of frantic screams faded. The horror receded. The soft normal sounds of night crept in.

Long moments later he turned to get dressed. There would be no more sleep tonight.

Once warmly clothed, he went to the motorcycle and climbed on board. A ride through the higher mountain roads would get him focused. He knew he was trying to outrun the demons. Nothing would ever erase that day from his mind. But he couldn't stay inside a moment longer. The wind rushed through his hair; the sting of cold air on his cheeks proved he was alive. And the lack of smoke was life-affirming. It was pure nectar after the hell he'd lived through.

Driving on the curving roads required skill and concentration. One careless moment and he could go spinning over the side and fall a hundred feet. The hills were deserted. No homes were back here, no one to see him as he made the tight turns, forcing the motorcycle to greater speed. He still felt that flare of exhilaration of conquering the challenge, his skills coming into play. At least he had this.

It was close to dawn when Cristiano approached the village. He'd made a wide circle and was heading back to home. A hot cup of espresso sounded good right about now.

He settled in on the road that curved around the lake. Soon he'd turn for the short climb to the family cottage. Then he smelt it.

Smoke.

His gut clenched. For a moment he thought he imagined it. He drew in a deep breath—it was in the air. Where there was smoke, there was fire. He slowed down and peered around. No one would have a campfire going at this hour; it was getting close to dawn. There, stronger now. To the left, near the lake.

For a moment indecision gripped him. Each breath identified the smoke as it wafted on the morning air. Forest fire? Building fire? He stopped the motorcycle, holding it upright with one foot on the ground. Every muscle tightened. He couldn't move. He felt paralyzed. Where were the village's firefighters? Why wasn't someone responding? Had the alarm even been sounded?

Seconds sped by.

Instinct kicked in. He slowly started moving, lifting his foot from the ground as the bike picked up speed.

He spotted a flicker of light where only darkness should be. He opened the throttle and raced toward the spot. In a moment, he recognized where he was—near the Bertatalis' row of cottages beside the lake. The flickering light came from the last one—the one Mariella and the baby were in!

He gunned the motor and leaned on the horn. In only a moment, lights went on in the Bertatalis' main house. He didn't stop, hoping they'd see the fire and respond. Seconds counted. Smoke inhalation could be fatal long before the actual flames touched anyone. Stopping near the cottage, he threw down the bike and raced to the door. He could see the fire through the living-room window almost consuming the entire area. The roof was already burning with flames escaping into the night. It would be fatal to enter that room.

Running to the back, he tried to figure out which window was the bedroom. Pounding on the glass, he heard no response. He hit his fist against the glass, but nothing happened. Quickly looked for anything to help; there—a large branch of a tree had fallen. Praying the baby was not sleeping beneath the window, he swung it like a bat, shattering the glass.

Smoke poured out. He could see the flames eagerly devouring the living room through the open bedroom door.

"Mariella," he shouted, levering himself up on the sill, brushing away glass shards, feeling the slight prick of a cut. He coughed in the smoky air.

"Huh?"

The sleepy voice responded. He jumped into the room and quickly assessed the situation. The door was open, the flames visible through the roiling smoke. Time was of the essence.

"Get up," he yelled, slamming shut the bedroom door, hoping it would hold the flames until he could get them out of the room. Where was Dante? He searched for the baby by touch in the smoke-filled room. There, near the wall, a cry sounded. He snatched up Dante and looked for Mariella. She was not responding. Had she already been overcome by smoke?

Stepping quickly as the crackling sounded louder, he found her still in bed and dragged her up.

"The cottage is on fire," he said as calmly as he could, trying to get through to her. He heard the sirens. Finally. Fear closed his throat as he looked overhead. An explosion paralyzed him. Was the tunnel caving in? Were there more bombs? Why wasn't his breathing mask working? He coughed in the smoke and moved toward the opening, pulling her with him. Echoes of men and women's screams sounded. The baby began screaming. Where was the little boy? Where was Stephano? Who could have done such a thing? How long did they have until everyone was safe?

"Cristiano?" Mariella's voice broke through. She coughed as she stumbled beside him. "What happened?"

"Don't know. Get out." They had reached the window and he scooped her up until she had her feet out the window, then pushed her gently until she jumped free. One leg over the sill, Dante in his arms, he didn't hesitate. A bright show of sparks and fire exploded as part of the front roof collapsed. Jumping free, he grabbed her arm and pulled her away from the cottage, the baby wailing in his arms. Past and present merged. Cristiano didn't stop running until he recognized the lake. Mariella kept up with him, coughing in the cold air.

The village volunteer firefighters were on their way. The sirens pierced the dawn air. Cristiano fought to keep his mind focused on the present, to be by the lake, to ignore the clamoring of his mind to relive the terror of a day in May.

In only moments the fire engine stopped, men scrambling to positions. Leaning against a tree, Cristiano stared at the fire, his throat tight. Tonight had not ended in tragedy.

"All my things," Mariella said, watching as the bedroom seemed to blossom with fire. "My laptop, my clothes. Dante's clothes. How could this happen?" She had tears running down her face. A moment later she was coughing again, shivering in the dawn light.

He pulled her closer, his arm around her shoulder, the baby screaming in his arms. "They are only things. You and the baby are safe, that's what's important." He offered up a quick prayer that he'd been able to save them. He'd faced his worst fear and come through.

Stephano and so many others hadn't been as lucky.

He watched the fire devour the cottage. In only moments it was completely engulfed in flames. He could feel the heat from where they stood.

She shivered again and he looked at her. The fire gave plenty of illumination. Shrugging out of his jacket, he wrapped it around her and handed her the crying baby. Her feet were still bare and must be freezing in the cold. Without a word, he picked them both up and headed toward the Bertatalis' main house. His ankle felt stiff, but it held. With grim satisfaction for the healing his body had done, he stepped carefully on the uneven ground, swinging wide around the burning cottage.

She coughed and tried to comfort the crying baby.

Signora Bertatali stood on the porch of her home, tears running down her cheek. When she saw Cristiano carrying Mariella and the baby, she hurried over.

"Thank God they are safe. Cristiano, thank you. Let me take the baby," she said, reaching out for Dante. "What happened?"

"I don't know," he said. "I saw the fire from the road and came to get them."

Mariella flung one arm around his neck. "I was asleep. Cristiano woke me up. How could the fire start?" She coughed again so hard, he almost dropped her.

"Try to take a deep slow breath. You're suffering from smoke inhalation."

"I don't know how this could happen. Oh, my dear, when I realized it was our cottage I feared the worst. Paolo has gone to help the firefighters. We'll know more after they tell us. Come, inside where it's warm. Did you leave the stove on or something?" Signora Bertatali asked, leading the way to her home. The warmth after the cold dawn felt wonderful. The baby stopped crying when in the light, blinking around, still looking as if he'd begin again in an instant.

"No. I turned it off after dinner," Mariella said.

"Oh, your poor feet. They're cut. Let me get some cloths and towels and take care of that," Signora Bertatali exclaimed, hurrying into the back bathroom, still jiggling the baby, trying to comfort him.

"I had to break a window to get into the bedroom. The living room was engulfed with flames when I arrived," Cristiano said, lowering Mariella down on a chair and kneeling in front of her to examine her feet as she began coughing again. She drew his jacket closer. A deep cut with a glass shard still in her left foot was bleeding; there were minor cuts on her right foot that had already stopped.

"This looks as if it needs stitches," he said, taking one of the towels Signora Bertatali brought and, after pulling the glass out, wrapped her foot.

The next while was chaotic. More volunteers arrived. Then the ambulance from Monta Correnti. Mariella and Dante were loaded up and taken to hospital while Cristiano stayed behind.

"I'll come to the hospital soon," he said as they drove away.

Now that the situation was under control, he watched from a distance until the fire was out. The adrenalin was wearing off. He could hear Stephano calling him. Feel the darkness closing in even as the sun broke on the horizon.

Retrieving his motorcycle, he roared off once more— trying to outrace the past.

CHAPTER THREE

MARIELLA braced herself against another bump as the ambulance sped toward the hospital. Dante cried until she picked him up to cuddle, trying to hold him around the oxygen nodules they both wore. He grew quiet at that and snuggled against Mariella. "Oh, sweet thing, we almost died." Tears pricked her eyes. She caught a sob. How could the cottage catch fire? And why had there been no alarms to alert them of the danger before it was too late? The first she'd known of the emergency was when she heard Cristiano calling her name. Smoke had filled their room and she'd almost passed out trying to get out of bed and to safety. Breathing had been almost impossible.

The next thing she remembered was stumbling into the yard with Cristiano while Dante cried. Thank God he was safe. They both were.

Her head pounded and her eyes watered again. Coughing, she felt she could not draw a full breath. A weight seemed pressed against her chest.

"We'll have you to hospital in just a short while. They'll bathe your eyes and continue the oxygen until morning," the EMT said, handing her a tissue to wipe the tears.

The baby had settled down, looked as if he was going back to sleep. She kissed his cheek, so grateful. Mariella wished she could drop off as he did and forget everything—if only for a few hours. Who would think such things happened while on holiday?

Once they reached the hospital, nurses swarmed around the ambulance. One gently took the baby, promising to take good care of him as she whisked him away to be seen by a doctor. Another helped Mariella into a wheelchair and pushed her quickly into the ER. It was quiet except for the two of them. In a short while a doctor had cleaned the cuts and stitched up the one on her left foot.

"Where's my baby?" she asked.

"He's in Pediatrics, on oxygen. A pediatrician has checked him out. Except for smoke inhalation, he seems fine. You can see him soon."

Mariella nodded. She already missed him. She needed to see again that he was all right. But patience was called for. For the first time she had a moment to think. Cristiano had saved them. She had no idea how he'd happened to be there, but she thanked God he had been. He was a hero. Without his intervention, she and Dante could have died.

After she'd been seen by the doctor, she was conveyed to a semi-private room by way of the pediatric ward. Once satisfied Dante was safely asleep, she allowed herself to be taken to her own room where she insisted she could bathe herself. After a quick shower, she gladly lay down, with oxygen, and tried to sleep—but the horrors of the night haunted her. What if Cristiano hadn't arrived? She and the baby could have been burned to death. What had caused the fire? What had brought Cristiano there at exactly the right time? It was much, much later before she fell into a fitful sleep.

Mariella stood by the window of the hospital room in the late morning gazing at the beauty before her. The gardens of the hospital gave way to the view of rolling hills that gave this area so much of its beauty. She knew the lake lay beyond her view. From her vantage point she saw only the edge of a bustling town and the distant serene countryside. The village was hidden behind a fold in the hills and no trace of smoke marred the crystal-blue sky.

Everyone went along with their daily lives. She had lost clothes and her laptop. And her photo of Ariana. Dante had only the sleeper he wore when they were rescued. Her livelihood depended on connections with her clients. She had to get another computer soon. She had backup files at home, so wouldn't totally start from the beginning. But this would certainly put a crimp in things.

The few hours' sleep she'd managed made her feel refreshed. She needed her wits about her to get back on track. Maybe she should consider returning to Rome immediately. But she wasn't sure when she'd have another break in her workload to look for Dante's father. If she didn't do some checking now, people would forget. Maybe they already had. But she owed it to the baby to find out anything she was able to.

Even with oxygen she still used she felt as though her lungs were on fire and it was difficult to breathe. Still, things were improving—she could go several minutes without the racking coughs.

She was declared healthy enough to be discharged, with a follow-up visit scheduled for a few days later.

She hurried to the pediatric ward, limping slightly because of the stitches in her left foot. She slowed in surprise to see Cristiano staring at the babies in the nursery.

"Cristiano?"

He turned and smiled when he saw her, giving her a critical look. "How are you today?"

She coughed, then smiled as she came up to him. "Much better. Doctor said I can go home and come back in a few days for another checkup." She looked into the nursery. "Is Dante in there?"

"No, these are newborns. Look how small they are."

She noticed the four babies and smiled. "Dante was tiny like that when he was born. Now look how big he's grown."

He turned and studied her again. "You really okay or are you pushing things?"

"I really will be fine. Let's find Dante."

Mariella was wearing clothes lent to her by a nurse on the night shift. Her feet didn't bother her much. The cut on the left gave her a bit of a limp, but the doctor had assured her it would heal quickly with no lasting damage. The scruffy slippers she wore needed to be replaced, too. Her mind spun with all she needed to do.

Cristiano led the way into the pediatric ward and in seconds they were in the room with the baby.

"The pediatrician made his round a short time ago," the nurse said. "Your baby's ready to go." She smiled at both of them. "He's a darling child. So attentive. But I know he misses his parents."

In a moment Mariella stood by the crib. Dante looked up at Mariella and gave her a wide grin. Lifting his arms, he came up easily when she reached out to pick him up. She held him closely, relishing the warmth of him in her arms. Her heart swelled with love. For a moment she almost broke into tears thinking about how close she had come to losing him. He was her precious son. The last link to her dearest friend. She gave silent thanks for his safety.

She turned to Cristiano. "You did a wondrous thing saving us. How could I ever thank you?" Mariella took a deep breath, taking in the sweet scent of baby powder and baby shampoo.

"Just get well fast. I'm glad I was there."

"And knew what to do. I don't even want to think about what could have happened."

"Don't. Let's get out of here," he said. "I'm not a big fan of hospitals."

As soon as they stepped outside he steered her to the black sports car parked nearby. Eying it dubiously, she asked, "Do you have a car seat for Dante?"

"The hospital is lending us one until you buy another. Then we'll bring it back. First thing, you need some clothes. Not that the outfit you're wearing doesn't have a certain cachet," he said, opening the door and pushing the passenger seat forward to access the baby's seat.

She laughed, then broke into coughing again. "Thanks. Nothing boosts a woman's ego more than compliments—" She stopped abruptly, before saying *from a man she cares about*. She had only just met the man. Taking the opportunity to end the statement while she put Dante into the carrier, she vowed to watch what she said in future.

Dante was oblivious to any tension. He babbled away in baby language and patted Mariella's face. Tangling his fingers in Mariella's long hair as she leaned over fastening the straps, he pulled.

"Ouch. You have to stop doing that," Mariella said with a laugh, grabbing his little hand and kissing the fingers. "That hurts!"

"He seems in fine form," Cristiano said.

Mariella smiled. "Seems as if no harm done. He's not even coughing."

Once she got Dante situated, she turned to Cristiano, so glad he'd come for her. "I have a million things to do. Are you sure you're up for it?"

"Who else?"

She bit her lip and nodded. Who else indeed? She had

no one except friends in Rome. If he was willing, she'd take all the help she could get.

"I have no identification—it burned in the fire. Along with all my money. I guess the first stop should be the bank, to see if I can get some cash."

"If not, I'll advance you some. Come on, it's breezy, let's get going."

Fifteen minutes later Mariella sat in a branch of her bank, talking with a manger to verify her identity and get money. Dante sat in Cristiano's lap, reaching for things on the manager's desk. He patiently pulled him back each time.

"That takes care of that,' the manager said as he hung up his telephone. "I'll get my secretary to bring you the money, and a temporary check book. You'll get imprinted checks sent to your home."

"Thank you. I appreciate all you've done for me."

The speedy transaction had been facilitated by Cristiano. The manager knew him and his family.

Once Mariella had money, Cristiano drove to a department store where she could get all she needed. He knew his way around Monta Correnti, for which she was grateful.

First purchase was a stroller for Dante, and a baby carrier. Once she no longer had to carry him, she felt better able to cope.

"Get a few things for him. I'll watch him, then, while you get your things," Cristiano suggested.

"You are a saint to do all this for me," she said. "I'm not sure I could have managed on my own."

He reached out and brushed back a lock of hair, tucking it behind her ear. The touch sent shockwaves running through her body. She smiled shyly and wanted to catch his hand and hold onto it, gaining what strength she could from him. But she kept still, treasuring the touch of his fingertips.

"You could have managed, I have no doubt. But why do it on your own?"

She nodded, knowing he'd made a special effort to help her. From comments Signora Bertatali had made, Cristiano had not left Lake Clarissa since he had arrived. She didn't know why he made an exception for her, but she was grateful.

"Next should be food for the baby. Once he's ready to eat, he lets everyone know in no uncertain terms—crying his head off."

"I bow to your assessment."

Mariella enjoyed shopping, the easy banter that grew between them. She held up baby clothes for his approval, which he gave after much mock deliberation.

"It really doesn't matter that much," she said, laughing at his posturing about the perfect outfit for Dante. "He's a baby. He doesn't know or care what he wears."

"Hey, he's special. He needs to make a statement—he's cool and he knows it."

She laughed again. Who could have suspected the devastation of the fire could lead to such a fun day-after? "I'll be sure to take pictures so he'll know when he's older."

Cristiano cocked his head at that. "Do you have a camera?"

"It burned."

"We'll get another."

"All the pictures I had on it are gone, too."

"All the more reason to make sure you start snapping new photos, so those won't be missed."

Her coughing was the only flaw in the day. She bought enough clothes to take care of a few days, shoes that didn't hurt her foot, and cosmetics—a definite necessity when she saw her face in the mirror. She probably should think about returning home to Rome. But she was enjoying every moment with Cristiano. She didn't want to think about being practical just yet.

Cristiano stood outside the dressing room, waiting for Mariella. Dante had been fed, changed, and was now asleep in the stroller. Idly he pushed it back and forth, but the baby didn't need soothing, he was out for his nap.

Glancing around the department store, he noted he was the only man, except for an elderly gentleman talking with his wife. If he'd ever suspected he'd be watching a baby this October day, that would have surprised him. Yet he couldn't imagine letting Mariella and Dante face this alone.

She came out of the dressing room wearing jeans that should have been banned—they made her figure look downright hot. The long-sleeve pink top highlighted her coloring and made her eyes seem even brighter silver. He could look at her all day. It wasn't just her looks that made it easy on the eyes. Her innate optimism shone from her eyes. He wished he could capture some of that for himself.

"Okay, I've gotten all I need, just have to pay for everything," she said, with a bright smile at him and a quick check for Dante.

"I'll be right here," he said, watching with appreciation as she walked away. Those freckles across her nose called to him. He wondered if she liked them. He'd heard from his sister when growing up that most women did not want freckles. He found them enticing. In fact, the more he saw of Mariella, the more he found enticing. She was pretty, sexy, and nurturing. He liked watching her with Dante. The baby seemed as fascinated with her as Cristiano was. "Probably a male thing," he murmured to the sleeping baby.

"All set," she said a moment later.

"Let's eat. You have to be hungry after all this and I know I am."

"Great. Where? Oh, dumb question, you probably always eat at your family restaurant."

Cristiano felt the comment like a slap. He had not been to Rosa for a long time. He'd been avoiding his cosseting family as much as he could, not wanting their sympathy over his injuries, and especially not wanting them to learn of his torment.

Excuses surged to mind. "I thought we'd eat closer to where we are. Rosa is across town. Then we need to get you two back to Lake Clarissa."

"Why? Where am I going to stay?"

"You could stay with me," he said. Then stared at her as the words echoed. Was he totally crazy? He'd been avoiding people to keep quiet about the flashbacks. He could not have anyone stay at the cottage. The first night he had a nightmare, the secret would be revealed.

"Thank you, really, but I can't stay with you. If the Bertatalis have another cabin available, maybe I'll stay a bit longer. I probably ought to return to Rome."

"Don't go."

He felt the intensity of her gaze. He could almost feel her mind working as she considered staying.

"Maybe for a few more days. I have no picture of Ariana to show around, few clothes, no computer."

"I have one you can use."

She slowly smiled. It was all Cristiano could do to refrain from leaning over and kissing her right in the middle of the department store. He caught his breath and forced himself to look away. Had he gone completely round the bend? He'd never felt such a strong desire to kiss a woman before. Obviously complete isolation was driving him more crazy than he already was.

"Then I'll stay for a few more days."

A man in his situation couldn't ask for more than that. At least not yet.

When Cristiano drove into the village by the lake, Mariella felt her stress level rise. The horror of the fire rose the closer they got to the resort. She wondered if she could ever fall asleep without fearing a fire would consume her lodgings.

He stopped the car near the Bertatalis' residence. The charred remains of the cottage could be seen clearly in the daylight. How had the fire started?

Signora Bertatali must have heard them as she threw open her door and rushed out to Mariella.

"Ah, Signorina Holmes. You are back." She hugged Mariella, baby and all. "I am so thankful. And the baby, he is well?" She greeted Cristiano and insisted on all coming into her home.

"We are devastated your cabin burned. Aye, when I think of what could have happened without the swift intervention of Cristiano. You will stay with us at no cost, we insist. That such a thing could happen is not acceptable. The fire chief thinks the heater's wiring overloaded. All are being inspected before we rent out another space. The electrician is here even now. I am so sorry. When I think of what could have happened—"

"We're fine, signora."

Cristiano nodded at her acknowledgment, staying near the door.

"Our insurance will cover everything. Please say you'll stay a little longer. We do not want you to remember Lake Clarissa with the horror from the fire. Do let us make it up to you. My husband has a contractor going over every inch of every cottage. They will be totally safe. I guarantee it. Please stay."

Mariella looked at Cristiano. "A day or two," she agreed.

"I am so grateful you are safe. And your baby. Come, let me prepare some tea and you sit. Please, come into the kitchen."

Signora Bertatali bustled around asking question after question. How did she feel? Did she get enough clothing?

"We are all so fortunate you saw the fire," she said to Cristiano. "How did you from your grandfather's cottage?"

He explained he'd been riding. Mariella wondered why he'd gone riding in the middle of the night. Not that it mattered. Thanks to him, they were safe.

Signora Bertatali poured the hot tea and sat at the table across from Mariella and Cristiano. Dante began fussing and Mariella reached into the baby bag to bring out a bottle. In short order it was ready.

"Let me. You drink your tea," Cristiano said, reaching for the little boy. Dante was light in his arms. For a moment Cristiano saw the baby he'd rescued. How was that child doing all these months later? He would have to see if he could find out.

"Thank you."

"And you, Cristiano, your family will be even more proud to learn of your rescue of last night. After that terrorist attack in Rome. I shiver every time I think about it."

He had no comeback. He didn't care if his family never knew of last night's fire. He was content to know he'd been able to function as his training had prepared him. No fear except for the woman and child.

Once Dante had been fed and changed, Signora took

them to the cottage right next door to the Bertatalis' home. It had been completely checked out and declared safe. Cristiano unpacked his car and brought in all her new clothes while Mariella put the baby down in the new crib.

Too tired to think straight, she thanked him and watched as he left, then fell on top of the bed and pulled over a blanket. Before she could mentally list any of the many steps she needed to take, she fell asleep.

The next morning Cristiano sat on the flagstone patio in front of the cottage and read from the latest manual his commander had sent him. Still technically on disability leave, he had plenty of time to keep up with the latest information and his commander agreed, sending him updates and reports to keep him current.

He heard a sound and looked up, surprised to see Mariella walking down the long graveled driveway. The sun turned her hair a shimmery molten gold shot through with strands of copper. She wore dark trousers and a sweater, though the afternoon was warm for October. He hadn't expected to see her here. How had she found the cottage? Not that it was hidden, lying right off the main road.

"Buongiorno," she called in greeting.

"Hello," he said, rising as he placed the manual face down on the small table. He hadn't expected her to make the long walk up a hill with a cut on her foot. Where was the baby?

"I came to say thank you for saving us," she said.

"You did that yesterday," he said, watching as she walked closer. He could see no lasting effects of the fire. Only the faintest hint of a limp showed.

"I know. I just wanted to see you again." She gave a shy smile and the effect on his senses was like the sun coming out after days of rain. For a moment, he felt elation. Then common sense intruded. He'd asked her to stay in Lake Clarissa, she had. Now she probably wondered why.

He glanced around. It was warm in the sun, but would cool down when the patio became shaded by the trees.

"Would you like something to drink?" he asked. He hadn't had anyone at the cottage since he had arrived. It felt strange to invite her inside.

"A glass of water sounds nice. It's warmer than I thought it would be today and that's a long walk."

"Especially with an injured foot."

She lifted her leg slightly and rotated the foot in question. "Actually, it didn't bother me that much."

He stared at the foot, then let his gaze wander up her body to those freckles. Her hair was curly and framed her pretty face. Her eyes were more silvery now than the other night. Then they'd been a stormy grey. The sun highlighted her hair, some of it the color of honey, some almost white gold. He wanted to touch those silky strands to see if they were as soft as they promised to be. Brush his fingertips across the freckles that dusted her face. Kiss her and feel the rise of desire being with a beautiful woman evoked. Prove to himself he was still alive, healthy and normal.

He resisted temptation. Dared he take the risk?

Every cell in his body clamored for closer contact with her. Temptation was never easily denied. He relished the feelings, the wanting, the anticipation, the desire. After staying alone for months, it was like an awakening, as if his body were coming alive after a long illness, painfully tingling. How ironic, he was attracted to a woman for the first time in ages and he dared not pursue the relationship. At least not beyond a casual friendship.

"Water's in the kitchen," he said.

She tilted her head slightly and smiled. "Usually is."

He led the way through the dark living area back to the kitchen. He opened the cupboard and stared for a moment. There were no glasses.

She followed him, looking around with curiosity. For a moment Cristiano scanned the room, noting the dirty dishes stacked in the sink.

He heard a giggle behind him and turned to find Mariella trying to hide her laughter. He scowled, knowing exactly what she was thinking.

"I've seen college kids with digs like this, but I never thought once people were grown up they'd continue to live this way. Or is it only guys?" she asked, the amusement bubbling in her voice.

"Dante would understand," he said, spotting a glass on the counter. He snagged it and quickly washed it. After it was rinsed, he filled it with tap water and handed it to her, still dripping. His sister would have his head if she ever saw the mess. His father would be speechless. Cristiano remembered how fastidious Luca had always been in the kitchen of Rosa.

She took the glass with a smile. "Thank you. I didn't mean to offend," she said. Drinking the entire glass in less than a minute, she held it out for more.

He filled it again. She coughed until she had tears in her eyes. Taking the glass, she sipped it more slowly this time, her gaze looking around the room as a smile tugged her lips.

"I've been recovering from an injury," he said gruffly, suddenly wanting her to know he didn't normally live this way.

Instant compassion shone in her face when she swung back. "I'm sorry. And on top of that you had the ordeal of carrying me away from the fire. I can't believe how fast the cottage burned."

"Entire houses can burn in less time given the right fuel and no safety precautions," he said. "How's the baby?"

"He's doing well. The Bertatalis are bending over backward to be accommodating. Did you know she has three children of her own, all grown now? She says she loves babies and almost begged to watch Dante for me while I walked here. Her husband has offered to take me on one of the fishing excursions on the lake."

"He leads fishing expeditions in the summer. Take him up on it if you get the chance—you'll like it."

"Hmm, maybe. It seems a little cool to be boating."

"I'll give you a ride back when you're ready to leave. Save walking on that foot."

"That would put you out. Which was not my intention. I truly wanted to thank you. You're a hero."

"No, I'm not." Why did people keep saying that? If they knew the truth— "I'll give you a ride," he said.

His motorcycle sat beneath the carport at the rear. Beyond that was a small building, door firmly closed.

Mariella followed, glancing around the kitchen again as she stepped outside.

"I could come back tomorrow and clean up the kitchen for you. As a token of appreciation."

Cristiano shook his head. "I don't need it."

He started the bike and helped her climb on. Instructing her to hold on tight, he didn't expect the jolt of awareness when she wrapped her arms around him. Her body was pressed against his back, her hands linked over his stomach. He closed his eyes, relishing the feel of her. Her hands were small, gripping over his belly. Her breasts pressed against his back and for a moment he wanted to turn around and pull her into a kiss.

"So how long will Signora Bertatali watch Dante?" he asked.

"No time limit."

"Want to take the long way home?"

"Sure."

"Will you be warm enough?"

"Oh, yes."

He started out slowly and then picked up speed when they reached the road. Turning away from the lake, he took the road he loved to ride when trying to outrun the demons and nightmares. It wound through the forest, dappled in shade in places, in full sunshine in others.

From time to time they could catch a glimpse of the lake sparkling in the distance. It was not as breezy today as other days and in places the lake looked like a mirror, reflecting sky and forest.

Mariella loved the ride. She felt free with the scenery whipping by. Seeing the lake when they turned from time to time was fabulous. Thankful for her rescue, she felt especially attentive to everything today. It was as if she were seeing things in a different light.

All due to Cristiano. And not only because he had saved them from the fire. But to take time yesterday to make sure she and Dante had all they needed was special.

But what she cherished the most was his request for her to stay.

He slowed and pulled off the road in a turn out that went to the edge of the open space in front of them.

"Oh wow," she said, gazing at the sight. The lake looked like a jewel nestled in a green setting. Beyond another hill and then another rose, until she felt she were on the rim of the world, looking out.

He stopped the motor. The silence was complete. Then the soft sighing of the breeze through the trees could be heard.

"This is beautiful," she said softly, so as not to disturb the moment.

"We can walk to the edge if you like," he said.

She hopped off the motorcycle and waited for him. Walking to the edge, she saw several rough-cut log benches.

"Others must come here for the view," she said, sitting on one sun-warmed log.

He sat beside her, gazing at the vista in front of them.

For several moments neither spoke, then Cristiano said softly, "I come here when I need to get away."

"A special place," she said, smiling, feeling as if she'd been given a gift. "I wish I had one. It gets overwhelming sometimes with Dante and working and trying to balance everything. I would love a place like this to just sit and be."

He nodded. "Maybe that's what is appealing, I can just be myself here."

She looked at him, tilting her head slightly. "Can't you be yourself everywhere?"

He met her gaze and slowly shook his head. "People expect certain things."

"And we always try to meet those expectations." She sighed. "Probably why I feel so inadequate with Dante. I expect to be wise like my mother and I'm not."

"She probably wasn't that wise when you were six months old," he said gently.

Mariella thought about that for a while. Was it true? Had her mother been learning as she went? "You might be right, but she always seemed to know what to say, how to explain things."

"You're a good mother to Dante. Don't doubt yourself."

Unexpectedly, Cristiano reached out and took her hand,

resting their linked fingers on his thigh. "It's beautiful here in winter when it looks as if powder sugar has been sprinkled on the trees. Now the trees are changing color, but spring will bring the new green of beginning leaves."

"Thanks for bringing me here," she said, returning her gaze to the magnificent view. The carefree feeling continued as if she had let all her worries vanish on the ride and the reward was this unexpected beauty.

They talked softly until the sun started slipping behind some of the trees and the temperature began to drop.

"Time to go," he said.

Mariella nodded, reluctant to end the enchantment of the afternoon. She would never forget this.

He continued the loop arriving in the village near the resort. He continued to the center of town to drop her by the small grocery store where she said she needed to pick up some things for Dante.

"Thanks for the ride home," she said, when she had dismounted. Giving into impulse, she kissed his cheek. "See you," she said and turned swiftly to enter the store.

Cristiano watched as she walked away, so alive and happy. He didn't want to think of the outcome had he not been riding that night.

But he felt like an impostor. He was no hero. He'd never tell her, or anyone, how fear engulfed him. How the nightmares of that incident in May haunted him unexpectedly day and night. Why couldn't he get the images out of his mind? Granted he could go several days without them. Just when he'd think he had it licked, they'd spring up and threaten to render him powerless.

Though he had been able to cope at the fire. Maybe, maybe, he was getting over it.

Mariella entered the grocery store and glanced back through the glass door. Cristiano sat on his motorcycle, staring at the door. Could he see her? She felt her heart beating heavily. She had never ridden a motorcycle before. She'd not known how intimate it felt, pressed against his hard body, feeling his muscles move against her as he drove the powerful bike. She still felt tingly and so aware of him. She hated to move, but people would begin to wonder if she stayed at the door staring like a moonstruck teenager at her latest heartthrob.

She almost giggled as she forced herself to move.

Would she ever get the chance to ride behind him again? Visit his special spot? Life seemed especially sweet today. It could almost as easily have been over for her. Instead, she had ridden with a sexy guy who intrigued her, fascinated her, set her hormones rocking.

She was curious about the injuries he was recovering from. Maybe he'd re-injured himself rescuing her, though he looked to be in perfect health to her. His broad shoulders and muscles beneath the shirt he'd worn attested to robust health. He looked as if he could jump mountains. And obviously was strong enough to carry her and the baby from a burning building.

With the loss of all her things—especially her computer—the sooner she returned home, the sooner she could pick up the pieces of her life. Maybe it was a sign she was not to look for Dante's father.

Fortunately her purchases fit into two bags and Mariella carried them back to the cottage. She also brought a bouquet of mixed mums for her hostess. She wanted to brighten the woman's day in gratitude for watching Dante for her. She wished the Bertatalis didn't feel so guilty. They had not known of the faulty wiring. All had ended well—except for the loss of her computer.

Was there a place in town she could use one? An Internet

café? Or, she could take Cristiano up on his offer and use his. Well, that was a no-brainer.

The next morning after tidying up, bathing and dressing the baby, Mariella set off for Cristiano's house. The road to the cottage was lightly traveled and easily navigated. However, it proved awkward pushing the baby stroller down the uneven graveled driveway.

The day was a copy of yesterday, sunny and balmy. Leaves had begun to change on some of the trees covering the hillside, bright spots of yellows and reds showed brilliant in the sunshine against the deep green of the conifers. She breathed the fresh air. What would it be like to live here year round? Nothing like New York where she'd been the past four years, with its concrete canyons and few open parks beyond Central Park.

Different from Rome, too. But that was home. Crowded, frenetic, yet comfortably providing all she really needed.

Rounding the bend, she saw the cottage. She studied it as she walked toward it. It was warm cream-colored stone, with a steep pitched roof of dark slate. The windows were wide with shutters on either side. It looked old, settled, perfect for its mountain backdrop. With an ageless look, it was hard to tell when it was built, but clearly a long time ago, she suspected from what she'd seen on the inside. He was lucky to have such a comfortable place to recuperate.

Cristiano was not on the patio this morning. She walked to the front door and knocked.

Cristiano opened the door a moment later and stared at her in surprise, then at the baby, his expression softening.

"What are you two doing here?" he asked, smiling at Dante.

"I came to take you up on your offer to use your computer. I need to check in with my clients."

"Come on in." He opened the door wide and she pushed the carriage in.

"It's dark in here," Mariella said, stepping into the living room. "Why is it all closed up?"

He looked around as if seeing the heavy drapes pulled over the windows for the first time.

"It suited me."

"How odd."

"They help insulate the windows."

"It's not that cold."

He stared at her a moment, then shrugged. "I'll get the laptop."

In less than five minutes, Dante was happily kicking his legs from the baby seat playing with a spoon and plastic cup while Mariella booted up the computer on the kitchen table. Cristiano had hooked it to a phone line. It wouldn't be the fastest connection, but at least she could check her email. Once Cristiano saw she was connected, he took off to give her privacy. She appreciated that, too aware of the man to concentrate on her work if he hovered nearby.

She gazed around the room while the computer booted up. It had a certain old-world charm that she loved. There was a huge fireplace, stone-cold now, at one end. She could envision a cheerful fire in the dead of winter when a sprinkle of snow might lie on the ground. How cozy this room would be. The large wooden table would seat a family of eight. The stone floor was cold, but, with a few rugs, could be comfortable in the winter months.

Which she would never see here in Lake Clarissa. For a moment the disappointment seemed too strong to bear.

CHAPTER FOUR

DANTE became fussy. Mariella prepared a mid-morning bottle and picked up the baby. She did not want to sit in one of the wooden chairs by the large table, balancing the baby and bottle, so she wandered into the living room. She'd like to tidy this room or at least open the curtains so she could see the magnificent views.

Sitting in a wing chair, she fed Dante, softly crooning to him as he ate. Maybe the dimness worked to her advantage as Dante began to fall asleep just as he finished the bottle.

Mariella continued to hold him after he fell asleep, relishing this quiet time with just the two of them. He was a beautiful child with dark brown eyes and dark hair. Ariana would have so loved this child of hers. Would Dante resemble her when he grew older? Or his unknown father? Tears threatened every time Mariella remembered her friend and her untimely death. How could she have borne having to leave this child behind? Love expanded within her heart and she wanted to hold the moment forever.

Cristiano came into the room from outside.

"Snack time?" he asked, studying her and Dante. He sat in the chair near her.

"Mid-morning feed." She gazed down at her sleeping baby. "I'll put him in the stroller and go when he wakes up. I still have to follow up on some work I was doing. I appreciate your letting me use your computer. We'll stay out of your way."

She rose and carefully placed the baby in the carrier, covering him lightly with a soft blanket.

"You're not in the way. Finish your work, then stay for lunch."

Cristiano knew he was grasping at straws, but he wanted her to stay. He wanted to talk to her, watch her laugh. Her skin was flushed slightly and looked soft and warm. Her hair curled around her cheeks, down her back. The sweater showed off the feminine body that awakened a need in his he'd thought long gone. When she was nearby, he had to fight the urge to find out more about her, see what she liked and didn't like.

And fight not to kiss her.

When he realized his thoughts had stayed on that point, he quickly looked away.

"You know that fire scared me. What if something happens to me? Who will take care of Dante?" she asked, covering the baby with a light blanket.

Cristiano's mother had died when he was a small boy. He remembered her smile, the fragrance she wore. The almost tangible love she'd given. No one got fully used to losing a parent. Had his father felt the same as Mariella? Worried about his children should something happen to him? Yet it wasn't the same. His father's sister lived in Monta Correnti, for most of his childhood Cristiano's grandfather had lived in this cottage with the rest of the family. There had always been family around. But one never got over the loss of his mother.

"My mother's dead, too," he said slowly.

"But not your father?"

"No, he's doing well." He guessed he was. Surely someone would have told him if he weren't. Not that he'd been very receptive to overtures from his family since he'd taken up residency in the cottage. His bossy sister had made sure he knew her thoughts on that from the messages she left.

The flashbacks happened without warning. He couldn't be around people who knew him for long—they'd see how messed up he was and cosset him so much he'd never get his life back. He had to beat this thing.

Mariella gazed at him as if expecting him to say more. He stared at her for a moment, wondering if he was finally moving on. He had handled the cottage fire. He had not had a nightmare since that night. He drew a breath, smelling the sweet scent of Mariella. It brought a yearning that grew in strength every time he was with her. Yet he could not fall for this woman.

"Are you the oldest child?"

"Yes, Isabella is a close second, incredibly bossy. Our mother died when I was a child. She took on the household work, and tried to keep us in line." For a moment he remembered some of the happy days they'd spent at the cottage, playing at the lake, just being with family. Life had thrown curves he'd never expected when he had been a child.

"Do your brother and sister still live close by?"

"Isabella still lives in Monta Correnti, along with Valentino," he said, smiling at the thought of his family.

"So you get to see them a lot. Must be nice. I was an only child."

He didn't reply. He had not seen them since they had visited him in the hospital after the bombing. His hospital stay had been lengthy and he'd missed his brother's wedding, and his cousin Lizzie's. Since his release from hospital Isabella called every so often trying to get him to go to family events. Mostly he let the answering machine take her call.

A lot had happened in his family over the recent months, including the startling revelation that his father had two older children by a first marriage. Cristiano still wasn't sure what to think about that. He had not met the two men—twins who had been raised in America. It was odd to think they shared the same father.

So far he'd found excuses that didn't raise undue suspicions. He was running out of time, however. How long could he keep his problem from his family? He wanted it to go away, wanted life back the way it had been.

He had loved this place as a child. It had been the first spot he'd thought of when wanting to retreat. His family was busy, fortunately. No one spent much time here anymore. Hiding hadn't changed a thing. Maybe he should open curtains. He was not in a tight subway tunnel, but had a view of endless miles.

"This is a terrific room. Do you use the fireplace when it gets cold?" she asked as she headed for the kitchen.

"Of course. It's the primary source of heat," he said, nodding toward the large wood-burning fireplace along an outside wall. He remembered rainy days in the fall when he and his brother Valentino would spend hours in front of the fire, trucks and cars zooming around. He hadn't seen his brother in months; he realized suddenly how much he missed him.

Cristiano followed her into the kitchen. She sat at the table and began checking her account. He crossed to the sink and leaned on the edge of the counter looking out the window over it. The view out back was opposite to the lake, to the rolling tree-covered hills that rose so high, offering peace and serenity. Dots of color presaged the coming of winter. Five months ago he had been working in Rome, settled with his life, his friends. Now he was practically a hermit, his closest friend dead, his job on hold.

But the hills didn't care. They remained the same year in and year out. Steadfast, secure, unchanging. It gave a longer perspective than short-time occurrence. Would he recover fully? Or was it time to begin to think of another way to earn a living? Would he return to Rome and the life he'd so enjoyed, or remain a virtual recluse cut off from friends and family?

"That was easy," she said a few moments later.

He looked over.

"Hardly any mail. I did send a note to two clients telling them I might be another day or two getting back in touch. Tomorrow I'll see about getting another laptop. Maybe in a shop in Monta Correnti."

"You are dedicated. I thought you were on vacation."

She looked at him. "I am, but I don't consider myself any more dedicated than you going into a burning building to save lives when you're recovering from injuries. You know I'll be forever grateful. Keep that in your heart. Now, do you have a printer?"

"Not here, why?"

"I wanted to print out a picture of Ariana. I found one I could use. The one I brought with me burned in the fire."

"Sorry. There's an Internet café in Monta Correnti, near the church on the plaza. They'd have a printer."

She shut down the computer and closed the top. "I'll go there, then. Thanks for the use of your computer today." She leaned back in the chair and looked at him. "So tell me, how did you get into firefighting? I think that's one of the most dangerous lines of work anywhere—pitting your life against a raging fire," she said.

"I like making a difference." A ready answer. It didn't explore the variety of reasons he chose fighting fires as compared to police work or mountain rescue. But all were similar kinds of jobs—first responders, never knowing what would await them. Challenges to be surmounted. Never boring.

She smiled, her eyes sparkling silver. Her hair shone in the sunshine pouring in through the side window.

Cristiano had a stronger urge to reach out and twirl some of those tresses around his fingers, feeling the silky softness, the heat from each warm strand. Those desires rose each time he saw her.

"Did your father want you to do something else?" she asked.

"Probably, though he never pressured any of us. My sister works with him at the family restaurant. My brother Valentino is home less than I am."

"Is your brother Valentino Casali? The racing daredevil?" She looked surprised.

Cristiano nodded. He knew Valentino had a reputation to match his daredevil ways. For the first time he wondered if their decisions had hurt their father. He took such pride in Rosa. It was a fine restaurant, but only Isabella had followed their father's path and worked in the family establishment.

"He got married recently, I saw that somewhere," she said. "Not my idea of a married man."

Cristiano shrugged. "What would be your idea of a married man?"

"Someone faithful."

"Valentino is fiercely loyal. He would always be faithful," Cristiano was quick to say.

"I'd also want my husband home more than he seems to be. And safe."

"Maybe now that he has a home and wife, he'll change. People do, you know."

She nodded.

"Other attributes?"

She frowned in thought for a moment. "Fun to be with, able to talk and share, and I'd want a husband to want the same things I do."

"Sounds like you've thought about it for a while."

"Ariana and I used to talk about our dream man. Hers turned out not to be the dream."

"And you?"

"Haven't met him yet. So what do you do here all day? Not working. No television I saw," she asked.

"This and that." He should tell her about the woodworking. Maybe later he'd take her to the shed to see.

"Did you always want to be a virtual assistant?" he asked, finding it an odd sort of job for such a bubbling personality like hers. He'd picture her surrounded by office workers, working as a team player, not in a solo job from home.

"When in university in New York, I planned to hit Madison Avenue big time. I majored in marketing—American style. But then my parents died, then Ariana. Things changed so much, I couldn't manage that on top of watching Dante. Maybe someday."

"I think I heard the baby," he said, hearing a noise in the living room.

Mariella jumped to her feet and went to check on Dante. Two minutes later she came back, carrying a bubbling baby.

"He was kicking his feet and saying something. I can't wait for him to talk."

"I'll start our lunch. I'll make you some of the world's best marinara sauce."

"The world's best?" she scoffed lightly.

"Hey, I challenge you to find better. It's from the family's restaurant. And you'll thank your lucky stars you get to have some."

"You made it?"

"No. My sister sends me care packages. I freeze the sauce until I'm ready to use it. It won't take long to prepare."

"Time enough for me to feed this little guy, then," she said.

"Again?"

"He eats a lot, that's why he's growing."

Cristiano took the sauce from the freezer, peeled off the wrapper and dropped it into a pan. Soon it began to simmer on the stove as he boiled water for pasta. He watched Mariella feed Dante while he worked. For the first time in months, he felt a touch of optimism. There was something about cooking long-familiar foods and sharing that touched that part of him that had once liked to spend time with friends. Stephano had loved the marinara sauce and every time he learned Isabella had sent some, he'd invite himself and his family over for dinner. He and the other guys at the station urged him to bring in enough for everyone.

For once the memory of his friend and the time they'd shared didn't hurt with the searing pain of loss. It was a bittersweet memory of times that would never come again. He missed his friend and probably always would.

But life went on. Stephano had loved life so much, he would have personally come to Lake Clarissa and knocked some sense into his head if he'd known Cristiano was secluding himself like this.

Except—the flashbacks were real.

Mariella's laugh pulled him from his thoughts and he looked up. The baby had something smeared all over his face, and his pudgy hands were spreading the mess to his hair.

"What is that?"

"Some kind of oatmeal cereal. The pediatrician is having me try it. Probably tastes like paste and feels better spread around outside than eating," she said, trying to catch Dante's hands to wipe them. She giggled. "He's a mess. I'm thinking this is not one of the better ideas the doctor had."

"You think? Hey, little man, would you like some of my papa's sauce?"

"He's not even six months yet. Too young for big people food."

"A taste won't hurt." Cristiano dipped his pinkie into the warming sauce and then carried it to the baby. Dante grabbed his hand and pulled it to his mouth. His frown of surprise had them both laughing.

"Maybe it's an acquired taste," Cristiano said.

The baby had eaten and Mariella settled him on a thick blanket on the floor when Cristiano served up their lunch.

"Wow, this was definitely worth waiting for," Mariella said after her first bite. "What makes it so great?"

"Family secret," he said.

"Ah. I bet Rosa has a line waiting for tables every night."

"The economy these days makes things unsettled. It does well enough, I think." Actually, from one or two comments Isabella had made, Cristiano wondered if that was true. Maybe he should check into it. If there was a problem, he might be able to help financially; he had some money saved.

"I know people are cutting back, but good food is always relished."

"My sister has been pestering me to talk about the situation for a while. It's her area, not mine. Whatever she decides is fine with me."

"Um. I just hope she decides to keep making this wonderful sauce. Does she sell it by the jar?"

He shook his head.

"She should. Maybe I can talk to her about that. She could consider an Internet mail-order business on the side. I bet folks would pay a premium. It obviously freezes well. I wonder how it could be shipped?"

"Ever the marketer?"

She nodded, but continued to look thoughtful.

"You said you went to university in New York? What was that like? Why there?"

"My dad was American, but he settled in Rome ages ago. Ever since I can remember the plan was for me to attend school there when I hit university level. After their death, it helped that New York is vastly different from Rome, so I didn't have lots of memories to deal with at every turn. Maybe it helped with the grief, too. To have the coursework to concentrate on."

"So now you're back settled in Rome?" he asked.

"I'm Italian, so is Dante. There is nothing waiting for us in New York. When he's older, I'll take him there and show him the sights. It's a fantastic city. But it's not home."

She looked up. "It was good to grow up in Rome, but I'm wondering if it might be even better to have a smaller town, where I could build a support group. A single mom will need help. I've lost touch with many of my friends from high school."

And lost her best friend, he remembered.

"I couldn't wait to move to Rome when I graduated. More vibrant, more things to do."

"Of course. But when you got hurt, you came home. There's a lot to be said for a country setting. Where in Rome can you get views like you have? Sitting on the patio, seeing the lake, the gorgeous hills. It's fantastic."

"Doesn't offer a lot of opportunity for young people, though."

"Ah, but that depends on what opportunities one's looking for. I have a job, a child. My opportunities now lie in different areas than when I was single and fancy free."

She smiled again and Cristiano was struck by her happy outlook. She seemed not to have a care in the world, though he knew differently. What was her secret to that optimistic outlook?

Not having to deal with post-traumatic stress disorder, for one thing.

"I think I'll take the baby to the lake later. Want to come with us?" she asked.

"Will it be warm enough for him?" he asked.

"In the sunshine. I guess you've done it a thousand times."

"It never gets old. The lake is beautiful all times of the year. My ankle was broken a while ago. I'm still getting it back in shape. The sooner I'm fit, the sooner I can return to work. Want to go Jet Skiing?"

She laughed and shook her head. "Sitting on the beach is enough."

CHAPTER FIVE

CRISTIANO drove them in the car back to the village. He and Mariella took the baby to the shore near the marina. The beach was a mixture of sand and pebbles sloping gently to the water's edge. There was a couple sitting in nearby chairs, reading. She waved to them while Cristiano settled on a spot some distance away so as not to disturb their tranquility with their presence.

He brought a blanket and soon Dante was taking tummy time facing away from the water, so he was facing up hill. When he grew frustrated, Mariella sat him up, holding him lightly so he wouldn't fall over. He could almost balance by himself. He settled in first gnawing on the plastic keys, then throwing them down. She retrieved them and handed them back.

Again

And again.

Cristiano stretched out beside them, laughing at the baby's antics. Mariella tossed him the keys.

"You try it," she said.

Dante turned to see the keys and grinned at Cristiano.

"Don't want to lose your keys," he said, dangling them in front of the baby. "Especially when you're older and that means wheels."

The tranquility of the setting soothed. Mariella coughed

again, wishing she'd get over the smoke problem soon. Her chest felt dry and tight. Taking a deep breath, she relished the clean air scented with evergreen. The sun sparkled on the water. In the distance she could see a boat bobbing near the center of the lake. Was that a fisherman?

Dante threw the keys again.

Cristiano retrieved them and handed them to Dante. He threw them again and looked at him, a wide smile on his face. Her heart contracted. She loved this precious baby.

"It's so lovely here, even if we can't swim today. Maybe we'll come back for a visit when Dante's older. Maybe continue the search for his father if we don't find him this time."

"How can you have spent so much time with your friend and not found out more information?"

"She was in the late stages of pregnancy and very ill. We spent more time talking about our shared memories, reliving good times. She changed the subject anytime I brought up who Dante's father might be. He could be named for the man, for all I know. She spoke of what she hoped for in Dante's future. The future she'd never see."

"Maybe she truly didn't want her son to know his father."

"Maybe." She wondered if she was doing wrong trying to find the man. He obviously wasn't as nice as Cristiano. She couldn't imagine any woman not want a child of his to know him.

"It's nice here," she said, turning slightly and fussing with the baby to cover the fact she was studying Cristiano's profile. He made her heart happy. He could have been in movies, she thought. The rugged hero rescuing the heroine from danger then kissing her silly. And her heart almost melted when he played with a baby. Why was a strong man giving his attention to a baby so sexy?

She sighed a bit, wishing he'd pay that much attention to her.

"Problem?" he asked, glancing at her, one eyebrow raised.

"No, just thinking how nice it is here and how horrible the other night was.' She shivered involuntarily. "We could have died."

"But you didn't." His voice came sharp.

She brushed her fingertips over Dante's head. He was perfectly content sitting on the blanket and throwing his plastic keys. She wished she could be so easily satisfied.

"I know that. As a firefighter, you've probably seen lots of death."

He frowned and sat up, resting an arm on his upraised knee. "It's not something anyone gets used to," he said.

"I imagine not." She could have bitten her tongue and not said anything. How many other lives had he saved, and how many had he not been able to save? There was more to firefighting than just pouring water on a fire.

"Do you think I can raise him?" she asked a few moments later.

"You can do anything if you want it enough. Remember that. From what I see, you are doing a fine job."

"Tell me more about growing up around here."

"Weekends are busy times for restaurants. My father worked hard. My mother with him, until she died. But even though we didn't see much of them our childhood was still magical. Especially when my grandfather was alive. His life was different from our everyday life. He knew the trees, the forest, fish in the lake."

She fell silent, thinking about the vacations she and her parents had enjoyed. It seemed so long ago and far away. Would visiting some of the spots bring the memories closer?

Or only emphasize she was alone? She wanted Dante to see all of Italy. They'd make new memories.

"I'm going into Monta Correnti tomorrow. The doctors at the hospital wanted to check me and Dante again, make sure there are no lasting effects. I need to get access to a printer so I can print up another picture of Ariana. Maybe check around in Monta Correnti to see if anyone recognizes her."

"Park near the town square. Easy to get to an Internet café, shops and the hospital."

"We'll find it," she said cheerfully, wishing he'd offered to drive them into town.

After visiting the hospital the next morning and getting a clean bill of health for both her and Dante, Mariella wandered the center part of Monta Correnti. First stop after the hospital was the Internet café where she was able to print a color photograph of Ariana. Staring at the picture of her friend, she remembered how vital she'd always been when younger. The illness had robbed her of so much.

Then she pushed the baby in the stroller, wandering down side streets, walking around the square. When she saw a likely tourist spot, she showed the photo. No one recognized Ariana.

It was after one when Mariella turned back onto the wide piazza and gazed at the buildings. Rosa seemed to leap out at her. That was Cristiano's family's restaurant—the one with the excellent marinara sauce. She pushed the stroller along, wondering if she dared try Dante in the restaurant. So far the baby had been in perfect harmony with all they'd done. But she'd hate to be in the middle of a meal and have him start screaming his head off.

As they approached, Mariella saw a nice open-air space

connected to the restaurant. Much better for the baby, she thought. The day was warm enough to sit outside.

Once seated, with a baby highchair for Dante, Mariella perused the menu. She'd try the tortellini with the famous sauce. She sat back to enjoy the ambiance while waiting for her order. The waiter had brought bread sticks and she gave one to Dante to drool on. He beat the table, put it in his mouth and looked surprised. She laughed. Hadn't he expected it to be food? He couldn't eat it, but she thought he could gum it a bit. Once it got soggy, she replaced it with another.

The courtyard was delightful. Tables were scattered around as if awaiting company, two others occupied. None too close to impede a private conversation. The bougainvillea spilled down a trellis, their flowers faded now as winter approached. She bet they were spectacular in the height of summer. A fountain's melody gave a pleasant sound to soothe and enhance enjoyment of the food. Mariella suspected the restaurant was a favorite of many.

When the meal was placed before her, Mariella smiled in anticipation. She looked at the waiter. "I can't wait to eat this. I had this sauce recently at Cristiano Casali's place. Do you know him?"

The waiter bowed slightly. "Of course. He is son of the owner, Luca." He frowned. "He has not been to visit recently. I shall tell his sister you are here."

Mariella took a bite of the tortellini. It almost melted in her mouth. The sauce was even better than she'd had at Cristiano's. She savored each mouthful.

"Signora?"

A pretty woman wearing an apron approached Mariella.

"Sì?"

"I am Isabella, Cristiano's sister. You are a friend of Cristiano?"

Mariella smiled. "He rescued me and my baby from a fire at Lake Clarissa. I consider him a hero."

"Ah. May I?" Isabella said, holding onto the back of a chair.

"Please."

"How is he?" she asked when she sat down.

"Fine. He said he is recovering from injuries?" How odd his sister asked a stranger for an update on her brother.

"He was a first responder to the bombing in Rome last May," Isabella said slowly.

"I knew that. That's where he was injured."

"A burn, a broken ankle. Yet it's taking a long time to heal. Does he walk okay?"

"Fine."

Isabella stared at Mariella for a long moment.

Growing uncomfortable, Mariella smiled again. "I had some of your marinara sauce at Cristiano's and so when I had to come to Monta Correnti and saw the restaurant, I thought I'd eat it again. It's delicious."

"Thank you. So you ate at Cristiano's home?"

"The cottage near the lake," Mariella clarified.

"I know where he's staying. Did he bring you here?" Isabella glanced around quickly.

"No, I drove," Mariella said.

Isabella looked at Dante. "What a blessing he is safe. Cristiano rescued him?"

"We're staying at the cottages rented by the Bertatalis. The unit we rented burned. Faulty wire in the heating device. I was asleep, so was the baby. We both would have been killed if Cristiano hadn't discovered the fire and come in to rescue us."

Isabella smiled. "So like my brother. You are going back to Lake Clarissa today?"

"Yes, for a few more days. I'm on a short holiday." She reached for her bag and pulled out Ariana's picture. "Have you ever seen her?" she asked.

Isabella looked at the photo and handed it back. "No. A friend?"

Mariella nodded. Another story too much to go into with everyone she saw.

"I have something for Cristiano. Would you take it to him for me? Things are hectic right now or I'd go myself. Not that he'd be happy to see me," Isabella said.

"Why ever not?"

"He's been avoiding me. Granted, I've had a few other things on my mind, but I wanted to make sure he was all right. He doesn't answer his phone most of the time. He was conveniently gone from the cottage the two times I went to visit. He's turning into a hermit."

Mariella laughed. "I don't think so. But he can be a bit moody."

"Cristiano? Doesn't sound like him. He has a very even disposition."

"Men hate to be sick. I know my father was grouchy when he was ill. My mother said not to worry, once he was better he'd be back to normal. Maybe Cristiano is frustrated with how long it's taking him to heal and is taking it out on family."

Isabella nodded. "Perhaps, but enough is enough. I shall get the letter and some more sauce. I'm glad to know he's eating what I left, anyway."

"It freezes well. I thought you might consider a mail-order side to the business. I'd love to be able to order this from my home and know I can have it whenever I wish."

"We are just a local restaurant."

"Think about it. I have a degree in marketing and could help set it up if you ever wanted to expand."

Isabella looked at her. "Would it cost a lot?"

"My contribution would be free. I owe Cristiano forever." She reached out and brushed back Dante's hair, smiling at the precious little boy. He rewarded her with a wide smile and drool on his chin mixed with breadcrumbs.

Isabella nodded. "If you would take the letter and sauce to my brother, it will be enough. Tell him his sister asks after him and to call me!"

By the time Mariella was ready to leave, a small bag containing a jar of sauce and an official letter was delivered to her table by the waiter. She placed in it the carry space of the stroller. After wiping Dante's face and hands, she placed him in the stroller and paid her bill. A few moments later they were walking around the square. She studied the restaurant that shared the small piazza with the family restaurant. It looked very upscale and trendy. Not the sort of place for a baby or a casually dressed tourist. Glad she'd had an excellent meal, and that Dante had not raised a fuss, she continued on her walk. There was more to see before returning to the lake.

The town was lovely, decidedly bigger than Lake Clarissa, yet nothing like New York or Rome.

But which appealed to her more these days—the big city excitement or the slower pace in these mountain towns? Would she like to raise Dante in a pastoral setting allowing him to experience nature in its raw beauty? Or would the experiences of museums, art galleries and opera be better to round his education?

Dante had fallen asleep by the time they returned to the car. Mariella couldn't wait to get him home and take a nap herself. The prognosis from the doctor had been good. But she still coughed from time to time.

* * *

The next morning, Mariella put Dante in the stroller, retrieved the sauce Isabella Casali had sent from the refrigerator and headed back up the road to deliver to Cristiano. Her nerves thrummed with anticipation.

On impulse, she stopped at the open-air market and bought a bouquet of mums. The fall flowers were vibrant bronze yellow and purple and she knew they would brighten the kitchen. She hoped he'd appreciate the gesture with the flowers. She wanted to brighten his day as he brightened hers.

Cristiano was sitting on the terrace when she arrived. She smiled when she saw him, already anticipating their time together. There was something about Cristiano that drew her like a lodestone. She watched his expression as it changed from surprise, to pleasure, to cautiousness. He rose and came to meet her.

"*Buongiorno.* We have brought you gifts," she said as she reached the terrace.

"I need no gifts." He watched her from wary eyes. He was several inches taller than she was and she had to crane her neck he was so close.

"Well, the flowers are from Dante, so speak to him about those. And this sack is from your sister, Isabella. She hopes you are well and you should call her."

"My sister?"

"Yes. She says you are becoming a hermit. I told her you weren't. Look how often we visit."

The amusement in his eyes lit a spark in her own.

Her spirits rose. She held out the flowers.

He stared at them and slowly took them. "Dante picked them out?" he asked.

"Well, that was the bunch he made a grab for. I figured they were the ones he wanted to give you."

"Or eat."

She laughed.

Cristiano stole another look at her. She was beautiful when she laughed. It was as if the sun shone from inside, lighting her eyes and making them look like polished silver. That pesky urge to wrap his hands in her hair and pull her closer sprang up again. He looked away before he did something stupid—like give into that impulse.

"And your sister sent you some more sauce." Mariella pulled a brown bag from the back of the stroller and held it out. Cristiano took it. Now both hands were full.

"I'll open the door so you can put the flowers in water and the sauce in the freezer or wherever you wanted to put it. I kept it cold. Delicious, even better made fresh. Still, I think your family could ship it frozen within the country at least. I think the sauce would do quite well—maybe they could send pasta, too. I printed a picture of Ariana, but no one I showed it to yesterday recognized her."

"Did you even take a breath in all that?" he commented, following her into the house and back to the kitchen. He put the sack on the counter, laid the flowers down and rummaged for something to put them in. Finally he settled on a tall glass. The flowers did look nice. But he wasn't used to getting gifts from women and wasn't sure how to handle this.

"I thought they'd look good on the table," she said.

"Sure." He set the flowers on the old table, struck by a memory of his mother doing the same thing. Now the forgotten memory flashed into his mind.

"My mother liked flowers," he said slowly.

"Most people do. I think they look happy. When we stopped at Rosa for lunch after our checkup yesterday, I told the waiter I'd had the sauce before and he apparently told your sister. She came out to meet me."

For a moment Cristiano wished he had given them a

ride, though he wasn't sure about visiting Rosa just yet. He realized he longed to see his father and sister. Find out how things were going at the restaurant. He had to make sure he was all right before risking it. "The outcome from the doctor?"

"We're both healthy. Though I still cough from time to time. The doctor said that would fade. So we had most of the day free after seeing him, so we set out to explore Monta Correnti. I recognized the restaurant as soon as I saw the sign. The food was superb. That's where I met Isabella. There's a letter in the sack for you as well."

Cristiano looked in the sack and took out the envelope. It was from the minister of the interior. Cristiano stared at it. It was addressed to his apartment in Rome and had been forwarded to the restaurant.

"Is it bad news?" Mariella asked, watching him.

"I have no idea." Although deep down Cristiano knew what this letter contained, but did not want to accept it.

"So open it and find out what it says."

He did. The letter confirmed what Cristiano had already known for a long time. He was being awarded a medal of valor for his rescue of the injured from the bombing. Immediately, he crushed the letter and threw it on the counter.

"Um, bad news," she guessed.

He shook his head. "It's a mistake, that's all."

Cristiano didn't want the medal, never had. Why him? Stephano had died. Others from his station had helped with the rescue. There had been so many who died. They had not been able to rescue everyone. Why would anyone want to award him a medal of valor? Especially if they knew of the flashbacks and attacks of sheer terror that gripped him. What kind of man deserved a medal when he couldn't handle all life threw his way?

"What's a mistake?" she asked.

"Never mind. Are you staying?"

"Gee, after such a kind invitation to visit and give you my impressions of Monta Correnti how can I refuse?"

She grinned that cheeky grin and Cristiano almost groaned at the sight. He wanted to pull her into his arms and kiss her until he forgot all the pain of the past. He wanted to feel that slim body against his, driving out the memories and offering an optimistic hope of the future. He wanted to lose himself in her and find that shining optimism she displayed.

He flat out wanted her.

Yet he had deliberately come to Lake Clarissa to avoid people until he could be sure the flashbacks had gone. Wasn't it risky to spend so much time with her? Yet she made him feel normal again, complete. And the baby was adorable. Cristiano wished he could remember when he was so young and innocent the future looked nothing but bright.

Dante began fussing and Mariella shrugged out of her sweater, tossing it on the counter, knocking off the letter. She picked it up and smoothed it out, her eyes drawn to the fancy letterhead. Skimming quickly, she widened them in shock.

"You're getting a medal! How cool is this!"

"I told you, it's a mistake. I don't deserve a medal. I certainly am not a hero!"

Mariella wasn't listening to him. Or attending to Dante, who looked as if he were working up to a fully-fledged screaming bout. She was reading every word in the letter.

"You saved seven people."

"Others saved lives as well."

"And at great personal risk you continued on with the last

two even though you were severely injured," she continued as if she hadn't heard him.

He didn't need the reminder. He saw it over and over every time he had a flashback. The shock, the anguish, the horror.

She looked at him, her eyes shining. "I knew you were a hero. Now it's been confirmed, and not just because of me and Dante. Wow, you must be so proud."

"I'm not going to accept it. It would be a farce."

"But—"

He snatched the paper from her hand, balled it up and tossed it into the trash before storming out of the kitchen.

CHAPTER SIX

MARIELLA was stunned at his reaction. But she had to see to the fussy baby before going after Cristiano. She lifted the baby from the stroller and tried to soothe him. Preparing a bottle one-handed, she soon shifted him to lie in her arm while offering the bottle. He fussed and pushed it away, wailing as if his world had ended. She jiggled him a little, singing softly as she tried the bottle again. Finally he took it, chewing on the nipple as much as sucking.

"Are you teething, sweetie?" She knew from the baby books that children began teething any time around five or six months, but this was the first time he'd pushed the bottle away. Maybe his gums hurt.

Finally Dante settled down to drink the bottle. Mariella walked into the living room, humming softly as he drank. The curtains were wide open today and sunshine flooded the room. It welcomed her and the baby. She sat in the chair that gave the best view of the lake and continued to hum as she fed Dante.

Her firefighter was an intriguing man. He was a hero, even the ministry confirmed that. Yet he seemed angry about it. Not at all satisfied with the heroic actions he'd performed.

So did that add to the fascination she felt around him? He was drop-dead gorgeous with his thick dark hair and haunted eyes. He looked fit enough to put out a blaze single-handed. She remembered those arms so strong when he lifted her and yet gentle enough for a small baby.

Her heart skipped a beat as she pictured the few times he'd smiled. She could watch him forever, she thought.

Except, he didn't seem to feel the same fascination with her.

Sighing softly, she tried to picture him as a child running around the piazza in Monta Correnti or the restaurant his father owned. She couldn't imagine it. She could see him here at Lake Clarissa, hiking in the woods, swimming in the lake in summer, racing Jet Skis. Chopping wood for a winter's fire. Chasing around a brother who looked like him.

Glancing around the room, she noted how family friendly it was. But she didn't see anything that looked as if it belonged to Cristiano alone. What were his interests? What did he do to combat the stress of rescuing people and battling blazes that threatened life at every turn?

Dante drifted to sleep. She rose and went to the door. As suspected, Cristiano was sitting on the patio, staring at the lake. She would always be able to picture him that way.

"Could you help me?" she asked softly.

He looked around.

"If you would release the back of the stroller, it lies down and I could put the baby there. He'll sleep fine in the stroller and be ready to go when I am."

The man nodded and rose. She watched him, no limp she could see, so why was he still on leave? Was he upset at taking so long to heal after being injured? Champing at the bit, so to speak, to get back to work?

She wondered why he was so adamant against the medal. Sure, others had died, but maybe they were also receiving a medal posthumously.

The stroller was still in the kitchen. He figured out how to recline the back and pulled the half canopy over it. He pushed the stroller, looking just a bit like a giant next to the tiny conveyance, over to Mariella.

She was swaying gently as she held the sleeping baby.

"Thanks, he's getting heavy."

He locked the wheels while she placed the sleeping baby down and covered him with a soft blanket.

"You take to being a mother," he commented, watching her. "Some women don't."

"It's still a struggle." She straightened and looked at the sleeping child with such an expression of love Cristiano caught his breath.

A strand of hair fell across her cheek. Before he could have second thoughts, Cristiano brushed it back, feeling the soft warmth of her skin. He tucked it behind her ear as she looked up and into his eyes. Her smile was warm. Her lips enticing. As if in a dream, he leaned across the slight distance and touched his mouth to hers. She was warm and sweet and so tempting. Kissing her lit a fire in his blood and he wanted the moment to go on forever.

Reality struck when she pulled back and blinked as she looked at him.

"I've wanted to do that for days," he said softly, his hands cupping her cheeks.

"I thought it was only me—I mean that the attraction was just one way."

"Oh, no," he said before he kissed her again, drawing her into his arms, holding her closely while the world seemed to spin around. Mariella was the only thing grounding him.

Rational thought vied with roiling emotions. The desire that rose whenever she was near had to be controlled. He refused to fall for Mariella. She was sweet and young and had bright expectations. He would never falsely lead her on when he had no clue if he could make it in the world again or not.

Holding her, touching her, kissing her, he could forget the horror of that day, the pain of losing his best friend, of the others in the squad that he'd been so close to. But it wasn't fair to her.

Slowly he eased up. They were both breathing hard. He wished for an instant the baby would sleep all afternoon so that he could whisk her into his bedroom and make love until they were both satiated.

"Wow," she said softly, the tip of her tongue skimming her lips. He almost groaned in reaction.

"Wow, yourself," he said, kissing her soft cheeks, seeing how long he could resist her mouth.

The baby awoke and started crying.

Mariella pulled away and hurried over to him.

"Oh, sweetie, what's the matter?" She picked him up and cuddled him.

"He was fussy eating, too," she said. "Maybe he doesn't want to sleep in the stroller. I'll take him home."

"I can drive you."

"No, we'll walk. It's still a pretty day. We'll be okay."

In only a couple of minutes they left.

He watched as she disappeared from view. Whether she knew it or not, the love she showed for the baby was strong. She would love that child forever. Her concerns on whether she was a good mother were for naught. When would she accept that?

He wished he could give her that knowledge.

Mariella pushed the carriage along the side of the road, not seeing the scenery, only halfway watching for vehicles. She was bemused with their kiss, concerned by the baby's fussy behavior. She was smiling, her heart still beating faster than normal, just thinking about Cristiano. She felt they were drawing closer. And he obviously felt that attraction she did, if his kiss was anything to go by. She wished they had not been interrupted.

"Not that you knew you were interrupting," she said to Dante. The baby was awake, fussy, his fist in his mouth.

She hoped Dante would nap in the crib. She wished to turn right around and go back to spend the afternoon with Cristiano. And share a few more blazing kisses.

Cristiano headed for the small shed in the back of the property. He entered, smelling the sawdust and polish. Slowly he relaxed. Whenever he came into the workroom he felt connected to his grandfather. His mother's father had been a craftsman in furniture making. He'd shown Cristiano the basics and had urged him to follow in his footsteps.

Cristiano had rebelled, as youth so often did, preferring the excitement of pitting his skills against that of a roaring conflagration and rescuing people from impossible odds— who would die if he hadn't been there. But always in the back of his mind were the quiet peaceful times he'd worked with his grandfather in this very workspace.

Since recuperating, Cristiano had built several small pieces of furniture. They were lined up against the side wall, polished to a high sheen, as if awaiting being taken home. He thought his grandfather would be pleased if he could see.

He went to the stack of wood against the opposite wall. He looked at each piece, selecting one of fine cherry wood. The overall dimensions were small, but would suffice for a project. Cristiano wanted to build a table and two chairs for Dante. The baby couldn't use a set for a couple of years, but Cristiano liked the idea of making something fine from Lake Clarissa. Once the boy was older, he'd learn of their visit to the lake. And Mariella could tell him of the fire-fighter who'd made him a table.

He put the piece of wood on the worktable, already envisioning the set. Small enough for a toddler, yet sturdy enough to last for years. Mariella would undoubtedly marry at some point—pretty women didn't stay single for long—and have more children. He hesitated a moment when thinking of her with another man. That idea didn't sit well. Unless he licked this hangover from the bombing, there would be nothing he could do about that.

He picked up a pencil and tape measure and began marking the wood for the first cuts.

When the phone rang half an hour later, Cristiano stared at it, debating whether to answer or not. It was most likely his sister or father. It might be Mariella. Though he had not given her the number, the Bertatalis had it. The ringing continued. Whoever was calling wouldn't give up. What had happened to the answering machine? He remembered—he'd unplugged it when hooking his computer to the Internet for Mariella.

Finally he reached for the phone to stop the sound.

"Ciao?"

"Finally. I was wondering if you'd ever answer," his sister's voice came cross the line. "How are you?"

"Fine." He leaned against the wall, wondering if he'd made a mistake staying away so long. Still, it was good to hear her voice.

"That's all? Fine. When are you coming here?"

"Why do I need to?"

"To see us. To see Papa. Surely you've recovered from your injuries by now."

"I have." At least the external ones. "But I've been busy."

"Come for dinner tonight."

"I told you I'm busy. I can't come for dinner."

"If not tonight, then later in the week?"

"Maybe." Not.

He heard her exaggerated sigh. "Tell me about your new friend, Mariella," she said unexpectedly. "I liked her."

He remembered their kisses. Swallowing, he hoped his voice came out normal. "She's visiting here, that's all."

"Where did you meet her?"

"I rescued her from a fire. She and the baby."

"She said she'd had the sauce at your house when you gave her lunch one day. That was unexpected. I sent another jar home to you with her."

"I know, thanks." The memory of their lunch surfaced. She had loved the sauce. If they shared a meal again, he'd get to see her delight in the flavor.

"Honestly, Cristiano, getting you to talk is like pulling teeth. Tell me something."

He laughed as a warmth of affection for his sister swept through him. He'd forgotten how much Isabella always wanted to know everything. Her curiosity knew no bounds. He missed her. "She came by to say thank you. I fed her lunch. End of story."

"So you're not going to see her again."

"Of course I am." A prick of panic flared at the thought of not seeing her again. One day soon, she'd return to Rome. But until then, he would see her again.

The surprised silence on the other end extended for several seconds. Then Isabella said, "I'm planning a family reunion at the end of the month. Actually, if you can keep it secret, it's a surprise for Papa."

"What kind of surprise? It's not his birthday." Cristiano was glad it was not a surprise party for him. Why did women want to have those?

"Just a surprise. But I don't want him to suspect, so, if

you're well again, I thought we could say it was a celebration of your recovery. That way he will know about it, but not that it's for him."

"I've been fine for a few weeks now."

"Not that any of us knew. I haven't seen you since you got home from hospital. If you're really okay, come by the restaurant one day. Come to dinner."

"I'll let you know."

"Keep the last Saturday free for the party."

Once he hung up, Cristiano almost groaned. Attending a party was the last thing he wanted. Yet how could he continue to deny his family? He missed them. He was fortunate to have a brother and sister, cousins. An aunt he didn't see much of. Still, maybe he could manage one evening.

He resumed his work on the child's table, thinking about the baby, trying to picture him growing up. The countryside was beautiful here. Maybe they could spend holidays in Lake Clarissa. There were endless acres of forest a young boy could safely explore. Water sports in summer on the lake. He worried Dante might dart into traffic in Rome or wander away and get lost and who would know him to help him home? No wonder Mariella worried—there was a lot to worry about when thinking of raising a child. His admiration rose at her willingness to take on that role.

He finished cutting the pieces by late afternoon, telling himself over and over their future had nothing to do with his. Cleaning up, he headed inside. The balmy fall weather couldn't continue forever. He'd eat his dinner on the patio if it wasn't too cold, watching the last of the sunshine as the shadows of night crossed the lake.

And he'd try to keep his mind off Mariella and the baby.

As he cooked dinner he realized it had been days since he'd had a nightmare or flashback. The night of the fire had been bad, but since then—nothing. Maybe he truly was getting better. Too early to know for sure. He'd gone several days between episodes before.

Still, if he continued this way, he'd make it back.

If not, he had a long, lonely life ahead of him.

Conscious of how fast her vacation time was speeding by, Mariella placed Dante in the stroller the next morning, making sure she had bottles and baby cereal, and headed out. The weather was ominous with dark clouds on the horizon and a breeze that was stronger than before. She hoped it wouldn't rain before she got to the cottage. Surely if it began after she arrived, Cristiano would give her a ride back to the village.

She wore her sweatshirt and jeans and wished when the wind blew that she'd bought a coat. But she had winter clothes back in Rome so had not needed to spend the money. She would have to return home sooner if the weather got worse.

Rounding the bend before the cottage, she shivered. It was growing colder by the minute and the dark clouds building on the horizon indicated it would surely storm before long. Maybe she should have stayed at the guest cottage. But her time with Cristiano was precious.

She reached the house and was disappointed not to find Cristiano sitting on the patio. Not that anyone in their right mind would be sitting out on a day like today, she thought. Knocking on the door, she blew on her hands. Unprotected while pushing the stroller, they were freezing. She checked Dante, and he smiled his grin at her. He was bundled up and felt warm against her fingers. Of course, they were so cold, how could she judge?

She knocked again.

There was no reply. Moving to the window, she peered

inside. The living room was empty; no lights were on even though it was growing darker by the moment. A gust of wind swirled a handful of leaves around, dancing near her, then moving off the patio.

Mariella heard a high whine from a power saw. She pushed the stroller around the cottage and heard the sound again, coming from a small shed at the far back of the cleared area. The stroller was hard to push on the uneven ground, but if Cristiano was there, she needed to find him. It looked as if it would pour down rain at any moment.

She found the door opened. Cristiano stood with his back to it, cutting a piece of wood. Pushing the baby inside, she was glad to be out of the wind. It felt much warmer in the shed, though she didn't see any sign of a heating unit.

She did see lovely pieces of furniture on one side. Cristiano cut another piece of wood and the baby shrieked at the sound.

He stopped suddenly and spun around.

"I didn't know you were here," he said with a frown. Reaching back, he turned off the saw. "Did you drive?"

"No, we walked. I think it's going to rain."

"It's supposed to storm." He took off safety glasses and tossed them on the wood. Walking over, he grinned at Dante.

"Hey, little guy. You warm enough?"

"Of course, I wrapped him well. I have a favor to ask." She had thought up the request on her walk up—to give herself a reason and not look so blatantly as if she couldn't stay away.

"What?" he asked warily, looking at her.

"Nothing dangerous, though I thought firefighters risked their lives daily for people. Are you telling me you wouldn't even do a little favor that does not involve risk of life or limb?"

"I'm waiting to hear what it is." He stood back up and crossed his arms across his chest, watching her.

Dante played happily with the plastic keys he was gnawing on. Mariella stepped around the stroller.

"Friday is Ariana's birthday. I wanted to go to the cemetery and put some flowers on her grave. A quick trip to Rome would enable me to get some winter clothes. Signora Bertatali said she'd watch Dante."

The thought of going with her to Rome made the bile rise in his throat. It was too soon. He wasn't ready. He stepped away, looking through the door, seeing the back of the cottage and the trees beyond. He couldn't see the lake from here. A moment went by. He wasn't flashing back to the subway tunnel. He took a deep breath, testing his reactions. Nothing. He could hear the baby with the keys, see Mariella from the corner of his eye. No flashback, no terror residual from the bombing.

He had to return to Rome sometime. What better than a fleeting visit knowing he could return to the cottage within hours? Maybe he worried for nothing. Maybe the worst was past and he could move on.

He could visit Stephano's grave.

Cristiano had not been able to attend Stephano's funeral. He'd been in hospital. Nor had he attended any of the many services for all the victims he had been unable to save. Rome had been in mourning for weeks. He'd escaped the worst of it drugged for pain and undergoing skin grafting for his burned hand.

He'd pictured it a thousand times, though. Stephano's coffin lowered into the ground. His wife weeping. His parents stunned with the loss of their only son. He drew in a breath, trying to capture the scent of sawdust to ground him in the present.

The faint hint of flowers caught his attention. Mariella's

special scent. He closed his eyes. The image of their kiss sprang to the forefront.

He opened his eyes, turned and looked at her, hungering for another kiss. He was lonely. Self-imposed or not, he didn't like staying away from his family or friends. Only the shame of not being able to handle things kept him isolated.

Until now.

She reached out and touched his arm, her touch light as a butterfly, yet as hot as a flame.

"Will you?" she asked.

He stared at her. He was thinking of kissing her, hugging her close to him, losing himself in her soft sweetness. And she was focused on a cemetery visit.

"All right, I'll go with you. For Dante. You can tell him you weren't the only one to mourn his mother's loss." He hoped he didn't have a flashback while standing by the graves.

A loud rumble of thunder startled them, causing Dante to begin to cry. Mariella rushed to him and lifted him from the stroller.

"There, there, little man, it's okay. Just noisy." She looked out the still opened door.

Rain poured down in torrents. The yard was already growing muddy as the rain splattered the dirt. The light was almost gone, making it as dark as twilight.

Cristiano breathed deeply the fresh, clean rain-laden air. The sky was a dark grey from horizon to horizon. The rain beat down ferociously. Mariella and the baby couldn't return to the village in this. In fact, they'd become soaked just running to his car. They were stuck for as long as the rain came so hard.

She came to his side, the baby settled on her hip and looking around. He gave his grin and lunged toward

Cristiano. He reached out instinctively to grab him and then was surprised when Mariella let go and he held the baby dangling in front of him. Bringing him close to his chest, he felt the light weight and looked at the baby. Dante gazed at him with dark brown eyes, as if studying a curious specimen. Then he grinned and bopped his head against Cristiano's cheek.

He was a goner. Who couldn't love a sweet baby like this?

"Rain," he said, pointing to the downpour.

The baby gurgled and patted Cristiano's cheek. He felt a tightening in his chest.

"His entire life is before him. What do you think he'll do when he grows up?" he asked softly as Dante settled against him to watch the rain.

"He can be anything he wants. I want him happy and healthy. And when he's older I'll tell him all I remember of his mother," she said, leaning against his left side. Cristiano put his arm around her shoulder. For long moments the three of them looked at the storm.

"And his father? What will you tell him about that man?" Cristiano asked.

"Ariana said he had vanished from their life. And the affair had been a mistake. But that, I would never tell their son. I'll just have to say he's gone."

"Do you think he's dead?"

"I have no idea. I had hoped I'd find something on this trip. People could have forgotten even if Ariana had been through here. Lots of tourists visit this area."

"Hmm."

"I hope it doesn't rain Friday," she said. "Cemeteries are sad enough without the heavens weeping as well."

"Well said. It rained on the day of Stephano's funeral. I think Heaven was weeping," Cristiano said slowly. He had never thought about it that way. He would have been weeping had he been at the church.

"Stephano was your friend?"

"My best friend."

"I'm sorry he died."

"He was killed in the bombing. We were on our third rescue foray when the second bomb went off. The roof of the tunnel completely collapsed, killing everyone still beneath it."

Cristiano wanted to step out into the rain, feel the cleansing of the water, feel the coolness, see the sky above him, know he was alive. But he held the baby, so remained sheltered in the doorway. The trust from Dante touched him. The baby knew the adults around him would care for him.

She reached around his waist, hugging him. "How horrible."

"The entire event was horrible."

"But you saved seven lives. If not for you, they would have perished in the second bombing."

"It wasn't enough. There were so many still trapped."

"It's amazing, that's what it is. How can you say it wasn't enough? It was more than anyone expected."

"I should have made sure Stephano was right behind me, not lagging behind—that he had not been in the tunnel when it collapsed. We lost seven men from our station." The anguish penetrated to his core. His duty was to save lives. His chosen way was to fight disasters and rescue people. He hadn't even been able to rescue his best friend.

She offered support the only way possible, her body warmth to chase the chill of torment. If only she could truly heal his sorrow. If only anyone could.

CHAPTER SEVEN

UNAWARE of the turmoil, the baby happily babbled, reaching out once or twice as if to touch the rain. The air grew chilled, but Cristiano didn't move. The child was well wrapped. He felt like the only warm spot in the world where he rested against Cristiano's chest. That and where Mariella touched him.

The silence extended. Yet it wasn't awkward. Instead, it was—almost healing. He took a breath, trying to let go the ache that plagued him with all the death and destruction.

"So how long were you and Stephano friends?" she asked.

Cristiano almost smiled. "I remember the first day I met him—it was at the training for firefighting. He came from Genoa, a man loving the sea. I came from here—hills and lakes. He was an only child, had a pretty wife and parents who doted on him. We both passionately loved soccer. We were paired up in training and the rest—"

He hadn't thought about those days in all the months since Stephano had died. Now, telling Mariella, he let the memories wash through him. They'd had fun times. They'd fought fires in Rome. Been sent to man the lines in raging forest fires worldwide. Practiced paramedical routines to save lives. And spent a lot of time together in their off hours.

"He was always up for adventure." Slowly Cristiano began to speak of his friend, remembering aloud the trips to the sea, the ski trip that had ended with both falling face first in the snow, and how quickly they'd progressed from that. The quiet times by a fire, sharing philosophies, plans for the future.

"His wife would probably like to hear from you," Mariella said as Cristiano wound down after telling her many of the shared experiences. "You haven't seen her since?"

He shook his head. "How can I face her when I lived and Stephano didn't?"

"You didn't kill him. The terrorists did. You and she have a shared love of the man—different, of course, but bonding nonetheless. I bet she misses you being around."

"I would remind her of Stephano."

"Maybe she wants to be reminded. Maybe she wants someone around who knew him, faults and all. Who can remember the happy times together. Celebrate his life, not ignore it."

"You don't understand."

She shrugged. The baby was growing more and more squirmy.

"He's probably hungry. I'll take him," she said, reaching for Dante.

He relinquished the child, feeling the cold air hit where the baby had been.

"What are you working on?" she asked, moving back to the workbench and looking at the wooden pieces.

Cristiano turned as well. The emotional toll started to overwhelm him. Needing a diversion, he crossed the small room and picked up one of the pieces that would be a chair leg. "A table and chair set for Dante."

"Wow, you can do that? Did you do all those?" She looked at the pieces lined up against the wall.

"It's been a long summer. I don't just ignore housework," he said, trying to lighten the mood.

"These are beautiful." She stroked a finger across the smooth polished top of a small half pie table. The cabriolet legs were elegant. The rich cherry wood gleamed even in the defused lighting.

"Those legs were hard to do. I ruined more pieces than I wanted." Temper had played a part, but he didn't need to tell her that. Impatient with his recovery, feeling helpless, he'd taken it out on the wood.

"And this, what a beauty this is. Did you make it for someone?" The small console table had classic lines and a band of inlay lighter wood in the perimeter.

"Just made them to kill time while recuperating."

"I'd buy this one if it's for sale," she said hesitantly.

"You can have it. No charge." He wondered where she would put it. Could he visit her one day and see how she was using it? It made him think of a connection between them. For as long as she held onto the table, she'd be holding onto a part of him.

He turned back to the workbench.

"Go on and work if you wish. Looks like we're going to be here a while with the rain. We won't get in your way," she said with a smile. "I can't wait to see what Dante's going to get. He's one lucky boy, isn't he?"

That damned optimism. Cristiano shook his head. How could she think that? The kid had no mother or father. No known relatives. He placed a terrible burden on the young woman now his mother. Yet Mariella seemed sincere in her comment.

Cristiano began working on the leg. At first he was conscious of Mariella watching him. But soon the pleasure he took in working with wood took over.

He was aware when she fed the baby, of the soft lullaby after he ate. Then when she put him down in the stroller for nap. She came back to stand beside him.

"Circle of life sort of thing, isn't it?" she said.

"What is?"

"You fight fire and destruction, and now create things of beauty. A balance. Is that why you do it? To balance out?"

"No. I do it because I like it. My grandfather taught me."

"And your father taught you to cook?"

"A bit. I do like good food prepared well."

"I can boil eggs," she said impishly.

He laughed. He couldn't help it. She'd been to America and back. Was capable of taking on an infant. And couldn't cook worth beans?

"So you and Dante will live happily ever after on boiled eggs."

"I might have to expand my repertoire," she said, wrinkling her nose. "Maybe you can give me some hints." She frowned. "You don't think that will be a problem in the future, do you? I mean, I can learn. And for now he's just beginning to eat baby food, so no worries."

"I'm sure that's not a condition of growing up healthy. Though to enjoy eating, you do need to know more than how to boil eggs." He shook his head. All the members of his family knew how to cook. Well, he wasn't sure about the newly found half-brothers from America. But if they lived alone at any time, they would cook for themselves.

"So tell me what you're doing now," she said, pressing closer. She was a toucher. He hadn't been touched since he left hospital. Until now. Every time Mariella came close, she reached out or bumped against him. He liked the human contact. The thought of pulling her into his arms grew stronger by the second.

He cleared his throat and began to explain, hoping talking would get his mind off what his body was craving—contact up close and personal with Mariella Holmes.

The worst of the storm seemed to be easing. The baby slept in the stroller. And Cristiano showed his work to an interested party. Mariella exclaimed over the craftsmanship and he felt the tightness ease. He might not be a hundred per cent yet, but he still had the ability to build something beautiful.

He glanced at his watch, surprised to see the morning had fled.

"I can give you a ride back. The worst of the rain seems over."

"Beats pushing the stroller. Plus it's decidedly colder after the rain."

Once in the car, Cristiano looked at her. "Since we're going out, what about lunch?" He surprised himself, then knew it was the right thing to do when she gave a happy nod.

"I would love that. I'm hungry. Do we have time to go to Monta Correnti? We could eat at your family's restaurant."

Cristiano hesitated. There was Pietro's in the village. He'd much rather eat there. He hadn't been to Rosa since long before the bomb. He felt a moment of panic. What if he had a flashback in the restaurant? What if he completely lost sight of reality and ended up beneath a table? His family would be horrified.

He knew he had to face his family at some time. The longer he delayed, the more suspicious his absence would become. His sister and father already complained they never saw him.

Yet, he wasn't ready.

Would he ever be?

"Never mind. Forget it. Pietro's is fine. Of course their sauce is not as good," she said.

"Fine, we'll go to Rosa." With any luck, his sister would be too busy to stop to talk to him. Though lunch during the week wasn't normally as crowded as dinners—or weekend crowds. With real luck, he'd act normal for the time it took to order and eat. Then get out of Monta Correnti and back to the safety of the cottage.

He drove through the intermittent rain testing his will power. He tried to gauge his feelings as they approached the town his family lived in. So far so good.

As they reached the outskirts of Monta Correnti she spoke for the first time since leaving the village.

"It's really pretty, even in the rain. I can see why Ariana spoke so fondly of it. And the memories I think were happy even though the end of their affair brought pain."

The closer he drove to the restaurant, the more the tension rose. It would be the first time he'd seen Isabella in months. The sporadic phone conversations didn't count. She would have a hundred questions. He'd be trapped until lunch was over. Had he made a mistake coming here?

They parked the car and walked quickly through the rain. Cristiano held a large umbrella he kept stashed in his car. She carried the baby and they moved in step, close together, to avoid the drizzle. It wasn't too late to turn back, he thought as they approached the door. He didn't know how he'd explain the situation to Mariella if he broke down, but he'd come up with something.

Entering the restaurant, Mariella took a deep breath.

"If we could bottle this aroma and pipe it into other

streets, people would flock here," she said. "It makes my mouth water."

Cristiano took a breath. To him it was home, as familiar as ever. The awkward stress grew until he felt it was almost tangible. He could taste the uncertainty and fear. One of the waiters came over. The two men greeted each other.

"We haven't seen you in a long time," the waiter said.

"It has been a while. Is my sister or father in today?"

"No. They are both at some meeting they had to attend."

"We'll sit in the back, if there's room," Cristiano said, letting the relief wash through him. One worry avoided. Now he just had to remain normal until the meal ended.

"Quiet today. Rain keeping people away, I think," the waiter said, leading them back to one of the small tables near the rear wall.

The wooden paneling gave the restaurant a cozy feel, contributing to quiet enjoyment, mixed with anticipation of the meal to come. When the waiter brought the high chair, Mariella strapped Dante in and handed him his plastic keys.

She opened the menu and scanned the offerings. Everything looked delicious. Choosing only one item wasn't easy.

Once they had ordered she leaned back and looked at Cristiano. "Do you know everyone here?"

Cristiano glanced around and shrugged. "I know most of the wait staff and I bet most of the people in the kitchen. My father has owned this place since before I was born."

"Sorry you're missing him today."

Cristiano pushed a glass toward the right a fraction of an inch. "It's just as well."

"Why?" she prodded.

He glanced up. "No reason."

She narrowed her gaze but didn't push the issue.

Breaking a bread stick, she handed half to Dante and began nibbling on the other half. She studied the decor. "When we ate here before we sat on the terrace. It's lovely. I really liked that. Too bad for the rain."

Just then there was a commotion by the door. Cristiano looked over and frowned.

Mariella turned around to see.

A woman in her early sixties was arguing with one of the waiters. She turned as if in a huff and then spotted Cristiano.

"Oh-oh," he said softly even as he began to rise as she stormed over.

"Cristiano." She reached him and kissed both cheeks. "I thought you were injured and recuperating." She ran her gaze from head to toe. "You seem fine to me. You were always such a good-looking boy."

"Aunt Lisa. I am fine."

"Hmm. So I see. Where is your father? What meeting is he attending?"

"I don't know. I expected him to be here."

She looked at Mariella. "How do you do? I'm Lisa Firenzi, Cristiano's aunt."

"Mariella Holmes."

"Holmes? Are you from around here?"

Mariella shook her head. "Rome originally. Most recently, New York."

"Ah, there they have fine restaurants that are appreciated by everyone." She looked around a bit and shook her head. "Cozy. Who wants cozy? Tell your father I want to talk to him. Or your sister. Perhaps Isabella would be easier."

Cristiano smiled slightly. "I'll make sure they know."

She gave a wave and headed back outside.

"Wow, a whirlwind," Mariella said.

"She actually owns the restaurant next door. Even though she's my father's sister, they have barely spoken to each other in years. I wonder what she wants."

"Maybe she appreciates the family she has. I wish I had family somewhere, besides Dante, of course."

"He's lucky to have you. Many people would not consider the child your responsibility. It's such an awesome one."

"Don't you want children?" she asked. "I mean after you marry and all."

He did not want to go there. On the surface, he looked normal. Only he knew what turmoil lurked inside his mind. He could not subject anyone to that. Fearful of what the flashbacks could lead to, he had to make sure no one came in harm's way. How could he enter any kind of intimate relationship with a woman if he could go off the rails without warning?

In fact, it was a risk to be away from the isolation of the cottage for this long.

Not that he'd had a problem since the night of the fire. Twice he'd thought he was coming close, but one look at Mariella and he'd staved off the threatening flashbacks.

For a moment he hoped he was recovering. Maybe he would be able to go back to work before long. It was still too early to say with complete confidence, but he might touch base with his commander in the next week or so.

"Maybe, if I marry," he replied.

"I'm so surprised you didn't go into this business. A ready-made family affair that you could take over when your father retires," Mariella said a short time later when savoring the first bite of her rigatoni. The sauce had a piquant flavor that she relished.

"It's my sister's thing. My brother and I couldn't wait to leave. It always felt too settled here, I guess you'd say."

"So you two chose the opposite extreme. You with your job, he with his races. Why do you both put your lives on the line like that? At least your actions are for some greater good, but just to challenge the laws of physics and risk death in car races seems a bit reckless."

"Ah, but there is that awesome feeling when he succeeds. Can't be measured."

"Is that how you feel about fighting fires?"

"It is always a challenge. No two fires are exactly the same."

"Scary."

He shrugged. He wouldn't admit it, but he had felt fear a few times. Overcoming it to come out on top was another kind of high. One that he could not achieve with the aftermath of the bombing.

"Enough about me and my family. Tell me about New York."

"It's so vibrant. I worked as an usher at theaters to get in to see the shows for free. Spent many rainy or snowy afternoons roaming the museums. I majored in marketing at university. I was not the only non-American in my classes. There were also students from the UK and Japan."

"You would have more chance of a high-paying job if you didn't have the baby."

"My entire life would be different if I didn't have Dante. I was set to partner with a fellow student in New York in a marketing firm."

"Must have been tough to give that up," Cristiano said.

"The reality turns out to be different from my dreams. I love Dante. I am gaining a bit of confidence. It's not forever. When he's in school, I can try something else, use the education I have. There are a lot of single moms out there. They all manage."

"And single fathers, but it still works better if there are two."

She fell silent. A moment later she looked up.

"I'll see if Signora Bertatali can watch Dante when we take a run up to Rome."

He'd take her to the cemetery, then swing by the station and talk to the commander. Check on his own apartment, which had stood empty these last months. He had held onto it with the intent of returning if he could lick the PTSD. And he'd go to see Stephano's widow.

He'd like to see where Mariella and Dante lived, too. He'd take her there to get her clothes. Then they could have dinner on the way back. For the first time in a long while, he felt the stirring of anticipation.

"We'll leave early."

She grinned at him. "How early is early?"

"Seven?"

"Fine. Are you going by the ministry to talk about the award?" she asked.

He'd forgotten about that. He shook his head. "No."

She narrowed her eyes. "Why not?"

"People died in that bombing. Good people. Men who tried to rescue others. I was luckier than most, I got out alive. But there were many more who didn't."

"You saved seven people. Including two children." She reached out to touch his arm. "It must have been terrifying as well as horrific. So many people lost their lives."

Including Stephano. Cristiano began to feel the stirrings of a panic attack. His vision was growing dark around the edges. His heart began pounding in remembered fear.

Her hand slipped into his and he gripped it, focused on her silvery eyes. And that dusting of freckles across her nose. What would it be like to kiss each and every one? She looked like happiness personified. He knew she'd had some hard knocks herself, but they didn't get her down. For a moment he envied her. He'd give anything to turn the clock back. To be the man he once was.

The moment passed. Another. The restaurant came back into focus—people enjoying the good food, the laughter and conversation conveying their pleasure. He drew a deep breath.

"Did you want dessert?" he asked, withdrawing his hand. Mariella was like a lifeline. Was that the clue? Not lock himself away but be with her all the time?

He'd give almost anything to do just that.

They decided against dessert. Soon they headed back to the car, glad the rain had stopped—if only temporarily. The dark clouds showed the storm had not completely passed.

She remained sitting in the car when Cristiano stopped in front of the Bertatalis' home. Dante was asleep in his car seat, the stroller folded in the trunk.

"It's been a nice day despite the rain. Thank you for lunch," she said.

"My pleasure."

"Your family's restaurant is so nice. I really like it. You're lucky to be a part of that, even if you don't work there."

That might change. If he couldn't return to firefighting, what would he do? Join his sister in the restaurant?

No public job. If he got that bad, he would never be able to be certain he wouldn't have another flashback. He gripped his hands on the steering wheel. Better he'd been killed in the bombing instead of injured. No one would ever have known about the reactions he couldn't control.

He would do his best to make sure no one ever found out.

"Thanks again," she said, opening the door.

"I'll get the stroller." Cristiano got out and retrieved the stroller from the trunk while Mariella took Dante, car seat and all, from the car.

The nightmare woke him again. Cristiano came awake amidst terror. He clenched his hands into fists and fought the tattered memory that wouldn't let go. Flinging off the blanket, he rose and went to the window. Breathing hard, he pushed open the window and drank in the cold night air. Gradually he calmed. He hadn't had a nightmare in days. He'd thought, maybe—was he forever doomed to relive the bombing?

He flung on some clothes and went to the kitchen for some coffee. No going back to sleep after that. He glanced around as he waited for the water to boil, feeling frustrated and angry. Noticing the laptop still on the table, he forced himself to remember Mariella using it. He could picture her blonde hair falling forward when she leaned closer to the screen. Her fingers had flown across the keys. Just thinking about her lowered his anxiety level. He almost smiled, wishing he could see her right now.

Of course starting any relationship with a woman he could scare to death if they slept together and he awoke in the throes of a nightmare would be foolish beyond belief. The kettle whistled and he turned to make the coffee. Still, the thought tantalized. She brought sanity into his life, made him hope for more than he had in a long time. He liked being with her. Wanted to know every speck of information about her life, her hopes, her dreams, now that she had a child to raise.

He wanted her in his life. Dared he risk such a chance?

Once he filled his cup, he prowled around the cottage. He considered going to the workshop and continuing with his project, but felt too edgy. Draining the cup, he grabbed the keys to the motorcycle. He'd ride through the remainder of the night and hope to find peace come dawn.

The roads were lonely, scarcely used even in the summer. No traffic. Few residences scattered miles apart. The world seemed different at night. No people. No animals he could see. Just the strip of asphalt illuminated by the headlight, the rest shadows whipping by, undefined vague splotches of black melding together as he increased the speed of the bike.

He made the circuit he'd completed many times before. Slowing as he approached the village, he looked toward the Bertatalis' cottages. The last time he'd done that one had been on fire. No sign of flames tonight. But the cottage Mariella was staying in was lit up; light spilled from every window.

He turned into the lane that led to the cottages. Stopping by hers, he considered his next step. Knock on the door to see if all was well? Would that scare her? A knock in the middle of the night? What if she'd merely fallen asleep with the lights on?

He glanced toward the east. A slight lightening of the darkness. Dawn was not that far away.

He heard the baby cry.

Quickly he went to the door and knocked.

A tearful Mariella and wailing baby opened the door.

"Cristiano, what are you doing here?"

"What's wrong?" he asked, stepping inside.

"He's been crying most of the night. I can't get him to stop. I've checked everything, given him warm milk, but he doesn't even want the bottle. I don't know what to do." With that she burst into tears.

"Here, give me the baby," he said, preferring dealing with a crying child than a woman's tears.

She complied and then wiped her cheeks. "I'll be right back." She fled.

The baby continued to cry and Cristiano juggled him, remembering another baby who had cried. The smoke and cement particles floating in the thick air had only exacerbated his distress. He would never take fresh air for granted again.

He bounced the baby gently. Watching Dante, he took a breath, testing the limits. Nothing but a warm cottage and a crying baby.

"Hey, little man, none of that. You've kept your mamma up all night by the looks of it," he said easily.

The baby scrunched up his face and looked ready to let fly again.

"Now, now, what's wrong?"

Cristiano rested him against his chest, upright so his head was by his own. Slowly he rubbed the baby's head with his cheek.

Dante hiccuped and then stopped crying, swaying back enough to look at Cristiano. His face was wet with tears, his eyes red. But he looked at Cristiano as if examining a wondrous thing.

"That's better. Give your mother a break. People normally sleep at night."

Mariella entered, having washed her face and pulled on a sweatshirt over her nightgown.

"What are you doing up so late at night? People normally sleep. And how did you get him to stop? He's been crying since before midnight!" Mariella peered at the baby. He still looked as if he'd start crying any second, but so far he was distracted by Cristiano.

"I woke early, took a ride."

"It's freezing outside."

He shrugged. Nothing colder than the way he felt after the nightmares.

"Well, I'm glad you did. Do you think he'll feel like going to sleep?" she asked hopefully, worried eyes studying the baby.

"I don't know, but you look like you could keel over without a problem."

She nodded and brushed her hand lightly over Dante's head. "I am *so* tired. But if he can't sleep, neither can I. I think he's teething. It's what the baby books say for this age. He won't eat, won't sleep, I don't know what else to do."

"Take a nap. I'll watch this little guy."

She looked at him.

The hope brimming in her eyes made Cristiano laugh. "Really?" she said.

He nodded.

She reached up and pulled his head down for a fleeting kiss. "Thanks. I'm so tired I can hardly stand on my feet. Call me if you need anything." With that she turned and went to the bedroom.

Cristiano watched, feeling the soft press of her lips against his. The lurch in his heart had surprised him. Without wanting it, without knowing it, Mariella had captured his heart. He'd give anything to have her kiss him every day. To share the tasks of caring for the baby, of seeing her sleepy and ready for bed. Desire shot through him and he shook his head. He had a cranky baby in his arms, she was dead tired, and all he could think about was her in that bed, alone. How her blonde hair would be spread across the pillow, soft and silky. Her skin would be warm and smooth.

He turned away from the door and his thoughts and he looked at Dante.

"Your mother weaves a spell on men, watch out," he said.

The baby looked as if he was dazed, his head weaving back and forth.

"Okay, let's get comfortable."

He put Dante down on the sofa to shrug out of his jacket. He hadn't even dropped it on the chair before the baby started crying again.

"Hey, none of that. Your mom needs sleep." Cristiano scooped him up and walked him around the small living room. The child was light and warm. Cuddling him gave Cristiano a sense of peace he hadn't had in a long time. He remembered the infant he'd saved. How was he doing these days? Would he ever have even the faintest remembrance of that awful day? He hoped Dante never had anything more difficult to face than teething.

A few minutes later Dante's head fell against his shoulder. Looking at him, Cristiano realized the baby had finally fallen asleep.

He sat on the sofa, careful not to disturb the sleeping child. Rubbing his back slowly, he let the peace of the cottage take hold. If he could bottle this and take it with him, any time a flashback threatened he'd be instantly cured.

Slowly dawn arrived. The baby slept; Cristiano relished the feel of him in his arms. But his thoughts winged to Mariella. He knew she was sleeping, but he wished she'd wake up and come talk with him. They could discuss options to make Dante's teething easier on all concerned. He wish he knew what the future held.

Even more than that, he wished he'd kissed her back when she'd kissed him.

The sun was well up when Mariella came back into the living room. She'd had several hours of much-needed sleep. Stopping in the doorway, she smiled at the sight. Cristiano was sprawled on the sofa, holding Dante. Both were fast asleep. Even in sleep, his arms cradled her son, keeping him safe.

She stared a long time, longings and wishes surging forward. He was a marvelous man. Strong, sincere and capable. Plus sexy to boot. The beginning beard gave him a rakish look. The muscular chest made the baby seem all the smaller—yet well protected and loved.

She went into the adjacent kitchen and quietly prepared coffee. While it brewed, she looked into the refrigerator for breakfast. She'd feed her savior of last night and send him on his way. She didn't want to impose on his time. He'd already helped more than she should have any reason to expect.

Hopefully Dante would sleep most of the day and she could get another nap.

She heard the baby fussing before she finished boiling the eggs she planned for breakfast. She knew she was no cook, but they could have eggs and toast. And coffee. She excelled in coffee.

"Something smells good," Cristiano said when he walked into the kitchen carrying Dante.

"Coffee. And I boiled us each an egg."

He laughed and, as naturally as if they did it all the time, he stepped closer, leaned in and kissed her sweetly on the mouth. Mariella savored the touch, too quickly ended.

"I like boiled eggs," he said a moment later.

Flustered Mariella could only stammer, "And toast. I can do toast."

"A feast indeed."

"Thank you for letting me sleep," she said, stepping away, feeling overwhelmed with the sensations spinning out of control. She wanted to put Dante in his crib and grab Cristiano with both hands. But she had responsibilities.

"Let me take him and feed him," she said.

"I can hold him while you get things ready. But I would take a cup of coffee."

"Done."

They worked together as if they'd done so before. Soon Dante was nursing on his bottle, but still fussy. Mariella encouraged him to eat, conscious of Cristiano only a few feet away. She wished she'd taken more care in dressing, had put on some makeup.

"I wish he could tell me for sure if he's teething. Babies start getting teeth at six months and he's almost that old already," she said as she teased his lips with the nipple. Dante chewed on it for a moment, then sucked some more, then looked as if he would cry.

"Ask Signora Bertatali what she did for her children— she had three," Cristiano suggested.

"Good idea."

When Dante fell asleep, Mariella smiled and kissed him gently. "Let's hope he stays asleep at least long enough for us to eat," she whispered, rising. "I'll put him in the crib."

Cristiano had started the toast when she returned. She quickly put the eggs into cups and set the table she used for dining.

"Best boiled eggs I ever had," Cristiano said.

She laughed. "Sorry, I'm just not a cook. I ate out mostly in New York—everyone seems to, or order in. My mother cooked at home, but I never wanted much to learn. I bet you're a great cook."

"Could be said by some. Not my father, but those not in the restaurant business think I can make some fine dishes," he agreed. Gazing into her eyes, he smiled.

Mariella felt her heart turn over, then begin to race.

"I could cook dinner for us tonight if you like," he said softly.

"I'd love that," she replied, still caught in the gaze of his dark eyes.

They finished breakfast and, by the time Dante woke again, white fluffy clouds dotted the sky. The chance of rain remained high, but for the short term it looked pleasant outside. Mariella fed and bathed Dante while Cristiano sat nearby to watch. They spoke of myriad things, from her favorite restaurants in New York, to his vacations skiing in the Swiss Alps.

"Come back to my place," he said when the baby was dressed for the day and had smeared oatmeal cereal everywhere.

Mariella merely laughed as she cleaned him up again, looking over at Cristiano. "To do what?"

"You can help me make the table and chairs."

"I know nothing about making furniture."

"Sanding doesn't take a lot of previous experience. Come on, it'll get you out of the house. But I can't bring you two on my motorcycle. You'd have to drive yourself."

"Or we can walk there. Dante loves the stroller."

"So I'll see you soon."

She smiled and nodded, glancing out the window again. "We'll be there soon. But if it looks like rain, we'll have to scoot for home. Maybe I can use your computer again. I want to check the status of the one I ordered. If it's already shipped it might be in Rome when we go up."

Cristiano waited until she had Dante bundled up and in the stroller. He took off on the motorcycle while she began to push the stroller up to the cottage. It was noticeably cooler than it had been. Tomorrow they'd zip into Rome. She'd do what she needed and he'd do what he needed and then she'd return to the lake to finish her vacation. She looked forward to spending the day with him without the baby. With just the two of them, and a carefree day, who knew what might happen?

When she reached the cottage, Dante was asleep. Poor thing, he was probably exhausted from being up all night. She went straight to the workshop in back. As she walked closer she could hear the raspy sound of sandpaper against wood. He had already started.

Parking the carriage just inside the doorway, she stepped further into the workshop. Better for Dante to be near the fresh air than one laden with sawdust. If it began to rain, he would be sheltered and she could get to him quickly.

Cristiano glanced up.

Taking a breath, she relished the scent of furniture oil and fresh-cut wood. "I love the way it smells in here."

"Me, too. Are we set for tomorrow?"

"I checked with Signora Bertatali and she said she'd be delighted to watch Dante. I'm looking forward to our drive. She also said it did sound like Dante is teething. She said to give him something cold to chew on, like a cold damp rag or a rubber toy that's been in the freezer."

He nodded, beckoning her over to watch as he continued with the sanding. She stepped closer and peered at the smooth piece that would become a leg.

Reaching out a finger, she rubbed it in the direction of the grain. "It feels like velvet," she murmured. She looked up. Her face was mere inches from Cristiano's. She could breathe the scent of his aftershave lotion. See the crinkles near his eyes from squinting in the sunshine. Feel the heat radiating from his body. Mesmerized, she gazed into his dark eyes, seeing tiny specks of gold near the irises. For an endless moment time seemed suspended.

A moment later Cristiano leaned forward the scant inches that separated them and kissed her. Mariella closed her eyes, relishing the warmth of his mouth on hers, the excitement that rocketed around within her. The way time felt suspended and only the two of them existed. This kiss was perfect: no pulling away, no fretful baby making noise in the background. Just a man and a woman sharing a special moment.

He pulled back, gazing into her eyes for a long moment, then took a breath and looked around—almost as if he weren't sure where he was.

She smiled and reached out to touch the wood again. Maybe she wasn't the only one knocked off her equilibrium by that kiss. She felt almost giddy with delight. The day seemed brighter than before. The colors more vibrant everywhere she looked. Cristiano seemed happier than she'd ever seen him. She loved watching him.

"Then we're set, we leave early in the morning," he said with a smile, his dark eyes gazing directly into hers.

CHAPTER EIGHT

CRISTIANO picked up some sandpaper and handed it to Mariella. "Rub it along the length of the leg. We want it totally smooth. No splinters for the little fella." His fingers deliberately brushed against hers in handing her the sandpaper. She smiled and nodded, feeling that tingling awareness that sparked whenever Cristiano was around.

Mariella had never done home projects so she was thrilled to be able to assist. She perched on the stool he had vacated and began rubbing the way he showed her. There was something soothing about the long, slow strokes. She couldn't wait to see the finished table and chairs. She'd never helped to build anything before. Glancing around, taking in everything, she would always remember the quiet time spent in this workshop.

Cristiano was focused on the piece he worked. The quiet was complete except for the sound of sandpaper and the rustling of the wind outside the door. She looked outside. It was growing overcast. She rose and checked the baby. He was fast asleep. Touching him, she knew he was warm beneath the fleecy blanket. She looked around. The beauty of autumn in the hills was evident everywhere she looked. Golden leaves, red leaves, and the occasional brown leaf looked a bit dull in the flat light beneath the clouds. She had seen them with the sun shining on them and they'd made her breathless.

Could she be happy in such a quiet setting?

"What do you do all day?" she asked, returning to the worktable.

"What do you mean?"

"It's quiet. Not many shops in the village, no nightlife to speak of. Do you listen to music or watch television?"

He shrugged. "No television broadcast service up here. Sometimes I listen to the news on the radio. I like the silence."

"Your family lives close enough though. How frequently do you visit them?"

"Not often. They have their lives, I have mine—"

"If I had a family who owned a restaurant, I'd eat there at least once a week. The pasta is so delicious and that sauce. Maybe you get tired of it if that's what you've known your whole life."

"I don't get tired of eating there. It's complicated."

"When do you go back to work?"

"Soon."

Dante began to fuss. Mariella dropped the chair leg she was sanding and went to pick up the baby. He rubbed his face and began to cry. She cuddled him close and walked around, rocking him gently.

"Does he need a bottle?" Cristiano asked, coming over.

"I don't know. He should be sleeping longer than this. If you could prepare a bottle, I'll try that. Maybe he's hungry because of being up so late last night."

Cristiano pushed the empty stroller to the kitchen. In only a moment, following Mariella's instructions, he had the bottle warmed for the baby.

Dante did not want the bottle. Taking the nipple, he

sucked for a moment then let out a wail. He pushed the bottle away and cried.

"Oh, honey, don't fret." Mariella held him up against her shoulder, walking around the stone floor. "Do you think it's more than teething?"

"I think your guess about teething is still likely. I remember Stephano's baby when he was teething. You could check with Signora Bertatali again, if you want. After that, if you aren't convinced, we can try the doctor."

She used his phone and checked with the woman again. When she hung up the phone Mariella looked at him. "She said it still sounds like teething. Give him something to chew on—soft so he won't hurt himself, but firm so he can feel it when he bites down. She said the process could go on for weeks or months."

"Oh, great. Do you have a rubber toy we could put in the refrigerator until it gets cold and let him chew on?"

She shook her head, jiggling him as Dante rubbed his face and cried.

"Maybe a cold washcloth?" she asked.

"That I have. I'll be right back."

In less then five minutes, Cristiano had a cold damp washcloth—soaked in ice water for a moment, then wrung out.

When he offered it to Dante the little boy stopped crying long enough to look at Cristiano. He lunged for him.

"Whoa." Surprised, he took the baby. Holding him in one arm, he offered the cloth again, wrapped around his finger. When Dante clamped down on it he smiled.

"He's got some bite. He keeps biting and releasing."

"At least he's stopped crying. Poor baby." Mariella brushed his downy hair. "This goes on for months? I'll never sleep."

"This might calm him down."

But as the afternoon wore on it was obvious to both adults the child had staying power. He chewed on the washcloth, then cried. They'd swap it out for another cold one, and he'd be content for a little while. Cristiano insisted on taking turns with Mariella as they walked the baby, trying to get him comfortable.

Dante drank a bottle, alternating between chewing on the nipple, crying and sucking. Finally, late in the afternoon he fell asleep.

Mariella held him close. "I think we should go home now," she whispered.

"I don't think the sound of our voices will wake him, he's out," Cristiano said. Hearing a noise, he looked at the windows. "It's raining again. Pouring more like. You don't want to take him out in this. Stay."

She looked at the rain. "So you're stuck with us."

He brushed his fingertips down her cheek. "No problem. The worst is behind us. I'll dash out and make sure the workshop is closed up. We can start dinner, eat a bit early and, when the rain stops, I'll drive you back to the cottage."

She nodded. "If this keeps up, I can't go to Rome tomorrow. I can't leave him when he's not one hundred per cent all right. I wanted to visit Ariana's grave on her birthday, but she'd understand I couldn't leave her son."

"Rome will be there whenever we go, no problem. Truth be told, I'm not sure I'm ready."

"Ready for what? Driving to Rome? Does your ankle hurt?"

"No, not that. I'm not sure I'm ready to face Stephano's wife. He had so much to live for. Why was he killed and not me?"

"We don't know why things happen. I'm sure every

family who was affected by that bombing questions why it happened."

"He saved several people before he was caught in the second blast."

"So he's a hero, too."

"Small help to his family now."

"There is comfort in knowing that, Cristiano," she said gently, reaching out to touch his arm. "I can only imagine how devastated his wife must feel, but she and her children can be proud of what he was doing when he was killed. And I know she would love to see you. I love visiting with friends of Ariana's who were close to her those last months when I was still in New York. Talking about her, remembering her hurts—but it also heals. She didn't have such a great life but she loved life. She was optimistic almost to the end."

"At least you had time to prepare."

"One is never prepared. Go to your friend's wife, talk to her of Stephano. You two probably knew him best in the world. She would want that contact."

He looked away, searched the ceiling, wondered how to truly convey the fear that flooded. "It's not that easy."

"No one said it was easy. It's just important."

"He was a good friend."

"So was Ariana. I think special friends are rare. I wonder if I'll ever have another that I feel as close to as I did with her."

He thought about it for a moment. "Probably not. Another friend that's close, I expect, but not as close. Stephano and I shared a strong bond from the training and the fires we fought together. We took holidays together. He and AnnaMaria always included me in family events."

"She must be hurt you haven't contacted her," Mariella said.

"I thought she wouldn't want to be reminded—"

"She'll need you for the memories you share. You can tell Stephano's children about their father. That'll be special for them."

Cristiano hadn't considered that. He missed his friend, but the best way to honor his memory was to make sure he was never forgotten. He hadn't given his friend's wife the attention she deserved. She would have been even more devastated to lose her husband than he had been to lose a friend. How could he have ignored her pain while dealing with his own?

"Cristiano?"

He looked at Mariella. "What?"

"You looked like you were in a trance."

"Just thinking about Stephano's family. I do need to see them."

"Yes. And your own."

"Why do you say that?"

"You're so lucky to have a big family to rally around when things are tough. They are there for you. I think the bombing must have been very hard on them. You need your family. You need people who know you, who love you, to support you no matter what. They are your support group that will never fail."

"Did you know I found out a few months ago that my father had a wife and two sons before he even met my mother? Yet he never told any of his second family about them. So maybe our family isn't as close as I once thought."

Mariella looked astonished. "You're kidding. What happened?"

"I don't know all the details, it all came out when my father and aunt were arguing. Isabella said the first sons live in America, but they have visited the family here, however I've never met them."

"How odd,' Mariella murmured. "How do you feel about that? I can't imagine learning I had siblings at this age. Is that why you aren't spending time with your family while you recover?"

He hesitated, the urge to explain growing stronger by the second. Yet he couldn't bear to see the disappointment in her expression when she realized he couldn't control his own mind. "It's complicated," he repeated.

"How?"

"For one thing, I can't believe my father never told us we had older siblings. Strangers who share our blood. Apparently he lost touch with them. Isabella didn't give a lot of details."

"So you have even more family than you thought. That's so cool."

He looked at her. "You have a most annoying habit of seeing everything through rose-colored glasses. What about my father's lack of trust in this family, his keeping them secret? His ignoring them for many, many years?"

"Maybe you should ask him why," she suggested. "I'd give anything to belong to a large family, to have people who loved me around to help when I need it. Or just to share good times with. What's wrong with being happy about things? Are you a pessimist?"

"No. A realist. Bad things happen to people. Things that can't ever change. Life is not all sunshine."

"True. But for the most part, it's an exciting adventure. There will be tough times, but happy times, as well. We need to search for the happy. Hold onto it as long as we can to balance the other times."

"Are you happy? You lost your friend, your parents, you're saddled with an infant, working at a job that's not what you planned for. No prospects for change in the near future that I can see."

She nodded and smiled at him. "Today I am happy. The baby is sleeping, you are cooking dinner for me, and I'm healthy. Just because I'm not doing what I thought I would be doing career wise right now doesn't mean I won't at some point in life. I've come to realize these last few days that I could never give Dante up. I will still look for his father so he'll know about him, but I don't know if I'll approach him. I need to make sure Dante stays with me. He's so precious."

"Don't you want to get married, have your own family?"

"Dante is my family. And, yes, I'd like to get married some day. But if that's not in the cards, I'm not going to pine away. Do you want to get married?"

He shrugged. "I'll let my brother and sister take care of future generations."

She laughed. "There's more to marriage than having children. I see it as a partnership of two people sharing their lives together. My parents had a great marriage. In a way, much as I wish things had been different, I'm glad they died together. I think either would have been lost without the other. That's the kind of marriage I want if I ever find the right man."

"Wonder if that's what my father thought he was getting—each time. The first wife left him. My mother died young. He's been a single dad most of his life."

"And, what, five kids? That's got to be sort of nice."

Dante fussed again and she went to quiet him down before he could fully wake up. Cristiano continued preparing the meal while the rain ran down the windows. Had his dad regretted the past? Wished he were closer to the grown sons he had in America. Cristiano had never doubted his father's love. But it seemed as if his entire world had gone topsy-turvy and he didn't like it.

"This is a nice place," she said when she had wheeled the stroller into the darkened living room. "Tell me some more about being a kid at the lake."

The rest of the afternoon passed with both sharing memories of happier times when they'd been younger.

Dinner was delicious.

"If you ever decide to give up firefighting, you could get a job cooking anywhere," Mariella commented as she complimented him on the pasta dish.

He looked at her sharply. "Why would I give up firefighting?"

"I don't know. It's not exactly the kind of job you do in your eighties, is it?" She licked her lips.

"No, it's not a job for an old man. But I've years ahead of me before I'm eighty."

She nodded, laughing softly. "I'll say."

Almost as if he knew dinner was finished, Dante began to cry again. He was not easily placated. They tried the cold washcloth for him to chew on. Tried rubbing his gums with their fingers, wincing when he bit hard. But nothing seemed to work.

Mariella fed him again, a hit or miss with him spitting out the nipple more than he drank from it. "I should be going," she said at one point.

"Stay a bit longer. No need for you to have to handle this alone. I can help."

"If this is like last night, you wouldn't get any sleep."

"We'll trade off. If he screams all night long, I'll take him for a while so you can sleep. I don't need much sleep."

"Thanks, but he's my problem."

"Actually, he's your son, not a problem. This situation can be shared. Let me help, Mariella."

She swayed from side to side trying to soothe the baby. "You don't know what you're in for."

"I do. I saw him last night. And today. We'll be fine. Let's try another cold washcloth."

As they took turns holding the baby and walking the floor with him, the hours slowly passed. A little after midnight Mariella gave into Cristiano's suggestion she go lie down in one of the bedrooms and sleep for a little while.

"What about you?"

"I'll be fine. I'll wake you when I need to go to sleep, unless this little guy finally gives in."

She nodded and closed her eyes for a moment. "I'm dead on my feet," she said. "Thanks, Cristiano. Which room?"

"None of the beds are made but mine. But there are fresh sheets and blankets in the closet along the hall."

"I'll make do."

It was almost three when Dante finally nodded off, tears still on his sweet face. Cristiano continued holding him in the large chair they'd been in for the last couple of hours. The child was in such discomfort nothing seemed to work. Now he would escape that by sleep. Cristiano envied him. He'd love to sleep and escape everything. But he never knew if the nightmares would rage or if the night would be restful.

The rain continued. The sound on the roof reminded him of days in the past when he and his brother and sister had to stay inside because of rain and how they'd railed against the weather.

He missed seeing them. Missed being a part of their lives. Valentino had married! He was trying to adapt to knowing his younger brother was married. And his sister, too! Mariella was right, he had a close family who would rally to his aid, if there were anything they could do.

Time and again he returned to wondering about the newly learned-of brothers. Dante lay across his chest. Cristiano brought up the baby blanket to cover him. He'd leave him right where he was for a while. He knew his father must have held those early babies—twins. Had his father planned a future for his sons? How devastated he must have felt when the boys had to go to America.

Had their mother had family to help out? Or had she been a single mother like Mariella? He'd want to share in all his child's growing—seeing him learn to walk, hear the cute sayings he'd come up with, watch as the amazement of learning blossomed on his face. If he ever married, ever had a child.

"What of you, little man? What will you become? Anything you want. A doctor? Maybe an artist.' He felt a pang when he thought of not seeing the baby again after Mariella left.

What of when Mariella left? He hadn't known her for long, but the feelings that had exploded had nothing to do with length of time knowing her. If things had been different, he'd make sure she didn't disappear back in Rome. He'd court her the old-fashioned way—flowers, dancing, long walks where they could talk about their hopes and dreams and fall in love.

Unfortunately, his future was on hold. Maybe gone.

He reached out and turned the lamp to the lowest setting, dimming the light. He'd see if he could doze a bit while Dante slept. Who knew how long he had?

Mariella woke in daylight. For a moment she wasn't sure where she was, then she remembered. Jumping out from beneath the duvet she'd drawn over herself last night, she hurried out to the living room. The house was silent. Where were Cristiano and Dante?

She stopped at the doorway. One lamp was on, giving little illumination. Cristiano was stretched out on the comfortable chair, his long legs straight out, his head resting on the back. Cradled against his chest, the baby was sound asleep, covered by one of his little blankets. Just like yesterday. She could get used to this.

For a long moment Mariella stared, imprinting the image on her mind for all time. She let herself dream for an instant that this was a usual occurrence. She'd be asleep and then awake to find Cristiano with the baby. She'd waken them and they'd spend their days together. And their nights. Dante would not always need extra care. He was good about sleeping through the nights normally.

She went into the kitchen to clean up from dinner and get something started for breakfast. If only coffee.

Then she needed to make plans to return home. Not for a brief trip, but back to their normal lives. She was falling in love with her firefighter and he was not falling for her. She blinked back tears, feeling the pain of disappointment deep inside. She wished he would, but there was an intangible barrier. Every time she thought they were drawing closer, he'd pull back.

What she felt for him went far deeper than any emotions she'd had before. From time to time growing up, she'd thought she was in love. A boy in high school. A young man in New York. But soon the feelings had faded. Knowing Cristiano showed her how pale the emotions before were compared to her feelings for him now. He was strong, generous, helpful. He saved people's lives. He was a hero several times over. And he made her feel so very special.

Which reminded her of the medal ceremony. He should attend. If not for himself, then for the others he spoke about who were heroes but couldn't be there. She wanted the world to know what a true hero he was.

She wondered how she could convince him to attend. Could his family help? She wasn't even sure they knew. To come right out and tell them seemed a breach of confidence, though Cristiano had never told her not to tell anyone.

She still had the letter. From what she'd read, the award was being made—whether Cristiano accepted it in person or not.

The cottage was quiet. Cristiano's computer sat on the table from before. Mariella turned on the computer, surrounded by the warmth of the cottage kitchen, redolent with the fragrance of coffee brewing. She checked messages, contacted her clients to let them know she was on top of things. Then she looked up the award ceremony. There was quite a bit of press about the event, honoring those who had responded to the bombing, both living and dead.

It would be held at the Parlamento addressing both the Senato della Repubblica and the Camera dei Deputati. The Prime Minister himself was presenting the awards.

The ceremony was given by a still-grieving nation doing what it could to honor those who had first responded at great personal risk and sacrifice.

The rain finally ended. She closed the laptop and rose to go to the doorway, opening it a crack and breathing in the fresh air, cool and damp. It raised her spirits. She had been on a fool's errand, trying to locate a man who had never wanted to know he had a son. If he'd left Ariana, she should have taken that as a sign. Longing for family of her own should not have had her going against her friend's wishes, however much Mariella wanted Dante to have an extended family. Her limited attempts to locate anyone who had known Ariana in this area had proved totally futile. Another sign?

She did not regret coming, however. If she hadn't, she never would have met Cristiano.

"Be happy, my love, whatever the future brings you," she whispered to the wind, wishing she dared whisper it to him face to face.

Time to go home.

CHAPTER NINE

THE phone rang.

"Get that, would you?" Cristiano called from the living room. Mariella hurried to the counter and picked it up.

The woman on the other end was obviously surprised when Mariella answered.

"Who is this?"

"Mariella Holmes." She recognized Cristiano's sister instantly.

"Where is Cristiano?" Isabella asked as soon as Mariella identified herself.

She explained how he was watching the fussy baby. "Hang on, I'll get him for you."

"A moment, please, Mariella. Do you know about the awards ceremony for those who rescued people in the bombing last May?" Isabella asked.

"Yes, I was just reading about it on the Internet, actually."

"You know Cristiano is getting a medal, don't you? Is he still refusing to attend?"

"I believe so." She was hesitant to confirm or deny anything. "You need to talk to him." Mariella hurried into the living room and held out the phone.

"It is your sister." She gently picked up the sleeping

baby and rocked him a bit, walking out of the room. But she could still hear Cristiano's side of the conversation.

He was arguing with his sister.

She knew he felt he'd done nothing extraordinary—it was his job to respond to any emergency. He should have done more at the bombing site. He focused on those who hadn't made it, not the ones he'd saved. Somehow he had to see he'd done more than most and merely because he lived didn't mean he hadn't been willing to give all. He hadn't needed to this time.

She heard an expletive, then silence. She stood by the back door, swaying with the baby. Was Cristiano angry with his sister? More likely just angry—at fate, at the way things had turned out.

She didn't know how long she stood there, but when she heard the car in the driveway a short time later she knew it had been long enough for Isabella to drive from Monta Correnti. Mariella watched as Isabella got out and walked quickly to the house. Her long wavy black hair blew in the wind. Her blue eyes looked stormy.

"Hello," Isabella said when she stepped inside.

"Cristiano is in the living room," Mariella said, wondering if she should leave or stay. "Do you want coffee?" She could put the baby in the stroller and prepare coffee—it would give her something to do.

"Yes, please." Isabella took off her jacket and draped it over the back of a chair, then headed to the living room.

Mariella was soon scooping coffee grounds and listening to the raised voices arguing in the living room. It wasn't anything she had not already heard. Cristiano did not want to accept a medal. He didn't feel he'd done anything special. He kept going on about those who had died.

Finally there was silence. Mariella checked the brewing

coffee and then stepped to the doorway. Brother and sister glared at each other.

"I think, Cristiano," Mariella said softly, "that this is something you have to do."

He began to protest, but she raised her hand. "I'm not finished. I've been thinking about it, and reading about it. It's a way for our country to honor those who went to help. What else can we do? We were not there with you. We did not die like your friends and comrades. We did not see the horror. What we did see was the bravery of the first responders who plunged into the inferno without knowing what they would find, or if they'd make it back out. You did—time and again and you saved seven lives to prove it."

"Stephano—" he began, but she raised her hand again and frowned at him.

"Listen to me! You must accept because of Stephano. He is not there to be awarded. Go and represent him and all those men and women you knew who died. Let our country honor your bravery, your courage and the unselfishness you demonstrated by risking your life to save strangers. Our country needs this, Cristiano. No matter what you think, the rest of us know you are a hero and we want to express our appreciation in a way the entire world will understand."

The anguish in his eyes was beyond her understanding. But she was steadfast in facing him. He needed to do this for himself and for those who had died. The tension stretched. Finally he gave an abrupt nod and turned to stride out the front door. "I'll think about it," was all he said.

"Whew," Isabella said, watching him leave. "Thank you, Mariella. You put it eloquently."

"It's only true. He carries this feeling he failed because his friends died, but he didn't. And I know every single one of the seven he saved will bless him all their days."

They returned to the kitchen to pour the coffee. Sitting at the table, Isabella looked at her for a moment, then said,

"His accepting the medal is an even better excuse to have the party. Dad will never suspect anything else."

"Like what?" Mariella asked, confused.

"What I'm telling you is in confidence. You can't tell anyone," Isabella said, leaning closer, dropping her voice slightly.

Mariella blinked. "Okay."

"My father and my aunt each own a restaurant in Monta Correnti. Many years ago, before I was born even, they were joint owners of Sorella. Then they had a major falling out. Dad left the restaurant to Lisa and started Rosa."

Mariella nodded. Where was this going?

"Economic times have been tough lately, people aren't eating out as much. Both restaurants have taken a hit, especially Rosa. For a while there we thought we'd have to close. One way to carry on is to merge the two and find economy of scale to have them both operated as one. They'd still keep their different menus, but economies can be achieved which would go a long way to turning things around. The restaurants would complement each other and continue to thrive."

"So is merging a problem? Are your aunt and father still feuding?"

"Actually, Dad turned the day-to-day operation of the restaurant over to us—Scarlett and me. I've been talking with my aunt and we've decided this is the best way to handle things. We wanted to surprise my father with this merger. I want a fait accompli. He loves the restaurant. I expect he'll go along with anything that keeps it open— even joining forces with his sister. Plus, there's another situation."

Mariella asked, "What is that?"

"Did Cristiano tell you about our American brothers?"

Mariella nodded slowly.

"I want a way to bring the entire family together—a reunion, if you would. So this is perfect. Everyone loves Cristiano. We've been worried about him these months. To celebrate this honor for him would raise no suspicions. I'll have Alex and Angelo visit from America and I'll make sure Aunt Lisa and her family are present. Then we can mingle, celebrate and announce the plans for the merger. It's perfect!".

"What's perfect?" Cristiano stood in the doorway.

"The excuse for the party I told you about. We'll change it to celebrating the medal."

Cristiano frowned. Isabella ignored him.

"Dad will be so proud of you. We'll have the celebration at the restaurant, of course. Everyone will come." She glanced at her watch. "I've got to go. I'll call you with details." Isabella glanced at Mariella, giving her a wink. "Bring Mariella as well."

When Isabella left, Cristiano sat at the table, looking drained.

"Are you all right?" Mariella asked. "Want some coffee? It's fresh."

He nodded. When he took the cup, he spoke, "There's things you don't know anything about. Other reasons I don't want to accept the medal."

She reached out and took his hand, feeling warmed when he turned to clasp hers. He studied their linked hands for a long moment, then raised his gaze to hers.

"Will you come with me?" he said.

"I can't go." She was stunned. "Someone close to you should go—Isabella or your father."

"You or I don't go at all."

She blinked. "Why me?"

"Because if you're ganging up with Isabella in pressuring me to go, I want you there. I'm sure families are allowed. I'll find out. Otherwise, the deal is off. I don't go."

"Okay, then. I'll go." She would be thrilled to be in the audience when he accepted the medal.

Dante woke and grew fussy. Mariella prepared him a bottle and then had the difficult task of getting him to eat when he was so miserable.

"Can I help?" Cristiano asked, watching them with concern.

"I'm getting the hang of it. You had him earlier."

"There's no time limit. I like that little guy," he said.

She smiled down at the cranky baby and kissed his fore-head. "He does grow on you, doesn't he? Go do some wood-working. We'll come out when he's finished eating."

"What makes you think I want to go work?"

"It'll soothe you, you said so—maybe not in so many words, but it shows."

Cristiano went to the shop in back and switched on all the lights. He was in turmoil; the thought of accepting the award not sitting well. And the worry he'd have another flashback in the midst of it all was enough to make him want to flee.

He was sincere in wanting Mariella there. He would look at her, not see in his mind's eye the devastation and horror of that day. He'd focus on her silvery eyes, her optimistic smile, and know he'd risk a hundred forays into hell to see her smile.

"It's an excuse, you know," Mariella said a short time later when she arrived pushing the stroller.

"What is?" He looked up, already feeling better for seeing her and the baby.

"Your medal celebration. Isabella wants a party to announce the merger of Rosa and Sorella."

"What?" He stared at her in stunned surprise. That was the last thing he'd expected to hear.

Quickly she told him what his sister had said.

"And Dad's okay with this?" he asked.

"Apparently it's to be a surprise, but Isabella said he turned things over to her and Scarlett and this is their decision."

"He'll flip."

"Or be proud of yet another offspring—for her business acumen. I still want to talk to her about a mail-order outlet for that sauce. Actually, the place could use a website just to let people know about it. I do have a degree in marketing— maybe I can help."

"Who will be at the party?"

"Just family, and me and Dante. Unless you don't want us to go."

"If I go, you go," he said, pulling her close with his arm around her waist. He leaned in and kissed her.

Wishes do come true, Mariella thought as she savored his kiss, giving back as much as she was able. Maybe she should start wishing for the moon. It could happen he'd fall in love with her, couldn't it? His month moved against hers, leaving to trail kisses across her nose.

"I've wanted to kiss those freckles since I first saw you," he murmured, trailing kisses across her cheek, down to her jaw, lower to the pulse point at the base of her throat, wildly beating as the blood rushed through her. She was floating in delight. Seeking his mouth, she sighed in contentment when he covered hers with his and deepened the kiss.

Long moments later they were both breathing hard. He pulled back a scant inch. "Is the baby okay?"

"I haven't heard him. I'll check."

Cristiano did not loosen his hold.

"Or maybe I'll just listen from here."

He kissed her gently.

"If he makes it through okay today, let's try Rome in the morning," he said. "We missed your friend's birthday, but it'll still be close."

She nodded, still in the circle of his arms, where she'd like to stay forever.

"You'll be okay about the medal?" she asked softly.

He groaned softly and rested his forehead against hers. "We'll just see, won't we?"

"What does that mean? Sometimes you're a bit cryptic."

"We'll just see."

Cristiano didn't want to talk. He wanted to hold her, kiss her, make love to her. His feelings were already entangled with Mariella Holmes. He couldn't take things any farther until he knew if he'd come through this a whole man.

He would never tie anyone to a man who couldn't function in today's world.

The thought seared his brain. He wanted her. He wanted what others had—a life's companion that would share the journey through the years. Share good times and bad, laugh with friends, children. He needed to affirm life, to relish the ordinariness of the day. Take what the day offered and not worry about the future. One day at a time. How far could that take them? Would it be enough?

Cristiano breathed deeply of the fresh, clean country air, the scent of wood and oil. The sun shone from a cloudy sky. The air was crisp and cool after the rain. It was a perfect day. And he vowed he'd spend it with Mariella and the baby. Time was fleeing, he had to make the most of every moment.

They took Dante for a walk in the stroller after lunch to

keep him occupied. Even though he was fussy, the change seemed to work. Cristiano had never imagined he'd be content to walk alongside a woman and baby on a quiet country road. Where was the adventure of Rome, the exciting life he'd demanded before? Stephano had told him how much richer life was married to AnnaMaria. He'd been over the moon when his son had been born, then his daughter.

"You're quiet," Mariella said.

"Thinking about Stephano's son. He's three now. His daughter is almost two."

"Go visit."

"When I drive you to Rome." It would be perfect, time constraints keeping it short. He could handle that. At least he hoped so. Would seeing AnnaMaria bring up all the anguish? Was she missing him as Mariella suggested? Or would she rather he not barge in? It had been six months; maybe she was getting on with her life and didn't need a part of the past.

"I was thinking of returning home. Not just for a quick trip," she said slowly.

That surprised him. "I thought you had some more vacation time."

"I do, or at least less demands on my time until my major clients return. But I'm going to stop trying to find Dante's father. The more I think about what you said, the more I question if I truly want him found. What if he tries to take Dante from me? I couldn't bear that. I used to think it would be okay, his father could tell him about Ariana. But they weren't together for long. And a man who could walk away like that isn't the one I want for a father for Dante. Better he stays with me. Some of my rationale in searching was the fear of being the sole person responsible for this child. But it looks as if that's the way it'll be. I think I can do it. I'll have to, won't I?"

"You'll probably marry some day. Then Dante will have a father. Pick a good one."

She avoided his eyes as they strolled along. Had he touched a nerve?

"Problem?"

"No."

He waited. Mariella usually wasn't so quiet. Something was wrong; even he could figure that out. "What?"

She glanced at him. "Nothing. Just—not many men will want to take on a ready-made family."

"Hmm, wonder if that's what kept my father silent all these years."

"What do you mean?"

"What would you do if you found out your father had been married before your mother, that all your life until you were thirty—well, all your life up to now—you thought you were the oldest of your father's children and suddenly you find out you have two older brothers?"

"I imagine I'd be thrilled. But then I think I have a different take on family than you seem to."

"It's not what it's cracked up to be."

"Why not?

"My grandmother made a mistake a long time ago, resulting in my father. His half-siblings never forgave her or him. It wasn't his fault he was born. But it still split the family. What I remember about my aunt and father was the constant fights and altercations. I know that when Dad hit a bad patch he asked his sister for financial help. She refused. So I should rejoice in finding more family?"

"If your sister asked for help would you refuse?"

"Of course not. I'd do anything for Isabella."

"And your brother?"

"Yes."

"How about your aunt?"

"Never."

She laughed. "Careful, she's going to be even closer tied if the merger goes through."

"That's another thing—what is Isabella thinking of?"

"Maybe of a way to get this split family back together acting like a solid family, with no secrets and no division. Who knows, you might like having older brothers."

"Twins."

She laughed again. "Oh, Cristiano, I wish you'd known them when you were younger. Think of the mischief four of you Casali boys could have gotten into. That would have given your father such joy."

"You have the most annoying habit of being right." He stopped her in the middle of the street and kissed her. "Okay, I'll go to the blasted awards and then Isabella's party and do my best to make nice with strangers, but if the twins start bossing me around—"

She hugged him. "Then you give back as good as you get. My money's on you every time."

The next morning when Mariella walked into the living room after a fitful few hours of sleep, Cristiano was balancing a happy baby.

"Come," he said, beckoning her over.

Taking her hand, he folded three fingers and held her index finger. Gently he rubbed it against Dante's lower jaw.

"A tooth!" she exclaimed. "Oh, baby, you have your first tooth."

"Don't let him bite down, it hurts," Cristiano said, smiling at the baby. "I know."

She opened the baby's mouth. "I can hardly see it."

"It just broke through during the night, I guess. Anyway,

until the next one, I think this kid is going to be back to his normally pleasant baby self."

"I hope I can sleep through the night."

"Me, too."

They grinned at each other.

Then Mariella said, "So I can head for Rome tomorrow. I can never thank you enough for everything. Saving my life—"

"Stop. I told you no debts."

"I know, but still. And helping these last few days with such a cranky baby."

"You sound as if you are saying goodbye."

"I am, sort of. I need to go home."

"Not yet. You have vacation time to finish. Stay, Mariella. Please?"

She hesitated, then wondered if she was thinking clearly when she agreed. "For a little longer." She didn't want to leave—not leave Cristiano behind. But he never mentioned returning to his life in Rome. How long would it take for him to fully recover? Then what? Was staying good or bad? Would she fall even more for the man only to face heartache a few weeks later?

"Today I'll finish the table. Tomorrow we'll go to Rome and take it to your place."

"No rush, it'll be a while before he can use it," she said.

"The table will be done. The chairs a little longer. I like knowing something I've made will be in your home. Maybe you'll think about me from time to time."

She couldn't speak. If he only knew! She loved him. She was going to hate returning home.

"I'll fix coffee," she said with a strangled voice. "And boiled eggs."

"I'll cook breakfast," he said quickly.

Mariella laughed, blinking to keep tears at bay.

The entire time Mariella fed the baby and then ate the delicious eggs Benedict that Cristiano prepared, she felt on the verge of tears. There was nothing to hold her in Lake Clarissa. She had her own life to get back to. But she didn't want to go. She wanted to stay with Cristiano. Was it a good thing he asked her to stay longer? Could they find a future together? Was he even thinking along those lines?

Yet she wanted to hold onto every moment, imprint every second on her mind in case there was not a shared future. The way Cristiano looked by the stove. The smiles he gave the baby, who was in a much better mood today. The way the sun shone on his dark hair when he passed by the window. Taking a deep breath, she smelled his scent, uniquely his. Her heart pounded and she had to take another breath to avoid breaking into tears. She longed for the right to ask him to hold her, kiss her. Make love with her. To be part of his breakfast every morning and sleep with him every night.

Soon after she ate, she insisted on returning to the rental cottage. She needed some breathing room and a serious talk with herself to make sure she didn't give away her feelings. She'd take a few more days' vacation and then return to Rome for good without ever letting him know how much she loved him.

The next morning Mariella kissed the baby goodbye and gave Signora Bertatali a dozen last-minute instructions.

"Go, have a good day. I know how to take care of *bambinos*." The older woman practically shooed her from the house.

Cristiano waited by his dark sleek speed machine. The instant Mariella sat inside she felt carefree and adventurous. She loved Dante to bits, but she was elated to be free of responsibility for a few hours.

It was an awesome car, much more suited to couples than families. And its driver drove as if he were in a grand prix or something. Smoothly taking the curves, accelerating on the straight ways. The ride was exhilarating.

"We'll be there in ten minutes, at this rate," she said.

"Too fast?"

"Not if you can handle it," she replied. For the first time in months she was totally on her own—no baby demanding her every moment. She missed Dante, but knew she'd be back with him in a few hours. She needed the break.

And who better to take it with than the man of her dreams? The car suited her image of him, fast and yet in control. Risking life and limb fighting fires, yet considerate and always looking out for others. He was a caring man and there were few of those around.

"Are you going to see Stephano's wife?" she asked.

"I'll see her once I drop you off at your place after we visit the cemetery."

She looked in the back and the small table wedged in. Reaching back, she ran her fingertips over the satiny wood. "It looks amazing. I can't wait to have it in the apartment. Who else will you see?" she asked. "Are you stopping by the ministry?"

"No. I called them yesterday and got all the information I need for the ceremony," he said. "We have to be there by seven. The actual ceremony begins at eight." He reached out and took her hand. "Wear something very pretty."

"And your family party is the next night. Tell me more about your family. If I'm to meet everyone, I need to know who's who, the relationships and how much you like them— or not," she said.

"What does it matter if I like them or not?"

"No sense wasting my time on people you don't like. I wouldn't like them either."

He laughed and squeezed her hand, then rested it on his thigh. "I don't know the older brothers, but I don't think I'll like them."

"Not fair, you have to meet them first. Who else?"

The rest of the drive was accomplished with Cristiano telling her about his aunt, his cousins, his brother and sister and what little he knew of the unknown men from America.

Reaching the outskirts of Rome, Mariella gave directions to the old cemetery. The visit was brief. Cristiano held back while Mariella went right to the small headstone marking the final resting place of her dearest friend.

He looked around. Stephano was buried in the cemetery closer to his home. He had yet to visit the grave. Maybe soon. But not just yet.

"Thank you. It was important to me," Mariella said when she rejoined him.

He nodded, wishing he could do more to ease her grief. Wishing his own would vanish.

She directed him to the apartment building housing her flat. It was on an older road, stone façade looking weathered and ancient.

He carried up the finished table. Entering, he looked around. "Nice." It was simply furnished, but every item was in good shape. The upholstered pieces looked comfortable. There was enough baby paraphernalia to tell the world a baby lived there, but not too much clutter in the small apartment.

"There, I think?" she said, pointing to a spot beneath the window. "When he's older, he'll have a place to play blocks or color with crayons. I can't wait."

Cristiano wished he could be there to see Dante toddling

around. Running in to tell his mother some exciting news, or bringing some friends over when he was older.

"I'll be ready to go after three," she said.

"I'll pick you up then." He brushed her lips lightly with a kiss and headed out. Time to stop in and see his chief and then go see AnnaMaria.

It was shortly before three when he stopped in front of Mariella's apartment building. The meeting with his captain had gone well. As soon as he received the release from the doctor, he was free to return to work.

AnnaMaria had welcomed him with open arms. Once the initial awkwardness had passed, he'd felt right at home. The only difference was he had expected Stephano to walk in at any moment. AnnaMaria had even commented on that. It helped her through the days, she said, imaging he was just away.

Their son had grown and talked a mile a minute. Cristiano couldn't help thinking of Dante in a few years. He'd be much like Stephano's son. Would the two boys like each other? In another time and place, they might have been friends like him and Stephano. The little girl was napping, but he could see Stephano's features in a feminine version on her face when he peeked in at her.

The afternoon sped by. Cristiano vowed to stay in closer touch with AnnaMaria and told her to call on him for any help she needed. They talked of the future, near and distant, and the fact Stephano was getting a posthumous award and she'd be there to receive it.

Arriving at Mariella's apartment a few minutes earlier than planned, Cristiano thought about waiting before going up—not wanting to appear anxious. "Forget this," he said, climbing out of the car. So he was early. If she wasn't ready to go, he'd wait in her flat. At least he'd be with her. Then they'd drive back, maybe eat dinner at Rosa, show his sister his face so she would be reassured. Talk about their day, make further plans for the award ceremony that he was now resigned to attend.

Mariella greeted him with a smile. "Come in. Want something to drink before we leave?"

"No. I'm not in a hurry."

"How did it go with AnnaMaria?"

He told her a little of the afternoon. "It was odd with Stephano not there. I always think of her with him."

"It must be hard for her."

He nodded.

"I'm almost ready. The new computer is set up. I had a lot of things stored on my backup drive, so could just reload." As she chatted about how she'd spent her afternoon, Cristiano settled in on the sofa, enjoying the normalcy of the moment. Feeling cautiously optimistic he wondered if he dared risk returning to work soon.

And if he dared take this relationship with Mariella another step.

"We could stop for dinner on the way home," he suggested.

"Terrific. In Monta Correnti?"

He nodded.

"Rosa?" she asked.

"Would you like to try Sorella? See the competition my sister wants to merge with?"

"Is it as good?"

"Not the sauce, but my aunt doesn't do anything by halves. No deadline to be home for Dante?"

"I checked with Signora Bertatali about a half-hour ago. He's doing fine."

She finished loading the computer. Shut it down and packed it in its carrying case. "I have this to take and another suitcase of clothes. I'm tired of wearing the few things I bought after the fire. And I have more for Dante. I think he's already outgrowing the clothes I bought last week."

"All set, then."

They headed out to the car. Cristiano placed the suitcase in the trunk, reached to take the computer from Mariella when the wail of sirens filled the air, growing louder by the second. The klaxons sounded at the intersection as two large fire engines roared down the street, the noise amplified between the buildings.

Suddenly the neighborhood vanished. He crouched low as the debris fell. The air was acrid with smoke, so thick he couldn't see two feet in front of him. The baby screamed in his arms, the child he carried whimpered softly, clinging fiercely. "Stephano," he yelled, fighting to keep going. The roof was collapsing. A second bomb had blown. Where were the stairs leading up from the subway station? Searing pain hit his leg, his ankle. He couldn't breathe, couldn't see. His helmet faceplate was broken, smoke and dust surrounded him, blinded him.

The wailing sirens filled his senses, the smoke impossible to see through. Heat scorched from behind from the fire. Concrete rained down. Chaos and confusion reigned. "Stephano?" He yelled again, heard nothing but the roar of the world collapsing around him. He couldn't move. Couldn't go forward, couldn't go back. He had two children to save. Where were his fellow first responders? Was he alone in a world gone mad?

"Cristiano!"

A voice called. It wasn't yelling. He could scarcely hear it over the klaxons echoing from the apartment façades.

"Cristiano, what's happening?"

He recognized that voice. What was Mariella doing in the subway? Had she been trying to catch a train?

"Cristiano, stop, you're scaring me." She shook him, patted his cheeks.

He closed his eyes and the world went black.

CHAPTER TEN

"CRISTIANO!" Mariella clutched his arm, shaking him again. She was stooped down beside him. When he fell against the car, she looked around. One of the men on the sidewalk hurried over. Panic filled her. What was wrong with him?

"Do you need help?" the man asked, leaning over.

Cristiano opened his eyes and gazed up at them, dazed.

"Yes. He's had a seizure. If I can get him standing, I think I can get him to my apartment," she said. "I can call an ambulance from there."

"No—no ambulance. I need to sit for a minute," Cristiano said, shaking his head as if to clear it.

The man helped Cristiano get to his feet.

"You sure? An ambulance could be here in a few minutes," he asked.

Cristiano nodded, his arm over Mariella's shoulder. "I've had this before. I know how to deal with it. I just need to sit."

"*Grazie,*" Mariella said, leading Cristiano into the apartment building. In only moments they were back in her apartment.

"I'll be okay," he said, still leaning slightly on her.

"Good. Sit on the sofa. I'll make some tea. Do you need to see a doctor? You scared me half to death."

"I don't need any doctor." He sank onto the sofa, elbows on his knees as he dropped his head into his hands.

"You scared me. Are you sure you'll be all right?"

"I'm sure," he said, his voice muffled.

Mariella watched him for a moment, biting her lip in indecision. Finally she headed for her kitchen. "Wait here, I'll make some tea."

She hurried into the kitchen, the initial fear fading. What had happened down there? It was as if he'd spaced out, ducking and yelling. She peeked back to the living room. He hadn't moved.

It seemed to take forever for the water to boil. As soon as she had the tea ready, she hurried back.

He still hadn't moved.

She placed both cups of tea on the coffee table and reached out to touch his shoulder.

He shrugged off her touch, rose and paced to the window. Gazing out, he still seemed dazed.

"Sorry about that," he said with some effort.

"Post-traumatic stress disorder," she said, picking up her cup to take a sip. Wanting her hands to have something to hold since he wasn't letting her hold him.

He swung around. "What do you know about it?"

"You forget, I spent the last four years in New York. America is home to PTSD. The terrorist attacks, hurricanes, major forest fires, earthquakes. Between first responders and the military, there are a lot of people suffering from PTSD. I have a friend whose brother was in Iraq and suffers from it daily. It can be quite debilitating. Is that what you have?"

He nodded. "Now you see why I am not a hero," he said,

turning to gaze back out the window at the scene on the street.

"What does that have to do with anything? You are a hero. Even more so, rescuing me and Dante after what you went through in May." She rose and crossed the room to stand beside him. Reached out to touch him, wanting contact; she wasn't going anywhere.

"Cristiano, you are a hero."

He hit his forehead with the palm of his hand. "Except I'm not right in the head."

She shook him slightly. "My friend calls her brother whacko, but loves him to bits. He does the same thing, goes off into the horror none of us can share."

"I can't get the images out of my head. I wake in the night. Sometimes during the day, out of the blue, I'm suddenly back in that hell. What kind of man does that make me?"

"Human."

He glanced at her, looked back out the window.

"Truly, I don't think we were designed to witness the horrors of modern life. The human mind can only absorb so much. Then it kicks in its defense mechanisms," she said.

"What are mine? Reliving the day forever? It's like I'm stuck in some repeat loop—the smoke, fire, crashing concrete, cries of the dying."

She hugged him, leaning slightly against him until he lifted his arm and put it around her shoulders. "I don't know that much about it. I've heard it can get better with counseling. Sometimes not. There are Vietnam War survivors still suffering from it forty years later. It's an awful payback for being heroic, for doing your best for others. I don't know how you can get over it. Maybe you never will, but it does not diminish who you are or what you've done."

"If I can't function in the world, they might as well lock me up and throw away the key," he said, letting his frustration show.

"Wait a minute—is this the reason you've become a recluse in Lake Clarissa? Does your family know?"

He turned and gripped her shoulders hard. "Do not tell them—do you understand?"

"Why not? It's nothing to be ashamed of. It's not something you can predict, or cure. It's not even something you caused."

"They think of me as some fearless, reckless adrenalin junkie. Daring danger in the line of work. I don't want them to know what a pitiful creature I've become."

"You are not the least pitiful. You are strong, brave, courageous and dependable." She gripped his wrists and shook him as much as she was able. "Pay attention, Cristiano, this isn't your fault. You are a fine man."

"Sure, like just now. Sirens go off and I'm a puddle on the pavement."

"A trigger, right? You heard them and flashed back to that day. From what I read on the Internet, it was horrible. You saw things you'll never forget, terrible things. People dying you couldn't save. Your own friends dying. You were almost killed yourself. Why wouldn't that bother you? You would be a very cold person if it didn't affect you."

"I can't get past it. It's been months. I need to get back to work. But I'm afraid that'll never happen. I ride the trucks that have the sirens. What good would I be if I have a flashback and put others in danger because I can't control what I see?"

Mariella didn't know what to say. Her heart ached for the burden he bore. She could tell by the anguish in his expression that this was something he'd been dealing with since May—alone. She encircled his waist with her arms.

For a moment he held himself rigid, then brought his arms around her. Clinging almost desperately.

"Your ankle was broken when the second bomb went off, wasn't it?" she asked, hoping she was going along the right track. She wished she knew more about PTSD, what triggered it, what might avoid an attack. How people moved beyond it.

"Yes."

"And it healed, but it took time. So, look at it as if your mind got bruised or something. It will take time but it will heal." She prayed she was right. She knew some men never got over the horrors they'd experienced. She hoped Cristiano wasn't one of them. But a man needed hope. She needed him to know that anything was possible.

"Have you seen a counselor?" she asked.

He shook his head. "The doctor at the hospital recommended one, but I left for Lake Clarissa as soon as I was out. There aren't any there."

"Monta Correnti?"

He shrugged.

"There's no shame in being injured," she said gently.

"There's shame when a man wants to be productive and dare not risk going among other people in case something like today happens. What good would I be anywhere? What if I'd been driving? I can't be a risk to others. I was a fool to leave Lake Clarissa today, to hope because I haven't had an episode recently that I was cured. To wish for a normal life like others. It isn't going to happen."

"You don't know that."

"I know I want what I had before—life that was carefree and suited me perfectly. Stephano and his family. My own family. The hope of falling in love and getting married. What of all that?"

"You can still fall in love and get married," she said.

"You still have your family and Stephano's wife and children."

"What woman would want to take on someone like me?" he bit out.

She stared at him. "I would," she said softly. Her heart ached for him. All the more painful for feeling his pain, his frustration when she had so much love to offer.

"Now you sound as crazy as I am," he said. Despite the words, he tightened his embrace and rested his head against hers, holding her firmly against him.

"Neither of us is crazy," she said, her voice muffled against his shoulder.

"If I weren't I'd court you like I were crazy," he said softly.

Her heart skipped a beat and then raced. "Don't play with me, mister," she warned.

He laughed. "I can't offer you anything. I will always cherish the days we spent together at the lake. But you need someone who's whole and free of flashbacks that could wind up injuring you or your son. I wish things were different, but they're not."

"So that's it? You are withdrawing from the world because everything is not perfect in your world?" She pulled back and glared at him.

"It has to be that way."

"No, it doesn't," she said, pushing free from his embrace. "You aren't the type of man to give up easily. Do you love me, Cristiano?"

"I have no right—"

"That's not what I asked." She glared at him. This certainly was not the way she'd expected to find out a man loved her. She had thought of roses and fine dining and dancing.

He took a deep breath, studying her face as if memorizing

it for all time. "I love you, Mariella Holmes. Your sunny disposition brightens my life. Your laughter makes my heart sing. Your devotion to your friend's son is heartwarming. I want you in the worst way—to spend nights in loving you, days in keeping you happy. But I have nothing to offer. I don't have a job I can go back to yet. I don't have the coping skills to make it with PTSD. I'm a mess."

She smiled at him and stepped closer. "I love you, too, Cristiano. I thought the way you were always pushing me away meant that you didn't care for me. But you do. Together we can face anything!"

"Didn't you hear me? There's no future together!"

"I'm ignoring what I don't want to hear. We can manage this. We can. I love you for who you are. I never knew you before, so this suits me perfectly."

"And if I have another meltdown like a little while ago?"

"Then we'll deal with it. Maybe you can start counseling to see if that helps. You can't be the only man from that day suffering from this. Who have you talked to about it? Who have you told?"

"No one."

She shook her head in exasperation. "I pictured you a fighter."

"I am. When there is something I can fight. This—I have no resources."

"So go find out all you can, find the resources to deal with it. Call your captain and tell him. Ask who else is having this problem and what they're doing about it. Oh, Cristiano, don't throw away what we could have together for some misguided notion you are in this alone. Your family would rally around in an instant. Your friends. Everyone. Me especially."

"I can't deal with it."

"Yes, you can. We can."

The silence stretched out for endless moments, then, with a soft sigh, he pulled her into his arms and kissed her. "What did I ever do to deserve this?" he said softly.

Sometime later he rested his forehead against hers and said, "It's not what I want for you. You should have a healthy, perfect man. You'd be getting damaged goods."

"How would I be getting that?" she asked saucily.

"I love you, sweetheart. Would you think—in the future, after we know more about this PTSD and what the prognosis is—would you consider marrying me?"

"Yes! And I don't need to wait for anything. I love you, Cristiano. I want to be with you always. No matter what, we can face it together. Besides, I come with baggage. Dante will need a father."

"Another thing that couldn't be better. I love that little boy. I want to see him grow up, see what kind of man he becomes. And have a part in that, showing him right from wrong, watching him discover the world."

"What better for him than a hero? Remember, you saved his life, it belongs to you."

"His biological father is a fool. I'd be honored to be Dante's father. So you'll marry me? As soon as we know—"

She put her fingertips over his lips. "As soon as we want. We're not waiting for some nebulous time in the future when you decide the stars align right or something. I want to be with you now, starting our memories and traditions. And helping if I can until you lick this thing."

"I have no job."

"I do. If we can live at the cottage for a while, we can manage. Don't say you don't want me unless everything is perfect. Love isn't like that. It takes good and bad, ups and downs. Now that I know you love me, I don't want to be apart. I'm alone in the world except for Dante. With you, I feel whole, complete, part of a family."

"What if I don't get better?"

"Cristiano, what would you do if I got sick?"

"I'd take care of you."

"Yet you want to deprive me of the same opportunity? I want to love you, be with you. Cristiano, that was a proposal and my answer is yes. Not yes someday, plain old yes!"

Her heart sang when he lifted her up to spin her around. "I love you!" he shouted.

She shrieked with mock fear as he spun them both around. "I love you!" she shouted back, then laughed with joy.

They spent the rest of the afternoon kissing, making plans, kissing, calling Cristiano's chief, kissing, and finally departed to return to Lake Clarissa.

"I can't wait to tell Dante," she said as she drove through the streets of Rome. Cristiano had insisted she drive, fearful of another episode if a siren sounded.

"He's six months old, what will he understand?"

"That you're going to be his daddy. That's so special."

"I think it's even more special that you're going to be my wife."

"Will your family approve? When will you tell them?"

He groaned. "Do you know every one of my cousins and siblings got married or engaged in the last six months. Must be something in the water."

"You're kidding!"

"Hey, we're all about the same age, natural, I guess. Only I didn't think I'd find anyone—especially after last May."

"So we can tell them at the party."

"After today I don't know if I should go. What if—?"

"Hey, they'll understand if something happens. You can't cut yourself off from the world. They'll be so proud of you receiving that medal."

"Oh, God," he groaned. "I can't go there."

"Of course you can go. I've known you for weeks and this is the first time I've seen you have a flashback. As long as there are no sirens, you'll probably be fine, don't you think?"

"What I think is if I can just look at you the entire time, I'll be able to do anything," he said, lifting her hand from the wheel and kissing the palm, then replacing it.

"Do you think your family will like me?"

"Yes."

She glanced at him. "That was positive."

"How could they not? You are adorable."

She laughed. "Keep that thought in mind forever."

"That's how long I'll love you. Forever."

CHAPTER ELEVEN

MARIELLA was dressed in a long gown, a rich dark burgundy velvet, suitable for the most formal of events. Her hair had been done up. Her nails polished to match the gown. She felt the butterflies in her stomach and knew Cristiano had to feel even more stress.

He was picking her up in another ten minutes. She had prayed all week that no sirens would mar the night. She so needed her man to receive his medal, to stand with those who had served beside him in rescuing all they could possibly save. And to stand in place of those comrades who had fallen and were only present in the memories of the minds of those present.

Promptly at the appointed time he knocked on her door. Her downstairs neighbor was watching Dante tonight. Nothing would interfere with the ceremony he so richly deserved.

She opened the door and exclaimed at how handsome he looked in his dress uniform.

"Wow, I'd want you to save me from all burning buildings," she said, leaning forward for his welcomed kiss. She'd only been alone for a day, but she had missed him as much as if they'd been parted a week or longer.

"Don't know if I ever will be able to do that," he murmured, pulling back to look at her. "You are beautiful."

The warm glow seeped through her. She hoped he always thought so.

"I'm ready," she said, reaching for her coat.

"That makes one of us," he said wryly.

"You'll do fine."

"If I end up a puddle on the floor, you'll be to blame."

She squeezed his arm, wishing she could take away every bit of turmoil and uncertainty. Wishing she could make him whole again. Perhaps time would do so, but not tonight.

Tonight was about Cristiano and Stephano and all the others, alive and dead, who had experienced the horror of the bombing together.

He'd hired a limo for the occasion and it was waiting outside her apartment. In only moments they arrived at the Parlamento building, brightly lighted for tonight's event. Reporters and cameramen flanked the cordoned-off entry, calling for sound bites and taking photos and videos of all entering.

"AnnaMaria will be there?" she asked as the limo stopped and Cristiano began to open the door.

"Yes. Her parents and Stephano's will be with her." He stepped out amidst the flashing lights and demands for tell-us-how-you-feel, coming from all directions.

"I probably should not confess to live cameras that I feel like I might throw up, hmm?" he said softly for her ear only.

She laughed and then smiled at the reporters. "I'm so proud to be here with you."

"Then let's walk tall and remember the fallen," he said, offering his arm and escorting her inside.

The buzz from outside was muted once inside the impressive building. Escorts took them to the Senato chamber where Cristiano moved to stand with other recipients while

Mariella was escorted to a seat in the second row. She saw him clearly when he walked in with the others, tall and proud. He looked amazing.

The actual event was full of pomp and ceremony. Television cameras captured everything. The national anthem was played. The Prime Minister spoke about the horror of the day, the attack on a country who had never anticipated such a cowardly assault, the great debt of gratitude the country had for those who had first gone in.

Mariella looked at Cristiano; his gaze was fixed on hers. She tried to relax, to be there for him as a means to hold on and not give way to the fear that plagued him. His eyes did not waver. She hoped he felt at ease.

The names of the men, women and children in the subway trains who perished were read. Relatives and friends sat in the audience. Mariella could hear quiet sobs as names were spoken.

The names of the first responders were then read, each one present stepping forward to receive their country's highest medal for bravery and service above and beyond the call of duty. She clapped wildly when Cristiano's name was called, when he stepped proudly forward to receive the medallion on a banner of Italian colors, green, white and red. He bowed slightly toward Mariella when he received them, his eyes glittering.

She was so proud he loved her. She wanted to stand up and tell the world that brave man had chosen her for his wife. But she merely clapped until her hands were red and stinging, and smiled as broadly as she could.

Then the names of the fallen responders were read. Mariella blotted tears at the moving ceremony, her heart aching for those men and women who had plunged into hell to save and ended up giving their lives. How fortunate their country was to have such brave people.

When the ceremony was over, everyone was invited to a reception. Cristiano found her as soon as the broadcast portion ended.

"Let's get out of here," he said, running his finger around his collar.

"No, first we go to the reception. Those you saved will be there. You must see them. For them to thank you and for you to know you did a miraculous thing that day."

"I don't want thanks."

"Sometimes you have to accept so others can give it. They need closure, too, Cristiano. Don't deny them that."

He drew in a deep breath.

"Very well, but we're not staying long."

The large reception hall was not crowded, though there seemed to be several hundred people present. Mariella met AnnaMaria and conveyed her sorrow on the loss of her husband. People came to congratulate Cristiano, to slap him on the back and some to give hugs. When a man came forward carrying a baby, Mariella watched closely. The child wasn't too much older than Dante.

"You gave me my son," the man said, reaching out to grasp Cristiano's hand. "How you managed I'll never know. I lost my wife, but I have my son, the best part of her. Thank you."

Cristiano smiled at the baby. "He doesn't look any worse for his ordeal. I'm glad."

A young boy came over, looking wary and overwhelmed. His grandparents were with him. "This is Emelio, the last one brought out—with the baby. He is our pride and joy, thank you," they said. "Our daughter and her husband perished, but we have our grandson."

"Thank you for saving me," the little boy said, grinning when Cristiano raised his hand in a high five, slapping it hard.

The young woman he'd first carried came over to thank him, and introduce him to her husband and daughter, both delighted to meet Cristiano and add their thanks.

So went the evening until everyone had greeted the man who had saved their lives.

"Tell me now you don't think you're a hero," Mariella said softly when the last man limped away.

"I was just doing my job. I wish I could have brought more out."

"I know. I think we could leave now," she said. She was exhausted with the emotions of the evening. How much more so must Cristiano be?

They found AnnaMaria and the rest of Stephano's family and said goodbye, with promises to get in touch when they returned to Rome.

Finally they were in the quiet of the limo, speeding through darkened streets.

Mariella squeezed his hand. "You did it, no episode at all!"

"Luck."

"Good luck, then," she said, snuggling close to him.

"I couldn't have done it without you, you know that."

"So we make a good team. I love you," she said.

"Not as much as I love you," he said, leaning over to kiss her.

Just one night later Cristiano parked his car near the piazza in Monta Correnti.

"I'm nervous," Mariella said, looking at the lights over the restaurants.

"We don't have to attend," Cristiano said as he switched off the engine and turned to look at her.

"Yes, we do," she said promptly. "Though if you felt

like this when we went to the medal ceremony, you're even
more a hero than I thought."

He reached for her hand and kissed her fingers. "I'd
just as soon forget the entire situation and go back to the
cottage. You, me and Dante. It's cold enough for a fire, we
could sit and talk until he's asleep and then make plans."

It was tempting. But she had to meet the rest of his
family some time and maybe it would be better all at once.
She had memorized all the names and tried to keep the
relationships straight. Plus she didn't want to disappoint
his sister. She had worked hard to make sure everyone was
there.

"The timing is perfect. We need to let your family celebrate. Besides, remember, this entire gathering is really
for your father, the medal award is the excuse."

"I know, but we'll still get more attention than I want
now." He took a deep breath. "I hope you're right about
their understanding."

"Oh, Cristiano, of course they'll understand. They all
love you. If one of them was hurt, you'd be the first there
to help. Let them have that same privilege."

"It's not quite as visible as a broken ankle."

"But just as real."

Mariella still marveled that this dynamic man loved her.
They had made plans for a quiet wedding before Christmas.
For the foreseeable future things would continue much as
they had been: she'd work her virtual-assistant job, Cristiano
would make furniture—and see a counselor to help him
cope with the PTSD. They were very hopeful in time he'd
be able to return to Rome and his job. It might take a few
months or maybe even a year or so. And if not, he had his
woodworking, which he enjoyed. Mariella was convinced
he could name his price for the fine pieces he made.

Mostly she was just glad he had not held firm on waiting

to get married until he thought he was cured. She couldn't wait to be his wife, spend her days and nights with him.

"Let's do it, then," he said, opening the car door. They took the baby carrier, though Mariella carried Dante. They'd use the carrier when Dante needed to rest.

In only a moment they were walking into the wide piazza that led to the restaurant. The large stone patio between the two restaurants was illuminated by soft lighting. The chairs were all empty as it was far too cold to sit out at night in November. The front doors of both establishments had prominent signs declaring they were closed for a private party. Mariella heard the voices from Rosa and felt a touch of panic. What if the family didn't want him to marry her? What if he changed his mind? Shaking her head impatiently, she knew she was acting stupid. As if anyone in the family could tell Cristiano what to do. She looked at him for support. She loved him so much she could scarcely believe it. And he loved her! That was the most amazing thing. She'd been deliriously happy these last weeks. And knew once married she'd be even happier. She would have her family—Cristiano and Dante. And maybe a few more babies. But if not, she would feel her world complete.

"Ready?" she asked with a smile.

"As I'll ever be."

With that he opened the door to his father's restaurant and the three of them entered.

"Feels like home," he murmured as they walked into the main room. The tile floor, warm wooden trim and fall colors in the decor were so familiar.

They were immediately spotted by his brother, standing with a small group on one side.

"The hero of the hour!" Valentino called, raising a glass in his honor.

Cristiano looked around. "I don't recognize half these

people. I thought Isabella said it was family," he murmured as he spotted his sister.

"About time. I was worried you wouldn't come," Isabella said, rushing over to give him a hug. "You haven't exactly been a frequent visitor since you started staying in Lake Clarissa." Then she hugged Mariella and Dante. "Welcome. We saw the presentation of the medals on the television. I cried through almost all of it. You looked so tall, so distinguished. I'm proud of you, Cristiano. It's not every day we have a hero in our midst."

Mariella saw him wince and stepped closer. "You've had him all along, maybe you just didn't recognize he was such a hero."

"Well said," Valentino said, giving Cristiano a bear hug as others crowded around, calling greetings. "You remember Clara," he said, reaching for the pretty woman at his side. The love shining from Valentino's face was obvious to the world.

"I remember you," Cristiano said. "Congratulations on marrying this guy. I hope he treats you right. If not, you let me know."

"Oh, he treats me really fine," she said. Rubbing her stomach, she smiled. "The truth will be seeing how he does when the baby comes."

"Congratulations, I didn't know," Cristiano said, shaking his brother's hand and slapping him on the back. "Beat you in the family department, though," he said with a smile at Dante.

"*Ciao*, Cristiano," another voice said.

"Scarlett, I haven't seen you in a while." He smiled at his cousin, and put his arm around Mariella's shoulders. "I'd like everyone to meet Mariella Holmes. My fiancée," he said proudly.

The exclamations and congratulations flew back and forth.

"We have news ourselves," his cousin Lizzie said, coming up to him. He hadn't seen her in years. She was glowing.

"You have new cousins you haven't met yet," she said, giving him a warm welcome. "They're sleeping right over there." She pointed to a double stroller sheltered in the one of the corners of the room, away from the main activity, but close by.

"Twins?" he asked.

"Yes. Must run in the family."

She gave him a hug and laughed. "You haven't seen anyone in a while from what I hear. Glad to see you made it out from that attack with only a broken ankle. That was horrible, for all of us."

The others greeted him, met Mariella and exclaimed in delight over Dante. The baby smiled his one-toothed grin and was soon being passed around as everyone seemed to want to hold the happy baby.

Then Cristiano looked across the room, seeing his half-brothers for the first time. The twins stood near each other, each with a beautiful woman beside him. They looked like their mutual father—only with lighter hair and lighter eyes. Almost as if it had been choreographed, the others parted as Cristiano and Mariella walked across the tiled floor to the two men.

"I'm Cristiano," he said, hesitating only a moment before putting out his hand.

"Angelo," the one with the blue eyes said, reaching out to shake his hand.

"Alex," the more muscular one said.

"Here's Aunt Lisa," his sister said, tugging on his sleeve. "We'll have lots of time tonight to catch up on everything.

Dad should be here soon. We're having drinks and appetizers here, then dinner will be at Sorella. Fingers crossed Dad accepts the merger."

"You can wrap him around your little finger. He'll be pleased things are going to continue, no matter how that happens."

He stepped back a bit and pulled Mariella closer.

"This is more than I expected. Everyone is either engaged or newly married, so we've just doubled the family. But I didn't realize they'd all be here tonight."

"A tribute to you and to your father," Mariella said.

Luca Casali entered the restaurant and greetings were called again. He made the rounds, clasping hands, hugging, getting kissed by most of the women. He looked pleased to see his American sons. Cristiano felt a twinge of uncertainty. He'd always been the older brother. Now he had two older than he. Still, he rejoiced for his father to finally connect with those children he'd had to give up so long ago. He glanced at Dante, being held by his cousin Jackie, and knew it would devastate him if he had to give up the child and never know if he'd see him again. He loved that little baby. He would be the best father he could be for him.

"Son," Luca said, reaching Cristiano. He gave him a big hug. "You have done us all proud," he exclaimed, smiling broadly. "Who knew those fearless escapades when you and Valentino were little would push you to become a man who does such daring rescues? I'm glad you came home to heal and hope you'll visit often after your return to Rome."

"There's something to talk about, Dad, but not here or now. I'm not going back right away."

"Good, I hope we see more of you than we have recently."

"From the looks of things, everyone has had plenty to keep them occupied."

"Luca." His sister Lisa came over. "So, we are united tonight as we have not been in many years. I think Mamma would be happy."

He nodded, glancing around. "I'm sure of it. All her grandchildren here, each with the one special person who will share life's journey with them. It is a happy day. And for me, especially to see my first sons again after so long."

"Attention." Isabella raised her voice above the conversations. Everyone stopped talking and looked at her. Smiles broke out. Glances to Luca were made, then back to Isabella.

"First, I'm so glad everyone could attend tonight. It means a lot to me and, I know, to my father." She smiled at him.

"We are gathered to celebrate my brother receiving a medal from the ministry for his heroic actions after the bombing last May. He was injured in the last moments, yet still managed to keep the children he carried safe and rescued a total of seven people. He also rescued Mariella and Dante from a fire at Lake Clarissa. And that sure had a happy ending."

Everyone laughed, Cristiano with them, leaning down to kiss Mariella quickly. He still had moments of doubt he was doing right by her, but her love was steadfast and he couldn't bear to turn his back on all she offered. He would always do his best to keep her safe and happy.

"But there is another reason we are gathered. Many years ago, my aunt Lisa and my father were left a restaurant by their mother, our grandmother Rosa. They ran it together for a while, then they parted. Different restaurants, different cuisine. Same family, however, though going in different directions. Now we come full circle."

All eyes turned to Luca. Cristiano hoped his father would be pleased.

"We are merging the two back. We will keep the differences in decor and menus, to attract a wide variety of patrons. But Rosa and Sorella will be operated as one unit. Dad, we do this for you. No one could have been a better father given all the setbacks and hardships you faced. This is our thanks to you."

Luca looked stunned. He looked at his sister, surprised to see her smiling.

"I don't know what to say," he said a moment later when no one else spoke. "I can't believe it. It's what Mamma wanted. After all these years—"

Lisa nodded. "You can blame me. I was at fault over a lot. But here's to good fortune for the family from today forward," she said, raising a glass of champagne high.

"Hear, hear."

Each raised a glass to join the toast and drank. Then laughter and conversations started again.

Cristiano walked to his sister. "You did it. He looks amazingly happy."

"I'm so glad. It's the best thing for both restaurants, but it was a risk. The breach was long."

"Healing comes through love," the man beside her said.

"Cristiano, meet Max—my husband," Isabella said.

Cristiano looked at Isabella. "You never introduced us before."

"You weren't exactly Mr. Approachable. And then I was more concerned with getting this off the ground."

Mariella took Dante from Jackie. "I hope he didn't drool on your beautiful suit," she said.

"Not at all and it wouldn't matter if he did. Have you seen my new nephews?"

"No, but I'd like to."

They went to the stroller. The babies slept peacefully, both adorable in their little blue sweaters and hats.

"The only bad part is they'll be growing up in Australia and I won't get to see them all the time. Lizzie has promised photos every day over the Internet. When they are all older, they and Dante can play together when they visit Italy."

"A ready-made family," Mariella agreed.

"Congratulations on your own forthcoming wedding," Valentino said, coming over to Cristiano as Max and Isabella moved to talk with Scarlett and her fiancé, Lorenzo Nesta. Cristiano knew Lorenzo from his years of working at the restaurant. The change in the man since the last time he saw him was amazing. He looked younger and far happier than Cristiano had ever seen him.

"Thanks. So you're going to be a father, Val. Hard to believe," Cristiano said.

"That's something, isn't it? Never thought it would happen," he said, his gaze focused on his wife halfway across the restaurant. "You know, I almost lost her before we got things straight. Life's fleeting. Look at our mother, dying so young." His face twisted in remembered pain.

"Let it go," Cristiano said gently. "She would be happy for all of us tonight." He knew Valentino always blamed himself for not being able to save their mother, but he'd been a small child. Even adults could not have saved her. "Mariella and I are adopting Dante."

"He's not her son?" Valentino asked in surprise.

Cristiano quickly explained things, then reached out to grip his brother's shoulder. "I want to make sure my son always knows he's mine, no matter who donated the sperm. You have always been Dad's son, no matter what. And always my brother."

Valentino nodded, looking for Clara again. "I've

changed. Love and family is the most important thing to me now. And whether it's by blood or love, families evolve and are there for us."

"Even brothers we have never met before?" Cristiano asked.

"I wasn't too excited about getting to know them when I first learned they existed. But the full story is sad. Dad did his best, couldn't keep them, so sent them to live with their mother. He couldn't afford anything until after he and mamma married. They have their own problems with the situation. I hope in time all of us feel the tie I know Dad does."

"Takes some getting used to."

"No more than realizing Lisa is actually welcoming the reunification of the restaurants and that Lizzie married an Australian and had twins," Valentino said.

Cristiano laughed, feeling things were getting back to normal. "Or Isabella married."

"To a prince, no less."

"What? Neither mentioned that."

"Prince Maximilliano Di Rossi," Valentino said.

"Does Isabella plan to leave the restaurant?"

"Not a chance. She's the best thing to happen to it. Who would take over completely if not Isabella?"

"Isn't that guy with Jackie the man she dated years ago?"

"Yes. Guess love's even better the second time around. He's okay. It's the Aussie I have trouble talking with. His Italian, as far as I can tell, is limited to I love you, my darling, which he says every so often to Lizzie."

Cristiano laughed. It warmed his heart to be with his family again. The PTSD hadn't abated. He could have an episode without warning, but Mariella had been right. If he did, the family would rally round. He'd forgotten that in his first months of hiding. He wasn't perfect, but neither was anyone in the family. They all did the best they could with what they had.

Mariella was walking his way, her smile lightening his heart. He would never tire of looking at her, or being with her. Whatever the future held, they were in it together.

"So, I've met the baby twins and the older twins. Now, do you think we run the risk of twins? I have to tell you, one baby is a lot to handle."

He brushed his lips across hers. "Whatever comes, we can face it together."

"Good answer. I love you, Cristiano."

"I love you, sweetheart. What a welcome to the family, huh?"

"Well, I've met an actress, a baseball player, two ranchers, a fashion designer. How is that for a diverse family?"

"Don't forget the prince."

"What?" she exclaimed, looking around.

He explained and laughed. "I hide away from the world for a few months and everything changes."

"All for the better. A few months ago I had no one, my best friend was dead, my parents gone. Now I have you and the baby and all these amazing relatives-to-be."

"And they'll have amazing you as part of their families. I will never be able to let you know how much I love you and how much your love means to me. You've given me back my life."

"You would have reclaimed it sooner or later. I'm just glad to be a part of it now and forever. Let's just promise we won't make any of the mistakes others have made. We will be happy forever."

"Forever."

Cristiano pulled her over to one side for a kiss. Behind the pillar, his aunt was talking with a man he hadn't yet met.

"It's a new age," he heard his aunt say.

"Same old Lisa," the man retorted.

"Single, but maybe thinking of marriage. I mean, look at everyone here tonight. I never saw so much love and devotion in one room," she said.

"You always wanted to be free," he said.

"I always wanted you," she replied. "Will you marry me?"

Cristiano peered around the column. The older man with his aunt had eyes only for her. Catching his movement, they both looked at him.

"Oh, don't you breathe a word," Lisa said. She glanced at the other man. "Rafe, are you going to answer?"

"Yes, but when we are alone," he said, his eyes dancing in amusement.

"It's time for dinner," Isabella announced.

"Ah, but first one more toast," Luca said, going to stand beside his daughter.

"To the legacy of our mother, Rosa," he said, raising his glass.

"To Mamma's legacy," Lisa echoed.

"To Rosa!" the entire family said as one.

THE BRIDESMAID'S BABY

BY
BARBARA HANNAY

Barbara Hannay was born in Sydney, educated in Brisbane and has spent most of her adult life living in tropical north Queensland, where she and her husband have raised four children. While she has enjoyed many happy times camping and canoeing in the bush, she also delights in an urban lifestyle—chamber music, contemporary dance, movies and dining out. An English teacher, she has always loved writing, and now, by having her stories published, she is living her most cherished fantasy. Visit her website at www.barbarahannay.com.

PROLOGUE

A PARTY was in full swing at Tambaroora.

The homestead was ablaze with lights and brightly coloured Chinese lanterns glowed in the gardens. Laughter and the happy voices of young people joined the loud music that spilled out across the dark paddocks where sheep quietly grazed.

Will Carruthers was going away, setting out to travel the world, and his family and friends were sending him off in style.

'Have you seen Lucy?' Mattie Carey asked him as he topped up her wine glass.

'I'm sure I have,' Will replied, letting his gaze drift around the room, seeking Lucy's bright blonde hair. 'She was here a minute ago.'

Mattie frowned. 'I've been looking for her everywhere.'

'I'll keep an eye out,' Will said with a shrug. 'If I see her, I'll let her know you're looking for her.' He moved on to top up other guests' glasses.

But by the time he'd completed a circuit of the big living room and the brightly lit front and side verandas, Will still hadn't seen Lucy McKenty and he felt a vague stirring of unease. Surely she wouldn't leave the party without saying goodbye. She was, in many ways, his best friend.

He went to the front steps and looked out across the garden, saw a couple, suspiciously like his sister Gina and Tom Hutchins, kissing beneath a jacaranda, but there was still no sign of Lucy.

She wasn't in the kitchen either. Will stood in the middle of the room, scratching his head and staring morosely at the stacks of empty bottles and demolished food platters. Where was she?

His brother Josh came in to grab another bottle of bubbly from the fridge.

'Seen Lucy?' Will asked.

Josh merely shook his head and hurried away to his latest female conquest.

A movement outside on the back veranda caught Will's attention. It was dark out there and he went to the kitchen doorway to scan the veranda's length, saw a slim figure in a pale dress, leaning against a veranda post, staring out into the dark night.

'Lucy?'

She jumped at the sound of his voice.

'I've been looking for you everywhere,' he said, surprised by the relief flowing through him like wine. 'Are you OK?'

'I had a headache.' She spoke in a small, shaky voice. 'So I came outside for a bit of quiet and fresh air.'

'Has it helped?'

'Yes, thanks. I feel much better.'

Will moved beside her and rested his arms on the railing, looking out, as she was, across the dark, limitless stretch of the sheep paddocks.

For the past four years the two of them had been away at

Sydney University, two friends from the tiny country town of Willowbank, adrift in a sea of thousands of strangers. Their friendship had deepened during the ups and downs of student life, but now those years were behind them.

Lucy had come home to start work as a country vet, while Will, who'd studied geology, was heading as far away as possible, hurrying overseas, hungry for adventure and new experiences.

'You're not going to miss this place, are you?' she said.

Will laughed. 'I doubt it.' His brother Josh would be here to help their father run Tambaroora. It was the life Josh, as the eldest son, was born to, what he wanted. For Will, escape had never beckoned more sweetly, had never seemed more reasonable. 'I wish you were coming too.'

Lucy made a soft groaning sound. 'Don't start that again, Will.'

'Sorry.' He knew this was a sore point. 'I just can't understand why you don't want to escape, too.'

'And play gooseberry to you and Cara? How much fun would that be?'

The little catch in Lucy's voice alarmed Will.

'But we're sure to meet up with other travellers, and you'd make lots of friends. Just like you always have.'

Lucy had arrived in Willowbank during their last year at high school and she'd quickly fitted into Will's close circle but, because they'd shared a mutual interest in science, she and Will had become particularly good friends, really good friends.

He looked at her now, standing on the veranda in the moonlight, beautiful in an elfin, tomboyish way, with sparkly blue eyes and short blonde hair and soft pale skin. A strange lump of hot metal burned in his throat.

Lucy lifted her face to him and he saw a tear tremble on the end of her lashes and run down her cheek.

'Hey, Goose.' He used her nickname and forced a shaky laugh. 'Don't tell me you're going to miss me.'

'Of course I won't miss you,' she cried, whirling away so he couldn't see her face.

Shocked, Will reached out to her. She was wearing a strapless dress and his hands closed over her bare shoulders. Her skin was silky beneath his hands and, as he drew her back against him, she was small and soft in his arms. She smelled clean like rain. He dipped his head and her hair held the fragrance of flowers.

Without warning he began to tremble with the force of unexpected emotion.

'Lucy,' he whispered but, as he turned her around to face him, anything else that he might have said was choked off by the sight of her tears.

His heart behaved very strangely as he traced the tears' wet tracks with his fingertips. He felt the heated softness of her skin and when he reached the dainty curve of her tear-dampened lips, he knew that he had to kiss her.

He couldn't resist gathering her close and tasting the delicate saltiness of her tears and the sweetness of her skin and, finally, the softness of her mouth. Oh, God.

With the urgency of a wild bee discovering the world's most tempting honey, Will pulled her closer and took the kiss deeper. Lucy wound her arms around his neck and he could feel her breasts pressed against his chest. His body caught fire.

How could this be happening?

Where on earth had Lucy learned to kiss? Like this?

She was so sweet and wild and passionate—turning him on like nothing he'd ever known.

Was this really Lucy McKenty in his arms? His heart was bursting inside his chest.

'Lucy?' Mattie's voice called suddenly. 'Is that you out there, Lucy?'

Light flooded them. Will and Lucy sprang apart and Mattie stared at them, shocked.

They stared at each other, equally shocked.

'I'm sorry,' Mattie said, turning bright red.

'No, it's OK,' they both protested in unison.

'We were just—' Will began.

'Saying goodbye,' Lucy finished and then she laughed. It was a rather wild, strange little laugh, but it did the trick.

Everyone relaxed. Mattie stopped blushing. 'Josh thought you might like to make a speech soon,' she told him.

'A speech?' Will sounded as dazed as he felt.

'A farewell speech.'

'Oh, yes. I'd better say something now before everyone gets too sloshed.'

They went back inside and, with the speed of a dream that faded upon waking, the moment on the veranda evaporated.

The spell was broken.

Everyone gathered around Will and, as he looked out at the sea of faces and prepared to speak, he thought guiltily of Cara, his girlfriend, waiting for him to join her in Sydney. Then he glanced at Lucy and saw no sign of tears. She was smiling and looking like her happy old self and he told himself everything was OK.

Already he was sure he'd imagined the special magic in that kiss.

CHAPTER ONE

THERE were days when Lucy McKenty knew she was in the wrong job. A woman in her thirties with a loudly ticking biological clock should not devote huge chunks of her time to delivering gorgeous babies.

Admittedly, the babies Lucy delivered usually had four legs and a tail, but that didn't stop them from being impossibly cute, and it certainly didn't stop her from longing for a baby. Just one baby of her own to hold and to love.

The longing swept through her now as she knelt in the straw beside the calf she'd just delivered. The birthing had been difficult, needing ropes and a great deal of Lucy's perspiration, but now, as she shifted the newborn closer to his exhausted mother's head, she felt an all too familiar wrench on her heartstrings.

The cow opened her eyes and began to lick her calf, slowly, methodically, and Lucy smiled as the newborn nuzzled closer. She never tired of this miracle.

Within minutes, the little calf was wobbling to his feet, butting at his mother's side, already urging her to join him in a game.

Nothing could beat the joy of new life.

Except…this idyllic scene was an uncomfortable reminder that Lucy had very little chance of becoming a mother. She'd already suffered one miscarriage and now there was a failed IVF treatment behind her. She was sure she was running out of time. The women in her family had a track record of early menopause and she lived with an ever growing sense of her biological clock counting off the months, days, hours, minutes.

Tick, tock, tick, tock.

Swallowing a sigh, Lucy stood slowly and stretched muscles that had been strained as she'd hauled the calf into the world. She glanced through the barn doorway and saw that the shadows had lengthened across the golden grass of the home paddock.

'What's the time?' she asked Jock Evans, the farmer who'd called her in a panic several hours earlier.

Instead of checking his wrist, Jock turned slowly and squinted at the mellowing daylight outside. 'Just gone five, I reckon.'

'Already?' Lucy hurried to the corner of the barn where she'd left her things, including her watch. She checked it. Jock was dead right. 'I'm supposed to be at a wedding rehearsal by half past five.'

Jock's eyes widened with surprise. 'Don't tell me you're getting married, Lucy?'

'Me? Heavens, no.' Peeling off sterile gloves, she manufactured a gaiety she didn't feel. 'Mattie Carey's the lucky girl getting married. I'm just a bridesmaid.'

Again, she added silently.

The farmer didn't try to hide his relief. 'I'm glad you haven't been snapped up. The Willow Creek district can't afford to have you whisked away from us.'

'Well, there's not much chance.'

'Most folks around here reckon you're the best vet we've ever had.'

'Thanks, Jock.' Lucy sent him a grateful smile, but as she went through to the adjoining room to clean up, her smile wavered and then collapsed.

She really, really loved her job, and she'd worked hard for many years before the local farmers finally placed their trust in a mere 'slip of a girl'. Now she'd finally earned their loyalty and admiration and she knew she should be satisfied, but lately this job hadn't felt like enough.

She certainly didn't want to be married to it!

For Will Carruthers, coming home to Willowbank always felt like stepping back in time. In ten years the sleepy country town had barely changed.

The wide main street was still filled with the same old fashioned flower beds. The bank, the council chambers, the post office and the barber shop all looked exactly as they had when Will first left home.

Today, as he climbed out of his father's battered old truck, the familiar landmarks took on a dreamlike quality. But when he pushed open the gate that led to the white wooden church, where tomorrow his best mate would marry one of his oldest friends, he couldn't help thinking that this sense of time standing still was a mere illusion.

The buildings and the landscape might have stayed the same, but the people who lived here had changed. Oh, yeah. Every person who mattered in Will's life had changed a great deal.

And here was the funny thing. Will had left sleepy old Willowbank, eager to shake its dust from his heels and to make his mark on the world. He'd traversed the globe more times than he cared to count, but now, in so many ways, he felt like the guy who'd been left behind.

From inside the church the wailing cries of a baby sounded, a clear signal of the changes that had taken place. Will's sister Gina appeared at the church door, jiggling a howling ginger-headed infant on her hip.

When she saw her brother, her face broke into a huge smile.

'Will, I'm so glad you made it. Gosh, it's lovely to see you.' Reaching out, she beckoned him closer, gave him a one armed hug. 'Heavens, big brother, have I shrunk or have you grown even taller?'

'Maybe the weight of motherhood is wearing you down.' Will stooped to kiss her, then smiled as he studied her face. 'I take that back, Gina. I don't think you've ever looked happier.'

'I know,' she said beaming. 'It's amazing, isn't it? I seem to have discovered my inner Earth Mother.'

He grinned and patted her baby's chubby arm. 'This must be Jasper. He's certainly a chip off the old block.' The baby was a dead ringer for his father, Tom, right down to his red hair. 'G'day, little guy.'

Jasper stopped crying and stared at Will with big blue eyes, shiny with tears.

'Gosh, that shut him up.' Gina grinned and winked. 'You must have the knack, Will. I knew you'd be perfect uncle material.'

Will chuckled to cover an abrupt slug of emotion that had caught him by surprise. Gina's baby was incredibly cute. His skin was soft and perfectly smooth, his eyes bright and clear. There were dimples on his chubby hands and, crikey, dimples on his knees. And, even though he was only four months old, he was unmistakably sturdy and masculine.

'What a great little guy,' he said, his voice rough around the edges.

Gina was watching him shrewdly. 'Ever thought of having a little boy of your own, Will?'

He covered his sigh with a lopsided grin. 'We both know I've been too much of a gypsy.'

Reluctant to meet his sister's searching gaze, Will studied a stained glass window and found himself remembering a church in Canada, where, only days ago, he'd attended the funeral of a work colleague. He could still see the earnest face of his friend's ten-year-old son, could see the pride in the boy's eyes as he'd bravely faced the congregation and told them how much he'd loved his dad.

Hell, if he let himself think about that father and son relationship now, he'd be a mess in no time.

Hunting for a distraction, Will slid a curious glance towards the chattering group at the front of the church. 'I hope I'm not late. The rehearsal hasn't started, has it?'

'No, don't fret. Hey, everyone!' Gina raised her voice. 'Will's here.'

The chatter stopped. Heads turned and faces broke into smiles. A distinct lump formed in Will's throat.

How good it was to see them all again. Tom, Gina's stolid farmer husband, was grinning like a Cheshire cat as he held baby Mia, Jasper's twin sister.

Mattie, the bride-to-be, looked incredibly happy as she stood with her bridegroom's arm about her shoulders.

Mattie was marrying Jake Devlin and Will still couldn't get over the changes in Jake. The two men had worked ~~~~~er on a mine site in Mongolia and they'd quickly become great mates, but Will could have sworn that Jake was not the marrying kind.

No one had been more stunned when Jake, chief breaker of feminine hearts, had fallen like a ton of bricks for Mattie Carey.

One look at Jake's face now, however, and Will couldn't doubt the truth of it. Crikey, his mate had never looked so relaxed and happy—at peace with himself and eager to take on the world.

As for Mattie…Will had known her all his life…but now she looked…well, there was only one word…

Mattie looked *transformed*.

Radiant and beautiful only went part way to describing her.

He couldn't detect any sign that she'd recently given birth to twins—to Gina and Tom's babies, in fact, in a wonderful surrogacy arrangement that had brought untold blessings to everyone involved. Mattie was not only slim once again, but she'd acquired a new confidence that blazed in her eyes, in her glowing smile, in the way she moved.

All this Will noticed as everyone gathered around him, offering kisses, handshakes and backslaps.

'So glad you could make it,' Jake said, pumping his hand.

'Try to keep me away, mate. I'd pay good money to see you take the plunge tomorrow.'

'We're just waiting for the minister and his wife,' Mattie said. 'And for Lucy.'

Lucy.

It was ages since Will had seen Lucy, and he'd never been happy about the way they'd drifted apart, although it had seemed necessary at the time. 'Is Lucy coming to the wedding rehearsal?'

'Of course,' Mattie said. 'Didn't you know? Lucy's a bridesmaid.'

'I thought Gina was the bridesmaid.'

Gina laughed. 'You haven't been paying attention, Will. Technically, I'm the matron of honour because I'm an old married woman. Lucy's the bridesmaid, you're the best man and Tom's stepping in as a groomsman because Jake's cousin can't get away.'

'I see. Of course.'

It made sense. If Will had given any proper thought to the make-up of the wedding party, he should have known that Mattie would ask Lucy to be a bridesmaid. She was a vital member of their old 'gang'.

And he was totally cool about seeing her again, even though their relationship had been complicated since his brother's death eight years ago.

He was surprised, that was all, by the unexpected catch in his breath at the thought of seeing her again.

Lucy glanced in the rear-view mirror as her ute bounced down the rough country road towards town. *Cringe.* Her hair was limp and in dire need of a shampoo and she knew she looked decidedly scruffy.

She'd cleaned up carefully after delivering the calf, but she couldn't be sure that her hair and clothes were completely free of mud or straw. Steering one-handed, she tried to finger-comb loose strands into some kind of tidiness.

She wasn't wearing any make-up, and she was already in danger of arriving late for Mattie's wedding rehearsal, so she didn't have time to duck home for damage control. Not that it really mattered; tomorrow was the big day, after all. Not today.

But Will Carruthers would be at the rehearsal.

He was going to be best man at this wedding.

And why, after all this time, should that matter? Her crush on Will was ancient history. Water under the bridge. He was simply an old friend she'd almost lost touch with.

At least that was what she'd told herself for the past three months, ever since Mattie had announced her engagement and wedding plans. But, as she reached the outskirts of town, Lucy's body, to her annoyance, decided otherwise.

One glimpse of the little white church and the Carruthers family's elderly truck parked among the other vehicles on the green verge outside and Lucy's chest squeezed painfully. She felt as if she was breathing through cotton wool and her hands slipped on the steering wheel.

Her heart thumped.

Good grief, this was crazy. She'd known for twelve weeks now that Will would be a member of the wedding party. Why had she waited until the last moment to fall apart?

She parked the ute, dragged in a deep breath and closed her eyes, gave herself a stern lecture. She could do this. She was going to walk inside that little church with an easy stride and a smile on her face. She couldn't do much about her external appearance, but at least no one need guess she was a mess inside.

She would rather die than let on that she was jealous of Mattie for snaring and marrying a heart-throb like Jake. And she wouldn't turn the slightest hint of green when she cuddled Gina and Tom's darling babies.

More importantly, she would greet Will serenely.

She might even drop a light kiss on his cheek. After all, if her plans to marry Will's brother Josh hadn't been cruelly shattered, she would have been his sister-in-law.

OK.

She was only a few minutes late so she took a moment to check that her blouse was neatly tucked into her khaki jeans. Her boots were a bit dusty so she hastily wiped them with a tissue. There were no visible signs of the barn yard, thank heavens.

Feeling rather like a soldier going over the top of a trench, she didn't wait for second thoughts. She dived through the church doorway, cheery smile pinned in place, apologies for her lateness at the ready.

Thud. Will was standing at the end of the aisle, in front of the chancel steps, chatting to Jake.

Surreptitiously, Lucy devoured familiar details—the nut brown sheen of his hair, the outdoor glow on his skin and the creases at the corners of his eyes and mouth, his long legs in faded blue jeans.

As if these weren't enough to raise her temperature, she saw baby Mia, in a froth of pink, curled sleepily into the crook of Will's arm.

Heavens, had there ever been a sweeter place for a baby to sleep?

The tiny girl and the big man together made an image that she'd guiltily pictured in her most secret dreams and the sight of them now sucked vital air from her lungs.

Somehow she managed to walk down the aisle.

'Lucy!' Mattie called. 'I was just about to ring you.'

'I'm sorry I'm late. I was held up with a tricky calving.' She was surprised she could speak normally when her attention was riveted by Will, not just by how amazing he looked with that tiny pink bundle in his arms, but by the way his head swung abruptly at the sound of her voice and the way he went still and his eyes blazed suddenly.

Lucy felt as if the entire world had stopped, except for the frantic beating of her heart.

Thank heavens no one else seemed to notice.

'Don't worry,' Mattie was telling her calmly. 'We haven't been here long. I've just been going over the music with the organist.'

Everything was so suddenly normal and relaxed that Lucy was sure she'd misjudged Will's reaction. He certainly looked mega-cool and calm now as he greeted her. His light touch on her shoulder as he bent to kiss her and the merest brush of his lips on her cheek scalded her, but Will's grey eyes were perfectly calm.

He even looked mildly amused when he greeted her. 'Good to see you again, Lucy.'

In a matter of moments the babies were handed over to the minister's wife and daughter, who cooed and fussed over them in the front pew, while the members of the wedding party were taken through their paces.

Will, as the best man, would partner Gina. Lucy would process with Tom. So that was a relief. At least she didn't have to link arms and walk down the aisle with Will at the end of tomorrow's ceremony.

Lucy had been a bridesmaid twice before so she knew the ropes, but the minister wanted to explain every step of the service, and the rehearsal seemed to drag on and on.

On the plus side, she had time to calm down. This wedding was going to be a cinch. Nothing to get in a twist about.

Anyway, it was the height of self-indulgence to keep thinking about herself. Tomorrow was going to be Mattie's big day. Lucy, along with the entire population of Willowbank, loved warm-hearted, generous Mattie Carey and the whole township would probably turn out to watch her marry the hunky man of her dreams.

Lucy didn't want a single event or unhappy thought to mar this wedding's perfection.

Will who?

By the time the rehearsal was over, it was already dark outside, with a fragile fingernail moon hanging above the post office clock. The group dispersed quickly. Gina and Tom wanted to hurry home to get their babies settled. Mattie and Jake had to dash away to a special dinner Mattie's parents were hosting for assorted members of both families.

And Lucy wanted to hurry home to her 'boys', as she affectionately called her dogs. The Irish setter and the border collie enjoyed each other's company but, if she was away for any length of time, they were always frantic to see her.

She was fishing in her pocket for her car keys when she felt a tap on her elbow. She swung around to find herself trapped by Will Carruthers's smile, like a startled animal caught in a car's headlights.

'I haven't had a proper chance to say hello,' he said easily. 'I wanted to know how you are.'

Lucy gulped. 'I…I'm fine.' She was grateful that the darkness disguised the flush in her face, but it took a moment to remember to add, 'Thanks.' And, a frantic breath later, 'How about you, Will?'

'Not bad.' He gave her another smile and the skin around his eyes crinkled, then he shoved his hands into his jeans' pockets and stood in front of her with his long legs comfortably apart, shoulders wide. So tall and big he made her shiver.

She managed to ask, 'Are you still working in Mongolia?'

'Actually, no.' There was a slight pause and the tiniest

hint of an edgy chuckle. 'I was there long enough. Decided it's time for a change, so I'm going to look around for somewhere new.'

The news didn't surprise Lucy but, after so many years, she'd finally got used to Will's absence. When he was safely overseas she could almost forget about him. Almost.

Without quite meeting her gaze, Will said, 'Gina tells me you've bought a house.'

Lucy nodded. 'I bought the old Finnegan place at the end of Wicker Lane.' She shot him a rueful smile. 'It's a renovator's delight.'

'Sounds like a challenge.'

'A huge one.'

He lifted his gaze to meet hers and a glimmer of amusement lingered in his eyes. 'You were always one for a challenge.'

Lucy wasn't quite sure what Will meant by this. He might have been referring to the way she'd worked hard at her studies during their long ago friendship at university. Or it could have been a direct reference to the fact that she'd once been engaged to his chick-magnet older brother.

She tried to sound nonchalant. 'I haven't managed many renovations on the house yet. But at least there's plenty of room for my surgery and a nice big yard for the dogs.'

'How many dogs do you have now?'

She blinked with surprise at his unexpected question. 'Just the two still.'

'Seamus and Harry.'

'That's right.'

A small silence ticked by and Lucy felt awkward. She knew that if she'd met any other old friend from her schooldays she would have offered an invitation to come back to her place. They could have shared a simple meal—probably pasta and a salad—eating in the kitchen, which she had at least partially renovated.

They could open a bottle of wine, catch up on old times, gossip about everything that had happened in the intervening years.

But her history with this man was too complicated. To start with, she'd never been able to completely snuff out the torch she carried for him, but that wasn't her only worry. Eight years ago, she'd made the terrible mistake of getting involved with his brother.

This was not the time, however, on the eve of Mattie and Jake's wedding, to rehash that sad episode.

From the darkness in the tree-lined creek behind the church a curlew's mournful cry drifted across the night and, almost as if it was a signal, Will took a step back. 'Well, I guess I'll see you tomorrow.'

'I dare say you won't be able to avoid it.'

Heavens, why had she said that? It sounded churlish. To make up for the gaffe, Lucy said quickly before he could leave, 'I'm so happy for Mattie. Jake seems like a really nice guy.'

'He's terrific,' Will agreed. 'And I'll have to hand it to Mattie. She succeeded in winning him when many others have failed.'

'Jake obviously adores her.'

'Oh, yeah, he's totally smitten.' Will looked suddenly uncomfortable and his shoulders lifted in an awkward shrug.

Lucy suspected this conversation was getting sticky for both of them.

'It's getting late,' she said gently. 'You'd better go. Your mother will have dinner waiting.'

He chuckled. 'That sounds like something from the dim dark ages when we were at high school.'

'Sorry,' she said, but he had already turned and was walking towards the truck.

He opened the squeaky door, then turned again and they both exchanged a brief wave before they climbed into their respective vehicles.

Lucy heard the elderly truck's motor rise in a harsh rev, then die down into a throaty lumbering growl. Will backed out of the parking spot and drove down the street and as she turned the key in her ute's ignition, she watched the truck's twin red tail lights growing smaller.

She remembered the times she'd driven with Will in that old truck of his father's, bumping over paddocks or down rough country lanes. Together they'd gone fossicking for sapphires, hunting for specks of gold down in the creek. At other times she'd urged him to help her to search for a new sub-species of fish.

They'd been great mates back then, but those days when Lucy had first moved to Willowbank with her dad after her parents' messy divorce felt like so very long ago now.

She had been sixteen and it was a horrible time, when she was angry with everyone. She'd been angry with her mother for falling in love with her boss, angry with her dad for somehow allowing it to happen, and angry with both of them for letting their marriage disintegrate in a heartbeat.

Most of all Lucy had been angry that she'd had to move away from Sydney to Willowbank. She'd hated leaving her old school and her friends to vegetate in a docile country town.

But then she'd met Will, along with Gina, Tom and Mattie and she'd soon been absorbed into a happy circle of friends who'd proved that life in the country could be every bit as good as life in the city.

OK, maybe her love of Willowbank had a lot to do with her feelings for Will, but at least she'd never let on how much she'd adored him. Instead, she'd waited patiently for him to realise that he loved her. When he took too long she'd taken matters into her own hands and it had all gone horribly wrong.

But it was so, so unhelpful to be thinking about that now.

Even so, Lucy was fighting tears as she reversed the ute. And, as she drove out of town, she was bombarded by bittersweet, lonely memories.

CHAPTER TWO

THE impact of the explosion sent Will flying, tossed him like a child's rag toy and dumped him hard. He woke with his heart thudding, his nerves screaming as he gripped at the bed sheets.

Bed sheets?

At first he couldn't think how he'd arrived back in the bedroom of his schooldays, but then he slowly made sense of his surroundings.

He was no longer in Mongolia.

He was safe.

He wished it had all been a nightmare, but it was unfortunately true. He'd been conducting a prospecting inspection of an old abandoned mine when it had blown without warning. By some kind of miracle he'd escaped serious injury, but his two good friends were dead.

That was the savage reality. He'd been to the funerals of both Barney and Keith—one in Brisbane and the other in Ottawa.

He'd been to hell and back sitting in those separate chapels, listening to heartbreaking eulogies and wondering why he'd been spared when his friends had so not deserved to die.

And yet here he was, home at Tambaroora...

Where nothing had changed…

Squinting in the shuttered moonlight, Will could see the bookshelf that still held his old school textbooks. His swimming trophies lined the shelf above the bed, and he knew without looking that the first geological specimens he'd collected were in a small glass case on the desk beneath the window.

Even the photo of him with his brother, Josh, was still there on the dresser. It showed Will squashed onto a pathetic little tricycle that he was clearly too big for, while Josh looked tall and grown-up on his first two-wheeler bike.

Will rolled over so he couldn't see the image. He didn't want to be reminded that his brother had beaten him to just about everything that was important in his life. It hadn't been enough for Josh Carruthers to monopolise their father's affection, he'd laid first claim on Tambaroora and he'd won the heart of Will's best friend.

That might have been OK if Josh had taken good care of Lucy.

An involuntary sigh whispered from Will's lips.

Lucy.

Seeing her again tonight had unsettled him on all kinds of levels.

When he closed his eyes he could see the silvery-white gleam of moonlight on her hair as they'd stood outside the church. He could hear the familiar soft lilt in her voice.

Damn it. He'd wanted to tell her about the accident. He needed to talk about it.

He hadn't told his family because he knew it would upset his mother. Jessie Carruthers had already lost one son and she didn't need the news of her surviving son's brush with death.

Will could have talked to Jake, of course. They'd worked together in Mongolia and Jake would have understood how upset he was, but he hadn't wanted to throw a wet blanket on the eve of his mate's wedding.

No, Lucy was the one person he would have liked to talk to. In the past, they'd often talked long into the night. As students they'd loved deep and meaningful discussions.

Yes, he could have told Lucy what he'd learned at those funerals.

But it was probably foolish to think he could resurrect the closeness they'd enjoyed as students.

After all this time, they'd both changed.

Hell, was it really eight years? He could still feel the shock of that December day when he'd been skiing in Norway and he'd received the news that Lucy and his brother were engaged to be married. He'd jumped on the first plane home.

With a groan, Will flung aside the sheet and swung out of bed, desperate to throw off the memories and the sickening guilt and anger that always accompanied his thoughts of that terrible summer.

But, with the benefit of hindsight, Will knew he'd been unreasonably angry with Josh for moving in on his best friend while his back was turned. He'd had no claim on Lucy. She'd never been his girlfriend. He'd gone overseas with Cara Howard and, although their relationship hadn't lasted, he'd allowed himself to be distracted by new sights, new people, new adventures.

He'd let life take him by the hand, happy to go with the flow, finding it easier than settling down.

The news that Josh was going to marry Lucy shouldn't have upset him, but perhaps he might have coped more easily if Lucy had chosen to marry a stranger. As it was he'd never been able to shake off the feeling that Josh had moved in on her just to prove to his little brother that he could have whatever he desired.

Unfortunately, Will had chosen the very worst time to have it out with Josh.

He would never, to the end of his days, forget the early morning argument at the airfield, or Josh's stubbornness, or the sight of that tiny plane tumbling out of the sky like an autumn leaf.

If only that had been the worst of it, but it was Gina who'd told him that the shock of Josh's death had caused Lucy to have a miscarriage.

A miscarriage?

Will had been plagued by endless questions—questions he'd had no right to ask. Which had come first—the engagement or the pregnancy? Had Josh truly loved Lucy?

A week after the funeral he'd tried to speak to her, but Dr McKenty had been fiercely protective of his daughter and he'd turned Will away.

So the only certainties that he'd been left with were Josh's death and Lucy's loss, and he'd found it pitifully easy to take the blame for both.

To make amends, he'd actually tried to stay on at Tambaroora after Josh's death. But he couldn't replace Josh in his father's eyes and he'd soon known that he didn't fit in any more. He was a piece from a flashy foreign jigsaw trying to fit into a homemade puzzle.

For Will, it had made sense to leave again and to stay away longer. In time, he'd trained himself to stop dwelling on the worst of it. But of course he couldn't stay away from his home and family for ever and there were always going to be times, like now, when everything came back to haunt him.

* * *

Lucy dreamed about Will.

In her dream they were back at Sydney University and they'd met in the refectory for coffee and to compare notes after a chemistry practical.

It was an incredibly simple but companionable scene. She and Will had always enjoyed hanging out together, and in her dream they were sitting at one of the little tables overlooking the courtyard, chatting and smiling and discussing the results of their latest experiments.

When it was time to leave for separate lectures, Lucy announced calmly, as if it was a normal extension of their everyday conversation, 'Oh, by the way, Will, I'm pregnant.'

Will's face broke into a beautiful smile and he drew her into his arms and hugged her, and Lucy knew that her pregnancy was the perfect and natural expression of their love.

She felt the special protection of his arms about her and she was filled with a sense of perfect happiness, of well-being, of everything being right in her world.

When she woke, she lay very still with her eyes closed, lingering for as long as she could in the happy afterglow of the dream, clinging to the impossible fantasy that she was pregnant.

Better than that, she was pregnant with Will's baby. Not his brother's…

The dream began to fade and she could no longer ignore the fact that morning sunlight was pulsing on the other side of her closed eyelids.

Reality reared its unwelcome head.

Damn.

Not that dream again. How stupid.

Actually, it was more like a recurring nightmare, so far divorced from Lucy's real life that she always felt sick when she woke. She hated to think that her subconscious could still, after all this time, play such cruel tricks on her.

In truth, she'd never been brave enough to let her friendship with Will progress into anything deeper. At university, she'd seen all the other girls who'd fallen for him. She'd watched Will date them for a while and then move on, and she'd decided it was safer to simply be his buddy. His friend.

As his girlfriend she'd risk losing him and she couldn't have coped with that. If they remained good friends, she could keep him for ever.

Or so she'd thought.

The plan had serious flaws, of course, which was no doubt why she was still plagued far too often by the dream.

But now, as Lucy opened her eyes, she knew it was time to wake up to more important realities. This wasn't just any morning. It was Mattie's wedding day.

This was a day for hair appointments and manicures, helping Mattie to dress and smiling for photographs. This was to be her friend's perfect day.

Get over it, Lucy.

Get over yourself.

Stifling a lingering twinge of longing for the dream, she threw off the bedclothes, went to the window and looked out. It was a beautiful day, cloudless and filled with sunshine. She smiled.

No more useless longings. No more doleful thoughts.

Surely clear blue skies were a very promising omen?

In Willowbank everyone was abuzz.

With the help of friends and relatives from around the

district, Mattie's mum had grown masses of white petunias in pots and tubs and even in wheelbarrows.

Lucy happily helped a team of women to unload containers of flowers from their cars and place them strategically in the church and the grounds, as well as the marquee where the reception was to be held in an allotment next to the church hall. The instant floral effect was spectacular.

After that, the morning passed in a happy whirl, much to Lucy's relief. First, she met up with Mattie and Gina at the hairdresser's, then they popped into the salon next door for matching manicures, and finally they dashed back to Mattie's for a delicious light lunch prepared by one of her doting aunts.

During lunch the phone seemed never to stop ringing and all kinds of messages flew back and forth. Gina's mum, who was babysitting the twins, reported that they'd been fed and burped and were sleeping beautifully. Nurses from the Sydney hospital where the babies had been born rang to wish Mattie and Jake all the best for married life. The caterer had a question about the positioning of the wedding cake on the main table.

Lucy had to admire the way Mattie seemed to float through it all. She was the most serene bride ever. Nothing bothered her or was too much trouble. Mattie had always been sweet and easy-going, but she'd never been as blissfully relaxed and happy and confident as she was today.

It must be love, Lucy thought, and she wished it was contagious.

Shortly after lunch, the excitement really began. Refrigerated boxes arrived from the florist, filled with truly gorgeous bouquets. Then it was time for the girls to put on their make-up, laughing as they took turns in front of

Mattie's bedroom mirror, the same mirror where years ago they had first experimented with mascara and eyeliner while they'd gossiped about boys.

Back then, Lucy, being older and from the city, had been considered to be wiser and worldlier. The other girls had looked up to her with undisguised respect and considerable awe.

How the tables had turned. Now Gina was married and a mother, and Mattie was about to marry Jake, while Lucy was...

No! She wasn't going to tolerate a single negative thought today.

When they'd achieved their best with make-up, Gina and Lucy slipped into their bridesmaid's dresses, which were simply divine. The palest pink duchess satin looked equally pretty on Gina with her dark hair and olive complexion as it did on Lucy, who was blonde and fair-skinned.

Then it was time to fuss over Mattie, to fasten the dozens of tiny satin-covered buttons down her back, to help to secure her veil and then to gasp in sheer astonishment when they saw the completed picture of their best friend in her wedding gown.

'You look absolutely breathtaking,' Lucy whispered.

Gina was emotional. 'You're so beautiful Jake's going to cry when he sees you.'

'Please don't say that.' Mattie laughed nervously. 'You'll make *me* cry.'

'And me,' moaned Lucy.

Already, at the mere thought of an emotional bridegroom, she could feel mascara-threatening tears about to spill.

Oh, help. Weddings were such poignant affairs. And

today Will was going to be there, looking dashing as the best man. How on earth was she going to get through the next few hours?

Dressed in matching dark formal suits with silver ties and orange blossoms in their lapels, Jake, Will and Tom were ushered into the minuscule vestry and instructed to wait till it was time to take their places at the front of the church.

Will anxiously patted a pocket in his suit jacket. 'The rings are still safe.'

Jake grinned and laid a reassuring hand on his friend's shoulder. 'That's the third time you've checked the rings in the past five minutes. Relax, man, they're not going to grow legs and run away.'

'Jake's the guy who's supposed to be nervous,' added Tom with a grin.

Will nodded and tried to smile. 'Sorry. Don't know what's got into me.' He shot Jake a questioning glance. 'Aren't you even a little nervous?'

'Why should I be nervous?'

'You're getting married.' Will wished his voice wasn't so hoarse. His sleepless night was really getting to him. 'It's par for the course for a bridegroom to have the jitters,' he said.

'But I'm marrying Mattie,' Jake responded simply, as if that explained everything. And his glowing smile made it patently clear that he knew, without doubt, he was the luckiest man alive.

Will wished he felt a fraction of his mate's happiness.

'So where are you heading for your honeymoon?' he asked. 'Or is that a state secret?'

Jake grinned. 'The exact location is a surprise for

Mattie, but I'll tell you two.' He lowered his voice. 'I'm taking her to Italy. She's never been overseas, so we're going to Venice, Lake Como and the Amalfi Coast.'

'Wow!' Tom's jaw dropped. 'That's so over the top it's fabulous. You'll have an amazing time.'

Jake nodded happily but, before he could say anything else, the minister appeared at the vestry door and sent them a smiling wink. 'Could you come this way now please, gentlemen?'

A chill ran down Will's spine. For crying out loud, what was the matter with him today? Anyone would think he was the one getting married, or that they were criminals being led to the dock.

'All the best, mate,' he whispered gruffly to Jake.

'Thanks.'

The two friends shook hands, then headed through the little doorway that led into the church, where an incredible transformation had occurred.

Not only was the place packed to the rafters with people dressed in their best finery, but there were flowers and white ribbons everywhere—dangling from the ends of pews, wound around columns, adorning windowsills and filling vases, large and small.

And there was organ music, billowing and rippling like the background music in a sentimental movie. Will tried to swallow the lump in his throat. Why was it that weddings were designed to zero straight in on unsuspecting emotions?

He glanced at Jake and saw his Adam's apple jerk.

'You OK?' he whispered out of the side of his mouth.

'I'll be fine once Mattie gets here.'

'She won't be late,' Will reassured him and again he nervously patted the rings in his pocket.

There was a flurry in the little porch at the back of the church and, as if everyone had been choreographed, the congregation turned. Will felt fine hairs lift on the back of his neck. His stomach tightened.

The girls appeared in a misty mirage of white and pink. Will blinked. Lucy, Gina and Mattie looked incredibly out-of-this-world beautiful in long feminine dresses and glamorous hairstyles, and with their arms filled with flowers.

He heard Jake catch his breath, felt goosebumps lift on his arms.

The organist struck a dramatic chord.

Lucy and Gina, apparently satisfied with their arrangement of Mattie's dress and veil, took their places in front of her, Lucy first.

Will couldn't be sure that he wasn't trembling.

Lucy stood, shoulders back, looking straight ahead, with her blonde head high, her blue eyes smiling. To Will she looked vulnerable and yet resolute and his heart began to thunder loudly.

It was so weird.

He'd seen countless weddings and endless processions of bridesmaids, but none of them had made him feel the way he felt now as the organist began to play and Lucy began to walk down the aisle with her smile carefully in place.

She'd always tried to pretend she was a tomboy, keeping her hair short and wispy and preferring to live in T-shirts and jeans, but today nothing could hide her femininity.

Her pastel off-the-shoulders dress and the soft pink lilies in her arms highlighted the paleness of her hair, the honey-gold tints in her skin, the pink lushness of her lips. She had never looked lovelier.

Except perhaps…that one night on a shadowy veranda, when she'd turned to him with tears in her eyes…

He willed her to look at him. Just one glance would do. For old friendship's sake. He wanted eye contact, needed to send her one smile, longed for one tiny link with her.

Come on, look this way, Lucy.

She smiled at the people in the congregation, at her particular friends, at Jake, but her gaze didn't flicker any further to the right. It was clear she did not want to see Will.

Or, perhaps, she simply felt no need.

CHAPTER THREE

LUCY'S eyes were distinctly misty as she watched Mattie and Jake dance the bridal waltz. They looked so happy together and so deeply in love. She was sure everyone watching them felt misty-eyed too.

It had been an utterly perfect wedding.

The beautiful ceremony had been followed by a happy procession across Willowbank's main street to the marquee where the reception was held. Champagne flowed, a string quartet played glorious music and the guests were served delectable food.

Jake's speech had been heartfelt and touching and Will's toast was appropriately witty, although he went embarrassingly over the top with his praise for the bridesmaids. Lucy had felt her face flame when curious eyes had swung in her direction and the cutting of the cake had been a welcome distraction.

Everyone had broken into spontaneous cheering for Mattie and Jake, and Lucy was thrilled. The wedding couldn't have been happier.

She was relieved that she'd survived without making a fool of herself. Which mostly meant avoiding Will—a tall order given that her eyes had developed a habit of sneaking in his direction whenever she thought he wasn't looking. She'd tried so hard to ignore him, but she'd always thought he was the best-looking guy ever.

She could still remember the day she'd first met him as a schoolboy down by Willow Creek, crouched at the edge of the water.

Even viewing him from behind, he'd been beautiful.

He'd taken his shirt off and he'd been squatting, reaching down, panning for gold in the water. Sunlight breaking through overhead trees had lent an extra sheen to his dark brown hair and to the smooth golden-brown skin on his back.

Lucy hadn't been able to help staring. His shoulders were wide, his hips narrow, his limbs long—the build of a swimmer.

Now, so many years later, he was even more irresistible in his dark formal attire. Lucy kept finding things she needed to check out—the manly jut of his jaw above the crisp collar, the neat line of his dark hair across the back of his neck, the stunning breadth of his shoulders in the stylish suit jacket…

Sigh…

Despite the wedding's perfection, the evening had been a huge strain and she was worn out.

She'd kicked off her high heeled shoes and they were now stowed under the table. She was thinking rather fondly about the end of the night when she could head for home. It would be so nice to greet her dogs, then curl up in bed with a glass of water and a headache tablet.

Tom leaned towards her. 'Lucy, it's our turn to dance.'

She winced. 'Is it really?'

Tom was already on his feet. 'Come on. Gina and Will are already up. You know the wedding party is expected to take a twirl on the dance floor.'

Bother. She'd forgotten about that. She suppressed a sigh as she fished beneath the table for her shoes. *Ouch.* They pinched as she squeezed back into them.

She looked over at the dance floor and saw that Tom was right. Gina was already dancing with Will and, for no reason that made sense, her silly heart began to trip and stumble.

'Lead the way,' she told Tom resolutely, slipping her arm through his. Thank heavens he was a reliable old friend. At least she could dance with Tom till the cows came home without being attacked by dangerous palpitations.

Unfortunately, Tom didn't seem to be quite so enamoured with her as his dancing partner. At the end of the bracket, other couples joined them on the dance floor and Tom leaned close to her ear. 'Would you mind if I asked Gina for a dance?'

'Of course I don't mind.' She took a step back to prove it. 'Please, go ahead. You must dance with your wife.'

Tom happily tapped Will on the back and Lucy retreated to the edge of the timber dance floor. Over her shoulder, she watched the men's brief smiling exchange. She saw Will's nod and her heart began to race as she guessed what might happen next.

It was logical—a common courtesy for Will to ask *her* to dance—but there were times when logic and courtesy flew out of the window. Times like now, when her out of date, unhelpful feelings for Will made simple things complicated.

On the surface, one quick dance with an old friend should have been a piece of cake. But on a super-romantic night like tonight, Lucy was trembling at the very thought of dancing publicly in Will Carruthers's arms.

She couldn't help thinking about that kiss all those years ago, when she'd made a fool of herself at Will's farewell party. She turned, planning to hurry back to her place at the table.

'Lucy!'

Will's voice sounded close behind her and she froze.

'I won't let you escape that easily.' His tone held a thread of humour, but there was also a note of command that was hard to ignore.

His hand brushed her wrist and the touch was like a firebrand. Lucy was helpless as his fingers enclosed around her, as he pulled her gently but decisively towards him. 'Come on,' he urged. 'We've got to have one dance.'

He made it sound easy, but when she looked into his cool grey eyes she was surprised to see a cautious edge to his smile, as if he wasn't quite as confident as he sounded. Which didn't help her to relax.

A number of wedding guests were watching them, however, and the last thing she wanted was a scene.

'One dance?' Lucy forced lightness into her voice. 'Why not?' She managed a smile. No way did she want to give the impression she was trying to dodge Will. One dance was no problem at all. She would dance with him till her feet fell off.

Will led her back onto the dance floor.

Gulp.

As soon as he placed one hand at her back and took her other hand in his, she knew this wasn't going to be any version of easy. She drew a jagged breath.

'Smile,' Will murmured as he pulled her closer. 'This is a wedding, not a funeral.'

He took the lead and Lucy obediently pinned on a smile.

She'd only danced with Will a handful of times, long ago. Even so, she could remember every single detail—his habit of enfolding her fingers inside his, the way he smelled of midnight, and the way her head was exactly level with his jaw.

Tonight, every familiar memory felt like a pulled thread, unravelling her poorly stitched self control. Being this close to Will played havoc with her heartbeats, with her sense of rhythm. She kept stumbling and bumping into him and then apologising profusely.

After the third apology, he steered her to the edge of the floor and he leaned back a little, and he smiled as he looked into her face.

Will said something, but Lucy couldn't hear him above the music and she shook her head, lifted her shoulders to show she had no idea.

Leaning closer, she felt her skin vibrate as he spoke into her ear. 'Are you OK? Would you like a break?'

That would be sensible, wouldn't it?

She nodded. 'Yes, please.'

A reprieve.

Maybe not. Will stayed close beside her as she returned to the table and, before she could resume her seat, he said, 'There are chairs outside. Why don't we go out there where it's cooler and quieter, away from the music?'

Lucy's heart stumbled again. Going outside where it was quieter suggested that Will wanted to talk.

Part of her yearned to talk with him, but she wasn't sure it was wise. What could they talk about now? They'd covered the basics last night after the rehearsal, and Will had been away for so long that they'd lost their old sense of camaraderie.

Besides, further conversation would surely lead to uncomfortable topics like her relationship with Josh. Wouldn't it be wiser to simply keep their distance now?

But the look in Will's eyes as he watched her sent a fine shiver rushing over her skin and she knew that wisdom would lose this particular battle and curiosity would win. She secretly longed to hear what Will wanted to talk about.

'I'm sure a little fresh air is a good idea,' she said and she went with him through a doorway in the side of the marquee into the moon silvered night.

They found two chairs abandoned by smokers and, as soon as Lucy sat down, she slipped off her shoes and rubbed at her aching feet.

Will chuckled softly.

'I'm not used to wearing such high heels,' she said defensively. 'You should try them. They're sheer torture.'

'I don't doubt that for a moment, but they look sensational.' He released a button on his jacket, letting it fall open. His shirt gleamed whitely in the moonlight and he stretched his long legs in front of him.

After a small pause, he said, 'I meant what I said in my speech. You look lovely tonight, Lucy.'

Her cheeks grew warm again. 'Thanks. Mattie chose our dresses. She has very feminine tastes.'

He let her self-effacing comment pass.

'It's been a perfect wedding,' she said to make amends, but then she was ambushed by an involuntary yawn. 'But it seems to have worn me out.'

'You've probably been working too hard.'

She shook her head. 'My work doesn't very often make me tired. Weddings, on the other hand…'

'Can be very draining.'

'Yes.'

He was watching her with a lopsided smile. 'It's not always easy to watch your friends tie the knot.'

'I…' Her mouth was suddenly dry and her tongue stuck to its roof. She shot Will a sharp glance, uncertain where this conversation was heading. She tried again. 'I'm really happy for Mattie, aren't you?'

'Absolutely,' he said. 'Marriage couldn't have happened to a nicer girl.'

Lucy nodded. A small silence limped by. 'I suppose weddings are tiring because they involve lots of people.' Hunting for a way to disguise the fact that Will's presence at this wedding was her major problem, she made a sweeping gesture towards the crowded marquee. 'I'm more used to animals these days. They're so much quieter than humans.'

'And I'm used to rocks.'

Lucy laughed. 'I dare say they're quieter too.'

'Silence is one of their better attributes.' Will chuckled again. 'Sounds like we've turned into a pair of old loners.'

'Maybe,' she said softly, but she knew it was hazardous for her to talk of such things with this man.

Quietly, he said, 'It's happening all around us, Goose.'

Goose…her old nickname.

Only her father and Will had ever called her Goose, or Lucy Goose…and hearing the name now made her dangerously nostalgic.

She tried to shake that feeling aside. 'What's happening all around us?'

'Friends getting married. Starting families.'

Lucy stiffened. Why did he have to bring up *that* subject? 'It's hardly surprising, given our friends' ages.'

'Yes, and we're older than all of them.'

Tick tock, tick tock, tick tock…

Lucy closed her eyes as the familiar breathless panic

gripped her. *No.* She wasn't going to think about *that* worry tonight. She'd declared a moratorium on all thoughts that involved babies, having babies, wanting babies, losing babies. She couldn't imagine why Will had raised such a sensitive topic.

Or perhaps he didn't know about her miscarriage. After his brother's death, she'd barely spoken to Will at the funeral and then he'd moved as far away from Willowbank as was humanly possible. Since then, if they'd run into each other, it had been by accident, or because their friends had invited them to the same Christmas party.

Will had always been polite but he'd kept his distance and Lucy had always been busily proving to him that she was managing damn fine splendid on her own.

So why this?

Why now?

Lucy knew her sudden breathless fear would not be helped by a continued discussion of marriage and babies with Will Carruthers.

'Is there a point to this conversation, Will?' She thrust her feet back into her shoes and grimaced as they pinched. 'Because I don't enjoy being reminded of how old I'm getting.'

She jumped to her feet, only to discover she was shaking violently. Her knees had no strength whatsoever and she had no choice but to sink down again.

She was too embarrassed to look at Will.

In a heartbeat, he was bending over her solicitously. 'I'm sorry. I thought I was stating the obvious. Marriages, births, christenings all around us. Are you all right? Can I get you a drink?'

'I'm fine,' she lied, dragging in oxygen. 'But I...I should go back inside. Mattie might need me.'

'Are you sure you're OK?'

She gulped another deep breath. 'I'm certain.'

Will's hand was at her elbow, supporting her as she got to her feet again, and she hoped he couldn't feel the way her body trembled.

With her first step she swayed against him. He put his arm around her and it felt amazingly fabulous to have his solid shoulder to lean on. 'I swear I haven't had too much to drink,' she said.

'I know that. You're just tired.'

She supposed he was right. What else could it be?

'As soon as this reception is over, I'll drive you home,' Will said.

'There's no need.'

'No arguments, Lucy. You don't have your car here, do you?'

'No,' she admitted. 'I left it at Mattie's place.'

'My vehicle's here. If you're tired, you need a lift.'

By now they'd reached the doorway to the marquee and Lucy could see Gina handing around a platter of wedding cake in pink and silver parcels.

'Oh, heavens,' she cried, slipping from Will's hold. 'I should be helping with the cake.'

'Are you sure you're up to it?'

'Of course.'

And, as she hurried to help, she knew that it was true. She was perfectly fine when she was safely away from Will.

That went well, Will thought wryly as he watched Lucy hand around platters of wedding cake.

Already she was smiling and chatting and looking a hundred times happier than she had a few minutes ago when he'd crassly reminded her that life was passing them by.

Watching her with a thoughtful frown, he recalled the countless conversations they'd enjoyed when they were friends. They'd shared a mutual interest in science, and so they'd been totally in tune about many things. It was only later, when they'd talked about life after university, that their friendship had run into trouble.

Lucy was adventurous and as curious about the world as he was, but unlike him, she hadn't been keen to get away. She'd apparently wanted nothing more than to get straight back to Willowbank, to settle down in a veterinary practice.

Her father was a doctor and she'd claimed that she was anxious to follow his example. She'd worked hard to get her degree and she looked on travel as a waste of time. Why work at menial jobs simply to earn enough money to move on to the next travel spot, when she could stay in Willowbank and build her career?

At the time, when Will had left on his big adventure with Cara in tow, he'd had a vague idea that he might eventually return and find work closer to home.

The news of his brother's engagement to Lucy McKenty had come out of the blue and he'd been shocked by how much it had worried him, by the urge that had hit him to hurry home. Not that he could blame Lucy for falling in love with Josh.

Everyone in the entire Willow Creek district had loved his outgoing, confident brother—and Josh Carruthers had a habit of getting what he wanted, especially when it came to women.

Will could easily imagine how his brother had flirted with Lucy. Hell, yeah. Josh would have charmed and courted her so expertly she wouldn't have known what had hit her. And Josh would have offered her the exact life she wanted—marriage and a family, with a sheep station thrown in as the icing on the cake.

But had Josh really, deeply cared for Lucy? Had he wanted to make her happy?

It surprised Will that he still let these questions bother him after all this time.

'You look down in the mouth.' Jake's voice sounded at Will's elbow. 'Everything OK?'

Will turned guiltily and forced a grin. 'It's been a fabulous night,' he said, hoping to avoid answering Jake's question. 'Ace wedding, mate.'

'Glad you've had a good time.' Jake nodded his head in Lucy's direction. 'She's a lovely girl.'

It was pointless to pretend he didn't know who Jake meant. Will nodded. 'Yeah.' He shoved his hands deep in his pockets, as if the action could somehow comfort him.

'Mattie told me you two used to be really close.'

'Close friends,' Will corrected and he did his best to dismiss this with a shrug, but Jake was watching him in a way that made his neck burn hotly.

Jake smiled. 'You look as miserable as I felt four months ago, before I sorted everything out with Mattie.'

'This is totally different. More like a mystery than history,' Will muttered glumly.

'Perhaps. But, in the end, it all comes down to the same thing.'

Will glared at his friend. 'I didn't realise that a marriage ceremony turned a man into an instant relationship guru.'

Jake's smile faded. 'Sorry. Was I sounding smug?'

'You were.' Will gave another shrug. 'But I'd probably be smug too, if I was in your shoes.'

'Except that you're right,' Jake said, looking more serious now. 'I know nothing about you and Lucy.'

A heavy sigh escaped Will and he realised that, despite his fierce reaction, he'd actually been hoping that his friend could reveal some kind of magic insight that would help him to clear the air with Lucy. Anything to be rid of this gnawing guilt he still carried.

'I think we're heading off soon,' Jake said. 'I guess I'd better find my wife and finish our farewells.'

They shook hands and Will wished his mate all the best and it wasn't much later before the guests started gathering on the footpath to wave the happy couple off.

In the light of a street lamp, Will could see Lucy's golden hair shimmering palely as she kissed Mattie and Jake, before she drifted back to watch their departure from the edge of the crowd.

Mattie was laughing as she stood at the car's open door and lifted her bouquet of white roses. Will saw Lucy backing even further away, almost trying to hide.

Then the roses were sailing through the air in a high arc. There were girlish squeals of laughter and hands rose to try to grab the flowers, but Mattie's aim was sure. The bouquet landed square on Lucy's nose and she had no choice but to catch it.

A cheer went up and Lucy gave a bashful smile and held the bouquet high, no doubt knowing that all of Willowbank would love to see their favourite vet married.

But she was probably grateful that everyone's attention quickly returned to the bride and groom. Jake was already helping Mattie into the car.

Over the heads of the crowd he sent Will a flashing grin and Will answered with a thumbs-up.

The car's exhaust roared as they took off and the rear window was covered in 'just married' signs written in toothpaste, which only served to prove how old-fashioned this town really was.

Will, however, was watching Lucy. She stood in the shadows at the back of the throng, clutching the wedding bouquet in one hand while she used the other hand to swipe at her tears.

CHAPTER FOUR

LUCY wished the ground would open up and swallow her. It was bad enough that everyone knew the bride had deliberately thrown the bouquet to her. To cry about it was beyond pathetic, but to do so in front of Will Carruthers was more embarrassing than she could bear.

Turning her back on him, she gave one final swipe and an unladylike sniff and she willed her eyes to stay dry. It wasn't a moment too soon.

Will's voice sounded close behind her. 'We can leave whenever you like,' he said.

She drew a deep slow breath and turned to him with a smile on her face. Any number of people would have given her a lift, but she was determined to show Will that his comments about the two of them being a pair of old loners had not upset her.

'Could you give me just a moment?' she said. 'I'd like to say goodbye to a few people.'

'By all means. I've said my farewells. Let me know when you're ready.'

'I shouldn't be long, unless Mrs Carey needs my help with anything else. Shall I meet you at the truck?'

'Sure.'

It was crazy the way her stomach tightened as she crossed the road to Will's parked truck. Crazier still the way her heart thrashed when she saw his tall figure waiting in the shadows beside the vehicle. He stepped forward when he saw her and the white shirt beneath his jacket glowed in the moonlight. Fire flashed in his light grey eyes.

'Let me help you up,' he said as he opened the truck's passenger door.

'I can manage.' Lucy was anxious to avoid his gallantry. If Will touched her now, she might self-combust.

But managing alone wasn't easy. With her arms filled with her bridesmaid's bouquet as well as the bride's white roses and with the added complication of her long straight skirt and precarious high heels, the whole business of clambering up into the truck was fraught with difficulties.

Will was full of apologies. 'I forgot how hard it is to climb into this damned thing.'

'If you hold the bouquets, I'm sure I can swing myself up.'

Without waiting for his reply, Lucy thrust the flowers into his arms. Then, grateful for the darkness, she yanked her skirt with one hand and took a firm grip of the door handle with the other. She stepped high and hauled herself up, and everything would have been fine if one of her high heels hadn't caught on the step.

In mid-flight she lost her balance and then lost her grip on the handle and, before she could recover, she was slipping backwards.

Into Will's arms.

She was crushed against his chest, along with several dozen blooms.

'I've got you.'

Lucy wasn't sure if the pounding of Will's heart and his

sharp intake of breath were caused by shock or the exertion of catching her.

Desperately, she tried to ignore how wonderfully safe she felt in his arms, how beyond fabulous it was to be cradled against his splendidly muscular chest. The wool of his expensive suit was cool and fine beneath her cheek. She could have stayed there...

'I'm sorry,' she spluttered. 'Anyone would think I was drunk.'

'The thought never crossed my mind.'

'You can put me down, Will. I'm quite all right.'

'I think it might be better if we do this my way.'

His face was in darkness so Lucy couldn't see his expression, but his voice was deep and warm, like a comforting blanket around her, and he hoisted her up onto the front seat of the truck with astonishing ease.

'Put your seat belt on,' he said, as if she was a child. 'And then I'll pass you what's left of the bouquets.'

Chastened, Lucy thanked him.

The glorious scent of crushed rose petals filled the truck's cabin as Will climbed behind the wheel and pulled the driver's door shut. But the fragrance couldn't disguise the smell of ancient leather and it couldn't block Lucy's memories.

This was the first time in ten years that she'd been alone in the dark with Will, and stupidly she remembered that embarrassing kiss on the shadowy veranda at Tambaroora. She could remember exactly how he'd tasted and the warm pressure of his lips, the sexy slide of his tongue...

He turned to her. 'Are you OK now?'

'Perfectly,' she said in a choked whisper.

'Are you sure?' he asked, frowning at her, watching her intently.

She pressed a hand against her heart in a bid to calm its wicked thudding. 'I was hobbled by this jolly dress and I slipped in the stupid heels.' She sounded more astringent than she'd meant to. 'After tonight, these shoes are going straight to the Country Women's second-hand store.'

Will chuckled softly, then started the truck and soon they were rumbling down the street. Lucy buried her nose in the roses, glad that he didn't try to talk all the way home.

But, in the silence, her thoughts turned back to their earlier conversation. Will had shocked her when he'd raised the subject of marriage and babies, but perhaps she shouldn't have been so surprised. It was, as he'd said, happening all around them. Gina and Tom had their twins. Mattie was married.

She had been so busy trying to back away from the topic, so scared Will would discover how hung up she was about these very things, that she'd cut the conversation short.

Now she was left to wonder. Had he actually been leading up to something he wanted to discuss? She'd always been hurt by Will's silence after Josh's death and the miscarriage. He'd never given her the chance to confess why she'd become involved with his brother.

Of course, it would be dreadfully difficult to tell him the truth, but she'd always felt guilty and she wanted to come clean. Perhaps then she would be able to put it behind her at last. She might, at last, stop dreaming about Will.

As the truck rumbled down country lanes, past darkened farmhouses and quiet paddocks, a number of questions bumped around in her head and by the time Will pulled up in front of her house, Lucy couldn't hold back. 'Will, what was the point you wanted to make?'

In the glow of the dashboard's lights, she could see his frown. 'I'm sorry, Lucy, you've lost me.'

'When we were talking at the wedding, you were carrying on about how old we are now and I got in a huff, but were you actually trying to make a point?'

He turned to face her, one hand draped loosely over the steering wheel. 'Nothing in particular.' He smiled shyly. 'I simply wanted to talk to you—the way we used to.'

A ghost of a smile trickled across his face. Then he looked out through the windscreen and tapped his fingers on the steering wheel. 'We have a lot to catch up on, but it's late. Why don't I give you a call some time?'

How could such a simple question send her insides into turmoil? It was so silly to be incredibly excited simply because Will Carruthers planned to talk to her again.

With difficulty, Lucy overcame her desperate curiosity to know what he wanted to talk about. She managed to speak calmly.

'I'll wait to hear from you, then,' she said as she pushed the door open.

'Don't move,' Will ordered, shoving his door open too. 'I'll help you out. I don't want you falling again. You're an accident waiting to happen tonight.'

A hasty glance at the huge step down to the road showed Lucy the wisdom of accepting his offer, but her heart skipped several beats as he rounded the truck and helped her down.

'Thank you,' she said demurely. 'My elderly bones couldn't have taken another stumble this evening.'

His soft laugh held the hint of a growl. 'Get to bed, Grandma.'

To her astonishment, Will's lips feathered the merest brush of a kiss against her temple. Her knees almost gave way.

'Perhaps I should escort you to the door,' he said.

'I think I'm still capable of tottering up my own front path.'

'I'll wait here till you're safely inside.'

After years of being fiercely independent, Lucy had to admit it was rather pleasant to have a lordly male watching out for her. With the bouquets bundled in one arm, she lifted her skirt elegantly and took careful dainty steps as she made her way up the uneven brick path.

She'd left her car and her other set of keys at Mattie's parents' house, but there was a spare key under the flowerpot on the porch. Tonight, however, there was more than a flowerpot on the porch. A hessian bag had been left on the doorstep.

Lucy saw it and sighed. Caring for wildlife wasn't part of her veterinary responsibilities, but people knew she had a soft heart and they were always bringing her injured bush creatures. Animals hit by cars were the most common and this was sure to be another one—a wounded sugar glider, an orphaned kangaroo, or perhaps an injured possum.

She was dead tired tonight, but now, before she could crawl into bed, she would have to attend to this.

She found the key, opened the front door and reached inside to turn on the porch light. Behind her, Will was waiting at the front gate and she sent him a friendly wave. 'Thanks for the lift,' she called.

He returned her wave and she watched as he headed back to the truck, then, with the flowers in one arm, she picked up the sack. The animal inside wriggled, which was a good sign. Maybe it wasn't too badly hurt and she wouldn't lose too much sleep tonight.

She heard her dogs scratching at the back door, but they

would have to wait a bit longer for her attention. She took the sack through to the surgery, put the roses and lilies in one of the huge metal sinks and set the bag down gently on the metal examining table.

First things first, she kicked off her shoes. That was *so-o-o-o* much better. Yawning widely, she unknotted the string around the neck of the bag.

A snake's head shot out.

Lucy screamed.

Panic flooded her!

A snake was the last thing she'd expected. The worst thing. She loved animals. She loved all animals. But she still couldn't help being terrified of snakes.

Her heart leapt in a rush of instinctive primeval terror. She couldn't deal with this.

Not now. Not alone in the middle of the night.

Paralysed by fear, she thought of Will driving off in his truck and seriously considered chasing after him, yelling for help. She whimpered his name and was ready to scream again when footsteps thundered up the path and Will appeared at the surgery doorway.

'Lucy, what's the matter?'

'A s-snake!' With a shaking hand she pointed to the sack.

'Let me deal with it.' He spoke calmly and, just like that, he crossed the floor to the wriggling hessian bag.

Lucy watched, one hand clamped over her mouth to hold back another scream, as Will carefully pulled the top of the sack apart, then, with commendable cool, gripped the snake firmly, just behind its head.

'It's a carpet python,' he told her smoothly as he lifted it out and took hold of the tail, while the snake thrashed wildly. 'And it's wounded.'

A carpet python.

Right. Lucy drew a deep breath. Her racing heartbeats subsided. Carpet pythons weren't poisonous. Actually, now that she was calming down, she could see the distinctive brown and cream markings on the snake's back.

'I'm afraid I panicked,' she said. 'Someone left the bag on my porch and I was expecting a small motherless furry creature.'

'Instead you have an angry snake with a nasty gash on its back.' The expression in Will's grey eyes was both tender and amused.

No longer trembling, Lucy came closer and saw the wound halfway down the snake's length. 'I'm afraid snakes are the one species of the animal kingdom I find hard to love. But this fellow's actually quite beautiful, isn't he?'

'As snakes go—he's extremely handsome,' Will said dryly. 'What do you want to do with him? Would you try to treat a wound like this?'

'I can at least clean it up. Maybe give it a few stitches.'

'Can you leave it till tomorrow? Shall I put it in a cage for you?'

She bit back a sigh and shook her head. 'The biggest threat for him is infection, so I really should see to the wound straight away.' Shooting Will an apologetic glance, she said, 'It won't take long, but I'm afraid I couldn't possibly manage without an assistant.'

He chuckled. 'No problem. I'm all yours.'

The sparkle in his eyes sent heat flaming in her cheeks. Tightly, she said, 'Thank you. If you'll keep holding him right there, I'll get organised. First, I'm going to have to feed oxygen and anaesthetic down his trachea.'

'You're going to knock him out just to clean up a wound?'

'It's the only way to keep a snake still. They're actually very sensitive to pain.'

As Lucy set up the gas cylinders, her mind raced ahead, planning each step of the procedure. She would place a wooden board between the python and the metal table to keep him that little bit warmer. And she needed something to hold the wounded section steady while she worked on it. Masking tape would do the least damage to the python's sensitive skin.

Quickly she assembled everything she needed—scissors, scalpels, tweezers, swabs, needles—and then she donned sterile gloves. 'OK, let's get this gas into him.'

Will held the snake's head steady while she fed the tube down its mouth, and she was amazed that she wasn't scared any more.

'How many pythons' lives have you saved?' Will asked as they waited for the anaesthetic to take effect.

'This is the first.'

He smiled. 'I can remember your very first patient.'

She frowned at him, puzzled. 'You were in Argentina when I started to work as a vet.'

'Before that. Don't you remember the chicken you brought to school in a woolly sock?'

'Oh, yes.' She grinned. 'The poor little thing hatched on a very cold winter's morning and I was worried that it wouldn't make it through the day.'

'You kept it hidden under the desk.'

'Until Mr Sanderson discovered it during biology and turned it into a lecture on imprinting.'

Their eyes met and they smiled and for a heady moment, Lucy was sixteen again and Will Carruthers was...

No, for heaven's sake.

Shocked by how easily she was distracted by him, she centred her thoughts on cleaning the outside of the python's wound with alcohol wipes and foaming solution. Then, when her patient was completely under, she began to debride the damaged tissue.

All the time she worked, Will was silent, watching her with a curious smile that she tried very hard to ignore.

'I guess this isn't quite how you expected to spend your evening,' she said as she finally began to suture the delicate skin together.

'Wouldn't have missed this for the world.' He chuckled softly. 'You have to admit, it's a unique experience. How many guys have watched a barefoot bridesmaid stitch up a python at midnight?'

Lucy couldn't help smiling. 'You make it sound like some kind of medieval witches' ritual.'

'The rites of spring?'

'Maybe, but then again, how many vets have been assisted by a hun—a guy in best man's clobber?'

Lucy thanked heavens she'd retracted the word *hunk*. For heaven's sake. It was the dinner suit factor. Stick the plainest man in a tuxedo and his looks were improved two hundred per cent. Will in a tuxedo was downright dangerous.

But she was grateful for his help. Working side by side with him again, she'd felt good in a weirdly unsettled-yet-comfortable way. They'd always worked well together.

'You're a tough cookie,' Will told her. 'You were white as a ghost and shaking when I came in and yet you morphed into a steady-handed snake surgeon.'

'It's my job,' she said, trying not to look too pleased.

She dropped the suture needles into the tray and snapped off her sterile gloves, removed the paper apron and rolled up the disposable sheet she'd used to drape over the wound.

'So where will we put this fellow while he sleeps off his ordeal?' Will asked.

'He'll have to go in one of the cages out the back.' Carefully, she peeled away the masking tape that had kept the snake straight.

'Shall I do the honours?'

'Thanks, Will. There's a cage in the far corner, away from the other patients. If you give me a minute, I'll line it with thick newspaper to keep him warm and dry.'

By the time the python was safely in its cage it was long past midnight but, to Lucy's surprise, she didn't feel tired any more. She tried to tell herself that she'd found working on a completely new species exhilarating, but she knew very well it had everything to do with Will's presence.

She'd felt relaxed and focused and it had been like stepping back in time to their student days. But, dear heaven, it was such a long time ago and they couldn't really go back, could they?

'Let's go through to the kitchen,' she said once they'd cleaned up.

She snapped the kitchen light on and the room leapt to life. She was rather proud of the renovations she'd made to this room, painting the walls a soft buttercup and adding hand painted tiles to the splashback over the sink. And she'd spent ages hunting for the right kind of cupboards and shelving in country-style second-hand shops.

'I'd better let the boys in.'

As soon as Lucy opened the back door, Seamus and Harry bounded inside, greeting her with doggy kisses and fiercely wagging tails, as if she'd been away for six months.

At last the dogs calmed down and she turned to Will. 'I think you've earned a drink.'

'I believe I have,' he agreed and he immediately began to remove his jacket and tie.

Lucy drew a sharp breath, already doubting the soundness of this idea. But she couldn't send Will packing after he'd been so helpful. Surely two old friends could have a drink together?

'What are you in the mood for?' *Oh, cringe. What a question.* 'Alcohol or coffee?' she added quickly.

She opened the fridge. 'If you'd like alcohol, I'm afraid there's only beer or white wine.'

Will chose beer and Lucy poured a glass of wine for herself. She found a wedge of Parmesan cheese and freshly shelled walnuts and set them on a platter with crackers and slices of apple.

'Come on through to the lounge room,' she said. 'It's pretty shabby, though. I started renovating the kitchen and then ran out of enthusiasm.'

Tonight, however, Lucy was surprised. She hadn't drawn the curtains and the lounge room, now flooded by moonlight, had taken on a strangely ethereal beauty. The shabbiness had all but disappeared and the garish colours of the cotton throws she'd used to cover the tattered upholstery had taken on a subtle glow.

'I might leave the lights off,' she said. 'This room is definitely improved by moonlight.'

'Everything's improved by moonlight.'

She studiously ignored this comment in the same way that she avoided the sofa and flopped into a deep, comfy single chair instead.

With a be-my-guest gesture she directed Will to the

other chair. Then, as the dogs settled on the floor, heads on paws, niggles of disquiet returned to haunt her. It was such a long time since she and Will had been alone like this.

'Try some Parmesan and apple,' she said, diving for safety by offering him the plate. 'Have you tried them together? It's a nice combination.'

Will obliged and made appropriately, appreciative noises.

Lucy took a sip of wine. In many ways this was one of her favourite fantasies—talking to Will late into the night. But in the fantasies there'd been no awkwardness. They had been as comfortable and relaxed as they were ten years ago, before they'd drifted apart.

Lucy wondered what they would discuss now. Will had hinted that he had specific things he wanted to talk about. Would he raise them now? She wasn't sure she was ready to hear his thoughts on marriage and babies and being over the hill.

Perhaps he still felt that tonight wasn't the night to be deep and meaningful. She searched for a safe topic that didn't include weddings, or honeymoons, or babies.

'So, have you started hunting for a new job?' she asked.

'I haven't put in any applications yet.' Will settled more comfortably into his chair, crossed an ankle over a knee. 'But I've found a few positions I might apply for. There's even one in Armidale, at the university.'

'In Armidale?' So close? To cover her surprise, Lucy said, 'I have trouble picturing you as an academic behind a desk.'

He shrugged. 'I thought it would make a nice change, after years of hiking over deserts and mountains looking for rocks.'

'There's that, I guess.' She couldn't resist adding facetiously, 'I suppose geology is a young man's job.'

Will smiled into his glass, took a swig, then set it down.

'I imagine your parents would like you to take up farming,' she suggested.

'They've never mentioned it.' He sighed. 'They're actually talking about selling up.'

'Really?' Lucy stared at him, horrified.

'My mother's been bitten by the travel bug.'

'She must have caught it from you.'

Will smiled crookedly. 'Perhaps.'

'But your family's been farming Tambaroora for five generations.'

'And now they've come to the end of the line,' Will said dryly.

Nervous now, Lucy chewed at her lower lip. Already they were treading on sensitive ground. Everyone in the district had always known that Will's older brother, Josh, was expected to take over the family farm.

Josh's death had changed everything.

She closed her eyes, as if to brace herself for the slam of pain that she always felt when she thought about that time.

'We've never talked about it, Lucy.'

She didn't have to ask what Will meant. The fact that they had never really talked since Josh's death had been like an unhealed wound inside her. 'There wasn't any chance to talk,' she said defensively. 'You went away straight after the funeral.'

'There were lots of good reasons for me not to stay. Your father didn't help.'

'My father?'

'After Josh's funeral, I tried to phone. I turned up on your doorstep, but your father wouldn't let me near you.'

Lucy stared at Will, stunned. 'I didn't know that.' Her

eyes stung and she blinked back tears. If she'd known Will had called, what would she have done? What might have been different?

Will's shoulders lifted in a shrug. 'Your father was probably right to protect you. I…I can't imagine that I would have been much help at the time.'

Lucy swallowed to ease the aching lump in her throat. She'd been in a terrible state after the funeral and the miscarriage. The really awful thing was that everyone thought she was grieving, and she was, of course, but a huge part of her distress had been caused by her overpowering feelings of guilt. 'Did you know…about the baby?'

'Gina told me at the time,' Will said quietly. And then, after a beat, 'I'm really sorry, Lucy.'

He sounded almost too apologetic, as if somehow he felt responsible. But that didn't make sense.

Lucy willed her hand to stop trembling as she held out the plate to him and he made a selection. For some time they sat in silence, nibbling walnuts in the silvered half-light, and then Will changed the subject.

'You've done so well here,' he said. 'I'm hearing from everyone that you're a fabulous vet.'

'I love my job.'

Will nodded, then he asked carefully, 'So you're happy, Lucy?'

From force of habit, a lie leapt to her lips. 'Of course.' She reached down and patted Harry's silky black and white head. 'I'm perfectly happy. I love this district. I love my work.'

'But is it enough?'

Oh, help. Lucy covered her dismay with a snappy reply. 'What kind of question is that?'

'An important one.'

'You answer it then.' She knew she sounded tense, but she couldn't help it. Will's question unnerved her. It was too searching, too close to a truth she didn't want to reveal. 'Are you happy, Will? Is your work enough?'

'Not any more.'

It wasn't the answer she'd expected and she took a moment to digest it. 'I suppose that's why you're looking for something different?'

'I suppose it is.' He circled the rim of his glass with his finger. 'I've had a bit of a wake up call.'

A swift flare of shock ripped through Lucy like a sniper's gunshot. 'Will, you're not sick, are you?'

'No, thank God, but I've had a close shave. I haven't told my family this. I didn't want to upset them, but there was an explosion in an old mine we were surveying.'

'In Mongolia?'

'Yes.' His face was suddenly tight and strained. 'The two men with me were both killed. Right in front of me. I've no idea how I escaped with a few scratches and bruises.'

'Oh, God, Will, that's terrible.' Tears threatened again as Lucy tried not to think the unthinkable—that there had almost been a world where Will didn't exist.

'I went to their funerals,' Will said quietly. 'And they really opened my eyes.'

'In what way?'

In the moonlight, she could see the sober intensity in Will's face.

'Barney was a bachelor, you see. No ties. So his funeral was a simple gathering of family and friends. There were a few words to say he was a good bloke and then a rather boozy wake. But Keith was a family man, always talking about his wife and three kids. And at the funeral his son spoke.'

Will sighed and rubbed at his forehead. 'He was such a courageous little guy. He couldn't have been more than ten years old. And he stood up there in front of us, with these big brown eyes, shiny with tears. His voice was all squeaky and threatening to break, but he told us all how proud he was of his father and how he wanted to live his life in a way that would go on making his dad proud.'

Lucy's throat ached at the thought of that little boy. She could picture his mother, too. The poor woman would have been so proud, despite her grief.

'I can't stop thinking about that kid,' Will said. 'He was like this fantastic gift to the world that Keith had left behind.'

Lucy reached for the handkerchief she'd tucked into the bodice of her dress and dabbed at her eyes.

'I'm sorry,' Will said. 'I'm being maudlin, talking about funerals when we've just been to a wedding.'

'No, it's OK.' She sniffed and sent him a watery smile. 'It's just happened to you, so of course it's on your mind. Anyway, that's what life's all about, isn't it? Births, deaths and marriages.'

He smiled sadly. 'I guess I'm a slow learner. It wasn't till I was sitting in that church that I suddenly got it. I could finally understand why Gina went to so much trouble to have a family, and why Mattie was prepared to undergo something so amazingly challenging as a surro-gate pregnancy.'

'Yes,' Lucy said, but the single word came out too loud and sounded more like a sob.

The dogs lifted their heads and made soft whining noises in her direction. With a cry of dismay, Will lurched to his feet.

'I'm so sorry,' he said. 'I should be more sensitive. I shouldn't be burdening you with this.'

He was referring to her miscarriage. Would he be shocked to hear that she still longed for a baby, that her need was bordering on obsession?

With an angry shake of his head, he went to the window, thrust his hands into his trouser pockets and looked out into the night.

Despite her tension, Lucy was mesmerised by the sight of him limned by moonlight. Her eyes feasted on his profile, on his intelligent forehead, on the decisive jut of his nose, his strong chin with its appealing cleft.

Without looking at her, he said, 'I'm surprised you haven't found someone else and settled down to start a family.'

Oh, help. Lucy stiffened. Again, Will had gone too far. Again, her chin lifted in defence and she hit back. 'I could say the same about you.'

'Ah.' He turned back from the window. His eyes shimmered and he said in a dry tone, 'But I'm the vagabond and you're the homebody.'

Too true.

However, Lucy couldn't help remembering how he'd come rushing back to Australia when she and Josh had announced their engagement.

She'd always wondered why.

But there was no way she could open up that discussion now. Not tonight.

She felt too vulnerable tonight and she was scared she might blurt out something she'd regret later. It would be too embarrassing and shameful to confess that she'd finally gone out with Will's brother, hoping that word would reach Will and spark a reaction.

If she told him that, she'd also have to confess that the plan had backfired when she'd become pregnant.

It was more than likely she would never be able to talk to Will about this.

Nevertheless, tonight's conversation felt like an important step. It was almost as if she and Will had picked up their friendship where they'd left off. He'd told her about the funeral, something he hadn't been able to share with his family.

It suddenly felt OK to say, 'I've actually become quite desperate to have a baby.'

Will spun around from the window and his chest rose and fell. Above his open white shirt, the muscles in his throat rippled. His eyes smouldered in the cool white light. 'You'd make a wonderful mother, Lucy.'

The compliment made her want to cry, but she gave him a shrugging smile. 'It's a terrible waste, isn't it?'

She hadn't expected to say more but, now that she'd started, it was surprisingly easy to keep going. 'To be honest, I worry constantly about the state of my ovaries and whether I can expect them to go on delivering, month after month.'

'The old biological clock?'

She nodded. 'Early menopause runs in my family. That's why I'm an only child.'

Will frowned. 'But I have it on good authority that you've turned down at least three proposals of marriage.'

Heat flooded Lucy's face. 'I suppose Gina told you that?'

He nodded.

'OK, so I'm fussy, but that's because I'm not so desperate that I'd settle for just any guy as a husband. Willowbank isn't exactly swarming with Mr Rights, you know. I'd rather be a single mother.'

Abruptly, Will came back to his chair and sank down

into it, long legs stretching in front of him. 'Why would you want to be a single mother?'

'Because it's better than not being a mother at all.'

He looked surprised and thoughtful.

Lucy made herself comfortable with her legs curled and an elbow propped on the chair's arm, her cheek resting on her hand. 'I've been to a fertility clinic,' she told Will. 'And I've already tried one round of IVF.'

'IVF?' he repeated, sounding shocked.

'Why not?'

'Isn't that a bit…extreme?'

'It seemed logical to me. I've inseminated hundreds of animals and it worked beautifully for Mattie and Gina. But, unfortunately, it didn't work for me.'

Will made a soft sound, a kind of strangled gasp.

'I'm sorry. That's probably too much information,' she said.

But Will shook his head and, a moment later, a smile played around his lips. He tapped at the arm of his chair. 'It's a pity Mattie can't have a baby for you.'

Lucy knew he was joking and forced a weak laugh. Uncurling her legs, she sat straight in her chair. 'Don't worry, that thought's occurred to me but I imagine Mattie has other plans now she has a husband.'

'I'm sure she has.' With a thoughtful frown, Will scratched at his jaw. 'But it's a pity there isn't someone who could help you out.'

'Do you mean a good friend? Someone like you, Will?'

CHAPTER FIVE

LUCY could not believe she'd just said that.

What had she been thinking?

How on earth could she have boldly suggested that Will could help her to have a baby—out of friendship?

What must he think of her?

The only sound in the room came from Seamus, the Irish setter, snoring softly at Will's feet. Lucy stared at the sleeping dog while her heart beat crazily.

'You know that was a joke, don't you?' she said in a small voice.

To her dismay, Will didn't answer and she wished she could crawl away and hide with her tail between her legs, the way Seamus and Harry did when they were in big trouble.

If only she could press a rewind button and take those words back.

When the silence became unbearable she looked up and saw Will's serious expression and her heart juddered. 'Will, I didn't mean it. It was my warped sense of humour. You know I've never been very good at making jokes. They always come out wrong. I'm sorry. Honestly, I feel so embarrassed.'

He looked shaken. 'For a moment there, I thought you were serious.'

'I wasn't, Will. You can calm down.'

Suddenly a cloud covered the moon and the room was plunged in darkness. Lucy turned on the lamp beside her and the return of light seemed to clear the air.

Will rose abruptly and stood towering over her. 'Perhaps I'd better get going before I say something outrageous, too.'

As Lucy stood she prayed that her legs were steady enough to support her. 'Thanks for helping me with the python,' she remembered to say as they crossed the lounge room.

Will smiled. 'My pleasure. I hope he makes a good recovery, and thanks for the drink and the chat. It was like old times.'

No, Lucy thought. Blurting out her desire to have a baby was not remotely like old times.

They went through to the kitchen, where Will collected his jacket and tie, and then on to the front door. His hand touched Lucy's shoulder and she jumped.

'See you later, Goose.' He dropped a light kiss on her cheek and then he was gone.

Will felt as if he'd stepped off a roller coaster as he started up the truck and drove away, watching the lights of Lucy's house grow smaller and more distant in the rear-vision mirror.

What a crazy night! In a matter of hours, he'd gone from being best man at a wedding to standing in as a veterinary nurse to fielding a request for his services as a father for Lucy's baby.

Not that Lucy had been serious, of course.

But bloody hell. The thought gripped Will and frightened him beyond belief. His heart had almost raced out of control when Lucy made that offhand suggestion tonight.

He was still shaken now, even though the subject had been laid to rest. Problem was, he couldn't let it go.

He kept thinking about how badly she wanted a baby. If he hadn't seen the emotional pain that Gina had been through, or if he hadn't so recently attended Keith's funeral, he might not have caught the genuine longing in Lucy's voice. In her eyes.

He might not have understood, might have simply thought she was selfish, wanting it all, when she already had so much.

But now he got it, he really understood that the desire to have a child came from somewhere deep, so deep that it couldn't be properly explained. And it shouldn't be ignored.

But should he be involved? For Pete's sake, he'd seen the haunted loneliness in Lucy's eyes and he'd almost grabbed her suggestion and moulded it into a realistic option.

They'd been such good friends and he'd wanted to help her.

But father her baby?

That was even crazier than the way he'd felt when he'd danced with her tonight at the wedding. It was the kiss on the veranda revisited. He'd been caught out by unexpected emotions, by an inappropriate desire to get too close to Lucy.

Every time she'd stumbled against him, he'd wanted to keep her close. He'd wanted to inhale the clean, rosy scent of her skin, to touch his lips to her skin, right there, in front of the wedding guests.

Thank heavens he'd had the sense to stop dancing before things got out of hand.

But it didn't really make sense that he was feeling this way about Lucy now. Why would he want to play second fiddle to the memory of his brother?

If he'd wanted Lucy as his girlfriend, he should have grabbed the chance when they were at university, before she got to know Josh. Problem was, he'd been too distracted by the sheer numbers of girls at Sydney Uni and he'd wanted to play the field.

And, truth be told, when he thought about those days, he had to admit that whenever he'd made a move in Lucy's direction she'd adroitly held him at a distance. She'd insisted that she was his buddy, not his girlfriend.

And yet she'd fallen for Josh quite easily. Will knew that was exactly why he mustn't think twice about her crazy suggestion.

Lucy had loved his brother. She'd been about to marry his brother and have his brother's baby.

Did he honestly think he could make amends by stepping in as a substitute?

The question teased him as he steered the truck over a single lane wooden bridge that crossed Willow Creek. He felt the familiar sickening slug of guilt he always felt when he thought about Josh and remembered the row they had on that last fateful morning before he'd died.

That was what he should have talked about tonight. He should have confessed his role in Josh's death.

Oh, God. The mere thought of telling Lucy the truth caused a sickening jolt in his chest. She would hate him.

He couldn't take that risk.

The next day, Sunday, dragged for Lucy. She wasn't on call so, apart from checking on her patients, including the python, who was recovering nicely, she couldn't distract herself with work.

She collected her car from the Careys' and spent a happy half hour discussing the wedding with Mattie's mum over a cup of tea. In the afternoon, she took her dogs for a lovely long walk along Willow Creek, but they weren't good conversationalists, so she was left with far too much time to brood over the huge gaffe she'd made during last night's conversation with Will.

She couldn't believe she'd actually asked her schoolgirl crush to help her to have a baby. Talk about a Freudian slip!

What must Will think of her?

Why in heaven's name had she blurted out such a suggestion when she'd once been engaged to Will's brother?

The question brought her to a halt, standing at the edge of the creek, staring down into the clear running water. She remembered the happy times she'd spent here with Will, panning for gold or sapphires. How excited they'd been over the tiniest speck of gold or the smallest dull chips of dark glass that signified sapphires.

She'd never once let Will see how much she loved him. She'd been too scared to risk losing him by telling him how she felt.

She was so totally lost in thought that she was startled when her dogs began to bark suddenly.

'Stop that, Harry,' she called. 'Seamus, what's the matter?'

Then she heard the snap of twigs and the crunch of gravel underfoot. Someone was coming along the track.

'Come here,' Lucy ordered but, to her dismay, the dogs ignored her. Their tails kept wagging and they yapped expectantly as a tall figure came around the bend.

It was Will.

A flare of shock burst inside her, as if someone had lit a match. Will looked surprised too, but he seemed to recover more quickly. He smiled, while Lucy's heart continued to thump fretfully.

'Fancy seeing you here,' he drawled.

'I brought the dogs for a walk.'

He grinned and bent down to give the boys a quick scruff around the ears. 'I needed to get out of the house.'

'Already? But you've just arrived home.'

'I know.' His grey eyes sparkled as he looked up at her. 'But I've had this crazy idea rattling around in my head and I needed to get away to think.'

'Oh,' Lucy said uncertainly.

The dogs, content with Will's greeting, went back to hunting for the delectable smells in a nearby lantana bush. Watching them, Will said, 'I've been thinking about your baby proposal.'

'Will, it wasn't a proposal. You know I didn't mean it.'

With a distinct lack of haste, he said, 'But is it such a bad idea?'

Lucy's mouth fell open. Surely he wasn't serious? 'Of course it's a bad idea. It's crazy.'

He looked about him, letting his gaze take in the silent trees and sky, the smooth stepping stones crossing the creek. 'You really want a baby,' he said quietly. 'You said so last night, and you're worried you're running out of time.'

Now it was Lucy who didn't answer. She couldn't. Her heart had risen to fill her throat. She'd never dreamed for a moment that Will would take her flippant comment even halfway seriously.

He stood, blocking her way on the narrow track,

watching her carefully. 'I'm sure you'd prefer your baby's father to be someone you know.'

She still couldn't speak. Her hand lifted to the base of her throat as she tried to still the wild pulse that beat there.

Will pressed his point. 'I imagine a friend must be a better option than an unknown donor in a sperm bank.'

'But friends don't normally have babies together.'

She couldn't see his expression. He'd turned to pluck at a long grass stalk and it made a soft snapping sound.

'People accept all kinds of convenient family arrangements these days,' he said. 'The locals in Willowbank have accepted the idea of Mattie's surrogacy very well.'

'Well, yes. That's true.'

But, despite her silly dreams, Lucy couldn't imagine having a baby with Will. He'd never fancied her. And, even if he did, he was Josh's brother.

'Look, Lucy, don't get me wrong. I'm not pushing this, but I'm happy to talk it through.'

'Why?'

A slow smile warmed his eyes. 'We haven't talked for years and we used to be really good at it.'

Lucy felt a blush spread upwards from her throat. Her mind was spinning, grasping desperately at the idea of Will as her baby's father and then slipping away again, as if the thoughts were made of ice. 'But what exactly are you saying? That you would be willing to…um…donate sperm for another round of IVF?'

Surprise flared in his face. He tossed the grass stalk into the water. 'If that's what you want.'

'I…I don't know.'

'Of course, there's always the natural alternative. If you've had trouble with IVF, that shouldn't be ruled out.'

Lucy bit her lip to cover her gasp of dismay. She watched the grass float away, disappearing behind a rock. The dogs began to bark again. 'They're tired of this spot and they want to move on,' she told Will.

'Let's walk, then,' he suggested.

There was just enough room on the track for them to walk side by side, and it should have been relaxing to walk with Will beside the creek—like in the old days. But today an unsettling awareness zapped through Lucy. She was too conscious of Will's tall, rangy body. So close. Touching close.

She couldn't think straight. She was so tantalised by the idea of a baby, but how could she even talk about having a baby with Will when she'd never admitted that she'd always had a crush on him?

She didn't want to frighten him away, not now when he'd made such an amazing suggestion.

Dragging in a deep breath, she said, 'OK. Just say we did…um…give this some thought. How do you actually feel about becoming a father?'

She glanced at Will and saw his quick smile. 'To be honest, fatherhood has been well down on my wish list. But I guess I'm seeing it in a new light lately. I've been hit by the feeling that I've been wasting my life.'

'Because of the little boy at the funeral?'

'Yes, that little guy really got to me. But there've been other things too—like Gina's twins. They knocked me for six. They're so damn cute.'

'I know. I'm eaten up with envy every time I see them. But you haven't answered me. Would you really want to be my baby's father?'

Will stopped walking. 'I can't promise I'd be a terrific

help, Lucy. I don't even know where I'm going to be working yet, so there's not much chance I'd be a hands-on father. But, if you want to have a child, I'd certainly be ready to help.'

She was so surprised she found her thoughts racing ahead. 'I don't mind managing on my own. It's what I'd planned anyway.'

Will smiled. 'So what does that mean? Do you want to give this some serious thought?'

'I...I don't know.' She was feeling so dazed. 'I know I was the one who started this, but I never dreamed you'd take me up on it.'

Even as she said this, Lucy wished she'd sounded more positive. This was her dream, to have Will's baby. OK, maybe the dream also involved Will falling madly and deeply in love with her, but surely half a dream was better than none?

'But I guess there's no harm in thinking about it,' she said.

His eyes were very bright, watching her closely. 'I wasn't even expecting to see you today. There's no pressure to make a decision now. We should sleep on it. If we decide to go ahead, we can fine-tune the details later.'

'Fine-tune?'

'IVF versus the alternative,' he said without smiling.

The alternative.

This time Lucy's skin began to burn from the inside out. She hadn't even been able to dance with Will last night without getting upset. How on earth could she possibly make love with him without a gigantic emotional meltdown?

The very thought of becoming intimate with Will sent flames shooting over her skin. She began to tremble.

'There's no rush,' he said. 'I could be around here for a

while yet, and if I move to Armidale it's only a couple of hours away.'

Lucy frowned at him. 'Armidale?'

'The job I mentioned. At the university.'

Oh. She expelled air noisily.

'Look, we both need time to think about this, Lucy.' Will watched her dogs running impatiently back and forth, trying to urge her to get walking again. 'And I should head back now.'

'All right.'

'I'm glad I ran into you,' he said.

Lucy nodded.

'So you'll give this some thought?'

'Yes,' she said, but a shiver rushed over her skin and she wrapped her arms around her as she watched Will walk away.

At the bend in the track he turned back and lifted his hand to wave. Then he smiled. And kept walking.

He hadn't been totally crazy, Will told himself as he strode back along the track beside the creek. He hadn't committed to a full-on relationship with his brother's ex. He'd simply offered to help her to have a baby.

This was purely and simply about the baby.

The baby Lucy longed for.

But it meant he'd be a father and he really liked that idea.

He'd be able to watch the baby grow. He'd help out with finances—school fees, pony club, whatever the kid needed. And who knew? Maybe, some day in the future, the kid might take an interest in Tambaroora, if it still belonged to the Carruthers family.

But the big thing was, the lucky child would have Lucy as its mother.

If any woman deserved to be a mother, Lucy did.

Will had dated a lot of women, but he couldn't think of anyone who was more suitable than Lucy McKenty to be the mother of his child.

And it wasn't such a crazy situation. Being good friends with his baby's mother was a vast improvement on some of the unhappy broken family set-ups that he'd heard his workmates complain about.

But the details of the baby's conception caused a road bump.

Will came to a halt as he thought about that. He snagged another grass stalk and chewed at it thoughtfully.

Any way he looked at this situation, leaping into bed with Lucy McKenty was stretching the boundaries of friendship.

But it was highly unlikely that she would agree to sex. Apart from the fact that Will was the brother of the man she'd planned to marry, and setting their friendship issues aside, Lucy was a vet. She used IVF all the time in her practice and she was bound to look on it as the straightforward and practical solution.

Except that she'd tried the clinical route once and it hadn't worked.

Which brought him back to the alternative. With Lucy.

Damn. He could still remember their long ago kiss on the veranda.

He should have forgotten it by now. He'd tried so hard to forget, but he could remember every detail of those few sweet minutes—the way Lucy had felt so alive and warm in his arms, the way she'd smelled of summer and tasted of every temptation known to man.

Hell. There was no contest, was there?

IVF was most definitely their sanest, safest option.

* * *

Lucy was in a daze as she walked back to her ute. She couldn't believe Will had given her suggestion serious thought. It was astonishing that he was actually prepared to help her to have her baby.

She couldn't deny she was tempted.

Tempted? Heavens, she was completely sold on the whole idea of having a dear little baby fathered by Will.

It was the means to this end that had her in a dither.

Sex with Will was so totally not a good idea. The very thought of it filled her with foolish longings and multiple anxieties.

She'd loved Will for so long now, it was like a chronic illness that she'd learned to adjust to. But to sleep with him would be like dancing on the edge of a cliff. She would be terrified of falling.

If only IVF was simpler.

She'd hated the process last time. All the tests and injections and clinical procedures and then the huge disappointment of failure. Not to mention the expense and the fact that, if she wanted to try again, she'd have to go back on that long waiting list.

Oh, man. Her thoughts went round and round, like dairy cows on a milking rotator. One minute she rejected the whole idea of having Will's baby, the next she was desperately trying to find a way to make it happen.

Could it work?

Could it possibly work?

Lucy remembered again how she'd felt when she'd seen Will at the wedding rehearsal, standing at the front of the church with tiny Mia in his arms. Just thinking about it made her teary. He would be such a fabulous father.

She drove home, but when she was supposed to be preparing dinner she was still lost in reverie, going over and over the same well worn thoughts.

She found herself standing at her kitchen sink, thinking about Will again. Still. She caught sight of her reflection in the window and was shocked to see that she was cradling a tea towel as if it were a baby. And her face was wet with tears.

The picture cut her to the core and, in that moment, she knew she had no choice. She wanted Will's baby more than anything she'd ever wanted in her life.

That precious baby's existence was a hundred times more important than the method of its conception.

Tomorrow, she should tell Will she'd made a decision.

Early next morning, however, there was a telephone call.

'Is that the young lady vet?'

'Yes,' Lucy replied, crossing her fingers. Calls this early on a Monday morning usually meant trouble.

'This is Barney May,' the caller said. 'I need someone to come and look at my sheep. Four of them have gone lame on me.'

Lucy suppressed a sigh. Lame sheep usually meant foot abscesses or, worse still, footrot, which was highly contagious. There'd been plenty of rain this spring so the conditions were ripe for an outbreak. *Darn it.*

'Could you come straight away?' Barney asked. 'I don't want a problem spreading through my whole herd.'

'Hang on. I'll have to check my schedule.'

She scanned through the surgery's diary for the day's appointments. It was the usual assortment—small animals with sore ears or eyes or skin conditions; a few vaccinations and general health checks for new puppies and kittens—nothing that her assistant couldn't handle.

'I'll be there in about an hour,' she told Barney.

'Good, lass. You know where I live—about ten kilometres out of town, past the sale yards on the White Sands Road.'

An hour later Lucy knew the worst. The sheep indeed had footrot and it had spread from the neighbouring property via a broken fence.

After paring the hooves of the unlucky sheep and prescribing footbaths, she had to continue her inspection and, all too soon, she discovered more evidence that the disease was spreading beyond the Mays' property, thanks to another farmer who'd really let his fences go.

Which spelled potential disaster.

Without question, it would mean a full week of hard work for Lucy. Her assistant would have to man the surgery while she toured the district, visiting all the farms as she tried to gauge just how far the problem ranged.

Each night she was exhausted and when she arrived home she had to face the surgery work that her assistant couldn't handle. By the time she crawled into bed she was too tired to tackle a complicated phone call to Will.

And, because the Carruthers family farm was at the opposite end of the district from the initial footrot outbreak, it was Friday afternoon before she got to Tambaroora.

It was a beautiful property with wide open paddocks running down to the creek and a grand old sandstone homestead, bang in the centre, surrounded by a green oasis of gardens. Lucy could never think about Tambaroora without seeing the garden filled with summer colour and smelling roses, jasmine, lavender and rosemary.

By the time she arrived, Will and his father had already completed a thorough inspection of their herd and they reported that their sheep were in good condition, but Lucy still needed to make spot sample checks.

Will hefted the heavy beasts she selected with obvious ease, and he kept them calm while she examined their hooves. She'd been dealing with farmers all week and she knew he made a difficult task look incredibly easy.

'For someone who doesn't think of himself as a farmer, you handle sheep well,' she said.

'Will's surprised us,' his father commented wryly. 'We didn't think he had it in him.'

A smile twisted Will's mouth as his father trudged off to attend to a ewe that had recently delivered twin lambs.

'I meant it,' Lucy told him. 'Not all farmers are good at handling stock. You're a natural.'

He looked amused. 'Maybe I was just trying to impress you.'

She rolled her eyes, but that was partly to cover the attack of nerves she felt at the thought of telling him she'd reached a decision about the baby. Her stomach was as jumpy as a grasshopper in a jar as he helped her to gather up her gear, then walked beside her to her ute.

'Do you have to hurry away?' he asked as she stowed her things. 'I was hoping we could talk.'

'About the baby idea?' She spoke as casually as she could.

There was no one around, but Will lowered his voice. 'Yes, I've been thinking it over.'

Her heart jumped like a skittish colt and she searched his face, trying to guess what he was going to tell her. If he'd decided to scrap the baby idea, she wasn't sure she could bear the disappointment. She'd become totally entranced by the thought of their adorable infant and she'd convinced herself that this time it would work.

With Will as her baby's father, she was confident of success.

She could be a mother. At last.

She forced a smile and willed herself to speak calmly. 'So, what have you decided?'

CHAPTER SIX

WILL'S eyes were almost silver in the outdoor light, so beautiful they stole Lucy's breath. 'I'd like to go ahead,' he said. 'I think you should try for a baby.'

'Wow.'

'So, are you keen too?'

'I am, yes.'

He smiled. 'Why don't we go for a walk?' He nodded towards the dark line of trees at the far end of a long, shimmering paddock of grain.

'Down by the creek again?' she asked, smiling.

'Why not?'

Why not, indeed? It had always been *their* place.

As Lucy walked beside Will, they chatted about her busy week and she tried to stay calm, to take in the special beauty of the late afternoon.

Cicadas were humming in the grass and the sinking sun cast a pretty bronzed glow over the wheat fields.

She tried to take in the details—the tracks that ants had made in an old weathered fence post, the angle of the shadows that stretched like velvet ribbons across the paddocks.

She really needed to stay calm.

It was ridiculous to be so churned up just talking to Will,

but now that they'd agreed to go ahead with this baby plan they had to discuss the more delicate details, like the method of conception.

How exactly did a girl tell a truly gorgeous man she'd fancied for years that she'd carefully weighed up the pros and cons and had decided, on balance, to have sex with him?

As they neared the creek she saw two wedge-tailed eagles hovering over a stick nest that they'd woven in the fork of a dead tree.

'I hope they don't plan to dine on our lambs,' Will said, watching them.

She might have replied, but they'd reached the shelter of the trees and her stomach was playing leapfrog with her heart.

It was so quiet down here. Too quiet. This part of the creek formed a still and silent pool and now, in the late afternoon, the birds had stopped calling and twittering. It seemed as if the whole world had stopped and was waiting to listen in to Lucy and Will's conversation.

'We need rain,' Will said as they came to a halt on the creek bank. 'The water level's dropping.'

Rain? How could he talk about rain? 'Now you're talking like a farmer.'

He pulled a comical face. 'Heaven forbid.'

Lucy drew a tense breath. 'Will, about the fine-tuning—'

'Lucy, I think you're probably right—'

They had both started talking at the same moment and now they stopped. Their gazes met and they laughed self-consciously.

'You first,' Will said.

'No, you tell me what you were going to say. What am I right about?'

'IVF. I know it's what you'd prefer and I think we should go that route.'

'Really?'

Oh, heavens. She hadn't sounded disappointed, had she?

Will's blue shirt strained at the shoulder seams as he shrugged. 'I can understand that it makes total sense to you and I'm prepared to do whatever's necessary.'

Lucy gulped as she took this in.

He watched her with a puzzled smile. 'I thought you'd be pleased.'

'Oh, I...I am. Yes, I'm really happy.' In truth, she couldn't believe the piercing sense of anticlimax she felt. 'I'm just surprised,' she said, working hard to cover her ridiculous disappointment. 'I spent the whole week worrying that you were going to back out altogether.'

Dropping her gaze to the ground, she hooked her thumbs into the back pockets of her jeans and kicked at a loose stone.

'So what were you going to say about the fine-tuning?' Will asked.

Lucy's face flamed. Now that Will had agreed to IVF, there was no point in telling him her decision. He'd never fancied her in that way, so it would be a huge challenge to become intimate.

'Lucy?'

'It doesn't matter now.'

'Why not?' Will swallowed abruptly and his eyes burned her.

'Honestly, Will, it's really great that you'd like to help with IVF. I'm very grateful. I couldn't be more pleased.'

His grey eyes were searching her, studying her. Suddenly they narrowed thoughtfully and then widened with surprise. 'Don't tell me you'd come around to...to the other option?'

'No, no. If you want to use IVF, that's good,' she said.

'I didn't exactly say it's what I *want*.' A nervous smile flickered in his face, then vanished. 'I was trying to look at this from your point of view. I thought it's what you'd prefer.'

'Thanks, Will. I appreciate that.' Lucy bit her lip to stop herself from saying more.

He stood very still, his hands hanging loosely at his sides, and she knew he was watching her while she continued to avoid his gaze.

'Or are you actually worried about IVF?' he asked cautiously. 'I know it didn't work for you last time.'

Lucy drew a sharp breath, and let it out slowly. Without meeting his gaze, she said, 'I can't say I'm in love with the idea of going through all those clinical procedures again.'

'The alternative is much simpler.'

'In some ways.' She knew her face must be turning bright pink.

To her surprise, Will looked as worried as she felt. He pointed to a smooth shelf of shady rock hanging over the water. 'Look, why don't we sit down for a bit?'

'Very well,' she agreed rather primly.

Despite the shade from overhead trees, the rock still held some of the day's warmth and they sat with their feet dangling over the edge, looking down into the green, still water. They'd sat like this many times, years ago, when they were school friends.

How innocent those days seemed now.

A childish chant from Lucy's schooldays taunted her. *First comes love, then comes marriage, then comes Lucy with a baby carriage.*

Now she and Will were putting an entirely new spin on that old refrain.

She picked up a fallen leaf and rolled it against her thigh, making a little green cylinder. 'Are we mad, Will? Is it crazy for us to be trying for a baby without love or marriage?'

She sensed a sudden vibrating tension in him, saw his Adam's apple slide up and down in his throat. He picked up a small stone and lobbed it into the water. 'I don't think it's a crazy idea. Not if you're quite sure it's what you want.'

She let the leaf uncurl. 'I definitely want to have a baby, and I really like the idea of having you as the father.' She rolled the leaf again into a tight little cylinder.

'But sex is a problem,' Will suggested and his voice was rough and gravelly, so that the statement fell between them like the stone he'd dropped in the water.

'It could be.' Lucy concentrated on the leaf in her hand.

'I know I'm not Josh,' Will said quietly.

Her head jerked up. With a stab of guilt, she realised she hadn't been thinking about Josh at all. Poor Will. Did he think he had to live up to some romantic ideal set by his brother?

If only he knew the truth.

But if she told him how she really felt about him, he might be more worried than ever.

No, this rather unconventional baby plan would actually work best if they approached it as friends.

Lucy looked down at Will's hand as it rested against the rock. It was a strong workmanlike hand, with fine sun-bleached hairs on the back. She placed her hand on top of his. 'I don't want you to be like Josh,' she said.

His throat worked.

'But this might be too hard,' she said. 'Friends don't usually jump into bed together.'

'But they might,' he said gently, 'if it was a means to an end. The best means to a good end.'

She sucked in a breath, looked up at the sky.

The best means to a good end.

A baby.

'That's a nice way of putting it,' she said, already picturing the sweet little baby in her arms. Oh, heavens, she could almost feel the warm weight of it, feel its head nestled in the crook of her arm, see its tiny hands. Would they be shaped like Will's?

'So what do you think?' he asked.

Lucy nodded thoughtfully. 'You're right. It's a means to an end.' After a bit, she said, 'It would probably be best if we took a strictly medical approach.'

Will frowned. 'Medical?'

'I can get ovulation predictors.' She was gaining confidence now. 'I'll need to let you know exactly when I'm ovulating.'

His eyes widened in surprise.

'You do know there are only a very few days each month when a woman is fertile, don't you?'

'Ah, yes, of course,' he said, recovering quickly. He sent her a puzzled smile. 'So what happens when it's all systems go? Will you send me a text message?' His smile deepened. 'Or fly a green flag above your door?'

Lucy saw his smile and she felt a massive chunk of tension flow out of her. To her surprise, she found herself smiling too. 'Oh, why don't I just go the whole hog and place a notice in the Post Office window?'

Now Will was chuckling. 'Better still, you could take out a full page ad in the *Willowbank Chronicle*.'

Suddenly, it was just like old times. Laughter had always been a hallmark of their friendship.

'What about hiring Frank Pope, the crop duster?' Lucy suggested. 'He's a dab hand at sky-writing. Can't you just see it written in the sky? Will Carruthers, tonight's the night.'

Laughing with her, Will scratched at his jaw. 'That's a bit too personal. What about a subtle message in code?'

'All right…let me see…something like…the hen is broody?'

'In your case it would have to be the Goose.'

Lucy snorted. 'Oh, yes. A broody goose.'

She collapsed back onto the rock, laughing.

Their conversation was ridiculous, but it was so therapeutic to be able to joke about such a scary subject.

Her anxiety was still there, just under the surface, but she felt much better as she lay on the warm rock, still chuckling as she looked up at the sky through a lacework of green branches.

She and Will would have to stay relaxed if this plan was to have any chance of working. Perhaps everything would be all right if they could both keep their sense of humour.

Will's mobile phone rang a week later, when he was sitting at the breakfast table with his parents. Quickly, he checked the caller ID, saw Lucy's name and felt a jolting thud in the centre of his chest.

'Excuse me,' he mumbled, standing quickly. 'I'll take this outside.'

His heart thumped harder than a jackhammer as he went out onto the back porch, letting the flyscreen door swing shut behind him.

'Good morning.' His voice was as rough as sandpaper.

'Will, it's Lucy.'

'Hi. How are you?'

'Fine, thanks.'

There was an awkward pause—a stilted silence broken only by a kookaburra's laughter and the whistle from the kettle in the kitchen as it came to the boil. Will's heartbeats drummed in his ears.

Lucy said, 'I was wondering if you were free to come to dinner tonight.'

'Tonight?'

'Yes, would that be OK?'

Will was shaking, which was crazy. This entire past week had been crazy. He'd been on tenterhooks the whole time, waiting for Lucy's call. He'd actually lent a hand with drenching the sheep, much to his father's amazement. He'd enjoyed the work, even though he'd originally made the offer simply to keep himself busy, to take his mind off Lucy.

'Sure,' he said now, walking further from the house, out of his parents' earshot. 'Dinner would be great. I'll bring a bottle of wine. What would you prefer? White or red?'

'Well, I'm making lasagne, so perhaps red?'

'Lasagne? Wow.' As far as he could remember, cooking had never been Lucy's forte. Perhaps she'd taken a course? 'Red it is, then.'

'See you around seven?'

'I'll be there.' And then, because he couldn't help it, 'Goose?'

'Yes?'

'Is this—?'

'Yes,' she said quickly before he could find the right words. Will swallowed. 'OK, then. See you at seven.'

He strolled back into the kitchen, body on fire, affecting a nonchalance he was far from feeling.

'I won't be home for dinner this evening,' he told his parents.

His mother smiled. 'So you're going out? That's nice, dear. It's good to see you catching up with your old friends.' She was always happy when she thought he was seeing someone. She'd never given up hope of more grandchildren.

Will's father looked more puzzled than pleased. This was the longest stretch his son had spent at home since he'd left all those years ago. Will knew they were both surprised, and expecting that he would take off again at a moment's notice.

But Gina and Tom's babies were to be christened as soon as Mattie and Jake returned from their honeymoon, so it was an excellent excuse for him to stay on.

As he tackled the remainder of his bacon and eggs he wondered what his parents would think if they knew he planned to help Lucy McKenty to become pregnant before he headed away again.

Half an hour before Will's expected arrival, Lucy's kitchen looked like a crime site, splattered from end to end with tomato purée and spilt milk, eggshells and flour.

She wanted everything to be so perfect for tonight and she'd actually had a brand-new whizz-bang stove installed. She'd even taken a whole afternoon off work to get this dinner ready for Will.

So far, however, the only part of the meal that looked edible was the pineapple poached in rum syrup, which was precisely one half of the dessert.

How on earth had she thought she could manage stewed

fruit and a baked custard as well as lasagne? She'd never been much of a cook and these dishes were so fiddly.

But now—*thank heavens*—everything was finally in the oven, although she still had to clean up the unholy mess and have a shower and change her clothes and put on make-up and set the table. She'd meant to hunt in the garden for flowers for the table as well, but the dinner preparations had taken her far too long.

She was never going to be ready in time.

Guys never noticed flowers anyway.

In a hectic whirl she dashed about the kitchen, throwing rubbish into plastic bags, wiping bench tops and spills on the floor, hurling everything else pell-mell into the dishwasher to be stacked again properly later.

Later.

Oh, heavens, she mustn't think about that.

The only good thing about being so frantically busy was that it had helped her not to dwell too deeply on the actual reason for this dinner. The merest thought of what was supposed to happen *after* the meal set off explosions inside her, making her feel like a string of firecrackers at Chinese New Year.

Hastily Lucy showered, slathering her skin with her favourite jasmine-scented gel and checking that her waxed legs were still silky and smooth.

Her hair was short so she simply towelled it dry, threw in a little styling product and let it do its own thing.

She put on a dress. She spent her working life in khaki jeans and she didn't wear dresses very often, but this one was pretty—a green and white floral slip with shoestring straps and tiny frills around the low V neckline. It suited her. She felt good in it.

A couple of squirts of scent, a dab of lip gloss, a flourish with the mascara brush…

A truck rumbled to a growling halt outside.

Lucy froze.

Her reflection in the bedroom mirror blushed and her skin flashed hot and cold. Frenzied butterflies beat frantic wings in her stomach.

Firm footsteps sounded on the front path and her legs became distinctly wobbly. This was crazy.

It's only Will, not Jack the Ripper.

Unfortunately, this thought wasn't as calming as it should have been.

Concentrate on the meal. First things first. One step at a time.

It was no good. She was still shaking as she opened the door.

Will was dressed casually, in blue jeans and an open-necked white shirt with the sleeves rolled up to just below the elbow. Behind him, the twilight shadows were the deepest blue. He was smiling. He looked gorgeous—with the kind of masculine fabulousness that smacked a girl between the eyes.

'Nice dress,' he said, smiling his appreciation.

'Thanks.'

With a pang Lucy allowed herself a rash moment of fantasy in which Will was her boyfriend and madly in love with her, planning to share a future with her and the baby they hoped to make.

Just as quickly she wiped the vision from her thoughts. Over the past ten years she'd had plenty of practice at erasing that particular dream.

Reality, her reality, was a convenient and practical parenting agreement. There was simply no point in hoping for more. She was incredibly grateful for Will's offer. It was her best, quite possibly her only prospect for motherhood.

'Something smells fantastic,' he said.

'Thanks.' Her voice was two levels above a whisper. 'I hope it tastes OK. Come on in.'

She'd planned to eat in the kitchen, hoping that the room's rustic simplicity and familiar cosiness would help her to stay calm.

Already, that plan had flown out of the window. She was almost sick with nerves.

'Take any seat, Will.' She gestured towards chairs gathered around the oval pine table. 'You can open the wine if you like. I'd better check the dinner.'

She opened the oven door. *Concentrate on the food.*

Her heart sank.

No, no, no!

The baked custard, which was supposed to be smooth as silk, was speckled and lumpy. Like badly scrambled eggs.

The lasagne was worse.

How could this have happened?

The lasagne had been a work of art when it went into the oven—a symphony of layers—creamy yellow cheese sauce and pasta, with red tomatoes and herb infused meat.

Now the cheese sauce had mysteriously disappeared and the beautiful layers were dried out and brown, like shrivelled, knobbly cardboard splattered with dubious blobs of desiccated meat.

It was a total, unmitigated disaster.

'I can't believe it,' she whispered, crestfallen. She'd spent hours and hours preparing these dishes—beating, stirring, spicing, testing, reading and rereading the recipes over and over.

'What's happened?' Will's question was tentative, careful.

Fighting tears, Lucy shook her head. 'I don't know. I followed the instructions to the letter.' Snatching up oven gloves, she took out the heavy lasagne pan.

Stupidly, she'd been picturing Will's admiration. 'It's disgusting,' she wailed.

'It'll probably taste fine,' he said gallantly as she dumped the hot dish onto a table mat.

Lucy wanted to howl. 'I'm sorry, Will.' Unwilling to meet his gaze, she retrieved the dreadful looking custard and set it out of sight on the bench, beneath a tea towel. 'They've opened a pizza place in town. I think I'd better run in there.'

'This food will be fine,' he insisted again.

Hands on hips, she shook her head and glared at the stove. 'I can't believe I spent so much money on a brand-new oven and I still made a hash of the meal.'

'It might be a matter of getting used to the settings.' He bent closer to look at the stove's knobs.

Lucy followed his gaze and squinted at the little symbols. Now that she took a closer look, she saw that a tiny wriggly line on one knob differentiated it from its neighbour.

She swore softly. 'I think I turned the wrong knob. Damn! I've been trying to grill the food instead of baking it.'

She'd been too distracted. That was her problem. She'd kept thinking about the *reason* for this dinner and a moment's loss of concentration was all it had taken to ruin her efforts.

Will's grey eyes twinkled, however, and he looked as if he was trying very hard not to laugh.

To Lucy's surprise, she began to giggle. She'd been so tense about this evening, so desperate for everything to be perfect and now, when she had to try to cover her disappointment, she could only giggle.

It was that or cry, and she wasn't going to cry.

Will flung his arm around her shoulders in a friendly cheer-up hug, and her giggling stopped as if he'd turned off a switch.

'Right,' she said breathlessly as she struggled for composure. 'If we're going to try to eat this, I'd better set the table.'

Will opened a long-necked bottle with a fancy label and poured dark ruby-red wine into their glasses. Lucy took the salad she'd prepared from the fridge. At least it still looked fresh and crisp. She removed the plastic film, added dressing and tossed it. She found a large knife and cut the lasagne and was surprised that it cut easily, neatly keeping its shape. That was something, at any rate.

'I told you this would taste good,' Will said after his first mouthful.

To Lucy's surprise, he was right. The lasagne's texture might have been a bit too dry, but it hadn't actually burned and the herbs and meat had blended into a tasty combination. She sipped the deep rich wine and ate a little more and she began to relax. Just a little.

'Have you rescued any more pythons?'

She shook her head. 'The only wildlife I've cared for this week is a galah with a broken wing. But I discovered who dropped the python off. It was one of the schoolteachers. Apparently, he accidentally clipped him with his ride-on mower. He's going to care for him for another week or so, then let him go again in the trees down near the creek.'

They talked a little more about Lucy's work, including the good news that the footrot hadn't spread to any more sheep farms.

'What have you been up to?' she asked. 'I hear you've been lending a hand with drenching.'

He sent her a wry smile. 'News travels fast.'

'I saw your father in town the other day and he was so excited. He said you haven't lost the knack.'

Will shrugged.

'I told you you're a natural with animals.'

'Are you trying to turn me into a farmer, too?'

She didn't want to upset him, so she tried another topic. 'Have you started job-hunting?'

Over the rim of his wine glass his eyes regarded her steadily, almost with a challenge. 'I'm going for an interview at Armidale University next Thursday.'

Lucy could feel her smile straining at the edges, which was ridiculous. She knew Will would never settle back in the Willow Creek district. 'That's great. Good luck.'

'Thanks.'

He helped himself to seconds, but Lucy was too tense to eat any more and she wasn't sure if she should offer Will the dessert. However, he insisted on trying her lumpy custard and rum-poached pineapple and he assured her it was fabulous.

'Very courteous of you to say so.' She took a small spoonful of the custard. 'Actually, this does have a scrumptious flavour, doesn't it?' She smiled ruefully. 'At least I had all the right ingredients.'

'And that's what counts.'

Something about the way Will said this made Lucy wonder if he was talking about more than the food. With a rush of heat, she remembered again what this night was all about.

The butterflies in her stomach went crazy as she stared at the mouthful of wine in the bottom of her glass. In a perfect world, people created babies out of love, but tonight she and Will were supposed to make a baby by having 'friendly' sex.

Leave your emotions at the door, please.

She wasn't sure this was possible for her. But, if she wanted a baby, she was going to have to pretend that she was OK about the 'only friends' part of their arrangement.

Cicadas started their deafening chorus outside in the trees and in the soft pink-plumed grasses, as they did every evening in spring and summer, calling to each other in the last of the daylight.

Lucy cocked her ear to the almost deafening choir outside. 'Those cicadas are just like us.'

Will's eyebrows lifted. 'They are?'

'Sure. Listen to them. They wait till the last ten or fifteen minutes of daylight, till it's almost too late to find partners, and then they go into a mad panic and start yelling out—*Hey, I need to pass on my DNA. I need a mate. Who's out there?*'

Will laughed and topped up their wine glasses.

A startling image jumped into her head of his white shirt slipping from his broad brown shoulders, of the fastener on his jeans sliding down.

Consumed by flames, she gulped too much wine. 'This would be so much easier if we were aliens.'

Will almost choked on his drink. 'I beg your pardon?'

'Oh, you've seen the movies.' She held out her hand to him, fingers splayed. 'If aliens want to have a baby, they just let their fingertips touch. Or they hook up by mental telepathy and *voila*! One cute triangular baby.'

Shaking his head, Will stood. He wasn't smiling any more as he collected their plates and took them to the sink.

Slightly dazed by this abrupt change, Lucy watched him with a mixture of nervousness and longing. His long legs and wide shoulders—*everything*, really—made him so hunky and desirable.

'Shall I put the leftovers in the fridge?' he asked.

Goodness. He was hunky and desirable and unafraid to help in the kitchen. Lucy was so busy admiring Will she almost forgot that this was her kitchen and she should be helping him.

She jumped to her feet. 'My dogs will adore that custard in the morning.'

They made short work of clearing the food away, then Will snagged the wine bottle and their glasses. 'Why don't we make ourselves more comfortable?'

'C-comfortable?'

He smiled at her. 'If you stay here chattering about mating cicadas and alien sex you're going to talk yourself out of this, Goose.'

Well, yes, she was aware of that distinct possibility.

'Where do you want to go, then?'

Amusement shimmered in his eyes. 'I thought we might try your bedroom.'

Lucy gasped. 'Already?'

'Come on.' Will was smiling again as he took her hand. 'We can do this.' He pulled her gently but purposefully across the room. 'Which way?'

'My room's the first on the right.' Lucy was super-aware of their linked hands as she walked beside him on unsteady legs.

Think about the baby. Don't fall in love.

Will stopped just inside her bedroom doorway. 'Very nice,' he said, admiring the brand-new claret duvet with silvery-grey pillows. She'd chosen the pillow slips because they were the colour of Will's eyes.

She was glad she'd turned on the bed lamps and drawn the new curtains. The room looked welcoming. Not too girly. Smart. Attractive.

Will put the bottle and glasses down on one of the bedside tables, then came and stood beside her. He took her hands.

Lucy's mouth was drier than the Sahara. How could he be so calm?

She felt a riff of panic, found herself staring at his shoes, thinking about them coming off and then the rest of him becoming bare. She could picture his shoulders, his chest, his tapering torso…

He was so gorgeous, but he was only doing this because he wanted to help her. He only thought of her as a friend. He couldn't possibly fancy her. She'd always known that.

If she'd ever doubted it, she only had to remember the way Will had kissed her on the night of his farewell party, and then left for overseas as if it hadn't meant a thing. Now he would be so much more experienced with women.

Oh, help. It was ages since she'd had a boyfriend. Why had she agreed to this? How had she ever thought this could be OK?

'Will, I don't think—'

'That's good.'

'Pardon?'

'Don't think,' he murmured and he smiled as he drew her closer.

Nervously, she looked down at their linked hands and watched his thumb gently rub her knuckles. She wondered if she should warn him she was scared—scared of not living up to his expectations. Scared of falling in love.

But no. He was so confident and calm about this, he probably wouldn't understand. She could frighten him off and she would end up without a baby.

'I want our baby to be like you,' Will said softly.

Lucy gulped. 'Do you? Why?'

'You're so sweet, so clever and kind.'

'You're all of those things too.'

She saw the stirring of something dark and dangerous in his eyes.

He touched her collarbone and she held her breath as his fingers traced its straight line. Her pulses leapt as he reached the base of her throat.

'Any baby who scores you as his mum will be born lucky.' His voice was a deep, warm rumble running over her skin like a fiery caress.

She could see Will's mouth in the lamplight. So incredibly near. She remembered that one time he'd kissed her and how she'd marvelled that his lips were surprisingly soft and sensuous compared with the rough and grainy texture of his jaw.

He trailed his fingers up the line of her throat to her chin and, for a hushed moment, his thumb rode the rounded nub, then continued along the delicate edge of her jaw.

She held her breath as he lowered his head, letting his lips follow where his fingers had led.

Despite her tension, a soft sigh floated from her and she closed her eyes as his breath feathered over her skin and she felt the warm, intimate pressure of his mouth on the hollow at the base of her throat.

He was unbelievably good at this. Her tension began to melt beneath the sweet, intoxicating journey of his lips over her throat.

He whispered her name.

'Lucy.'

His lips caressed her jaw with whisper-soft kisses. He kissed her cheek, giving the corner of her mouth the tiniest lick, and she began to tremble.

Please, Will, please…

At last his lips settled over hers and Lucy forgot to be frightened.

Her lips parted beneath him and he immediately took the kiss deeper, tasting her fully, and she decided it was too late to worry about what Will thought of her. About having babies or not having them. She just wanted to enjoy this moment. This, now.

Will framed her face with his hands and he kissed her eagerly, ardently, hungrily and Lucy returned his kisses, shyly at first but with growing enthusiasm, eager to relearn the wonderful texture and taste of him.

His voice was ragged and breathless as he fingered the straps of her dress. 'How do I get you out of this?'

'Oh, gosh, I forgot. Sorry.' The spell was broken as Lucy remembered that her dress had a side zipper. She had to lift one arm as she reached for it.

'I've got it,' Will said, his fingers beating hers to the task.

She heard the zip sliding south, felt his hands tweak her shoulder straps and suddenly her dress was drifting soundlessly to her feet. She wasn't wearing a bra and she felt vulnerable and shy, but Will drew her close, enfolding her into a comforting embrace.

With his arms around her, with his forehead pressed to hers, he whispered, 'Your turn, Goose.'

'My turn?'

'Take off my shirt.'

'Oh, yes. Right.'

Her eyes were riveted on his chest as she undid the buttons to reveal smooth masculine muscles that she longed to touch. She felt breathless and dizzy as she slid the fabric from his shoulders.

Her breath caught at the sight of him. She'd known he was beautiful, but she'd forgotten he was *this* beautiful.

Will kissed her again, letting his lips roam over hers in slow, lazy caresses that made her dreamy and warm so that again she gave up being scared. Still kissing her, he drew her down to the edge of the bed and then he took her with him until they were lying together, their limbs and bodies touching, meshing, already finding the perfect fit.

Bravely, she allowed her fingers to trail over his chest and felt his heart pounding beneath her touch. She smelled the long remembered midnight scent of his skin and she closed her eyes and gave in to sensation as he kissed her ears, her throat, her shoulder.

Every touch, every brush of his lips on her skin, every touch felt right and perfect and necessary.

She wasn't sure when she first felt the hot tears on her face, but she smiled, knowing they were tears of happiness.

How could they be anything else? This was her man, her passionate, hunky Will, and she was finally awake in her dream.

CHAPTER SEVEN

THEY sat in a pool of soft golden lamplight.

Will moved to the edge of the bed, shaken by what had happened.

He'd known that making love to Lucy would be a sweet pleasure, but he hadn't expected to be sent flying to the outer limits of the universe.

He felt an urge to ask her: *Does this change…everything?*

But that was lovers' talk and she expected friendship from him. Nothing more.

His thoughts churned while Lucy lay very still, with her knees bent and her shoulders propped against the pillows. She looked deceptively angelic with her short golden curls and a white sheet pulled demurely up to her chin.

'I mustn't move,' she said.

'Why can't you move?'

'I want to give your swimmers their very best chance of reaching my egg.'

He smiled at the hopeful light in her blue eyes, but his smile felt frayed around the edges.

It was hard to believe that this folly had been his idea. His foolish idea.

Lucy had been joking when she'd first suggested this, but he'd turned it into something real. He'd thought he was so damned clever. But he hadn't known, had he? Hadn't dreamed that making love to Lucy would turn his world upside down.

Was this how it had been for Josh?

He forced himself to remember why they'd done this. 'So I guess it's now a matter of wait and see?' he asked.

Lucy nodded. 'My period's due in about two weeks.'

So matter of fact.

Two weeks felt like a lifetime. 'I'll wait for another phone call then,' he said. 'And I'll hope for good news.'

Her eyes shimmered damply. Shyly, she said, 'Thank you, Will.'

His abrupt laugh was closer to a cough.

A tear sparkled and fell onto Lucy's flushed cheek, making him think of a raindrop on a rose. Reaching out, he gently blotted the shining moisture with the pad of his thumb. 'You OK, Goose?'

'Sure.'

She smiled to prove it and he launched to his feet and dragged on jeans. 'Can I make you a cup of tea or something?'

Lucy looked startled.

'I just thought…' He scratched at his bare chest. 'If you're planning to lie there for a bit, I thought you might like a cuppa.'

'Oh…um…well, yes, that would be lovely. Thank you.'

He went through to her kitchen, filled the kettle, set it on the stove and, as he rattled about searching for teabags and mugs, he saw a familiar piece of framed glass hanging in the window.

It was dark outside so he couldn't see the jewel-bright

colours of the stained glass, but he knew the dominant colour was deep blue.

Memories unravelled. He'd given this to Lucy as a graduation gift, to remind her of the times they'd spent as schoolkids fossicking for sapphires.

She'd always been fascinated by the change in the chips of dark sapphire when they were held up to the light and transformed from dull black into sparkling, brilliant blue.

The same thing happened when sun lit the stained glass.

But he hadn't expected her to keep this gift for so long, or to display it so prominently, as if it was important.

Now, Will looked around, trying to guess which piece among Lucy's knick-knacks had been a present to her from his brother.

Lucy managed not to cry until after Will had left. She heard the front door open and close, heard his footsteps on the front path, the rusty squeak of the front gate, the even rustier squeak of the truck's door and then, at last, the throaty grumble of the motor.

As the truck rattled away from her house, she couldn't hold back any longer.

The mug of tea Will had made for her sat untouched on the bedside table, and the tears streamed down her face.

She should have known.

She should have known this was a terrible mistake. Should have known Will Carruthers would break her heart.

Her sobs grew louder and she pulled a pillow against her mouth to muffle them, but nothing could diminish the storm inside her.

She loved Will. Loved him, loved him, loved him, loved him.

She'd always loved Will, and she'd wrecked her whole life by getting involved with his brother in a bid to make him jealous. She felt so guilty about that. And even now her memories of her mistakes cast a shadow over what had happened tonight.

Almost two weeks later, Lucy bought a packet of liquorice allsorts.

It was an impulse purchase in the middle of her weekly shopping. She saw the sweets, felt the urge to buy them and tossed them into her supermarket trolley. It wasn't until she was unpacking her groceries at home that she realised what she'd done and what it meant.

She only ever had the urge to eat sweets on the day before her period was due.

Which meant…

No.

No, no, no.

This didn't mean she wasn't pregnant, surely?

She'd been tense all week, alert to the tiniest signs in her body. But she hadn't noticed any of the well-known symptoms. No unusual tiredness. No breast tenderness. And now—she was having pre-menstrual cravings!

She couldn't bear it if her period came. She so wanted to be pregnant.

Just this week she'd delivered five Dachshund puppies and two purebred Persian kittens and each time she'd handled a gorgeous newborn she'd imagined her own little baby already forming inside her.

Heavens, she'd imagined her entire pregnancy in vivid detail. She'd even pictured the baby's birth and Will's excitement. She'd pictured bringing the little one home, watching it grow until it was old enough to play with Gina and Tom's twins. She'd almost gone into Willowbank's one and only baby store and bought a tiny set of clothes.

She *had* to be pregnant.

But now, on a rainy Friday night, she sat curled in a lounge chair with the bag of liquorice in her lap, aware of a telltale ache in her lower abdomen.

She was trying to stay positive. And failing miserably.

She'd had so much hope pinned on this one chance. She couldn't risk another night in bed with Will, couldn't go through another round of heartache. She really, really needed that one night to have been successful.

Time dragged for Will.

November, however, was a hectic month on a New South Wales sheep farm so, even though he couldn't stop thinking about Lucy, he found plenty of ways to keep busy.

Now that the shearing was over, all the sheep had to be dipped and drenched, prior to the long, hot summer. It was time to wean lambs and to purchase rams for next year's joining. To top it off, it was also haymaking time.

Will found himself slipping back into the world of his childhood with surprising ease.

In his wide-ranging travels, he'd seen breathtaking natural beauty and sights that were truly stranger than fiction, but it was only here at home that he felt a soul-deep connection to the land.

He supposed it flowed in his blood as certainly as his DNA. He'd always been secretly proud of the fact that his great great-grandfather, another William Carruthers, had bought this land in the nineteenth century.

William had camped here at first and then lived in the

shearers' quarters, before finally acquiring sufficient funds to build a substantial homestead for his bride.

Will found himself thinking more and more often about Josh, too. His brother had been the family member everyone had expected to work this land as their father's right hand man. The man who had won Lucy's heart.

He remembered the fateful morning Josh had woken him early, proclaiming that this was the day he was going to fly the plane he'd worked on for so long.

It had been too soon. Will had known that the final checks hadn't been made by the inspector from the aero club, but Josh had been insistent.

'I'm not waiting around for that old codger. I've put in all the work on this girl. I know she's fine. This is the day, Will. It's a perfect morning for a first flight. I can *feel* it.'

Will had gone with great reluctance, mainly to make sure Josh didn't do anything really stupid. As they drove through the creamy dawn towards the Willowbank airfield, he'd conscientiously reread all the flying manuals, anxious to understand all the necessary safety checks.

'I still don't think you should be doing this,' he'd said again when they'd arrived at the hangar.

'Give it a miss, little brother,' Josh had responded angrily. 'Just accept that we're different. I'm my own man. I go after what I want and I make sure that I get it.'

'Is that how you scored Lucy McKenty?' Will hadn't been able to hold back the question that had plagued him ever since he'd arrived home.

Josh laughed. 'Of course. What did you expect? In case you haven't noticed, Lucy's the best looking girl in the district. I wasn't going to leave her sitting on the shelf.'

'She's not another of your damn trophies.'

'For God's sake, Will, you're not going to be pre-cious, are you?'

An unreasonable anger had swirled through Will. His hands had fisted, wanting to smash the annoying smirk on his brother's handsome face. 'You'd better make bloody sure you look after her.'

'Don't worry.' Josh laughed. 'I've already done that.' He was still laughing as he climbed into the pilot's seat. 'Now, you sit over there and stay quiet, little brother, while I take this little beauty for her test flight.'

Once more, Will had tried to stop him. 'You shouldn't be doing this. You only have to wait for one more inspection.'

Josh had ignored him and turned on the engine.

'I'm not going to sit around here like your fan club,' Will shouted above the engine's roar. 'If you're going to break your bloody neck, you can do it by yourself.'

From the cockpit, Josh had yelled his last order. 'Don't you dare take the car.'

'Don't worry. I'll bloody walk back.'

They had been his parting words.

The plane had barely made it into the air before it had shuddered and begun to fall. Will had seen everything from the road.

So many times in the years that followed, he'd regret-ted his actions that morning.

He'd washed his hands of his brother, turned his back on him, but he should have stood up to Josh, should have found a way to stop him.

But then again, no one, not even their father had been able to stop Josh when he'd set his mind on a goal.

Lucy wouldn't have stood a chance either.

* * *

The next morning, Lucy knew the worst.

She sent Will a text message.

Thanks for your help, but sorry, no luck. We're not going to be parents. L x

She felt guilty about texting him rather than speaking to him, but she was afraid she'd start blubbing if she'd tried explain over the phone.

If Will's parents were nearby when he took the call, it would be really awkward for him to have to deal with a crying female who wasn't actually his girlfriend.

But it was a Saturday morning and she wasn't working, so she wasn't totally surprised when Will turned up on her doorstep within twenty minutes.

She hadn't seen him in two weeks and when she opened her door and saw him standing there with his heart-throb smile and blue jeans sexiness she felt a sweet, shivery ache from her breastbone to her toes.

'I guess you got my text,' she said.

Will nodded. 'I'm really sorry about your news, Lucy. It's rotten luck.'

She quickly bit her lower lip to stop it from trembling and, somehow, she refrained from flinging her arms around Will and sobbing all over him, even though it was exactly what she needed to do.

Instead she took two hasty steps back, tried for an offhand shrug. 'I guess it wasn't meant to happen.'

Will shook his head. 'I can't believe that.'

Her attempt to smile felt exceptionally shaky.

As they went through to the kitchen, she couldn't help remembering the last time they had been here together on *that* night.

'I should warn you, Will, I'm rather fragile this morning.'

Her hands fluttered in a gesture of helplessness. 'Hormones and disappointment can be a messy combination.'

'Maybe we were expecting too much, hoping it would all happen the first time.'

'I don't know. Maybe I should have more tests. I'm so scared that my eggs aren't up to scratch.'

Before she knew quite what was happening, Will closed the gap between them. His arms were around her and she was clinging to him, snuffling against his clean cotton T-shirt and inhaling the scents of the outdoors that clung to his skin. Trying very, very hard not to cry.

His fingers gently played with her hair. 'I'm sure your eggs are perfect. I bet they're the healthiest, cutest little goose eggs ever.'

She muffled a sob against his chest.

'We might have to be patient,' he said.

'Patient?' She pulled away. 'What do you mean?'

His eyes reflected bemusement. 'In a couple of weeks we can try again, can't we?'

No. No, they couldn't. She couldn't do this again. It had been a mistake.

'No, Will.' Lucy swallowed. 'I'm afraid we can't try again.'

Unhappily she slipped from the haven of his arms and turned away from the puzzled look in his eyes.

'But surely you're not ready to give up after just one try?'

'Yes, I am. Perhaps nature knows best.'

'What are you talking about?'

'Perhaps friends shouldn't try to be parents.'

'Lucy, that's not rational.'

'I'm sorry if you're disappointed, but I couldn't go through this again.'

Not with Will. It would be a huge mistake to sleep with

him again. It was too painful, knowing that he was only being a friend to her, that he didn't love her.

In the agonising stretch of silence he stood with his arms folded, frowning at a spot on the floor. Eventually, he said, 'You're disappointed right now. That's understandable. But you're sure to feel differently in another week or so.'

Lucy shook her head. 'No, Will. I'm sorry. This isn't a snap decision I made this morning. I'd already made up my mind last week. I decided I should give up on the whole idea of a baby if there was no pregnancy this month.'

'But that doesn't make sense.'

Tears threatened, but she kept her expression carefully calm. 'It makes sense to me.'

If only she could explain her decision without confessing that she had always been in love with him. But that meant talking about Josh and she felt too fragile this morning to go there.

Perhaps it was better to never talk about it. If they stopped the friendship plan now, they could leave the past in the past, where it belonged.

Somehow she kept her voice steady. 'It was a great idea in theory, but I'm afraid it's not going to work, Will. I might take months to fall pregnant. *Friends* don't keep having sex month after month, or possibly several times a month, trying to becoming parents.'

'But I thought you really wanted to have a baby.'

'Well, yes, I did want a baby. But—' Oh, help. What could she tell him? 'Maybe sex is different for guys,' she finished lamely.

'I wouldn't be so sure about that.'

Lucy's heart stuttered as she watched a dark stain ride

up Will's neck. Knotted veins stood out on the backs of his hands as he gripped the back of a kitchen chair.

Lucy knew she mustn't cave in now. She should have recognised from the start that this convenient baby idea could never work. She should have known that her emotions would never survive the strain of making love to him when he'd only ever offered her friendship and a fly in, fly out version of fatherhood.

She should have heard the warning bells then. She'd been foolish to agree.

Even so, a huge part of her wanted to remain foolish. She longed to rush into Will's arms again. She longed for him to kiss her, longed for a future where Will Carruthers figured in her life, no matter how remotely.

'So,' he said tightly, 'you're quite certain you want to ditch our arrangement?'

'Yes, that's what I want.'

His jaw clenched tightly and a muscle jerked just below his right cheekbone. For a moment he looked as if he wanted to say more, but then he frowned and shook his head.

'Will, I do appreciate your—'

He silenced her with a raised hand. 'Please, spare me your thanks. I know what this is all about. It's OK.' Already he was heading back down the hallway to her front door.

Puzzled by his sudden acceptance, but aching with regret, Lucy followed. On the doorstep, she said, 'Gina's invited me to the twins' christening. I guess I'll…see you there?'

'Of course.' He smiled wryly. 'We're the star godparents.'

It occurred to Lucy that this christening would be like the wedding—another gathering of their friends and families. Another ceremonial rite of passage. Another occasion when she and Will would be in close proximity. But she wondered if either of them could look forward to it.

The heaviness inside her plunged deeper as she watched Will swing into the truck. It was only as the driver's door slammed shut that she remembered she hadn't asked him about his job interview.

She ran down the path, calling to him, 'Will, how was the interview in Armidale?'

His face was stony. 'I didn't end up going.'

Shocked, she clung to her rickety front gate. 'Why not?'

'When I really thought about working there, shut up in a building all day, preparing lectures, marking papers, talking to academics, I knew I wasn't cut out for it.'

Before she could respond, he gunned the truck's motor and sent it rattling and roaring to life. Without smiling, he raised his hand in a grim salute. Dust rose as he took off.

Miserably, Lucy watched him go.

Soon he would probably disappear completely, off to another remote outpost. Now, too late, she realised that she'd been secretly hoping he'd get that job in Armidale and stay close.

At least Will had been honest with himself. He was right—unfortunately—Armidale wouldn't have suited him. Alaska or Africa were more his style. Anywhere—as long as it was a long, long way from Willowbank.

The christening was perfect—sweet babies in white baptismal gowns, white candles, a kindly vicar, photos and happy onlookers.

But it was an ordeal for Will.

Lucy was a constant distraction in a floaty dress of the palest dove grey, and Gina and Tom's obvious pride in their beyond cute, well behaved babies was a poignant reminder of her recent disappointment.

Spring was at its best with clear blue skies and gentle sunshine, but Will felt like a man on a knife edge. He so regretted not being able to help Lucy to achieve her goal of motherhood.

He was deeply disappointed that she wasn't prepared to have a second try. In fact, the depth of his disappointment surprised him. It was disturbing to know that she'd found the whole process too stressful.

Will reasoned that his relationship to Josh was the problem. He was too strong a reminder of the man she'd loved and lost. Why else had she looked so miserable when he'd tried to convince her to keep trying?

After the church service, the Carruthers family held a celebratory luncheon at Tambaroora. Long tables were covered in white cloths and set beneath pergolas heavy with fragrant wisteria. Everyone helped to carry the food from the kitchen—platters of seafood and roast meat, four different kinds of salads, mountains of crispy, homemade bread rolls.

Two white christening cakes were given pride of place and crystal flutes were filled with French champagne to wet the babies' heads.

Will chatted with guests and helped with handing the drinks around and Lucy did the same but, apart from exchanging polite greetings, they managed to avoid conversing with each other.

It seemed necessary given the circumstances, as if they both feared that a conversation might give their strained relationship away.

Fortunately, no one else seemed to notice their tension.

Everyone was too taken with the babies, or too eager to hear about Mattie and Jake's honeymoon travels in Italy.

Gina's father-in-law, Fred Hutchins, broke off an animated conversation with Lucy to catch Will as he passed.

'Great to see you again,' Fred said, shaking Will's hand. 'We old-timers have been following your exploits in Alaska and Africa and Mongolia. It all sounds so exciting.'

'It's been interesting,' Will agreed, without meeting Lucy's gaze.

'Good for you. Why not enjoy an adventurous life while you can? I should have headed off myself when I was younger, but it just didn't happen. I'm pleased you didn't get bogged down here, Will. I suppose, in some ways, we look on you as the one who got away.' Fred chuckled. 'When are you heading off again?'

'Pretty soon.'

Fred clapped Will on the shoulder. 'Good for you, son. Don't hang around here. It's too easy to grow roots in a place like this.'

Will caught Lucy's eye and saw the sad set of her mouth and the thinness of her smile. He wondered, as the laughter and chatter floated about them, if he was the only one who noticed the shadowy wistfulness in her eyes whenever she glanced in the direction of the babies.

Unlike the other women, Lucy hadn't begged for a chance to cuddle little Mia or Jasper and Will's heart ached for her.

When it was time for dessert, silver platters piled with dainty lemon meringue tarts appeared.

'Lucy, these are divine!' Gina exclaimed with her mouth full.

For the first time that day, Lucy looked happy. 'They turned out well, didn't they?'

'Did you make these?' Will was unable to disguise his surprise, which he immediately regretted.

Lucy's smile faltered. 'Yes.' She tilted her chin defensively. 'As a matter of fact, I made them entirely from scratch—even the pastry.'

'What's got into you, Will?' Gina challenged. 'Are you trying to suggest that Lucy can't cook?'

The eyes of almost every guest at the table suddenly fixed on Will and he felt the back of his neck grow uncomfortably hot. He smiled, tried to mumble an apology. 'No, no, sorry. I…I…'

To his surprise, Lucy came to his rescue. 'Back when Will and I were at uni, I used to be an atrocious cook.'

This was greeted by indulgent smiles and nods and comments along the lines that Lucy was an accomplished cook now. As general conversation resumed, Lucy's eyes met Will's down the length of the table. She sent him a smile, nothing more than a brief flash, but its sweet intimacy almost undid him.

Shortly afterwards, the babies woke from their naps and the christening cakes were cut and glasses were raised once again. Tom made a short but touching speech of thanks to Mattie for her wonderful gift of the surrogate pregnancy and, just as he finished, baby Mia let out a loud bellow of protest.

'Oh, who's a grizzly grump?' Gina gave a theatrical groan. 'She probably needs changing.'

To Will's surprise, Lucy jumped to her feet and held out her arms. 'Let me look after her,' she said.

'Oh, thanks, I won't say no,' Gina replied with a laugh.

Lucy was smiling as she scooped the baby from Gina's lap.

Will watched her walk back across the smooth lawn to the

house and thought how beautiful she looked in her elegant dress with its floaty grey skirt, the colour of an early morning sky. Her pale blonde hair was shining in the sunlight, and the baby was a delicate pink and white bundle in her arms.

Without quite realising what he'd done or why, he found himself standing. 'I'll fetch more champagne,' he offered, grasping for an excuse to follow her.

'No need, Will,' called his father, pointing to a tub filled with ice. 'We still have plenty of champers here.'

'I…er…remembered that I left a couple of bottles in the freezer,' Will said. 'I don't want them to ice up. I'd better rescue them.'

As he entered the house he heard Lucy's voice drifting down the hallway from the room that used to be Gina's. Her voice rippled with laughter and she was talking in the lilting sing-song that adults always used with babies. For Will, the sound was as seriously seductive as a siren's song and he couldn't resist heading down the passage.

In the doorway he paused, unwilling to intrude. The baby was on the bed, little arms waving, legs pumping as she laughed and giggled and Lucy was leaning over her.

Will couldn't see Lucy's face, but he could hear her soft, playful chatter. It was such a touching and intimate exchange. A painful brick lodged in his throat.

Lucy was laughing. 'Who's the cutest little baby girl in the whole wide world?'

Mia responded with loud chuckles and coos.

'Who's the loveliest roly-poly girl? Who's so chubby and sweet I could gobble her up?'

Will felt a twist in his heart as he watched Lucy kiss the waving pink toes, watched her gently and deftly apply lotion to the petal soft skin, then refasten a clean nappy.

Aware that he was spying, he stepped back, preparing to make a discreet departure, but just at that moment, a choked cry broke from Lucy and she seemed to fold in the middle like a sapling lashed by a storm.

She sank to her knees beside the bed.

'Lucy.'

He didn't want to startle her, but her name burst from him.

Her head jerked up and she turned and her face was white and wet with tears. She looked at Will with haunted eyes and then she looked at the baby and she tried to swipe at her tears, but her emotions were too raw. Her mouth crumpled and she sent Will a look of hopeless despair.

In a heartbeat he was in the room, dropping to his knees beside her. He pulled her into his arms and he held her as she trembled and clung to him, burying her face, warm and wet with tears, against his neck.

It was then that he knew.

He knew how deeply she longed for a child.

He knew how very much he wanted to help her.

Most of all, he knew that Lucy's need was greater than her fear.

'We can try again if you like,' he whispered close to her ear. 'Lucy, why don't you try again?'

'Yes,' she sobbed against his shoulder. 'I think I have to. Please, yes.'

His arms tightened around her.

In a few minutes Lucy was calmer. She stood and went to the bathroom to wash her face while Will held Mia.

It was quite something the way his little niece snuggled into him, with her head tucked against his chest and one chubby starfish hand clutching at the fabric of his shirt.

Will tried to imagine a son or daughter of his own. A tiny person like this. Mia smelled amazing. She smelled… pink.

Yes, if pale pink was a fragrance, he was sure it would smell like this baby. Warm and fuzzy and incredibly appealing.

The baby was wearing the gold bracelet he'd bought for her christening—a little chain with a heart shaped locket—and it almost disappeared into the roly-poly folds of her wrist. Her skin was so soft. Peach soft.

No, softer than a peach.

Wow. No wonder fathers wanted to protect their daughters.

'Oh, gosh, Will, that baby really suits you,' Lucy said, almost smiling as she came back into the room.

'Not as well as she suits you.'

He handed the tiny bundle back to Lucy and she buried her nose in Mia's hair. 'I'd bottle this smell if I could.'

Turning, she checked her appearance in the mirror above the dressing table. 'I just need a minute to compose myself. It's a pity I don't have my make-up with me.'

To Will, Lucy looked absolutely fine just as she was, but he offered to fetch her handbag.

'No, it's OK,' she said. 'You'd better go back to the party. Gina will be wondering why we're taking so long.'

CHAPTER EIGHT

LUCY'S words were prophetic. Will had barely left before Gina appeared at the bedroom door.

'Oh, there you are,' she said. 'I was wondering—' She stopped and frowned. 'Is everything OK, Lucy?'

'Yes.' Lucy dropped a swift kiss on the baby's head. 'Mia's fine.'

But gosh, she couldn't quite believe that she'd actually agreed to try again for a baby with Will.

'But what about you?' Gina asked. 'You look upset.'

Lucy tried to shrug this aside.

'You've been crying.' Gina came closer, her dark eyes warm with concern.

It was too hard to pretend. Lucy tried to smile but her mouth twisted out of shape.

'Lucy, you poor thing. What's the matter?'

'I'm just emerald green with jealousy, that's all.' She looked down at Mia, curled in her arms and this time she managed a rueful smile. 'I would so love to have a little one like this for myself.'

'Oh.' Gina made a soft sound of sympathy. 'I know how awful that longing can be. It just eats you up, doesn't it?'

That was the great thing about Gina. She wasn't just a good friend. She really understood. She'd been through years of painful endometriosis before her doctor had finally told her that she needed a hysterectomy. The news that she could never have children had broken her heart, but then Mattie had stepped in with her wonderful surrogacy offer.

Now, just as she had when they'd been school friends, Gina plopped down on her old bed and patted a space for Lucy, who obeyed without question. She was so totally in need of a girly heart-to-heart and where better than Gina's bedroom, still painted the terrible lavender and hot pink she'd chosen when she was fourteen?

'Are you thinking about tackling another round of IVF?' Gina asked.

Lucy shook her head and hastily weighed up the pros and cons of confiding in Will's sister. Quite quickly she decided it was necessary. Out of any of the women in her circle of friends, Gina would most understand her longing for a baby. And she also understood her history with Will.

'I'm trying for a baby, but not with IVF,' she said.

To Gina's credit, she didn't look too shocked, although she was understandably puzzled. 'So how's that work? You have a secret boyfriend?'

'Not exactly.' Lucy settled Mia's sleepy head more comfortably into the crook of her arm. 'Actually, Will's offered to help me out.'

This time, Gina did look shocked.

Momentarily.

'Will's helping you to have a baby?'

'Yes.'

'Wow!' Gina gasped. 'That's…that's…far out. You and

Will.' She gave an excited little squeal. 'Gosh, Lucy, that's wonderful.'

'Unconventional is probably the word most people would use.'

Gina frowned. 'Excuse me? I'm lost.'

'Friends don't usually plan to have a baby together.'

'Friends?'

'Yes. Will and I are still only friends. But he's quite keen to be a dad and he knows how I feel, so he wants to help me to have a baby. It's actually rather convenient.'

'Right.' Gina frowned as she digested this. Then she smiled. 'But friends often fall in love.'

Lucy felt bad, knowing she was about to watch Gina's happy smile disintegrate.

'Not this time,' she said. 'There's no chance.'

For a moment Gina seemed lost for words. She traced the pattern of pink and lavender patchwork squares on the bed quilt. 'I guess it must be awkward,' she mused, 'because you were engaged to Josh.'

Unwilling to dwell on that subject, Lucy tried to steer Gina's thoughts in a different direction. 'The thing is, Will's not a settling down kind of guy. You and I both know that. We've always known it.'

Gina pulled a face. 'Will's annoying like that, isn't he? I really love my brother but, I have to admit, he's always been a bit of an outsider in our family. Middle child syndrome, I guess.'

'I wouldn't know. I was an only child.'

'In our family, it was always about Josh, as the eldest son. He was the heir apparent. And I was the spoiled baby girl. Poor old Will was caught in the middle, neither one thing nor the other.'

Gina lowered her voice importantly. 'Even though I was the youngest, I could see how it was. Dad spoiled me rotten. Gosh, when I was little, he used to take me out on the tractor every night just to get me to sleep. I'd sit up there with my security blanket and my head in his lap, while he went round and round the paddock.'

'Lucky you,' Lucy said.

'And then Josh was always trailing after Dad like a faithful sheepdog and the old man adored it. They were always together, working with the sheep, tinkering with machinery. They had a special bond and I'm sure Will felt left out. I think that's why he drifted towards books and study, rather than helping out on the farm. And then he started taking off on his own to fossick for rocks.'

'Which he's still doing, more or less,' Lucy suggested.

'I guess.' Gina let out a loud sigh. 'It's not fair on you, though.' She pulled at a loose thread in the quilt. 'Will might still feel as if he's living in Josh's shadow.'

Bright heat flared in Lucy's face. 'I hope he doesn't,' she said quietly.

'What is it with my brothers? Why do they both have to mess up your life?'

'Because I let them?'

Gina's face softened and she reached out to touch her daughter's hair as she slept in Lucy's arms. 'Well…for what it's worth, I think this baby idea is fabulous. OK, maybe it's a tad unconventional, but it's still fabulous. I do wish you luck.'

'Thanks.' Lucy smiled. It was good to know she had someone on her side. 'You won't say anything to Will?'

'Heavens, no.' Gina threw a reassuring arm around

Lucy's shoulders. 'A little sister's advice would be the kiss of death, and I really want this to work.'

After the last of the guests had left, Will helped with the dismantling of the trestle tables and the stacking away of the chairs in a storage room below the hayloft. As he worked, his thoughts were focused front, back and centre on Lucy.

It wasn't possible to think about anything else. His heart had cracked in two today when he'd seen her weeping beside little Mia.

Mattie had achieved the impossible for Gina and Tom and no doubt that made Lucy's situation all the more distressing. But what upset Will was the fact that she'd told him last week she wanted to call off their plan, when it was so obvious that she still wanted a baby.

There could only be one reason, of course. She wasn't happy about having to sleep with him again. He'd created a problem for her.

For possibly the thousandth time Will thought about that night. He'd been a lost man the minute he'd touched Lucy McKenty. That was his problem. One caress of her skin, one brush of his lips against her soft, sweet mouth and he'd forgotten his plan to have simple, 'friendly' sex with a focus on procreation. Damn it. He'd been so carried away, he'd practically forgotten his own name.

Problem was, he'd put their kiss of ten years ago out of his mind. He'd gone into this without thinking about how Lucy might taste, or how she'd react. He certainly hadn't expected such a passionate response from her.

Was that how she'd been with Josh?

Hell.

Will was shocked by the violent force of his feelings when he thought about Josh and Lucy together.

He tried to stop thinking about them but, with the last chair stacked, he strode to the end of the home paddock. He looked out across the valley to where the distant hills were blue smudges on the horizon and he drew a deep breath and caught the sharp tang of eucalyptus and the dusty scent of the earth.

He looked up at the wide faded blue of the sky, searching for answers to the turmoil inside him.

Some answers were easy. He knew exactly why Lucy loved this land, and he knew that he wanted his child to live here with her.

It felt right that Lucy should be the mother of his child.

It felt good.

But was he fooling himself? Was it madness to think he could replace his brother?

No, he decided. It was actually a greater madness to dwell on the Josh-Lucy scenario, to keep letting the past haunt him.

For more than twenty years he'd lived in Josh's shadow, but it was time to get over that. His task now was to concentrate on the living. To do the right thing by Lucy.

Heaven knew she deserved to be treated well. She was a wonderful girl. Gutsy and clever. Sweet and fun.

She was his friend.

And she needed his help.

And he needed—

Hell, he wasn't sure what he needed from Lucy. He had the feeling though, that he couldn't stop wanting to help her.

But, if that was so, if they were going to keep trying until

Lucy was pregnant, he had to make this baby plan easier for her. Which meant he had to make sure that their next rendezvous was as friendly and functional as possible.

Will let out a sigh—which he smartly decided was a sigh of relief. He felt marginally better now that he had his thoughts straight.

All he had to remember was that he was Lucy's friend, not her lover.

Friendship gave them clear boundaries and boundaries were good. Breaking the boundaries could completely mess up her life.

In line with that thinking, he should start making plans to get a job outside this district. That way Lucy would know he wasn't going to crowd her once their goal of pregnancy was achieved. He'd heard of jobs in Papua New Guinea that he could apply for.

PNG wasn't too far away, so he could come back to Willowbank from time to time to play whatever role in their baby's life that Lucy wanted.

Good. Will was glad he had that sorted.

It always helped to have a plan.

Three days later he received a text message from Lucy:

Can you come over tonight? I have evening surgery, so can't offer dinner. Is 9.30 too late? L x

He sent a hasty reply:

I'll be there.

I'll be there...

All day Will's message drummed inside Lucy with a pulsing, electrifying beat.

She knew she was weak. She was supposed to be giving up on this baby idea and protecting her emotions, but she'd only spent five minutes with little Mia and her brave plans to abandon the project had toppled like bowling pins.

She shouldn't have jumped at Will's offer to try again for a baby, but heavens, if he hadn't offered, she might have begged him.

Now, she couldn't stop thinking about him arriving on her doorstep tonight, coming into her house, into her bed.

For the first time in her professional life she found it hard to concentrate on her work. She was excessively grateful that the tasks were routine, so she could more or less function on autopilot.

But, by the time the hands of the clock eventually crawled to nine-thirty in the evening, she was jangling with tension and expectation.

And she was falling apart with insecurity.

She wished she knew how Will really felt about this second night, but it was such a difficult question to broach. And she might not like his answer.

She told herself that she should be grateful he was willing to help, and she should be pleased that he hadn't pressed her to talk about Josh. If she started down that track, she might reveal too much about her feelings for Will. She could complicate the delicate balance of their friendship. Spoil everything.

Perhaps Will was nervous too, because he arrived two minutes and thirty-five seconds early, but Lucy opened the door even before he knocked.

'Evening, Lucy.' His smile was shy, yet so charming, she was sure it was designed to make her heart do back-flips.

She ran her damp hands down the side seams of her jeans. 'Come on in.'

Will came through the doorway but then he stopped abruptly. 'I've brought you a little something,' he said, holding out a slim box tied with curling purple ribbons.

'Oh.' Lucy gulped with surprise. 'Thank you.'

'I know rocks don't really have special powers, but see what you think.'

Her hands were shaking and she fumbled as she tried to undo the ribbon, pulling the knot tighter, instead of undoing it.

'Hey, I'll get that.'

The brush of Will's hands against hers sent rivers of heat up her arms. Her heart thumped as she watched the concentration in his face, the patience of his fingers as he deftly prised the knot free. Finally, he lifted the lid and showed her a neat little pendant on a pretty silver chain.

'Will, it's gorgeous. Is it an amethyst?'

'Yes.' He sent her another shy smile. 'Apparently, amethysts have traditionally been linked to fertility.'

'Oh, wow. That's so thoughtful. Thank you. It's beautiful. I love it.'

He smiled gorgeously. 'Let me do up the clasp for you.'

Lucy decided it was quite possible to melt just from being touched. She was burning up as Will fastened the pendant. She turned to him.

'It suits you,' he said. 'It brings out the deep blue in your eyes.'

To Lucy's surprise he looked suddenly nervous. Bravely, she stepped forward and kissed him. On the mouth.

Gosh. When had she become so brave?

Will returned her kiss carefully, almost chastely, and she felt a cold little swoop of disappointment.

She lifted her hands to his shoulders and felt him tense all over. 'Will,' she whispered, 'what's wrong?'

CHAPTER NINE

WILL knew he could do this.

All day, he'd rehearsed in his mind how he would make love to Lucy as her friend. He'd thought about nothing else as he'd driven the tractor up and down the paddocks at Tambaroora and the whole idea had seemed solid and plausible.

Now, however, Lucy was close—kissing close—and his certainty evaporated.

Or, rather, his certainty shifted focus. And the focus was *not* on friendship. Far from it.

He wanted nothing more than to gather Lucy in to him, to kiss her with the reckless frenzy of a lover, to kiss her slowly, all night long, to lose himself in her fragrant softness.

He wanted to forget *why* they were doing this. He wanted to forget her past history with his brother. He wanted to think of nothing but...

Lucy.

He wanted *her*.

Tonight.

She was simply dressed in jeans and a tomboyish grey T-shirt. No pretty floral dress. No sexy high heels.

It didn't matter. She was Lucy. And he wanted her.

Too much.

Her disappointment was clear as she stepped away from him and nervously fingered the amethyst, feeling the smooth facets beneath her fingertips. Her blue eyes were cloudy. Understandably perplexed. 'Will, there's something wrong, isn't there?'

'No,' he muttered and he forced his thoughts to focus on restraint.

'You don't want to…' she began, but she couldn't finish the sentence.

'I don't want to hurt you, Lucy.'

Cringe. Had he really said that? The only way he could hurt Lucy was by walking away and denying her the chance to become a mother.

Or perhaps that was the only way he could save himself from eternal damnation? Why the hell hadn't they stuck to the IVF option?

His throat worked.

Lucy looked away. They were still standing in her hallway, for heaven's sake.

'Would you like a drink?' she asked.

'A drink?' he repeated like a fool.

'To…er…relax.'

He shook his head. He would need a whole bottle of alcohol to douse the fire inside him.

Lucy looked as if she wanted to weep and he knew that, at any minute now, she would thank him for the gift and send him home. It was exactly what he deserved.

She dropped her gaze to the empty box in her hands. 'I thought a drink might help with…um…getting in the mood.'

With a choked sound that was halfway between a groan

and a sick laugh, Will fought back the urge to haul her against his hard, aroused body. 'There's nothing wrong with my mood, Lucy.'

'Right,' she whispered hoarsely, but she looked upset, a little shocked. And maybe just a tad angry. Her chin lifted and her unsmiling eyes confronted him.

His heart slammed inside his chest. He couldn't believe he'd been so cool about this last time. What a poor naïve fool he'd been. Back then, he hadn't known what it was like to take Lucy into his arms. He'd forgotten how dangerous it could be to get close to her, to know that the slim curves pressed so deliciously against him were Lucy's.

Until then, he'd innocently assumed that their kiss on the veranda all those years ago had been an aberration.

Now, Will knew better.

Now, he knew that kissing Lucy, making love to Lucy could all too easily become a dangerous addiction.

With a soft sigh, she set the box and purple ribbon on the hallstand, and when she looked at him again, she set her hands on her hips and her eyes were an unsettling blue challenge. 'What do you want to do, then?'

'Kiss you.'

The answer jumped from Will's lips before he could gather his wits. He saw the flare of confusion in Lucy's eyes, the soft surprised O of her mouth. But his hands were already reaching out for her and then he kissed her as if this were his last minute on this earth.

He kissed her as if at any moment he might lose her.

For ever.

Lucy couldn't quite believe this.

She hadn't dared to hope that Will could possibly want her with such intensity.

One minute he'd looked as if he wanted to bolt out her front door, the next his mouth was locked with hers. His hands cupped her bottom and he pulled her against him and suddenly she stopped worrying.

All the fantasies she'd lived through that day—actually, all the romantic fantasies she'd dreamed about her entire adult life—rolled into one sensational here and now.

Never had she experienced such a hot kiss. Flashpoints exploded all over her skin. Recklessly, she pushed even closer to Will, winding her arms around his neck, seeking the closest possible contact. To her relief, he most definitely didn't seem to mind.

Gosh, no.

His fever matched hers, kiss for kiss, and a kind of wonderful madness overcame them.

Together they made it down the hall, bumping against the walls in a frenzy of kissing and touching, until they reached the first doorway.

It led to the lounge room, and it seemed that would have to do.

They stumbled to the sofa, sinking needfully into its velvety cushions.

Bliss.

Bliss to help and be helped out of clothing. Bliss to lie together at last with Will, to run her hands over the satin of his skin as it stretched tightly over hard bands of muscle.

Even greater bliss when Will took charge and deliberately held back the pace, stilling her seeking hands and kissing her with unhurried, leisurely reverence.

It was sweet, so sweet. He kissed her slowly and deeply, drawing her gradually but relentlessly down into an intimate dark cave where only the two of them existed.

And everything was fine. It was perfect. Because this time she knew that Will Carruthers was the one man in the world she could trust to fulfil her innermost secret longings.

Will woke as the pale buttery light of dawn filtered though the curtains in Lucy's bedroom. He didn't move because she was still asleep with one arm flung across his chest and her soft, warm body nestled against him, her breath a sweet hush on his skin.

Staying with her till morning had not been part of his plan. Hell, practically none of last night had been part of his plan, although he had rationalised that he should make the most of this one night.

Tomorrow he was flying out to Papua New Guinea to check out job prospects.

At that thought Will suppressed a sigh, but perhaps Lucy felt it for she stirred against him and her blue eyes opened.

'Morning, Goose.' He thought about kissing her, but decided against it. This morning was all about seriously backing off.

Lucy looked at her bedside clock and groaned. 'I've slept in.'

He thought guiltily about the amount of time he'd kept her awake.

'I'm going to have to hurry,' she grumbled, reaching for a towelling robe draped over a nearby chair.

Will swung his legs over the edge of the bed.

Lucy tightened the knot at her waist and stood. She ran a hand through her tumbled curls and sent him an uncertain smile. She let her gaze travel over him, and it seemed to settle rather sadly on his bare feet.

He looked down. 'Yeah...I worry about that too.'

'What?'

'Whether the baby will inherit my freakishly long second toes.'

'Oh.' She laughed. 'It might end up with my freakishly tiny ears.'

He fought back an urge to pull her to him, to nibble and taste those neat little ears. 'Cutest ears in the southern hemisphere,' he said.

'But they might not look too flash on a boy.'

She bit her lower lip and touched the pendant at her throat. 'I wonder if it's happening, Will. I wonder if I'm pregnant.'

'You're sure to be,' he said and he did the only thing that was right.

He reached for his clothes.

Lucy held back her tears until after Will left, but she'd never felt so desolate. To watch him walk away was like cutting off a lifeline and she felt like an astronaut, adrift in endless emptiness.

But there was no point in letting him see how much she'd hated to let him go. He was heading off to Papua New Guinea tomorrow and he was sure to get a job there. She'd always known he was never going to be tamed and kept in one place.

He was a catch and release kind of man, like the wild bush creatures she cared for and then set free.

Will telephoned when he got back a week later. 'Have you started tucking into the liquorice allsorts?'

Lucy was relieved to report; 'Not yet.'

'Any symptoms?' he asked hopefully.

'Hard to say. It's still too soon, but I've been rather tired and I need to go to the bathroom in the middle of the night.'

'They're promising signs, aren't they?'

'Could be.'

Problem was, Lucy had become hyper-aware of her body, anxious to discover the slightest hint of change. She was sure she felt different this month, but she couldn't be certain that the differences were real and not simply the result of her overactive imagination.

Just in time she bit back an impulse to tell Will she'd missed him. But it was true, of course. She'd missed Will terribly. Desperately. The longer he'd stayed away the more she was certain that making love to him on a second night had been even more dangerous than she'd feared. She loved him.

Still.

Always.

With all her heart.

She could no longer hide from the truth and she had no idea how she could go on pretending anything else.

But she had to accept that Will was never going to change, never going to settle down. He might be attracted to her, but he'd always been restless and he would always need to keep travelling, seeking new sights and challenges.

When she was younger, she'd known this, and she'd tried to protect herself by simply being his friend. Now she'd thrown caution to the wind and she had to accept that her love for him was a weakness she'd have to learn to adjust to and live with—the way other people adjusted to a disability.

'How was your trip to Papua New Guinea?' she asked, keeping her voice carefully light.

'Oh, there's plenty of work up there. I've had a couple of offers, so it's a matter of deciding which job to take.'

'That's great.' Good grief, she hoped she didn't sound as unhappy as she felt. 'A very fortunate position to be in.'

'No doubt about that,' Will agreed. 'So...about you. This week is the week of the big countdown, right?'

'Yes.' Lucy let out a sigh. 'I wish I didn't have to wait. I'm afraid I've become mildly obsessive. I've taken to reading my stars in every magazine I can find. I've even thought about going to see Sylvie.'

'Who's Sylvie?'

'The hairdresser in the main street. She tells fortunes as well as cutting hair, but I'm not quite desperate enough to trust her talents. I'm actually trying very hard to be sensible and philosophical.'

'Will you use a home pregnancy test?'

'Oh, yes. Definitely. I've a carton of tests ready and waiting, but I'm holding off till next Friday. If I try too soon, I might get a false reading and I don't think I could bear the disappointment.'

'Lucy, I want to be there.'

The sudden urgency in his voice made her heart jump.

'You want to be here when I do the test?'

'Yes. Is that OK?'

She pressed a hand against her thudding heart. She shouldn't be surprised. The baby would be as much Will's as it was hers, but somehow she hadn't expected this level of interest from him.

'It doesn't seem right that you should be all alone when you find out,' he said.

She couldn't deny it would be wonderful to share her news with Will. If it was good news they could celebrate, and if she was disappointed again he would be there to comfort her.

'You'd better come over first thing on Friday morning,' she said and her voice was decidedly shaky.

Friday morning produced an idyllic country dawn. As Will drove to Lucy's place, the paddocks, the trees and the sky looked as if they'd been spring cleaned for a special occasion, and the landscape had a gentle and dreamy quality as if he was viewing the scene through a soft focus lens. The air was balmy and light.

A pretty white fog filled the bowl of Willow Creek and he watched it drift from the dark cluster of trees like magician's smoke. He felt keyed up, excited, anxious, hopeful.

Torn.

He longed for good news, but in many ways he dreaded it. If Lucy was pregnant, he would have no choice but to take a back seat in her life.

He found that prospect unexpectedly depressing so he tried, instead, to enjoy the picture perfect scenery.

It shouldn't have been difficult. The road from Tambaroora wound past a small forest of pines, then over a low hill before it dipped to a rustic bridge where another arm of Willow Creek was bordered by yellow and purple wildflowers.

But he was still feeling edgy when he reached Lucy's place, even though her dogs rushed to the front gate to greet him with excited barks and madly wagging tails.

Lucy was dressed for work in a khaki shirt and trousers, but he could see the amethyst pendant sitting above the open V of her shirt collar.

Valiantly, he ignored the urge to pull her in for a kiss.

'How are you feeling?' he asked her.

'Totally nervous,' she admitted. 'I didn't sleep very well.'

'Neither did I.'

She looked surprised. 'I…I'm assuming you'll stay for breakfast? I've started sausages and tomatoes.'

'Thanks. They smell great.'

'And I've made a pot of tea. Why don't you help yourself while I…er…get this done? I can't stand the suspense.'

'Off you go,' he said, but as she turned to leave he snagged her hand. 'Hey, Goose.'

Her blue eyes shimmered. 'Yes?'

'Good luck.'

To his surprise she stepped closer and gave him a swift, sweet kiss on the jaw. The room seemed intolerably empty when she left.

Will poured tea into a blue pottery mug and walked with it to the window, saw the stained glass feature winking bright blue in the morning light and felt shocked by the tension that filled him.

For Lucy's sake he really wanted this test to be positive.

He wondered about that other time, eight years ago, when she'd discovered she was pregnant. Had she been ecstatically happy? Just as quickly he dismissed the question. There was little to be achieved now by reminding himself that he could only ever be a second best option after Josh.

It was time to be positive, to look forward to the future. A new generation, perhaps.

When he heard Lucy's footsteps he set his mug down, unhappily aware that she wasn't hurrying. She hadn't called out in excitement.

He turned, arms ready to comfort her, and his heart stood still in his chest as he prepared himself for disappointment.

He didn't want to put extra pressure on her, so he

summoned a smile and tried to look calm, as if the result really didn't matter either way.

Lucy came into the kitchen and he saw two bright spots of colour in her cheeks. Her eyes were huge and shiny with emotion.

She waved a plastic stick. 'There are two lines.'

'What does that mean?'

'It means—'

She looked as if she was going to cry. Will's throat tightened.

'We did it, Will.'

She didn't look happy.

'You mean—' He hardly dared to ask. 'You're pregnant?'

'Yes!'

He wasn't sure if she was going to laugh or cry.

'Congratulations,' he said and his voice was choked. 'You clever girl.'

Tears glistened in her eyes but at last she was smiling.

And then she was grinning.

'Can you believe it, Will? I'm pregnant!' With a happy little cry she stumbled towards him and he opened his arms.

'Thank you,' she cried as she hugged him.

'Congratulations,' he said again.

'Congratulations to you, too. You're going to be a father.'

He grinned shakily.

A soft look of wonder came over her face as she touched the amethyst pendant, then pressed her hands to her stomach. 'I'm going to be a mother.'

'The best mother ever.'

'I don't give a hoot if it's a boy or a girl.'

'Not at all,' Will agreed, although he realised with something of a shock that he would love to have a son.

Happiness shone in Lucy's eyes as she looked around her kitchen, as if she was suddenly seeing it with new eyes. She grinned at the table that she'd set for breakfast, at the dogs' bowls on the floor near the door. 'Oh, gosh, Will, I'm pregnant!'

He laughed, but it felt inadequate.

'Thank you,' she said again, and her smile was so sweet he wanted to sweep her into his arms, to hold her and kiss her and murmur endearments, all of which were completely inappropriate now that they were reverting to friendship.

Lucy's mind, however, was on a more practical plane. She looked over at the stove. 'I've probably burned the sausages.'

'They're OK. I turned them down low.'

'Well done. Thanks.' She glanced at the clock and sighed. 'We'd better eat. I still have a day's work ahead of me.'

'That's something we need to talk about,' Will said. 'You need to look after yourself now.'

She frowned at him, then shrugged. 'We can talk while we eat.'

It felt strangely intimate to be having breakfast with Lucy—pottering about in the kitchen, buttering toast, finding Vegemite and marmalade.

When they were settled at the table Lucy looked at him across the seersucker tablecloth, her blue eyes wide and innocent. 'Now, what were you saying about my work?'

'You're going to need some kind of support now you're pregnant. You can't manage such a big workload on your own.'

'I have an assistant.'

'But she can't take on the tough jobs like delivering difficult calves. And she's not qualified to operate. I don't like the thought of you standing for long hours over difficult surgery.'

'Are you going to get bossy already?'

'You had a miscarriage once before,' he reminded her gently. 'And you're quite a bit older now.'

'Thanks for bringing that to my attention.' Lucy's mouth was tight as she spread Vegemite on her toast. 'Isn't it a bit hypocritical of you to be worrying about my age and personal safety?'

'Hypocritical?'

Her eyes blazed. 'You're not exactly taking care of yourself.'

'How do you mean?'

'You're about to become a father. You barely escaped with your life from your last job and you told me you'd learned a big lesson. But now you're heading off to Papua New Guinea, where a mudslide wiped out an entire village last summer. And everyone knows how often planes crash in the highlands. The airstrips are the size of postage stamps and they're perched on the edge of massive deep ravines.'

'I'm not going to the highlands.' Will rearranged the salt and pepper shakers like pieces on a chessboard. 'And I'm not the one who's pregnant. Your safety is more important than mine.'

Lucy opened her mouth as if she was going to say something more, but apparently changed her mind. She shrugged. 'Actually, I'd already been planning to cut back on work if I became pregnant. I can use locums. I have quite a few city vet friends who love it out here.'

'What kind of friends?' Will felt foolish asking, but he'd been attacked by an unreasonable fit of jealousy. 'Married couples?'

'Chris is a bachelor,' she said in a matter of fact tone. Her eyes were defiant as she looked at him. 'Leanne and

Tim are married. If I have time later today I'll phone around and send out a few feelers.'

'I think that's wise.'

Lucy concentrated on piling tomatoes onto her fork. She looked upset and they finished their breakfast in uncomfortable silence.

Will felt upset too, but he wasn't sure why. He and Lucy had achieved their goal and now they were moving onto the next stage of their plan. She was going to be a single mum and he was going to visit their child from time to time.

That was what he wanted, wasn't it? Fatherhood without strings. He should have been on top of the world.

From the start he'd said that he would remain an outsider in their child's life. The silent scream inside him didn't make sense.

He heard the sound of a car pulling up and a door slamming.

'That's Jane, my assistant, ready to start work,' Lucy said pointedly.

Will got to his feet. 'I'd better get out of your way.' He indicated the breakfast dishes. 'Can I help with these?'

'No, don't worry.'

She walked with him to the front door and waved to her assistant, who was using a side gate to reach the surgery. 'I'll be there in a minute, Jane,' she called.

'Don't hurry,' Jane called back, smiling broadly when she saw Will.

Lucy looked unhappy. 'Make sure you come and see me before you go,' she told him.

'Yes, of course.'

Her mouth trembled and she blinked.

He said inadequately, 'Thanks for breakfast.' And then he dipped his head and kissed her cheek.

Lucy mumbled something about a very busy day, gave him a brief wave and shut the door.

After Will left, her day proved to be even busier than she'd expected but, every so often as she worked, she would remember.

I'm pregnant.

Excitement fizzed inside her and she hugged herself in secret glee. She'd been waiting for this for so long. She couldn't help thinking about all those busy little cells inside her, forming their baby.

Their baby.

Wow.

There was no time to celebrate, however. As well as her usual line-up of patients, she had to perform emergency surgery on an elderly dog and she found the work unusually stressful. She was very fond of this sweet black and white cocker spaniel. He'd been one of her first patients when she'd started working in Willowbank.

She would do what she could for him now, but she feared he was nearing the end of his days. His owner would be distraught when his time was up.

If that wasn't enough to dampen Lucy's spirits, she was upset about Will. She couldn't stop thinking about him, felt utterly miserable about him going away.

Again.

How could she bear it?

The threat of his impending departure had made her snappy with him this morning and she felt bad about that, after he'd been so excited. But how could she not be upset by the thought of saying goodbye?

She loved Will.

Letting him go felt like cutting out a vital organ. Whenever she pictured him leaving, she grew angry again. How could Will pretend to be terribly concerned about her and then take off to the wilds of a New Guinea jungle?

How could he leave her so soon? So easily?

All day, her mind churned with things she wished she'd asked him, as well as things she wished she'd told him. But the crux of her message was hard to admit—their friendship plan was a farce.

It was rubbish.

Sharing responsibility for a child required a commitment that went way beyond friendship.

And she and Will had already shared a beautiful intimacy that she could never classify as friendship.

Maybe it was easier for guys to be interested in sex without actually being in love, but she'd never been brave enough to be honest with Will about her feelings, so wasn't it possible that he'd hidden some of his feelings, too?

Should she try to find out?

It was crazy that she was still afraid to admit the truth about her feelings. She'd always been so worried that her disclosure might shock him, that she might alienate him completely. But today she felt different.

Determined.

She'd been hiding behind fear for too long. She was going to be a mother now and that required courage.

For her baby's sake, she should tell Will how she really felt and then face the consequences bravely.

Her confession might not make any difference. There was a chance it could make everything worse but, as the day wore on, Lucy became surer and surer that it was time to take the risk she'd shied away from for too long.

At lunch time Gina popped her head around the surgery door, her dark eyes brimming with curiosity. 'Mum's minding the twins while I do my shopping, so I thought I'd duck in quickly to see how you're going.'

'You must have a sixth sense about these things,' Lucy said, smiling.

Gina's eyes widened.

'Come and have a cuppa.' Lucy took her through to the kitchen.

'Do you have some news?' Gina asked as soon as the door that linked back to Lucy's office was firmly shut.

'I only found out this morning.'

'That you're pregnant?'

Lucy couldn't hold back her grin. 'Yes.'

Gina squealed and knocked over a kitchen chair in her rush to hug her friend. 'Oh, Lucy, I'm so excited for you.'

'I know. It's fantastic, isn't it? I have to keep pinching myself.'

'Our babies are going to be cousins,' Gina gushed.

Lucy smiled again, but this time there wasn't much joy behind it.

'I'm assuming that Will is the father,' Gina said less certainly.

'Yes, he is, and he knows about the baby. But I haven't told anyone else yet, so keep it under your hat.'

'Of course.'

The kettle came to the boil and Lucy was aware of Gina's thoughtful gaze as she poured hot water over the teabags.

'So how are things between you and Will?' she cautiously asked as Lucy handed her a mug.

'Hunky-dory.'

'Oh. That doesn't sound too promising.' Gina took a sip of tea. 'I suppose Will hasn't admitted that he loves you.'

Lucy felt the colour rush from her face. 'Don't talk nonsense, Gina. He doesn't love me.'

'Do you really believe that?'

'Yes. He can't love me. If he did, he wouldn't be taking off for PNG.'

Gina sighed. 'Is he really going away again?'

'Yes.'

'Sometimes I could wring his neck.'

'He's the man he is,' Lucy said, surprised that she could sound philosophical about a sad fact that was breaking her heart. 'Everyone in Willowbank knows Will doesn't belong here.'

'I'm not so sure about that, actually. But, anyway, he could always take you with him when he goes away.'

'I can't take off for some remote mining site when I'm pregnant. I certainly couldn't live there with a tiny baby.'

'Well…no. I don't suppose you could.' Gina gritted her teeth. 'So, do you need me to wring my brother's neck or try to hammer some sense into him?'

'No,' said Lucy, crossing her fingers behind her back. 'Leave it to me.'

By mid-afternoon the pace in the surgery wasn't quite so hectic and Lucy sent her father a text message:

Are you busy? Can I phone you?

The two of them had always been good mates and she wanted him to know her news.

Almost immediately, he called her back. 'Darling, I have five minutes. What can I do for you?'

'I just wanted to share some good news, Dad. I'm pregnant.'

She waited for his shocked gasp, but he surprised her. 'That's wonderful news. Congratulations.'

'Really, Dad? You don't mind?'

'Do *you* mind, Lucy?'

'No. I'm actually very, very happy.'

'Then so am I. I'm delighted. Couldn't be happier.'

Lucy was amazed that he didn't immediately bombard her with predictable questions about the baby's father, or when she was planning to be married.

Her dad simply asked, 'Are you keeping well?'

She grinned. First and last, Alistair McKenty was a doctor. 'It's very early days, but I'm feeling fine. I have good vibes about this pregnancy.'

'You'll see Ken Harper?'

'Yes, Dad.' Ken Harper was Willowbank Hospital's only obstetrician. 'And, as you know, Ken will give me top antenatal care.'

She heard a chuckle on the other end of the line and she waited for more questions. When there was silence, she said, 'In case you were wondering, Will Carruthers is the baby's father.'

'Ah.'

'Ah? What does that mean?'

'I noticed that Will's been home for rather longer than usual.'

Heat suffused Lucy. 'Is that all you can say?'

'No. I'm actually very pleased. I like Will. I always expected you two to get together.'

'You did?'

'You used to be such terrific friends, but then you took up with that older brother.'

'Yes.'

'I never understood that, Lucy. Josh Carruthers had girl-friends all over the district.'

'Dad, I don't really want to go back over that now.'

'I'm sorry. You're right. It's all in the past.'

'Actually, there is one thing about that time I've been meaning to ask you.'

'What's that, dear?'

'Why didn't you tell me that Will telephoned and tried to visit me after Josh died?'

A sigh shuddered down the phone line. 'You were so dis-tressed, Lucy, and I was upset too. Your mother wasn't around to advise, and I suppose I went into over-protective mode.'

'But Will was my friend.'

'I know, dear. I'm sorry, but I did what I thought was right. Mattie was there almost every day, and she was a huge help. And, to be honest, Will wasn't his normal self at the time. He was acting quite strangely. Extremely tense. Distraught, actually. I didn't see how he could do you any good.'

Lucy pressed two fingers to the bridge of her nose to hold back the threat of tears. She knew there was no point in getting upset about this. It wasn't her father's fault that Will had taken off again, without leaving her any hint that he'd wanted to keep in touch.

It wasn't her father's fault that her own feelings of guilt had driven her to silence, adding more strain to an already tense friendship.

'Well, things are still complicated between Will and me,' she admitted.

'Is he planning to continue working overseas?'

'Yes.'

'How do you feel about that?'

'OK.' Lucy forced a smile into her voice. 'It's what we planned.'

'So this baby was planned?'

'Yes. Will and I decided we'd like to have a baby together, but we'll just remain friends.'

There was a significant pause. 'Are you really happy with that arrangement, Lucy?'

She couldn't give a direct answer. 'Dad, I knew what Will was like when we started talking about this.'

There was another sigh on the other end of the line. Another pause. 'My big concern is that you must look after yourself.'

'I will, Dad. I promise.'

'I'm afraid I have to go now. Come and see me soon. Come for dinner.'

'I will. Thanks. Love you, Dad.'

Lucy was about to disconnect when her father spoke again. 'Lucy.'

The tone of his voice made her grip the phone more tightly. 'Yes?'

'I've always thought that if two very good friends fall in love, they should grab their good luck with both hands.'

Lucy couldn't think of anything to say.

'It's the greatest happiness this life can offer,' her father said.

And then he hung up.

CHAPTER TEN

IT HAD been a long hot day and a summer storm broke late in the afternoon. By the time Lucy closed up the surgery, it was raining and thunder rumbled in the distance.

It was still raining heavily half an hour later when she set out for Tambaroora. She was nervous, but she was determined to see Will this evening before she chickened out again.

It wasn't yet six but the sky was already dark and her windscreen wipers had to work overtime. The winding, unsealed country roads had quickly turned to slippery mud so, despite her impatience, she had to drive very slowly and carefully.

She could see wet sheep clustered beneath the inadequate shelter of skinny gum trees. Thunder rolled all around the valley and white flashes of sheet lightning lit the entire sky. She was relieved when she finally saw the lights of Tambaroora homestead.

As soon as she pulled up at the bottom of the front steps she made a dash for the veranda.

Will's mother, wearing an apron, greeted Lucy warmly and she could smell the tempting aroma of dinner cooking. 'You were brave to come out in this terrible storm,' she said.

'I know it's not a good time to be calling, but I was hoping to see Will.'

Jessie Carruthers smiled. 'He's told us your news.'

'Are you pleased?' Lucy asked.

'Very,' Jessie said. 'Especially when Will told us that you were so happy about it.'

Lucy held her breath, wondering if Jessie would make a reference to her previous pregnancy with her elder son. But she said simply, 'Will and his father have spent the whole afternoon out in the shed, working on the tractor.' She smiled. 'You know what boys are like with their toys.'

'You must be pleased that Will's taking an interest.'

'Well, yes, I am, actually, and he's still at it. Robert came back a few minutes ago and he's in the shower. But Will's still out there, tinkering away.'

'I'll drive over and see if I can find him.'

'All right, love.' Jessie gave a wistful sigh. 'I suppose you're as disappointed as I am that Will's going away again so soon.'

'Well…I'm not surprised.'

'You might be able to talk him out of it, Lucy.'

Lucy stared at Will's mother, surprised. 'I could try, I guess. But I'm afraid it might be like trying to persuade a leopard to change his spots.'

Jessie frowned. 'I don't understand young people these days.'

'I'm not sure that we understand ourselves,' Lucy admitted.

Jessie accepted this with a resigned shrug. 'Anyway, it's lovely to see you, dear. And you must join us for dinner.'

Lucy thanked her and then drove her ute around to the back of the house, past garden beds filled with blue hydrangeas and a vegetable plot where tomatoes and fennel and silverbeet had been drenched by the heavy rain.

From there, she went through a gate, then followed muddy wheel tracks across a wet paddock till she reached the old galvanised iron structure that served as a machinery shed.

There was a light inside the shed and her heart was as fluttery as a bird's as she turned off her ute's motor. Consciously gathering her courage, she hurried to the lighted doorway.

The rain was making a dreadful racket on the iron roof so there was no point in knocking. She went inside and the smell of diesel oil seemed to close in around her. The shed was almost a museum of ageing tractors and the walls were hung with relics from the past—an ancient riding harness, the metal steps of a sulky, even a wagon wheel.

She saw the top of Will's head as he bent over a modern tractor engine, tapping at it with a spanner.

The storm battered against the iron walls and Lucy began to wonder why she'd thought it was so important to hurry over here. She'd never seen Will working at any kind of mechanical task and she felt like an intruder. He was probably trying to get the job finished by dinner time and he might not appreciate her interruption.

'Will,' she called.

He looked up and his eyebrows lifted with surprise. 'Lucy, what are you doing here?'

Setting down the spanner, he grabbed at a rag and wiped his hands as he hurried around the front of the tractor.

His shoulders stretched the seams of a faded blue cotton shirt. Weather-beaten jeans rode low on his hips and everything about him looked perfect to her.

He smiled and she felt a familiar ripple of yearning, but

she felt something deeper too—the painful awareness of
how very deeply she loved this man.

That love hurt.

'Is everything all right?' he asked.

'I'm fine, Will. Still pregnant.'

His face relaxed visibly.

'I needed to talk to you, but it's been a busy day. I came
as soon as I could get away.'

'You should be sitting down.' He frowned as he looked
about the untidy shed. 'We used to have a chair out here
somewhere. Oh, there it is.'

He freed a metal chair from a tangle of tools in the
corner and wiped cobwebs and dust from it with a rag.
Then he carefully tested the chair's legs and, finally satisfied, he set it on the concrete floor.

Lucy thanked him and sat with necessary dignity.

She thought, for a moment, that Will would remain
standing, towering over her and making her more nervous
than ever, but he found a perch on the tractor's running board.

'So you've had a busy day,' he said, still wiping the last
of the grease from his hands. 'Have you had time to tell
anyone your good news?'

'Gina called in at lunch time and I told her about the baby.
She's over the moon, of course. I rang my dad, and I spoke
to your mother just now. Everyone seems really pleased.'

She dropped her gaze to her hands, clenched white-
knuckled in her lap. 'But they're all a little mystified when
they realise you're still going away, Will. Somehow we're
going to have to explain our arrangement to them. They
need to understand we won't be living together as tradi-
tional parents.'

She wished she didn't feel so sick and nervous. Outside, a gust of wind caught a metal door, slamming it against the shed wall.

'Actually, I've changed my mind about going away.'

Lucy's head snapped up and she stared at him. Her heart hammered and she wasn't sure she could trust what she'd heard.

'I've rung the PNG mining company,' he said. 'It's all arranged. I'm not going.'

'But I've just spoken to your mother and she—'

'Mum doesn't know about it yet. My father should be telling her right now.'

'Oh? I…I see.'

She felt faint. Dizzy.

'I've spent most of the afternoon talking about it with my father,' Will said, 'and it's all planned. I'm going to take care of this place, while Dad takes Mum on the trip of a lifetime to Europe.'

Oh…so his reason for staying had nothing to do with her or the baby.

Lucy tried to swallow her disappointment. 'Your mother will love that,' she said. 'I heard her plying Mattie with questions about Italy at the christening. She's dying to go overseas.'

The faintest of smiles glimmered in his eyes. 'And I don't want to be too far away from you.'

Lucy's heart leapt like an over-eager puppy, bouncing with too much excitement.

'I need to keep an eye on you now,' he said.

'I see.' She twisted her hands in her lap, hating the re-alisation that at any minute now she might burst into tears from tension.

'I want to court you.'

'Court me?'

Lucy was sure she'd misheard Will, but then she saw a flush creeping upwards from his shirt collar.

'I thought that perhaps we should go out on dates like other couples,' he said. 'To find out—'

He stopped, as if he was searching for the right words.

'To find out if we can fall in love?' Lucy supplied in a cold little voice she hardly recognised.

'Yes,' he said, clearly grateful that she understood.

Lucy was devastated. She was fighting to breathe. Will had been her friend since high school. For heaven's sake, he'd slept with her on two occasions. He was the father of her baby, and yet he still needed to take her out on dates to find out if he loved her.

A cruel icy hand squeezed around her heart.

'I really don't think dating would work,' she said, miserably aware that her life and her silly dreams were falling to pieces. 'If you were ever going to fall in love with me, it would have happened by now.'

'But, Lucy, I—'

'No!' she cried and the word sounded as if it had been ripped from her.

She held up her hands to stop him. 'I'm an expert when it comes to falling in love, Will.' Despair launched her to her feet.

Will's face was as pained as it was puzzled. He stood too.

Tears clogged Lucy's throat and she gulped to force them down. 'I know all about trying to manipulate love.'

'What do you mean?'

She saw the colour flee from Will's face and for a moment she almost retreated. Why should she force Will to hear her confession?

He wasn't going to PNG any more. Perhaps that was enough. She should be grateful for small mercies.

But no, she'd promised herself that she wouldn't be a coward. Will was, after all, her baby's father. Her confession wouldn't change that.

She took a deep breath and dived in. 'I tried to make you fall in love with me once before, Will, but it didn't work.'

Dismayed, he shook his head. 'I don't understand.'

'I'm telling you something rather terrible, actually.' She fixed her gaze on a huge muddy tractor tyre. 'I started going out with Josh because I was hoping you'd hear about it and be jealous.'

She heard the shocked sound Will made, but she couldn't look at him.

'My plan backfired,' she said. 'Josh was more than I'd bargained for.' Her cheeks flamed. 'Then I discovered I was pregnant.'

Shyly, she lifted her gaze.

Will's eyes were wild, but he held himself very still, hands fisted. 'Please tell me that Josh didn't force you.'

'No, he didn't use force, but I was young and he was very persuasive.'

A harsh sound escaped him. He began to pace, but then he whirled around to face her. 'Is that why you became engaged to Josh? Because you found out you were pregnant?'

'Yes.' Tears spilled suddenly.

Tears of shame.

And relief.

It was so good to have her confession out in the open at last.

'I was such an idiot, Will, and I ended up being trapped by my mistakes.'

'Goose.' With a choked cry, Will closed the gap between them, pulling her roughly into his arms. 'I thought you were in love with Josh.'

She shook her head and pressed her damp face into the curve of his neck.

A groan broke from him. He enfolded her against the wonderful warmth and strength of his chest and she could feel his heart knocking against hers.

'I was so angry with Josh,' he said. 'I was scared he wouldn't love you enough. Scared he wouldn't try hard enough to make you happy and keep you happy.'

'Oh, Will.'

'We had a terrible row just before he took off in the plane.'

Lucy leaned back and looked up at him, saw horror and tenderness warring in his eyes. 'How awful.'

'I still feel sick every time I think of it.'

'That's a terrible burden to have carried all these years.'

'Yes. I've blamed myself for a long time.'

She wanted to ease the pain in his eyes. 'But it wasn't your fault. Josh always made his own decisions.'

He nodded sadly. 'Short of holding a gun to his head, I couldn't have stopped him.'

Lucy shivered and took a step out of the comforting circle of Will's arms. She thought about the way that one event had shaped their lives. Wished that her confession had brought her a sense of peace.

It would be too much to expect a similar avowal of love from Will.

'It was nice of you to offer to court me,' she said and she pressed a fist against her aching heart, as if somehow she could stop it from bleeding. 'But if you don't mind, I think I'd rather not go on those dates.'

'But—' Will began.

Lucy hurried on. 'I think it would be better if we stick to friendship.'

'Why?'

Why? How could he ask that? After everything he'd had to say on the subject of friendship.

Lucy gave a shrug of annoyance. 'We've managed very well as friends for a long time now.'

'But you said you loved me.'

Oh, God.

Her heart stopped.

Will sent her a bewildered little smile. 'You don't have a monopoly on mistakes, Lucy.'

She felt rooted to the floor and her body flashed hot and cold. 'What do you mean? Have you made mistakes?'

His smile tilted with faint irony. 'Self delusion tops my list.'

Tears burned her eyes but she dashed them away because she wanted to see the raw emotion in Will's face. She'd never seen anything more beautiful.

'I've always cared about you, Lucy. I've always wanted to make you happy, but somehow—' He gave a sad shake of his head. 'Some *crazy* how—I couldn't see what that caring really meant.'

His eyes shimmered brightly. 'I made my first terrible mistake when you kissed me goodbye.' He reached for her hand. 'That was the kiss to end all kisses. I should have bound you to my side and never let you out of my sight. Instead, I was a fool, and I took off overseas.'

'I didn't know you liked that kiss,' she whispered.

He gave an abrupt laugh. 'I tried to tell myself I'd read

it wrongly. That maybe you were a particularly talented kisser, and that you kissed everyone that fabulously.'

'Not a chance, Will.'

'I spent far too much time on that first trip trying to forget you.' He tucked a curl behind her ear. 'I think that was about mistake number thirty-three.'

Lucy could hear the frantic beating of her heart and she realised the rain and the wind had stopped. 'Were there any more mistakes?'

'Dozens,' he admitted with a rueful smile. 'Every time I talked to you about friendship I was being an idiot.'

She felt the warmth of his fingers stroking her cheek. He touched her chin, lifted her face so that she was lost in the silver of his eyes. 'We should have been talking about love, Lucy.'

She couldn't speak.

'I love you,' he said again, and she tried to smile but she sobbed instead.

'I love you, Goose.'

Will kissed her damp eyelashes. 'You're the most important person in the world to me. That's got to be love, hasn't it?'

She could feel a smile growing inside her. 'It does sound promising.'

His eyes shone. 'I want to protect you and your baby.'

'Our baby,' Lucy corrected, and yes, she was definitely smiling on the outside now.

'I want to make you happy every day. I want to sleep with you every night and have breakfast with you every morning.'

'That definitely sounds like more than friendship, Will.' Smiling widely, she reached up and touched the grainy skin of his jaw. 'And I should know. I've loved you for so long I don't know any other way to be.'

His hands framed her face and his eyes were shining. With love. 'Do you think you could marry me, Lucy?'

She smiled as a fleeting memory from a time long ago flitted through her mind—pages of a school book filled with her handwriting: *Lucy Carruthers. Mrs Lucy Carruthers.*

'I'd love to marry you, Will.'

He punched the air and let out a war whoop. 'Sorry,' he said, 'but I couldn't help it. I just feel so damn happy.'

And then Will kissed her.

He poured his happiness and his love and his soul into the kiss and Lucy discovered that an old shed with a leaky roof was the most romantic place in the world.

CHAPTER ELEVEN

THEIR baby chose to be born on a crisp clear winter's day in July.

Will rose early when it was still dark. He built up the fire in the living room so it could heat the whole house and, with that task completed, he returned briefly to his bedroom doorway. He smiled at the sight of Lucy still sleeping, the tips of her blonde curls just showing above the warm duvet.

He continued on to the back door, donned a thick, fleecy lined coat and heavy boots and went out into the frosty dawn to the first of his daily tasks—checking the condition of the pregnant ewes and any lambs born during the night.

The sun was a pale glimmer on the distant horizon and the sky was grey and bleak, his breath a white cloud. Grass underfoot was crisp with frost. Last week he'd started spreading hay and feeding their flock with winter grain stored in their silos.

Farming was constant work, but Will loved his new life. Loved being in the outdoors, loved working with the animals and the land, planning the seasonal calendar of tasks required to keep the business running smoothly.

Best of all, he loved sharing every aspect of farm life with Lucy.

His wife was a walking encyclopaedia when it came to sheep and there'd been plenty of times when he'd had to humbly ask for her advice. But lately Lucy had been endearingly absent-minded, her attention turning more and more frequently inward to their baby.

And that was the other grand thing about Will's life these days—the pregnancy.

Of all the adventures he'd enjoyed, this surely had to be the greatest. Will never tired of watching the happy light in Lucy's eyes, or the proud way she carried herself as their baby grew and grew. Never tired of seeing the baby's movements ripple across her belly, or feeling stronger and stronger kicks beneath his hand.

Together Will and Lucy had converted his old bedroom into a sunny nursery, with yellow walls and bright curtains and a farmyard frieze.

'The kid will only have to look out the window to see a farmyard,' Will had teased.

But Lucy wanted farm animals so that was what they had, along with a wicker rocking chair and a fitted carpet, a handmade quilt lovingly pieced by his mother, as well as a white cot with a soft lamb's wool rug.

And any day their baby would arrive and they'd be a family.

At last.

This morning, Will refilled the water troughs and pulled down extra bales of hay which he spread for the pregnant ewes, and he checked the three healthy lambs that had been born overnight.

Satisfied that all was well, he returned to the warm

kitchen, ready for breakfast, and found Lucy already up and busy at the stove. His heart lifted as it always did when he saw her.

She was wearing one of his baggy old football jerseys— blue and yellow stripes—over blue maternity jeans and her feet were encased in fluffy slippers.

'Hey there,' she said, turning to smile as he entered.

He came up behind her, slipped his arms around her and kissed her just below the ear. 'How's my favourite farmer's wife?'

'Fat, pregnant and in the kitchen.' Lucy laughed as she leaned back against him and lifted her lips to kiss the underside of his jaw.

'That's exactly how I want her,' Will growled softly, dipping his lips to trap hers for a longer, deeper kiss.

When they sat down to eat, he was surprised to see that Lucy had nothing besides a mug of tea.

'Aren't you hungry?' he asked, feeling guilty that he'd already started on his mushrooms and toast.

She smiled and shook her head.

'That's not like you.'

'It's just a precaution.'

He felt a stab of alarm. 'A precaution?'

'I've been having contractions.'

Will almost choked on his food. 'Lucy. My God, what are you doing, sitting here watching me eat breakfast? I've got to get you to hospital.'

'It's OK, Will. There's no rush.' She smiled at his dismay. 'The contractions are still twenty minutes apart.'

'Twenty minutes?' He couldn't have been gone much longer than twenty minutes. 'How many have you had? When did they start?'

'They began around four this morning.' She must have seen the panic in his face and she laughed. 'Don't worry. With a first baby it might take ages. I could go on like this all day.'

'But you might not. And it's a good hour's drive to the hospital.' How could she sit there looking so calm? Was she crazy? 'Shouldn't you ring the doctor?'

Lucy nodded. 'I'll ring him when I'm certain that it's not a false—'

She didn't finish the sentence. Without warning, her entire manner changed. She sat very still, her face concentrated. Inward. Breathing steadily but deeply. In, out. In, out.

Nervously, Will watched his wife. If Lucy was in labour he wanted her safely in hospital, surrounded by a team of medical experts.

'Phew,' she said at last. 'That was stronger.'

'What about the timing? How far was it from the last one?'

She looked at the clock. 'Gosh, it was only ten minutes.'

'That's it then.' Will lurched to his feet. 'Come on, we've got to leave *now*.'

Lucy caught his hand. 'Are you sure you don't want your breakfast?'

'Not now.'

Lucy's suitcase had been packed and ready for some weeks. 'I'll put your bag in the car,' he said, grateful that they'd bought a comfortable all wheel drive station wagon some months back.

'OK. I'd better get the rest of my things.'

He gave her a tremulous smile, but there was nothing tremulous about Lucy's grin. Her face was alight with exhilaration. 'Isn't this exciting, Will? Our baby's coming.'

A tidal wave of emotions flooded him. Glorious love for

her. Chilling fear and a desperate need to protect her. Closing the gap between them, Will took her in his arms. 'I love you so much.'

'I know, my darling.' She touched a gentle hand to his cheek.

He clasped her to him, his precious, precious girl. 'I'm going to get you there safely, Lucy. I promise.'

Will drove with his heart in his mouth. Despite Lucy's calm assertion that all was well, he knew her contractions were getting stronger and he suspected they seemed to be coming closer. He could tell by her bouts of deep breathing and the way she massaged her stomach and he knew she needed all her concentration just to get through the pain.

Now he cursed himself for not making better contingency plans. He'd tried to suggest that Lucy stay in town with her father for these final weeks, but she'd insisted she'd be fine. He'd read the books on childbirth. He knew every case was different. Hell, he shouldn't have listened to her.

'Sorry, this is going to be bumpy,' he said as they came to the old wooden bridge crossing Willow Creek.

'It's OK,' she said, smiling bravely. 'I'm between contractions.'

But they had only just made it to the other side of the bridge when Lucy gave a loud gasp.

'What's happening?' Will sent her a frantic sideways glance.

She couldn't answer. She was too busy panting.

Panting? Didn't that mean—?

'Lucy!' he cried, aghast. 'You're not in transition already, are you?'

'I think I might be,' she said when she'd recovered her

breath. For the first time she looked frightened. 'First babies shouldn't come this fast.'

She no longer sounded calm. All too soon, her eyes were closed, her face twisted with pain, one fist clutched low, beneath the bump of the baby.

Oh, God. They were still thirty minutes from the hospital. Will felt helpless and distraught as he pressed his foot down on the accelerator. His heart began to shred into tiny pieces.

As they rounded the next curve, Lucy cried out and the guttural animal force of the sound horrified Will. Seizing the first possible chance to pull off the road, he brought the car to a halt.

'I'll ring for an ambulance,' he said, already reaching for his mobile phone.

Lucy nodded and managed a weak smile. 'Good idea. I…I think the baby's coming.'

Will choked back a cry of dismay.

The voice on the other end of the emergency hotline was amazingly calm as he explained their situation and gave the necessary details, including their location.

'The ambulance is on its way,' he said, wishing he felt more relieved.

Lucy nodded and fumbled with her door handle.

'What are you doing?' he cried as her door swung open. Had she gone mad?

Leaping out of his seat, he hurried around the car and found his wife slumped against its side, panting furiously.

Helplessly, he tried to stroke her arm, to soothe her, but she pushed him away and shook her head. He stood beside her, scared she might collapse, arms at the ready.

When the panting was over she opened her eyes. She looked exhausted. Sweat beaded her upper lip. 'It's too painful sitting in that front seat. I think I need to get into the back.'

'Right,' he said, biting back his fear. 'Let me help you.'

He hated to see Lucy's pain as he struggled to help her with the unwieldy transfer. Her contractions were fast and furious now and there seemed to be no spaces between them. He found a cushion for her head and helped her to lie along the back seat.

In a tiny lull, she sent him a wan smile. 'I'm sorry. I didn't dream it would be this fast.'

'Our baby can't wait to get here,' he said, doing his best to sound calm. 'He knows what a great mother he's getting.'

After the next contraction Lucy said quite calmly, 'Do we have any towels? Can you get the baby blanket out of the suitcase, Will?'

The baby blanket? He must have looked shocked.

'In case we beat the ambulance,' she said.

No, no. That couldn't happen, surely?

But by the time he'd found a beach towel—freshly washed, thank God—and retrieved the baby blanket from the hospital suitcase, Lucy was panting so hard she was in danger of hyperventilating.

'It's coming!' she cried. 'Will, help me!'

With frantic hands, she was trying to push her clothing away in preparation for the baby's imminent birth.

Oh, God it was actually happening. This was it. The birth of their child. On the side of the road beneath a river red gum.

Over the past nine months Will had imagined this birth, but he'd always pictured himself watching from the side-lines while medical experts did the honours. Mostly he'd seen himself emerging from a delivery room wearing a green hospital gown and a beaming smile as he shared the good news with their waiting families.

But, to his surprise, as soon as he accepted that he had no choice about where their baby might be born, an unexpected sense of calm settled over him. The terror was still there like a savage claw in the pit of his stomach, but Lucy needed him and he had to pull himself together.

Before they'd left home, he'd promised to protect her. He'd never dreamed what that might involve, but this was the moment of reckoning. She needed him to be calm and competent.

He could do this. For her. For their baby.

'OK, Goose, you're doing really well,' he said as he settled the folded towel beneath her.

Lucy merely grunted and went red in the face. Her right hand was braced against the back of the front seat. With the other she clung to an overhead strap.

She held her breath and grimaced, and Will couldn't bear to think how much this was hurting her.

Then he saw the crown of their baby's head.

Lucy finished pushing and let out an enormous gasp as she wilted back against the cushion.

'Good girl,' he said. 'Our baby has dark hair.'

She tried to smile. 'I'm going to have to push, Will. I can't hold back any longer. If you can see the baby's head, that means I can push without doing any harm.'

'Tell me what to do,' he said, ashamed of the hint of fear that trembled in his voice.

'Just be ready to catch. Support the head.' Lucy sent him an encouraging smile before her belly constricted and she was overtaken by the force of another contraction.

Inch by inch, their baby emerged.

'You're brilliant, darling,' he told her. 'I can see the eyebrows, eyes, nose.' Excitement bubbled through him now. 'I can see the mouth. It's kinda scrunched but cute.' He held his hands at the ready. 'OK, the head's out.'

Somehow he managed to sound calm. 'It's turning.'

With the next of Lucy's grunts, he gently but firmly held his child's warm damp head. He saw a slippery shoulder emerge and then another. In the space of three heartbeats, he was steadying his baby as it slipped from its safe maternal cocoon.

He and Lucy had chosen not to know the baby's sex, but now his heart leapt with incredible joy.

'Lucy, it's a boy.'

'A boy?' Her eyes opened and a radiant smile lit up her face. 'Oh, the little darling. I had a feeling he was a boy.'

Will's throat was too choked to speak as he lifted his son onto Lucy's tummy. Their son had thick dark hair, and his little arms were outstretched, tiny fingers uncurled, as if he was reaching out for life, or bursting through the winner's tape at the end of a race.

'Oh, Will!' Lucy whispered, looking pale but happy. 'Isn't he handsome? Isn't he gorgeous?'

'He looks like a champion,' Will agreed, but then he frowned as a new fear worried him. 'Should I do anything? Is he breathing OK?'

'I think he's fine.' Lucy spoke calmly as she rubbed the baby's back and, as if to answer her, the little fellow began to cry, with a small bleat at first, then with a loud gusty wail.

She grinned. 'He's got a terrific set of lungs.'

'He's got a terrific mum,' Will said as he helped her to wrap their son in the soft white blanket dotted with yellow ducklings.

The whine of a siren sounded in the distance and Will felt a weight lift from his shoulders.

'Help is on its way,' he said.

Lucy smiled. 'I've already had all the help I needed.' With a wondrous, soft expression she touched the top of their son's head. 'Thank you, Will. Thank you.'

By midday Lucy was happily ensconced in a private room in Willowbank Hospital in a lovely big white bed, with her darling baby boy, wrapped in a blue bunny rug, beside her.

Surrounded by flowers.

Surrounded by so many flowers, in fact, that she felt like a celebrity.

'You *are* a celebrity,' Gina told her. 'Think how many puppies and kittens and ponies and sheep you've looked after in this district. Every household in Willowbank is thrilled that you now have your own dear little boy.'

'And he's such a beauty,' said Mattie, gazing fondly at the sleeping little cherub in the crib.

Lucy watched the soft glow in Mattie's eyes, watched the reverent way Mattie stared at little Nathan, at the way she gently touched his cheek, and she felt a tiny current of excitement inside her.

The excitement grew as Lucy saw the meaningful glance Mattie sent to her husband, and a thrilled shiver ran through her as she witnessed the warm intimacy of Jake's answering smile.

They had important news. Baby news. Lucy could feel it in her bones.

'Mattie…' she said, but then she stopped, not sure how to continue.

Mattie smiled, almost as if she was encouraging Lucy to question her.

'You're not?' Lucy began and then she stopped again.

'Yes!' Mattie exclaimed and she was smiling broadly now. She reached for Jake's hand and their fingers twined. Her eyes glowed. 'I'm three months pregnant.'

'And we couldn't be happier,' said Jake, backing up his words with a huge grin.

The room suddenly erupted with excited questions and congratulations.

'That's the most perfect news,' Lucy said and she knew she was beaming with joy as she looked around the room, filled with the people who were so important to her—Gina and Tom, Mattie and Jake—and Will, her darling Will. And now, dear little Nathan William Carruthers.

'There's going to be a whole new generation of the Willow Creek gang,' Tom said, grinning.

Everyone laughed and, from his vantage point near the door, Will sent his wife a conspiratorial wink. He thought Lucy had never looked more beautiful.

He looked around the room at their friends and he marvelled at the sense of completion he felt. He thought about the long and roundabout journey he'd taken to reach this satisfying moment.

And he knew at last that he was finally home.

* * * * *

A sneaky peek at next month...

By Request

RELIVE THE ROMANCE WITH THE BEST OF THE BEST

My wish list for next month's titles...

In stores from 21st June 2013:

❏ The Hudsons: Max, Bella and Devlin –
Emilie Rose, Maureen Child & Catherine Mann

❏ Housekeepers Say I Do! – Susan Meier

In stores from 5th July 2013:

❏ New York Nights
– Kathleen O'Reilly

3 stories in each book - only £5.99!

Available at WHSmith, Tesco, Asda, Eason, Amazon and Apple

Just can't wait?

0613/

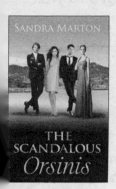

The World of Mills & Boon®

There's a Mills & Boon® series that's perfect for you. We publish ten series and, with new titles every month, you never have to wait long for your favourite to come along.

Blaze

Scorching hot, sexy reads
4 new stories every month

By Request

Relive the romance with the best of the best
9 new stories every month

Cherish™

Romance to melt the heart every time
12 new stories every month

Desire™

Passionate and dramatic love stories
8 new stories every month